Bootleg
Broadway

by

Diana Rubino

The New York Saga, Book Two

Bootleg Broadway

Cover Art by *Diana Carlile*

The Wild Rose Press, Inc.
PO Box 708
Adams Basin, NY 14410-0708
Visit us at www.thewildrosepress.com

Publishing History
First Vintage Rose Edition, 2015
Print ISBN 978-1-5092-0128-0
Digital ISBN 978-1-5092-0129-7

The New York Saga, Book Two
Published in the United States of America

Dedication

To my husband Chris

Acknowledgments

Many thanks to "Uncle Junior," Aunt Ceil, Aunt Angie, Aunt Mare, Aunt Edna, Aunt Doris, Uncle John, Aunt Ida, Angela Rosati, and Vivian Cuenca for the wonderful stories about "the good old days." No history book can come close to your memories. To Linda Unger, a bottomless well of theater expertise, Dawn Falsinotti for the Italian cuisine, and Rose Bengardino for the Italian "insults."

Saluti per cent'anni.

The cop poked his head into the car. "What's in the briefcases?"

I stiffened, paralyzed. My breath caught. "Uh—I dunno. I'm doing an errand for somebody."

"Yeah, I'll bet you dunno. Step aside, please."

Now he pissed me off. "Hey, you got a search warrant?" I demanded.

But demanding a search warrant from a New York City cop was like demanding a shot of Scotch from Satan in the middle of Hell.

I didn't want to look. I turned my head and flattened my palms on the roof of the car, like I was being searched. I heard the clicks as he sprang the latches and his not-so-surprised "mm-hmmm" as he checked out the contents.

"Who you doing this errand for, sonny boy?" He turned to me.

What was the "sonny boy" bit? He wasn't much older than me. I knew he just wanted to humiliate me. Screw that. I've been called a lot worse by much better cops than him. He obviously didn't know who I was. "Uh—I'd better get a lawyer or something."

His "You'd better come with me" didn't sound like a suggestion.

"Look, uh—you wanna just take a few bills outta there and forget it?" I asked, real generously. "I mean, uh—we're all in this mess together, ya know—"

"Bribing an officer of the law is a very serious offense, sonny boy," he scolded me, shaking his finger in my face. "Park your car there, please."

"There?" I gestured at the curb. "But there's a hydrant there. I'll get a ticket."

Praise for *BOOTLEG BROADWAY*

"Diana Rubino has blended the history of the Depression and Prohibition, romance and the realities of getting mixed up with the mob into one compelling read. This may not be you typical romance, but it is one magnificent story."

~Deborah Brent, Romantic Times (5 Stars)
~*~

"Fine addition to the home library if you enjoy historical fiction filled with a touch of romance, and a whole lot of action. Enjoyed the read, happy to recommend."

~Molly Martin, The Author's Den
~*~

Other books by Diana Rubino
available at The Wild Rose Press, Inc.
Fakin' It
A Bloody Good Cruise
For Love and Loyalty
~*~

Other books in the New York Saga
at The Wild Rose Press, Inc.
The End of Camelot
From Here to Fourteenth Street (soon to be released)

Prologue

New York City, May 1935

Billy moseyed out of The Stork Club whistling "I'm In The Mood For Love" because he was. The rain-slicked pavement glistened under the streetlamps. A cold drizzle tickled his face as he plopped his hat on. Fishing his keys out of his pocket, he stepped off the curb and headed for his new Packard.

An engine's roar came at him from the darkness. "Hey!" He leapt out of the way, but not in time. He got hit so hard he went flying, landing on his side. He lay crumpled in the street, choking on the exhaust. The wheels screeched away.

Bodies hovered over him, but it was all a blur.

"You all right, buddy?"

"Stand back, give him some air!"

"Is he dead?"

"Somebody call an ambulance!"

He shut his eyes against the unbearable pain and, mercifully, slipped away.

****

The fingers brushing his cheek roused him, and he struggled to part his eyelids. They felt glued shut. He tried sitting up, but his entire body was wrapped like a mummy. He struggled to move. Panic hit him.

"Billy—it's okay, I'm here." His wife's voice

sounded a million miles away.

"Greta, what happened? What's all this? Where am I?" He didn't even recognize his own voice, a hoarse croak.

"You were hit by a car. You're in the hospital in a body cast." Her fingers grasped his, but lightly, as if she feared she'd break him. "You might be laid up for up to six months, but you're under the best possible care."

"Hit by a car? Oh, God…" Emerging from the initial shock, he remembered leaving the Stork Club, but nothing else.

He licked his cracked lips. "Anybody know who hit me?"

"No, Billy, it was a hit-and-run."

Terror seized him and chilled his blood. He shivered. "They're after me, Greta. They found out what I did and they came to get me!"

"No, Billy—"

He cut her off. "Yes, Greta. They won't quit till I'm dead!"

"Billy, it was probably just some drunk…"

He tuned out his wife's soothing, loving voice as horrible scenes flashed before his eyes: putrid corpses rotting on the ground, machine-gunned bodies drained of blood, closed caskets hiding the mangled messes inside…

The mob finally wanted their revenge. But facing death was easier than running from it. So he lived every single moment like it was his last—just in case it was.

"Hold my hand again," he whispered.

She clasped her fingers around his.

"Greta—kiss me."

She leaned over. Her lips brushed his, like a

feather. "Get some rest. I'll be right here by your side. I love you, Billy." Her singsong voice calmed him.

Before drifting off, he thanked God for the short life he'd been given. If it was ending now, at least he'd done more in the last few years than most people did in decades. From Tin Pan Alley to Broadway to riches beyond his wildest dreams, to the tragedy that ended it all…

And it had started so innocently…

Chapter One

March 1932

"The intricate and mysterious rites observed before patrons are allowed to enter seem to be chiefly intended to add romantic excitement to the adventure, since the authorities are not likely to remain long unaware of their existence. Introduction by someone who has been there before is usually required. Then there is the business of registering the new patron's name and perhaps the issuing of a card of admittance to be presented on the next visit. It is sometimes made even more important-looking by a signature or a cabalistic sign on the back of the card. Many persons about town carry a dozen or more such cards.

"The devious means employed to protect the entrances to speakeasies probably adds to the general mystification. Bells are to be rung in a special way. A sliding panel behind an iron grill opens to reveal a cautious face examining the arrivals…"

—The New York Times

Billy sat at his piano composing another sentimental ballad when the buzzer went.

He wanted to finish writing out the measure, but the buzzer wouldn't let up. Were they leaning on it or what?

"Okay, I'm comin'. Keep your pants on." He opened the door.

His girlfriend stepped in and collapsed on him. "Pru! What's the matter? What?"

She buried her face in his sweater. "I'm pregnant, Billy," came her muffled voice.

Wrapping his arms around her, all he could say was, "Huh?"

Her breathing came in short gasps. "I ran all the way from Eighth Avenue. I just went to the doctor, and I'm three months already. What are we gonna do?"

"It's okay, Honey Bear. We'll manage somehow." He held her close and kissed her slender neck.

"Never mind somehow. How?"

"Come over here." He sat her down on his bed and held her till she relaxed. "I should've known, Billy," she sobbed. "My chart said to watch out for it. I should've been careful."

"Aah, come on." He didn't believe in that star stuff but held a grudging respect for it and for all things otherworldly. Maybe she'd gone to his fortunetelling sister.

"It did! Mercury went into Sagittarius at three twenty-six p.m. on December third, and the moon, in Capricorn, created a first quarter at twelve degrees at ten fifty-five. Almost the exact moment I conceived." She wiped her teary jade eyes on his sleeve.

"How do you know what moment it was?" He handed her his hankie.

She tilted her head and eyed him up and down. "In the bathtub—remember?"

"Oh, yeah." He remembered, all right.

The traditional route wouldn't be an option here.

5

She was a nocturnal bohemian who packed her one satchel every few months and hopped from SoHo loft to SoHo loft with every artist's dream: displaying her canvases in the staid galleries of Paris. He had his own erratic habits—work till three a.m., wolf down breakfast at Billy Haas's Restaurant, and sleep all day. Revolving their lives around an infant would take some rescheduling.

"So, you wanna tell your parents first?" He clasped her hands. "Or we'll both tell them together." New York City was Sodom and Gomorrah to her Bible-thumping parents. They'd condemn her soul to hell for this mortal sin. "I'll go with you. I'll do anything you want." He nearly sang the words, in a voice as soothing as he could muster. "You know us Libra guys," he joked, but didn't get a smile out of her.

"I don't think I'd better tell them. They'll disown me," she wailed. "They'll say I disgraced them. I'll say I'm going to Europe or something."

"When you show up with a bundle of joy in six months, they might wonder. You gotta tell them sometime. How can they turn away from their own grandchild?" His voice gathered volume as his blood began to boil.

"It took all my courage to tell *you* about this!" She pressed up against him, her lips found his, and he soared into orbit. "I thought you'd be so mad when I told you," she whispered when they came up for air.

"Uhhh…" What were they talking about? Oh, yes. The baby. "Mad? Me? Nah, of course not. Surprised, maybe, but not mad. I wasn't expecting this to happen. I never planned for something like this. I mean, what guy does?"

She looked up at him, and he detected a pang of hurt darkening her eyes. He could read every emotion in those eyes, from the annoyance of a hangnail to the agony of grief. Her eyes always said it all for her, as his songs did for him.

"No, I didn't mean it like that—you know what I meant." Oh, why did everything he say come out like mush?

"I always know what you mean, Snuggles," she cooed.

When she called him Snuggles, he knew all wasn't lost. He grinned widely enough to produce his dimples for her. Her eyes brightened to the color of leaves under a spring sun. The whole situation was beginning to look like a minor inconvenience to him. The upshot was that she'd be his forever. No man would want to mess with a woman who'd been "tampered with" and saddled with an infant.

"Look at the bright side. This is the beginning of our life together, Honey Bear." He nibbled her earlobe, gathered her hair in bunches, and brushed his cheek with it. Rich as mahogany, all that bobbing kept it full and bouncy.

"But I wasn't planning on having children till we were much older." She bowed her head, looking so proper, so guilty. "We should move in together. I want the baby to have his mom and dad home with him under the same roof."

Billy calculated rapidly: now his parents entered the picture. He could see them holding their grandchild and wishing they could call the mother of this angel their daughter-in-law.

When would be the time to reel off his news to

them?

So he wasn't destined to be a bachelor forever. Younger fellas than him handled sudden manhood.

Her gaze locked into his. For his next words, he'd have to rely on raw talent; there was no time to write this down and polish it.

He clasped her hand, dropped to one knee, and cleared his throat for the most important recital of his life. "You're the essence of my being. I want to spend the rest of my life with you, and even after that. Now you're carrying my child, and I want us to be a real family. Pru, will you marry me?"

She threw her arms around his neck and smothered him with pink lipstick kisses. "Oh, of course! How can I refuse such a beautiful proposal?"

Whew! He wiped his sweaty palms on his backside. It worked! It was one of his most ambitious efforts, if he did say so himself. He wiped away a tear at this moment he'd always remember. If he'd put it to music, it would've been even more stirring. Best of all, it wasn't the way his father proposed to his mother. Da had popped the question in the Breevort Hotel cafeteria and whisked her to the altar the next day to keep her father from marrying her off to some creep.

"...and we can have a nice church ceremony, and maybe a small reception afterwards..."

But he wasn't listening. He was fretting: Where would they live? Could they afford three rooms? How much did diapers cost?

"We'll have to get a cradle and stuff like that," he broke in, but she was still stuck on the wedding plans.

"Do you think it would still be proper if I wear white?"

"You can wear anything you want." He nodded.

"Can we go on a honeymoon?"

"Sure." He shrugged.

"Niagara Falls?"

"Anyplace you want." That's where his father had taken his mother. He hoped the similarities would end there.

"Oh, Snuggles, I love you." Her lips found his. They fell onto his bed and celebrated their engagement.

From the moment he first saw her in P.S. #132's lunchroom, sitting alone and drawing instead of wolfing down a bologna sandwich, he knew Prudence Muller was the girl he wanted to love, honor, cherish, and endow with his worldly goods: a Wurlitzer upright and a mechanical clown bank. By grade 8a-1, he finally got up the guts to serenade her under the fire escape of her Leroy Street walkup. In high school they started courting, which meant shared eggcreams at Fenucci's Drugstore while playing footsie under the table. Smitten with his tall blond good looks, girls followed him home and made him all kinds of tempting offers. But he wanted only the shy Iowa farm girl who always got detention for drawing instead of listening in class. He wrote songs for her; she drew pictures for him. After smooching through a Lillian Gish filmfest in the balcony, they gave each other pet names: Honey Bear and Snuggles. He'd saved himself for her, and after three years of serious discourse about morality and even more serious begging, they consummated their passion in his Horatio Street basement apartment. An adolescence of frustrated desire exploded in splendor that seared the night in that hovel across from the furnace. He'd choreographed that tryst like a production of *Romeo and Juliet*: after his pal Charlie Burp delivered a veal parmesan dinner and vanished, Billy had doused himself with watered-down piano wax as a cologne stand-in, uncorked a bottle of his mother's homemade wine, and donned the silk underwear he'd begged and borrowed from his sister's boyfriend. The fella let him keep it, bless his soul.

The long-awaited event couldn't have gone more perfectly if he'd written music and lyrics, built a stage and lined it with floodlights. He followed the flawless performance with two curtain calls.

Now, only five years later, the fairytale romance collided head-on with reality.

He tucked her into his bed and wanted to get back to composing, but the piano would disturb her. So he got out his journal. One thing he and his father had in common besides their last name: keeping a journal. It was Billy's outlet for the baffling feelings that plagued every young man.

Another reason he wrote everything down—orally, he was a bumbler. But give him anything to write on, from bathroom tissue to cream parchment, and his words could move a career gangster to tears. In between the heartfelt prose were some catchy song lyrics. By eighteen, he was playing New York's best clubs and had a nice catalog of published songs under his belt.

Now, at twenty-five, he was adding the role of family man to his repertoire, one of life's little surprises.

An event like this deserved music. So naturally this journal entry became another song: a love ballad about a woman who tells her man she's carrying his baby. It would start in A minor, then modulate to C, to end in that bright key. He couldn't wait to sing it to her.

****

"Hey, Billy, shouldn't you be gettin' home to the wife?" fellow musician Ziggy Elman asked Billy as they finished another round of drinks. They were sitting in Piano's, the speakeasy Billy ran with his sister Susan in the basement of her brownstone. Tonight was Susan's turn to work.

"Don't have to. She's not my wife yet." Even if she was, he wouldn't want to go home; he was still trying to unwind from the gig they'd just played uptown.

"Well, I gotta get home to mine. I come in too late, she puts me out on the fire ex-scape." Red drained his drink. "Enjoy your final days of freedom, pal." He clapped Billy on the shoulder and headed out.

A mild shock went through Billy at those words "final days of freedom." Would he ever get used to diaper pails and wheeling a carriage through the park? And sleeping on the fire escape if he came in too late?

Susan came over and sat across from Billy. "Here's your take for the week." She dropped a billfold on the table. Ever since Pru's announcement, he'd been socking money away. Times were tough out there, and he didn't want his child to ever know there'd been a Depression. "Had a good week. Must've been the new shipment from that ladylegger in Jersey City." She lit a cig.

"Mrs. Arnone?" He swept the bills into his pocket. "The redhead who owns all the apartment buildings?"

"She's the one." Susan nodded. "But we're on more friendly terms now. I call her Josie and she calls me Suzie. She gave me some hot stock tips, too. She's quite a shrewdie."

"Then how 'bout celebrating?" He gestured at his empty glass.

"Expectant fathers shouldn't imbibe." She smiled and tousled his hair.

He glowed in her comforting warmth. Close kin distanced him from the poverty and misery on the streets. A vision of his father appeared in his mind, and he chased it away. Not all kin was so close.

She ordered another Scotch for him and a Pink Lady for herself. "You should buzz Ma. When you didn't show up last Sunday for dinner, she almost had kittens. I had to convince her you weren't sick or dead or—even worse—not hungry."

"Yeah, I will. Tomorra." He knew what this was leading to. "I hadda stay with Pru. She wasn't feelin' too great."

"Well, that's fine, but I think Ma has a right to know she's a grandma-to-be."

With only two years between them, he and Susan got along great, only she repressed what he let grow and thrive. He knew Susan envied his bohemian life, but her business sense overshadowed any artistic whims.

She ran a clothing store with her husband Irv and already had two homes, three servants, and enough jack to retire on. But tonight she looked the hostess part she liked to play: black velvet dinner dress with flared skirt and attached sash. A velvet cloche hat dipped over one eye. Her wedding rings dazzled on her left hand; a diamond doorknob sparkled on the right.

Susan understood him more than anybody; she never scoffed or laughed at his dreams to be famous and travel the world with his own orchestra. She didn't utter so much as a syllable of disapproval at his untimely upcoming fatherhood.

He lit a cig off hers. "I'll just go over there. I won't call first. Ma likes that, when I just turn up and surprise her."

"It'd be nice if you go when Da's home." She took a drag and blew out a stream of smoke.

"After the last blowup, I think it'd be better if I didn't." Deep in his heart, he regretted that he and the retired Chief of Police weren't like other fathers and sons. But since he'd hit about fourteen they never saw eye to eye on anything, and the last squabble drove him away for good. His mother's refereeing amounted to a lecture about money management as she slipped him a few simoleons.

Their drinks came and he took a long swig. "He might not show it, but he misses you, Billy."

"I got nothing more to say to the man, Suze, nothing. He can't accept me for who I am, that's his decision." He flicked an ash.

With a sigh, Susan glanced at her watch and stood. "Let's not start this now. I need to add up tonight's take." She ground out the butt in the ashtray and went to the back, taking her drink with her.

Their assistant answered a discreet rap at the door, pushing aside the peephole cover that a detective, of all people, had installed. Billy heard their password, *parlo pianissimo*—"I speak softly"—and in walked a few fellas from the neighborhood, along with some dames they romped with. One of them, a Jean Harlow blonde, had gams that could put the Ziegfeld Follies to shame. The others were poor man's versions of her.

Another guy swaggered in with them and removed

his gray fedora. He could've been a prize fighter; his nose looked like a crooked weathervane permanently facing west. Could've been anywhere between thirty-five and fifty. Enough grease to lube the Erie Lackawanna Railroad coated his coal black hair. He gimped in his blue-and-cream lace-up shoes like he was trying to hide a limp. His double-breasted wool blazer with its flap pockets fit like it was painted onto his bulky build. Anyone who wasn't from around here would think this guy had class, but Billy knew better. With that Chicago look about him, he was either a Fed or a hood.

"Excuse me, is the chair opposite you taken?" he asked Billy as the group settled at the next table.

"Nope. It's all yours."

"Be right wit'cha, Toots," he said to the dame with the gams, and he turned back to Billy. "I know you from someplace." He wagged a finger. "Didn' you just play at the Back Stage Club? The piana player, right?"

"Yeah, that was me," Billy answered. "I play clubs when I'm not runnin' this place."

"Oh, so you must be Susan's brother." He took the proffered chair, turned it around, and straddled it. So he wanted to stick around and beat his gums. That was all right with Billy; he wasn't tired, and he wanted to stretch out his final evenings of singledom.

"Rosario Ingovito. Rosie Ingo for short." Rosie's diamond pinkie ring cut into Billy's hand as they shook. He couldn't imagine why any guy would want to be called Rosie, especially one that looked like him.

Just then Susan came by. "Hi, Rosie. Sorry I was in the back when you came in. So you've already met. Rosie's a regular customer at the store, Billy." Hence the natty suit.

"I have a joint in East Harlem, Billy," he said. "Ever hear of Rosie's?"

Billy nodded. "Yeah, I heard Red McKenzie and his Mound City Blue Blowers play there. Nice room."

"You want a gig there anytime, it's yours." He gave Billy a cuff on the chin.

"Oh, so you're that Rosie?" He never would have believed it. "I thought some ladylegger ran it. Thanks, I'd like to come down and play there sometime."

"How 'bout tomorra night?"

"I run this place three nights a week, and I'm on tomorrow night." He couldn't resist adding, "I write a lot of those songs I play."

A flash of gold caught the light as Rosie smiled his approval. "Then gimme a call when you're ready. Your playin' killed me over there."

"Why, thanks." Billy relaxed. The fella was okay. He had to be, if he shopped in Susan's store and paid his tab. Susan didn't put up with deadbeats. He was on the up-and-up; he wasn't about to raid the joint.

But Billy soon found out that Rosie Ingo was the farthest thing from a Fed on two feet.

****

"Aah, come on, Tess, you know I don't go for any of that mumbo jumbo." Billy and his younger sister sat at their mother's dining room table. Coffee percolated on the sideboard. Four dessert places were set, but their father wasn't expected home till later. That was fine with Billy. He just wasn't up to facing the old fella right now. He couldn't explain why, even on paper that morning.

Tessie shook her head, trying to conceal a worried

frown as she studied the arrangement of cards before her. "It don't look good, Billy."

"Then shuffle 'em again till it does look good." He sat back and stretched his legs.

Her green eyes, identical to his, bored into him. "That's not the way it works, Billy. This is the reading, right here. You don't wanna know what it says? You a-scared?"

"I ain't a-scared of a pile a cards. I just think they're all wet. How can a pile a cards know who I am and what's gonna happen to me?" He sensed the cards were symbolic of his relationship with his father. Da didn't know who Billy was either.

"They represent the spirit guides." Tessie looked down and studied the spread. "It's not the cards talking, it's the spirits talking through them."

Just then their mother came in carrying a tray of cannoli and cheese-filled cupcakes for which there was no English word, *pasta ciotti.*

"Hey, I'm still full from lunch, Ma. One *busta chut* and I'll bust. But I can squeeze in half a cannoli." He grabbed one and sucked the cream from the middle.

"It was good to see you *mange.*" She bent down to embrace him, and he rested his head against her softness, breathing in the powdery scent that brought back his earliest memories. He had no qualms about his mother hugging him like a little kid, as long as it was at home. "Well, I don't always have time for a feast."

"I hope Pru's eating enough for two. Is she taking care of herself?" Ma draped a napkin across his lap.

"Yeah, real good." He nodded and chewed. "She went to the doctor yesterday."

Ma smoothed back a few of his stray locks like she

always did, but she no longer licked her hand first. "I'm so glad you found the right girl."

"Yeah, I know." The thought of Pru as the mother of his child gave him a sense of pride he'd never felt before. Now he could prove he was grown up. "I already wrote two songs about us. I'll play them before I go."

"Ma, he don't wanna listen to this reading I'm doing on him. It looks onim—ominous." Tessie gave a resolute nod with the new word she'd just mastered.

"Teresina, don't make him worry. Maybe he just doesn't want his good mood spoiled. To be honest, I'd rather not hear it right now either. I just found out I'm going to be a *nonna* and you're going to be a *zia*, so let's keep the atmosphere happy. Tell the spirits to let up a little, or to go back to the other side for a while." Ma's tone was never stern, never authoritative, but its convincing quality made a person do anything she asked; that's how she got so far in politics. If she ever became President, her nickname would be The Great Persuader. It made Billy proud of her; she'd done all right. His father never would've made Chief of Police if it wasn't for her; he'd have spent his career pounding a beat at Five Points. But he didn't judge his father for his shortcomings. He just thanked God he didn't inherit any of them.

"But, Ma, look what it says here!" Tessie pointed a beringed index finger at a card with a goofy-looking Ethel drawn on it, draped in medieval robes and holding a long stalk with what looked like asparagus sticking out of it.

"Who's he?" Billy asked. "He don't even look like me. Thank goodness."

"It's the Nine of Rods. Upside down," Tessie explained.

"He ain't upside down."

Tessie rolled her eyes. "Not to you it isn't, but to me it is. I'm the reader."

"Then straighten him up." Billy took another bite of pastry.

"No, they have to stay the way I turn them over. The Nine of Rods upside down means obstacles, adversity, problems, displeasure, calamity, disaster, barriers to overcome, ill health. That's the sphere of influence that's coming into your future, in a broad sense."

"Come on, Tess. If I listened to you every time you read my fortune, I'd be…" He stopped himself by shoving the hollowed-out pastry into his mouth. He couldn't argue, because every damn thing she'd ever predicted about him had come true. And Susan, and their parents, and their ex-stepgrandmother, who'd run off with the creep their mother was supposed to marry. Tessie had a knack. She'd predicted that he would drop out of school in his senior year, which he did, that he'd get very sick, which he did—with chicken pox—and last year, she'd turned over a card that foresaw a birth in his future. He'd howled with laughter. Now there wasn't so much to laugh at. Sometimes she spooked their parents, the way she claimed to talk to the dead— and not just any dead, but famous people, like George Washington and Rudy Valentino.

Why couldn't her cards ever come up with the trifecta winners at Belmont Park?

"Your cards say anything that's not gloom and doom for a change?" Billy challenged.

"Susan's gonna make a lotta money in the next year." She swept her cards into their wooden box.

"I coulda told you that, and I ain't got no cards. I got news for you. She's gonna make a lot the year after that, and the year after that, too. And her husband's gonna die countin' it. The guy'll be found smothered under a pile of pennies. Tell Susan, if Irv disappears for more than three days, to look in the attic before calling missing persons."

"Don't knock them, Billy, just because they're business minded. They don't criticize the life you chose." Ma poured him another cup of joe.

He looked away and sucked on another cannoli so he wouldn't talk back. The life he "chose." Like it was a choice.

"Yeah, Billy, I wish I was as smart as her," Tessie chimed in.

He couldn't help speaking up before he swallowed. "She'll never admit it to nobody else, but she wishes she could be like me. But the almighty dollar tells her what to do. She divides her time into fifteen-minute blocks, 'cause her time is lettuce. Me, I don't even know what day it is, never mind the time. That I can usually guess. If it's gettin' light out, I go to bed. When it's dark, I go to work. When it's cold, it's winter, when it's hot, it's summer. When I don't take an umbrella, it rains."

"You'll know it's two a.m. when your baby starts wailing," Ma replied with a wistful smile. "If he's anything like you were, he won't let you sleep a wink."

Actually, he did know what day it was—he had exactly thirty-one days till the wedding. He didn't count his days forwards like most people; he was counting backwards.

Just then the door slammed shut and footsteps echoed down the hall toward them. That steady tattoo of beat cop footsteps was ingrained into his memory.

"Hi, my lovely ladies," Da greeted them. Ma got up and hugged him. "And who's this stranger? Feeding vagrants again, Vita?" With a hint of joshing in his tone, he smiled down at Billy.

Billy stood and acknowledged his father's presence. "Hi, Da." His flat voice expressed neither gladness nor reluctance to see him. Soon enough he'd be out of here and back to the life he "chose." He only had to endure this for another couple minutes.

"Billy has some fabulous news, but I think father and son should be alone now," Ma said, ushering Tessie out.

So father and son stood facing each other. Seeing his own reflection in the mirror above the sideboard, Billy looked at his father and himself at the same time. He was starting to look like the old boy: the same lanky build, the same crease over the brow, the generous heap of hair. But it ended at looks.

"So what's your fabulous news?" Da asked, like he was doing a routine questioning.

Billy cleared his throat. "I, uh—" He knew how his father would want to hear it phrased, so he thought it out as best he could, looking down at his feet. "I'm settling down, with Pru, finally. We're, uh, that is, she's—she's gonna have a baby." He looked up. "Mine," he added for emphasis, and to quelch the possibility of a sarcasm match.

To his surprise, Da smiled and tugged Billy's left ear, something he hadn't done in twenty years. "You never cease to amaze me, son of mine." He beamed like Billy had never seen before. Was he proud that his son could impregnate a female and obey the code of honor? To his father, this was a real rite of passage. To Billy, it was a detour on his road to fame.

"So when's the big day?" Da asked.

"The birth or the wedding?"

"Should've qualified that one." Da chuckled. "What's coming first?"

"The wedding, of course!" Billy glanced at the kitchen doorway for eavesdroppers.

"Well, how'm I supposed to know? Did you expect me to?"

Billy drummed on the chair rung. "Nah, I guess not. But she's making all the plans. I don't even know what church it's at or anything."

"So when is it?" Da asked.

"Uh—" He didn't know the calendar date. "Just— thirty-one days from today. That'll be April, I guess."

"Anything you want to talk about before you take that plunge, son? I mean, the plunge down the aisle." He winked. Now he wanted to be Dear Old Dad again. Last time they saw each other, his final words had been, "Go ahead, write songs. You'll starve, I tell you! You'll wind up on a bread line with the rest of 'em!"

"I ain't exactly proud of you, either!" had been his last retort to his father that day as he slammed out of the house.

But at this moment Billy felt like an only son. He was glad Da had come home early and found him there. He didn't want advice on his personal life; that was the last thing he needed from a guy who'd beat up a rival for his mother's affections. He didn't know quite what

21

he wanted from this man who'd raised him with nineteenth-century values yet backed away from every display of his son's uniqueness and, finally, refused to accept it.

"So you're happy for me?" Billy didn't know why he cared, but he did.

"Sure, I'm happy you're going to have a wife and a child and a home life." He nodded. "As long as you can provide for them. Is it what you want?"

"Well, I didn't plan it." Billy looked everywhere but into his father's eyes.

"You don't plan to cross a street till you're halfway across." Not insulting, just matter-of-fact.

Now Billy's eyes met his father's. "Yeah, but I'm diving in head first, and I'm looking forward to it."

"I think she'll straighten you out." Da leaned on the sideboard. "She's a levelheaded gal. You could do a lot worse."

And just where do you, in all your wisdom, believe I need this "straightening out"? Billy wanted to snap out loud. But he knew what that would start. So he bit his tongue and, instead, reminded his father, "She could do a lot worse, too."

Da didn't agree or disagree. Instead he changed the subject. "You staying for supper?"

"Nah, I gotta work tonight. This joint in Harlem I never played before." He jerked his thumb in the northerly direction.

"Well, be careful up there," Da warned.

He nodded. "I'm always careful." That was hardly true, but the less his father knew about his "chosen" life, the better.

A long but comfortable silence followed. Da went

for the coffeepot. "You okay for money?"

"Swell. I even got Susan to sock some away in the stock market or whatever market she puts her dough into."

"Good. She's done just great since the market recovered after the crash. She's one smart cookie—a real businesswoman." Da poured himself a cup.

Which means I'm just a musician with beans for brains perched at the tip of his tongue. But once again something stopped him. He'd done pretty well not to start an argument up to this point. Maybe being in the last thirty-one days of bachelorhood did that to a man.

He felt like sharing that revelation. "Hey, I think I'm growing up, Da. Really. I mean, not intentionally. It's just that since—well, I feel like I'm on the outside looking in—or maybe, down. I'm looking at things through my son or daughter's eyes now. And the world looks like a pretty shitty place to be a kid."

"Things'll get better. They always do." Da sipped, his eyes shut. "I'm thinking back to when I was your age. It was worse than this, and there was no Great Depression going on. Everybody was just poor. Not like we were rich one day and poor the next. I mean, we were poor always." He focused on Billy. "But I was determined to escape that trap, because I wanted to have a family and show them a good life. It happened in reverse for you, okay, so you'll have to work harder at it. But now you're living for your family, and your life will revolve around that. You might not be able to give your kids everything money can buy, but give them something more important. Your time."

"Yeah." Billy nodded. "I will. But still—it's miserable out there."

"You can only do your best, son. Surround your kids with your music, and happiness, and love. That'll keep the elements at bay most of the time." He sipped his coffee.

This was the first time his father had referred to his music as a positive thing, or even uttered the word "music" in the same sentence with a reference to him. What had changed in the last ten minutes? Was impending grandfatherhood even more profound than fatherhood? After all, if Billy felt old now, he could imagine how his father felt.

"Hey, maybe the three of us can do stuff, when he's old enough. Assuming it's a boy," Billy said, a hopeful note in his voice, thinking the three of them should get along better than the two of them.

"I would love nothing better." He gave Billy a genuine smile.

So that was it. This baby was going to bind them, bridge their differences, be the common bond.

"We'll see. Hope for a boy, then, Da. But if not, I'd like a few sons later. A pitcher, a shortstop, and a first baseman!"

"Then eat broccoli," came his sage advice.

So he stayed for supper. And he ate broccoli.

****

He showed up at Rosie's joint for his gig, armed with tooth powder to mask his garlicky breath. As the other cats warmed up on stage, the place filled up. He wondered if somebody important was playing here tonight, or if some politician or mob boss was throwing a bash.

Rosie knocked and entered the tiny room where Billy changed into his "play clothes." Dressier than his street clothes, the double-breasted red satin jacket with black velvet lapels and black trousers looked real natty on stage.

"Who's the guest of honor?" Billy expected the answer to be Benny Goodman, Glenn Miller, Tommy Dorsey, or even Mayor Walker.

Rosie pointed an index finger at him, thumb up, like aiming a pistol. "You, kiddo."

Billy halted with his pants pulled just past his knees. "Me? This is the first time I've ever played here."

"Oh, I spread the word aroun'. Worda mouth's the best way to get famous, ya know. Told everybody I know to come down and hear this piana player. They're all here, every one of 'em—Larry Fay, some o' the Tammany boys, Walter Winchell might even show up. And if you want dames, you can have one a minute if you want."

"Wow! Winchell might write about me in his column?" He couldn't think of a better start than a mention in the *Daily Mirror*. He couldn't take it all in at once. "Me?" is all he could say, standing there with his pants now puddled around his ankles. Never mind the dames. "I mean—I'm good, but—to headline a place like this—oh, and I have a dame—a girl. I'm getting married. So thanks for the offer. But the other cats in the band—"

"They don't look like they go for dames." Rosie snickered. "But you—you got a real future ahead a you, kiddo. Now I ain't no musician, but I know what I like. I heard you play, and I know good music from schlock music, and a good musician from a schlock musician. I know what people wanna hear and what they don't wanna hear. You wanna have your own club or your own band someday, you can do it. You got it."

Coming from a big shot like Rosie, that was encouraging. But it was scary to hear it, at any rate. Now he knew Tessie's cards were phonus balonus. Obstacles? Adversity? Barriers? Says her! Yesterday, he was just another Tin Pan Alley songwriter; now one of the premier nightclub owners in New York was gushing about how brilliant he was.

"Well, thanks, uh—I don't know what to say." He stood there and shrugged, not thinking to pull his pants up.

"Come out here and say *ciao* to your audience. Er—when you're dressed." Rosie backed out and shut the door. Billy stood in the light of a bare bulb, shaking his head in amazement. Tonight he would give it all he had.

****

Billy lounged on a couch in The Park Avenue Club, on the uptown side of 75th Street, a Scotch in one hand, a cigarette in the other. His head was too fuzzy to talk business. They'd been at it since Rosie's driver brought him there in a Pierce-Arrow. It had to be going on five a.m. His rumbling stomach wanted breakfast. But all Rosie Ingo's partner wanted to do was knock back booze and talk turkey.

These fellas were opening a new joint, on West 52nd Street, and planned to call it Swing Street. A dance club in front, speakeasy in back. But by the gist of the conversation, Billy knew who the clientele would be: the same as the owners. They offered him part ownership if he'd just play there, hire a band and slick it up, get real tight, with fancy matching suits, a glitzy-looking piano, and upbeat, danceable numbers.

How could he refuse? More importantly, how would he tell Susan he wouldn't have time to run Piano's with her, and how would he tell Pru he was now in business with these guys? But after all, this was their future, and his shot at the big time. Once he got there, he could open a theater, make records, tour the world with his own orchestra. Those dreams he always entertained now resembled reality.

As a leggy brunette slipped another Scotch into his hand, he found himself nodding, all right, but nodding off. He pitched forward, out of exhaustion, and spilled eighty-five proof contraband all over Biaggo Gazzola's silk tie.

At least something good came out of it when they propped him up—he referred Biaggo to Susan's store for a new suit, on him—Susan always gave him a 10% referral fee.

****

As Billy and Pru sat on his bed, he ripped open his second pack of the day. Cigarettes calmed him. But not now.

"What do you mean, you don't like the looks of this?" He halted, about to light a match. "This is the chance I've been waiting for!"

"To run a nightclub with a bunch of gangsters?" Her eyes stabbed him. "Susan's basement is one thing, but this—this could get dangerous. I read about the raids in the papers—you could go to jail, or worse—you heard what happened in Chicago."

"Do you think I was born yesterday?" he shot back. "I'm a musician, not a gangster, just 'cause I'm goin' in partners with 'em. Who do you think supplies the booze for Susan's place? You think a bunch of little old bootlegger nuns hide John Barleycorn in the convent for us? No, we get it from these guys, after they get it from who knows where. But that's the way it is. I ain't puttin' us in any more danger than anybody else in New York is in. I'm a businessman, pure and simple."

"There's nothing pure or simple about it, Billy. This sounds bad." Her hands shook as she fumbled with a button on her blouse. "I hear all kinds of stories about these guys."

"Yeah, and that's prob'ly just what they are. Stories." Heaving a frustrated sigh, he flicked the cigarette butt out the window and held her. "Just trust me. It'll be all right. We're gonna have a nice place, nice furniture, nice clothes, even maybe live as good as Susan and Irv. And all they have is a clothes store. A joint like this can rake in a lot more."

"At least Susan and Irv aren't running their store with gangsters." Her body stiffened as he held her.

"Yeah?" He struck a match and lit another cig. "Who do you think *buys* most of those silk suits? Especially these days? Not the down-and-outers on the bread lines, I'll tell you that much! Susan ain't stupid. She knows who her customers are." He took a drag and blew out a stream of smoke.

"But she doesn't own the place with them!" She pulled back. "Unless Irv is involved in something we don't know about. Is there a Jewish mob?"

He laughed. "Of course. And an Irish mob and a Chinese mob and probably a Zulu mob. But Irv's not in it, you can count on that. Look, Pru, you have to trust me. It'll be all right, I swear. I know what I'm doin'."

She rolled her eyes as if to say, "I've heard that one

before," and spread her fingers over her middle, which was just beginning to swell. He looked at the small mound and couldn't help but gape in amazement. "Hey, a life is growing in there, a part of me," he marveled with a powerful surge of protectiveness, another new emotion. Now he had two more lives to look after, and he wanted only the best for them. "You're not letting me do what I'm s'posed to do. I'm s'posed to be the provider here."

"You just want to be famous and see your name in lights." She gave him a cynical cock of her brow.

He shrugged and nodded. "Well, yeah, that too. It's what I always wanted. Besides you, of course. I mean, I've always wanted to be famous *and* be with you. I never thought I'd be lucky enough to have both. And this young! Look at me, I'm like—you know what Rosie called me? The *wunderkind.* That's German. That's what they called Mozart, you know. I learned that in my first piano lesson."

"*Wunderkind*, huh?" She smirked. "I didn't think he could manage all those syllables."

"Well, he did. And the joint was packed, and they all loved my playing, and the dames all—uh—" He nearly choked on his words.

She stabbed him with those sharp eyes. "The dames all what?"

"Well, there were dames there, but I didn't pay any attention to 'em. I was too busy playing. Er, I mean, I don't pay attention to 'em when I'm not playing, either, but—"

"Forget it, Snuggles!" She held her palm up, her fingers stained with blue paint. "I wasn't born yesterday either. There will always be women hanging around you. I'm sure young Mozart had the same problem." She gave him a half smile. "But these characters you're getting involved with—" She sighed, clasping her hands together. "Please, God, look after my two babies!"

****

"Billy, I got some things out of the attic: your christening gown, which my brother Dominic wore, the silver rattle Aunt Eileen gave you for your first birthday, and the cradle Grampa and Jadwiga made from scratch when Susan was born." Ma showed him the items in the hall before he even got to the table.

"Hey, they're nice. I didn't know you saved that stuff," Billy said as Pru hung back, clasping his hand.

"Oh, there's loads of treasures up there." She waved toward the trapdoor in the ceiling. "Why don't you kids go exploring later?"

Kids. He wished she wouldn't call them that anymore. Okay, Tessie was a kid. But not him and Susan. *I guess I'll always be a kid to her*, he groused. *Even after I become famous.*

"I love this cradle, Mrs. McGlory." Pru knelt and rocked it, tilting her head, a thoughtful expression softening her features. "Can I refinish it? I'd like to varnish it white, and paint the baby's name in little pink flowers on the sides."

"Of course, honey, you can do whatever you want." She smoothed down Pru's hair. "It's yours."

Da came out and nodded at Billy in greeting as he gave Pru a fatherly hug. "How's the bride-to-be?" Not mother-to-be, of course.

"Fine, Mr. McGlory. I love these things." She shook the rattle.

"Yeah, these kids had more than we ever had." Da's tone took on that soft reminiscing lilt. "We never had toys. Billy, you know your mother didn't have any dolls, so she dressed up the kitchen table instead? Sewed it a pretty tablecloth and decorated it real nice. I was lucky to have a brass paperweight in the shape of a bunny to play with. Hey, Vita, where's my brass bunny?"

"Right up on the shelf there, dear," she called from the dining room.

"That's a hint, Pru," Billy half-whispered. "Make sure we spoil the kid rotten."

"Oh, I will, don't worry!" She rubbed her tummy, and Billy looked over at his father.

He saw the old fella's eyes sparkle in wonder. Then Da tossed his head in the direction of the dining room. "C'mon, dinner's almost ready. Billy, go wash your hands."

****

On early Monday mornings, Billy enjoyed walking the empty streets. As the first day of the week, it had an innocence to it, like a newborn, not yet tinged or tainted with the world's filth and corruption. This morning greeted him with a warm embrace when he opened the club's back door and stepped outside. He listened as his footsteps echoed down the deserted Fifth Avenue like a solitary drumbeat.

He took a deep breath. Even the air was clean, somehow untouched, this early. Nobody was out to dirty it up yet. He didn't even want to light a cigarette. Only the night people, like him, were still up. They slept when the serious stuff was going on. His were the dark hours, of entertainment, boozing, and hedonism—

the hours of the night.

"Oops! I almost forgot!" He snapped his fingers, spun on a heel, and went back to the club, heading for the office. "Rosie, I'll be a little late comin' in tonight. Can you get one of the other cats to cover for me?"

Rosie sat at his desk counting the night's take, smoothing out dollar bills, an iron resting on a hot plate. Like the tailor pressed his clothes, Rosie pressed his money. Then he folded it in half before slipping his gold money clip over it. He'd handed Billy his first payment with a wax coating. It had felt counterfeit, so he went outside and stomped on it, scraping it along the sidewalk to get the wax off. But he knew Rosie had his reasons. Like Billy's parents, Rosie had grown up in poverty; he was probably Billy's age before he held his first dollar bill instead of loose change.

"I wish you told me sooner, Billy." Rosie looked up. "It's your crowd. They want to see you, ya know. Those other fellas in the band, they're just decoration."

"I'll ask Jazzy Lou Grecco if he can play till I get here," Billy offered. "I'll only be an hour or so late."

"Why? Whatcha doin' tonight that's more important than performin'?" Rosie gave Billy that warm, gold-toothed grin that came much more freely since they'd opened the club together. Rosie had no children or siblings; Billy knew he needed a youngster to watch over, like a kid brother. Billy liked the arrangement, too. He looked up to Rosie, in a strange kind of way. Sadly, in a way he could never look up to his own father.

"Well, I'm, uh—" He shuffled his feet. "I'm gettin' married this afternoon."

Rosie almost spit out his cigar. "Says you!"

"No, really," Billy assured him. "Even I wouldn't joke about something like this."

"This afternoon? And you wait till now to tell me? Somebody out there wit' a shotgun or somethin'?" Rosie grinned.

"No, no, I just—" Billy kicked a cigarette butt out of the way. He threw his head back, stretching his stiff neck. "I, uh—kinda forgot. Till now."

Rosie chuckled, expelling puffs of smoke, reminding Billy of a locomotive, and that went for the way he was built, too. "So you'll be doing a different kind of performin' tonight, then. Take the whole night off. For a honeymoon." When their eyes met, Rosie winked. Then he took the top bill off the pile, newly ironed, and tossed it to Billy. "Here's a weddin' present."

Billy reached over to retrieve it. It was a C-note. "Hey, thanks, Rosie. I appreciate it. It goes out as fast as it comes in, you know."

"Yeah, I know how these brides are. Just wait till you're married a while. She'll take ya for every cent ya got. Take some advice from me—always stash a little away for yourself, don' matter where—under the floorboards, in your shoes, just somewhere she won' fine it. You'll need it, trust me."

Rosie wasn't big on marriage, having had his own annulled after six months. But Billy frowned at the thought of hiding anything or fibbing to Pru about something as superficial as money. Everything had become theirs from the day she told him their baby was inside her—no more "mine" and "yours."

"I don't have to hide nothin' from Pru." He shook his head as he slipped the bill into his pocket. "She's not like that."

"None of 'em are 'like that' till later. Sometimes much later." He sat forward. "I'm just tellin' ya—you know why they call it mad money."

But maybe he should heed his older, wiser friend who'd seen much harder times than Billy ever would. Rosie had come over in the bowels of an immigrant ship, like Billy's parents, and those tales of poverty and privation never stopped swimming in his head. What was the harm in stashing a little dough away? He knew how Pru didn't believe in hoarding for a rainy day. So he began slipping the hundred back out. "Okay, I'll start with this." He walked over to the safe, concealed behind a portrait of the Mona Lisa. They each had a key that opened a different lock. Neither of them could open it without the other. Not that they didn't trust each other—Rosie said this was how everybody did it. Billy fished his key out, and Rosie got up to open the door with his. The musty smell of money wafted out. Billy wished he could talk Rosie into investing it, but he wouldn't hear of it. "After '29, my money stays safe. You know why they call it a safe?" he'd once said, tossing another wad inside.

Rosie didn't want to hear that the stock market eventually recovered and became a field of bargains. Susan had snapped up a bunch of cheap stocks that were worth a bundle again. So Billy played it "conservative" as he called it: half the money went into the vault, the other half into the portfolio she'd set up for him. He liked the idea of having a "portfolio"—it made him feel like he had some business savvy.

"It gonna be a big wedding?" Rosie asked nonchalantly enough, but Billy could detect the underlying question: "Why wasn't I invited?"

"Nah. Just my family. Hers ain't attending. They're kinda against it. They're rubes from Iowa—well, they're a little high-hat, too, but we did a few things bass-ackwards, you know." Billy placed the C-note in his half of the safe, shut it, and covered it with the Mona Lisa. "They think she's a woman of loose morals, now, and I'm the spawn of the devil. Bunch of Bible-bashers. Beware the flames of hell and brimstone."

Rosie nodded the whole time. "I know the story. You don't hafta tell me. Shame. You're holdin' up your honor, marryin' her. Never mind what her family thinks. Don' ever let another person judge you, Billy. 'Specially your in-laws. You know what in-law means? Just what it says. And they're made to be broken. Some of 'em." He cast Billy a sideways glance, and Billy felt a strong sense of connection at that moment. Sometimes they spoke half-sentences and didn't have to finish.

"The trick is in knowing which ones, right, Rosie?" Billy winked as he straightened the Mona Lisa. "What the hell is she smiling about anyway?" he wondered out loud.

"Maybe DaVinci took good care a her," Rosie said. "I'll see ya tomorra then. Congratulations."

"Thanks." He headed out the door, back into the innocent morning, feeling as clean as the new day. Then it hit him—*Today is your wedding day*. Nothing would be the same after today. Not the way he looked at himself, at Pru, or at the world.

He leaned against the door for a moment, lowered his head, and shed a few tears. Then he pulled himself together and moved on.

****

Crossing 14th Street, Billy saw the sign, bigger and higher than any other on the block, FINK'S, the letters stacked vertically—upright, imposing, yet plain and sharp. Refreshed from his four-hour nap, he hoped there'd be no customers pawing through the racks, so he could spend some time alone with Susan. This was their last visit before the wedding. They'd spent some private time before she married Irv, and mostly they'd reminisced about their childhoods, which seemed like ancient history even then. He'd felt grown up, and that was five years ago already. Now he needed a talk with his sister more than any stag party or wild night out with the guys.

The door was still locked, but he spotted her in there arranging hats on a rack. As he rapped on the glass, she looked up and tore around the counter to open the door. Bells clanged. "Billy! I was hoping you'd come by early!"

"Yeah, well, I wanna make sure the suit fits, and talk, maybe." He stepped inside the empty store.

"Let me go get it. Then you can try it on, and we'll have a whole hour before opening time. You're going to be a regular Joe Brooks with that suit!" She dashed to the back to fetch his wedding suit, which at the last fitting had made him feel like the Prince of Wales. All his clothes came from her store, but this wedding suit was the fanciest—and most expensive—he'd ever bought. He knew how important all this was to Pru, especially after her parents gave their final boycott notice in a letter addressed to both of them *and* his parents. Pru had read it and then used it to wipe her paintbrushes on.

Susan handed him the suit, and he held it up to himself, looking in a full-length mirror. "My kid brother, getting married!" Her eyes welled up, and she blotted the tears with a lace hankie.

"I don't feel like such a kid anymore." He actually felt pretty old at this moment. "Don't get all teary on me, Suze. I gotta get through this with Ma, too. Not to mention Pru. She cries at a parting of the clouds these days."

"Your top hat is over there." She ran to get it, sweeping it off the head of a male mannequin bowing to a lady mannequin at the entrance to her menswear department. "It came out so nice, I wanted to display it. I hope you don't mind."

"As long as he don't mind." He pointed to the now bareheaded gent, his bald pate exposed. "Give him a toupée or something."

"I'll put one of Irv's on him." Susan placed the gray hat on Billy's head. He tilted it to a rakish angle. "That's not the way you wear a top hat!" She slid it back into the correct position.

He glanced into the mirror again. "This hat makes me look like a giant. I don't know about this, Suze. I'm wearing this to get married, not deliver the Gettysburg Address."

"It looks classic and imposing," she insisted, brushing a speck of lint off his tails. "Now put this on, and here are the gloves and walking stick, and you're New York's newest fop."

He wasn't used to dressing classically or imposingly. Or foppishly. Putting on the suit, he felt stiff and unnatural. "How do I sit down in this thing? What do I do with the tails when I sit?" he asked from behind the dressing room curtain.

"Nothing. They sit with you."

He came out, and she gasped in delight. "Oh, *mama mia*, I didn't recognize you!" She placed the hat on his head again, thrust the gloves and walking stick at him, and he strode over to the mirror. The transformation astounded him. Seeing himself look so different made him feel different. He turned to the left, then to the right, in the single-breasted gray wool tailcoat with double-breasted lapels. Underneath it he wore a single-breasted collarless waistcoat that matched the black-and-gray striped pants. Lastly, he put on his new black shoes and gray spats.

"How'd I get into this, Suze?" He turned to her, and they laughed. "Did you ever imagine me looking like this?" He turned back to the mirror and, for a brief flash, thought he saw his father looking back at him. He swept the hat off for reassurance. The blond locks once again dominated his appearance, and he relaxed. He was still Billy.

"Come on back to my office." She took his arm. "We'll have some coffee and crullers before I have to open."

They sat in her throne room, an oasis befitting a society matron rather than the back office of a clothes store. She'd decorated it exactly like her lounge at home—the same velvet burgundy drapes, the same flowered carpet, even the Queen Anne sofa and end tables were identical to what she had at home. The only thing not duplicated was her nineteenth-century marble fireplace—here, she'd used *scagliola*, the Italian art of mixing marble dust, paint, and resins to make plaster look like marble. She was her mother's daughter, all right; she never passed up a chance to economize. But she had a comfortable setup here, considering it was her workplace. Cramming himself into nightclub dressing rooms wasn't exactly his idea of glamour, either. But once he was famous…

"Nervous?" She rubbed his back up and down.

"Me? Nah." He didn't want to admit his stomach was churning like an overloaded washing machine. He slid out his silver hip flask and emptied it into his coffee cup. She fetched a bottle from her portable bar and placed it on the cocktail table in front of him.

"For a refill." She sat back, crossed her legs, and admired him, nodding her approval. "My baby brother. A husband and a father."

"Cut it out, Suze." He flicked his hand. "You know I wasn't ready for this. It happened to me when I wasn't looking."

"You never would've been ready. But you'll have no regrets."

"Why?" he asked. "It'll make me grow up even more?"

"You want to grow up even more?" Susan looked him in the eye.

"Well, yeah, I was planning to. Soon. But not this soon. I thought I'd knock around New York a few more years, head to Europe, try to get my name made…" He trailed off, knowing it wouldn't happen so fast now.

"Plenty of musicians have families, Billy. Look at all the kids Bach had."

"Everybody had servants in those days. Us, we're just gonna do it ourselves. She'll take time off to raise the kid, then I'll do what I gotta do." He sat back, tugged on the pants, and crossed his legs.

"I'm sure Rosie and your other partners will understand. Family comes first." She took a sip of her drink.

He studied his sister in her navy-and-white crepe dress with the V-neck and pointed cuffs. She eased up the scalloped hem of her bias-cut skirt. Her matching beret sat on a dummy head on her desk.

He wasn't sure he'd heard right. Family comes first? They never saw her anymore—she was always here. Or running Piano's. Or on a buying trip. Or at some three-day stock market seminar. "Whose family?"

"Yours, of course," she answered. "Your family is your wife and child now. When the child is sick, you rush home to take care of him. When the child starts school, you help him with his homework. Then there are the school plays, the ball games, the teachers' meetings. You know. Things that come with raising a child. All the things Ma did for us. She took lots of time off her city job to take care of us, didn't she?"

"Yeah, but she's the mother." He sat forward, flustered. "That's the mother's job. Where was the old fella when one of us got sick or somethin'?"

"I like to think differently, Billy. Irv and I share equally. You see the way we're raising Rachael and Thomas. Irv stays home part of the time, takes them to school, the things the mother traditionally does. I run the store and the speak, but I still go to the school functions, come home when they're sick, all that stuff."

He had to admit they did a great job of raising their twins, who had just started school this year. Irv and Susan were equally close to the kids, their roles very blurred. But it seemed to work. Those kids were bright as hell, and enjoyed both parents' company.

"You think that'd work for us? But you know the way I am. I don't even know what day it is. Well, I know what day today is, but I usually don't. I go by the phases of the moon, almost. That's what scares the hell out of me." His voice shook. "I wanna be a good father, I wanna know my kid, go to ball games, and the whole bit. But who the hell has time? All I have time for is work and sleep."

"If all you had time for was work and sleep, you wouldn't be expecting a baby." She re-laced her coffee.

"Okay, work and bed. Besides, we won't have a maid and a chef and a butler and a driver and a bottle washer like you guys."

"Is that what you want?" she asked. "I'll hire you a live-in maid. That'll be my wedding present to you."

"Cripes, no." That made him laugh. He could just see a maid flouncing around their third-floor Jane Street walkup. "Where the hell would we put her? Out on the fire escape? I'm not the master type, and neither is Pru. She's looking forward to the mother part. She wants to do all that nurturing stuff. Me—I don't know if it's in me. Changing diapers? I don't even know if I'd get the right end—of the baby, that is."

"You'll learn, believe me. There's no mystery to it. There are two of you. But even if you had to do it alone, you'd do just fine." She seemed to take too quick a sip after that, as if to hide what she'd just said.

"Now where did that come from? Is this from another one of Tessie's visions?" He wiggled his fingers in the air.

"No, course not. I'm just saying you're a lot more capable than you give yourself credit for. It was just..."

He waved his hand, inviting her to finish the

sentence.

"A poor choice of words, that's all."

He glanced at the clock. He could no longer count off his remaining bachelor days; now it was hours. That thought made his heart thud against his chest like it wanted to get out. He swiped her bottle off the table and took a swig.

"You want a glass and some ice or water with that?" she asked.

"Nah, straight from the bottle and down the hatch is better sometimes." He held it up in a toast. "More direct. *Salut*."

"You need to stay awake for a few more hours, you know. We don't want to have to carry you down the aisle," she warned.

"I'm not gettin' squiffed. I just need to calm down." He grabbed a cruller and stuffed it into his mouth.

"You want to tickle the ivories a little, relax you?" She gestured at the piano across the room.

"Yeah. That's a good idea." He got up and went over to her upright Steinway, another replica of what she had at home. She even had them tuned at the same time, although this one didn't have the kids banging on it every day. He ran a few scales and arpeggios to warm up. Lost in his own musical world, he played some of the request numbers he did in the clubs: "Body and Soul," "I Got Rhythm," and one of his favorites, "Happy Days Are Here Again." He only stopped once, to slide his feet out of his shoes, which were pinching him. But he kept playing, now completely calm and himself once again, until Susan poked her head in the doorway and told him it was time to go.

"But I only started."

"Billy, it's one o'clock." She tapped her watch.

"Christ in a bottle." He grabbed his hooch and went to get married.

****

The ride to the church went by too quickly; he didn't even have time to think.

The back door to Susan's car opened and someone helped him out. He looked up into the eyes of his father, smiling down at him with approval, for once. He nodded and gulped.

Da walked him down the dark aisle to the altar. They had no ushers or bridesmaids. No one was giving Pru away. This was the two of them—the three of them—against the world.

The bridal march was in the key of F. The organist hit a few bum notes as Pru came into focus in her white dress with a pearl-edged neckline, a gift from Susan. Her gauzy veil reached halfway to the floor, gathered from a fabric cap trimmed with little roses. She looked like she'd come straight from heaven.

It all happened so fast. He repeated a few words, said "I do," and slid a gold band onto her third finger as she did to him. Never having worn a ring in his life, he hoped it wouldn't get in the way when he played the piano.

They stood for what seemed like a long moment. "Is that all?" he whispered to the priest, and he nodded.

"Yeah."

"We can go now?"

"Go in peace, my son." The priest raised his hands, palms up.

"Okay, thanks, Father."

Billy turned and looked into the eyes of Mrs. Virgilio McGlory for the first time. It all seemed right.

After the small reception at his parents' house, Susan's chauffeur took them back to their tenement. Billy saw Rosie's Morris Cowley Tourer parked outside the door. He waved Susan's chauffeur off just as the driver's side of Rosie's car opened. He recognized Fritz, Rosie's driver. "Fritz! Something the matter?" He instantly pictured Rosie full of bullets somewhere.

"No, Mr. Ingovito just wanted me to give you this wedding present." He proffered two jingling keys on a gold keyring that glinted in the streetlamp.

"Keys? To what, the car?" Or maybe the safe. Was this his way of telling Billy all the money was his to keep?

"No, to a residence. He gave me the address and told me to take you there. Uh—" He pulled a crumpled piece of paper from his pocket. "Nine-Twelve Fifth Avenue. Penthouse A."

"Why, that's—the Upper East Side." He felt Pru tugging at his sleeve and heard her clearing her throat to get his attention.

"It's your new home. Congratulations, partner." He held out his hand, and Billy shook it. He glanced at his bride glaring at him.

"Uh—can we have a moment, Fritz?" Billy mumbled.

Pru turned and entered their building. He followed on her heels. Halfway up the stairs, she spun around and pointed a finger.

"Billy, I'm not taking any gifts from him. A penthouse on Fifth Avenue? You know what that must cost?" Her voice echoed in the empty stairwell.

"Come on, Pru, he's loaded. It means nothin' to him. He's just bein' nice, I'm his partner, and he's always generous with all of us in the band. He gave Floody a trip to Europe, gave Jinji a new Caddoo."

"But a penthouse?" She grasped the banister. "Why?"

"Why not? I deserve it." Sure, the hundred simoleons was nice, but... "I'm the club's headliner. I'm his partner. I make a lot of jack for the place. It's always mobbed. You should see it some time." He couldn't help commenting on her continued refusal to attend the club.

"Did you know about this?" Her eyes narrowed.

"Of course not. But come on, Pru, we can use a nice place. You wanna bring up a kid here?" He gestured toward the top of the narrow stairs at a door so rotten it hardly closed.

"We did just fine. I fixed it up nice." A defensive tone crept into her voice.

"Yeah, it's nice. But compared to what he's giving us, it's a dump. Let's face it. The Upper East Side and this dive is like night and day. And what a beautiful way to start our life together. In the lap of luxury." He moved to embrace her, but she pulled away, gathering her gown, as if the stairs would contaminate it. Not like she'd ever wear it again. He couldn't wait to get out of this suit, classy as it was, and into a bed with his new wife.

"I don't want to go there, Billy, luxury or not. I don't want anything from the likes of him." She sliced the air with her hand.

"Come on, Pru." He expelled an exasperated breath. "You refuse this, he'll be insulted. I like being in business with the guy, and I don't wanna do nothin' to piss him off. Refusing his wedding gift will be like a snub."

"And accepting it will be like you owe him a favor. I know the way these people operate." She took a step up.

He rubbed his temples. "It's a gift, Pru. Nothing to do with favors or payback or any of that stuff. Where do you get these kooky ideas? You read too many of them penny dreadfuls."

"I'm not going, Billy." She stood there in the dark stairwell, glowing in her white gown. The only light shone from a bare bulb on the landing. She turned, the gown gathered in her fist.

He clutched her arm. "Pru, we'd better go. I don't wanna get on the wrong side of him. Look. Just for tonight. Then I'll tell him—I don't know, you're allergic to the paint or you're afraid of heights or something. But we can't flat out refuse. Let's just get Fritz to take us over."

She jerked her arm away and fished the apartment key out of her white satin bag, holding the envelopes from the wedding. "Tell him what you want, but I'm not having anything to do with that slimy gangster. They're all the scum of the earth as far as I'm concerned."

"Look, Pru, he does have a heart, you know. He is a human being," he snapped. Now she annoyed him, judging Rosie for no good reason.

"You like him so much, you stay there!" She fled up the stairs in a swoosh of satin. Her footsteps echoed and died above.

"Pru! God dammit!" But she'd already entered

their apartment. Their door slammed shut. Man, she was touchy these days. "All right, I will!" But he stood there for a long time, torn between his wife of five hours and his powerful business partner. Finally, he went back out and slid into the passenger's side next to Fritz.

"Uh—she's ill. She's—you know—expecting. Doesn't think she'd make the trip up there. Just take me there. Go back to Rosie and tell him I'm—we're settled in and thank you."

Fritz nodded and started the engine.

So Billy spent his wedding night alone in his beautifully furnished new palace at Nine-Twelve Fifth Avenue, Penthouse A.

Chapter Two

"It is impossible to tell whether Prohibition is a good thing or a bad thing. It has never been enforced in this country. There may not be as much liquor in quantity consumed today as there was before Prohibition, but there is just as much alcohol. At least 1,000,000 quarts of liquor is consumed each day in the United States. In my opinion such an enormous traffic in liquor could not be carried on without the knowledge, if not the connivance, of the officials entrusted with the enforcement of the law. I believe that the percentage of whiskey drinkers in the United States now is greater than in any other country of the world. Prohibition is responsible for that."

—Fiorello LaGuardia,
Hearings before the Committee on the Judiciary,
U.S. Senate, 69th Congress, 1st Session

"You like your new digs?" Rosie sat at his desk chewing on his cigar, counting money, when Billy came in.

"Oh..." He splayed his fingers in a gesture of wordlessness. "What can I say? It's the elephant's eyebrows, the butterfly's boots, and everything in between. Fit for a king. And queen. That bathtub is like a swimmin' pool. It was just too generous of you, Rosie."

"Hey, this is only the beginning. Want some fried calamari?" He pointed his cigar to a plate covered with a monogrammed napkin.

"No, thanks." Billy still hadn't talked to his bride, and it was five o'clock the next afternoon. They'd been married twenty-four hours already.

"The missus like it too?"

"Uh—well, she, uh—why, she found it very difficult to even set foot in there." Billy didn't dare tell his powerful partner that his bride refused to move into the home he'd given them, much less all the venom she spewed about him.

"Yeah? Don't she think she deserves the finer things in life?" Rosie dished out bills into separate piles like a dealer in a poker game.

"Well, you know, starving artist and all that. But thanks again for your generosity." He went out to the piano, the only thing he could face right now. He didn't want to call on Pru; what would that accomplish? She'd only start another shouting match and give Rosie the razz some more. Let her cool off, he decided, as he ran through all his scales. Letting the sounds take over, he closed his eyes and let his fingers do their magic over the keyboard. Then he sang a few Irving Berlin tunes, to him the best composer out of Tin Pan Alley. He wished Mr. Berlin were here right now; he could use some creative interaction. He improvised a few lyrics off the top of his head, but decided they were dreck. Slamming the lid down over the keys, he spun around on the stool and looked across the empty room. The chairs sat upside down over the tables, the sun struggled in through the skylight splattered with pigeon droppings. "This is only the beginning," Rosie had said.

Only now did that register. They were making good money; Rosie never kept a dime from Billy that was his. That penthouse must've cost at least a hundred Gs, but he was earning it; it was his name that drew the crowds every night. Without Rosie's connections and backing, it would've taken him years to get where he was now. Why couldn't Pru appreciate that?

With a few hours till the joint opened, he went behind the bar, filled his flask, then went outside to lean against the brick wall and watch the world go by. This entire scene was foreign to him, this workforce who made their living by day and slept by night. A life he wasn't cut out for. Bored with watching that after two minutes, he walked toward the Columbus Circle subway, passing all the briefcase-toting workaday stiffs in suits. He glanced at the tired and haggard faces. And these were the lucky ones—they had jobs.

The subway reeked of stale urine, and for the first time in years, he had to stand and be a straphanger. The train swayed and jolted. The lights dimmed and blacked out, on and off. He lost his balance several times, bumping into bodies pressed up against him; he couldn't have fallen if he'd tried. He mouthed silent thanks he'd been born with musical talent; he'd go off his nut if he had to live like this.

He got off at 14th Street and crossed over, the FINK'S sign welcoming him. Susan would still be here; she never left before six at night. The bells jangled as he opened the door and stepped in. They did a respectable business, but in better times the place would've been almost as mobbed as his club.

He went straight back to Susan's office and knocked. The polished brass nameplate announcing

"Mrs. Irving S. Fink" matched the doorknob.

"Who is it?" came her voice, sounding impatient.

"Billy."

In a second the door opened. She pulled him inside. "Billy, what on earth are you doing here? Aren't you supposed to be—well, what are you doing here?"

He went straight for the half-filled bottle on the table and took a swig. "We had a lovers' quarrel."

"You must be joshing." She set her fists on her hips. "You're married barely twenty-four hours and you're telling me you had a lovers' quarrel?"

"Oh, no, we had it when we were married six hours and forty minutes." He took another swig from the bottle.

"Well, for the love of God, what happened?" Now she went for the bottle and filled the monogrammed highball glass right next to it.

Just then Tessie came in, carrying a bundle of clothes. "Suze, these all fit, I'm gonna—Billy!" She nearly dropped her fashions on the floor when she saw him standing there, jingling coins in his pockets, looking down at his leather lace-up shoes.

"Yeah, it's me. Just stopped by to say hi." He didn't want to discuss any of this with Tessie around. She was only sixteen; he still wanted to protect her from the mess out there. He didn't want her to know about marital tiffs and gangsters and murders and bootleggers and how the hungry had to beg for a slice of bread these days. Of course she could see it for herself; all she had to do was walk down the street and get hit up by no less than a dozen panhandlers. But still, he wanted her to enjoy being a kid, far from all the grownup crap she'd have to face soon enough.

"You don't look right. In fact, you look sick. Have you been sick? You looked fine yesterday." She placed the apparel on the sofa and went over to take his wrist. She liked to play family doctor. So he let her take his pulse, he stuck out his tongue, said *aah* and she inspected his eyeballs.

"I'm not sick, Tess. Nothing for you to worry about." He waved her away and, with one more tipple, nearly emptied the bottle.

"You and Pru had a fight," Tess zeroed right in, eyes narrowed.

He glanced at Susan, who raised a brow and folded her arms across her chest.

"No, we didn't." He turned away.

"Yes, you did," she insisted.

"Cut out all the psychic applesauce, all right?" He turned and stared out the window.

"There's nothing psychic about it," Tessie went on. "She was here."

"When?" Both Billy and Susan said together, as if on cue.

"'Bout an hour ago. I was picking out dresses for the fashion show. She came in and looked around, took an armful of the most expensive clothes, tried them on, then put it all back."

"Maybe she just wanted to shop to console herself," Susan offered.

"Yeah, that's what she looked like," Tessie said. "Like she needed to console herself. She looked even worse than you do, Billy."

"Did you talk to her?" Susan asked. It was getting to be girl talk, so he shut up.

"Yeah, I went over and said hi, is everything okay,

and she said she was feeling under the weather. I asked her how Billy was, and she said he left early that morning, and she didn't get up till noon, and he was already gone," Tessie said.

So she hadn't blabbed about spending their wedding night apart. He expelled a relieved *whoosh.*

"Billy, you'd better get home in case she's not okay," Susan mildly admonished him.

"Yeah, Billy, what are you doing here anyway?" Tessie demanded, and by now he didn't feel like answering to either of them.

"All right, I'm goin'." He would tell Susan about the mess later.

As he turned to leave, Susan grabbed his sleeve. "Wait. Tess, let me talk to Billy. Go help out on the floor."

Alone with Susan again, he sat at the edge of the sofa and took a pre-speech slug of whiskey. "Well—it was like this. We got back to our place, and Rosie's driver was out there waiting for us with these keys, see…"

After he'd retold the events of his wedding night, she refilled their glasses. "Maybe you'd better dissolve this partnership, then, if she's that dead set against them."

"Are you *pazzo* or something?" he exploded. "This is the chance of my lifetime. I'm drawing crowds it takes better musicians than me years to get. Rosie treats me like a brother—almost a son, even!" He realized his glass was empty. He hadn't even tasted it going down.

"So that's what you want, a father figure?"

"Don't go into the Sigmund Freud routine, Assunta." He only called her by her given Italian name when he was at the end of his rope, which he was now, with the entire world hanging around his neck. "No. I don't need another father. God knows I got more than my share of those. But Rosie gave me my first break, and we're in business together. Pru has nothin' to be afraid of—she thinks there's gonna be another Saint Valentine's Day Massacre in the place or something."

"Well, it can happen, Billy," she warned. "This is New York."

"I refuse to worry about that. I'm too busy makin' a name for myself, and doin' what I was born to do." He paced the room, waving his hands.

"Well, now there are a few other things besides music that should be taking up your time." She followed on his heels.

He shook his head and flipped a quarter over and over. It slipped and rolled under the sofa. He left it there. "I gave up my bachelorhood—okay, I can live with that, because I love her. But I am not givin' up a Fifth Avenue penthouse. Or refusing Rosie his generosity 'cause of a naïve little pantywaist who can't see the world for what it is. Yeah, I wanna shield my son or daughter from the muck out there as much as I can, and I even wanna protect Tessie as long as she's a kid, but when you're Pru's age, it's time to face the world and see it for what it is."

"Just because she shuns mob figures and bootleggers doesn't mean she's naïve." Susan's tone stayed firm. "It means she's moral. More than we are, it seems."

"Whatever it is, the bottom line is that we're married one day, she's there and I'm here, and I spent my wedding night alone in one bed while she spent it in another. Never mind who's moral or proper or who's a saint or a sinner. How the hell do I get outta this?" he pleaded.

Susan laughed, and when he glared at her, she clammed up. "I'm sorry, Billy. I'm so sorry, I didn't mean to laugh, it's just that—" She took two slim cigarettes from a monogrammed silver case, offered him one, and lit them both with a matching lighter. "If I had a nickel for every time you said, 'How do I get outta this?' this store would stretch from here to Union Square."

"You're a big help, you are." He puffed on the cigarette, pacing back and forth. Then, with the cig still in his mouth, he sat down at the piano, always his last refuge. But he didn't play a note. Just sitting at a keyboard made him feel special, knowing he had a gift. He pitied the poor tin-eared souls who had no passion for song.

"You're a very clever fella, Billy." She dusted the piano with a rag. "You always manage to get out of your scrapes. But this one's an adult scrape, when all your past ones were kid stuff. This is something you'll have to resolve with your wife. The first of many, believe me."

He rested the cigarette in a crystal ashtray on the piano lid. "If this was Irv, how would you handle it? I mean, if he didn't want us running Piano's, or didn't like the way you invested your money or—anything. Would you walk out on him?"

She lowered her eyes, as she always did when deep in thought. He didn't think the question was so loaded; after all, she'd been married to him for five years—she should know about everything regarding Irv, so wrapped around her finger Billy called him her Jewish Bauble. "Probably talk it out, then reach a reasonable compromise."

"How the hell can you compromise on your dreams?" He threw his hands in the air. "Or the best way to get a decent income? Or where to live?"

"Tell Pru if she keeps the apartment on Jane Street, you'll keep the Fifth Avenue place, and you can go there to flop when you're tired. The rest of the time, you can spend at Jane Street, where you can raise the baby, keep all your things, just use the Fifth Avenue place for yourself. She never has to set foot in there. You can have your musician cats up there at all hours, so it won't disturb her or the baby, Rosie won't feel slighted, she'll be happy you're not completely caving in to him and letting him drag you down to the bowels of the underworld, and you'll have two apartments. Try it on for size."

He stood and jangled his pocket change. He always kept change in both pockets to balance the sound when he jangled it; instant music for him. "That was my idea, to set her up in a place and continue the way it was. It was her idea to move in together. She wants the kid to have a stable home."

"It'll be plenty stable. Lots of couples have two homes, two careers, so now you've got it. Now get off your coolie and go tell her. Talk it over. Write a song about it and sing it to her." Susan shook the dust rag into the trash can.

He smiled. A million lyrics buzzed around in his head about a man whose new bride runs out on him, but the song's ending was a happy one. It was Tin Pan Alley perfection. Even if she never came back to him, he'd probably have a hit song on his hands. "Okay, I'll go over there now. Thanks, Suze. Compromise. I'll remember that word. I might even set three music notes to it so I can sing it." He picked up the cigarette and puffed away.

"Well, some things can't be compromised," she gave him her lecturing tone. "Sometimes you have to bend all the way, some things just can't be met in the middle. But that's what marriage is about. Giving in to the spouse, and the spouse giving in to you when it's impossible to meet halfway. And not keeping score."

"Oh, so that's what it's about." A lopsided grin tugged on his lips.

"Didn't you listen to the vows you spoke yesterday?"

"Yeah, but it was all about being faithful and sticking it out when you're sick and poor." He plinked a few black keys.

"You weren't really listening, then. There's much more to it than that, Billy." The lecturing went on. "If vows included everything we're supposed to do, wedding ceremonies would take two days."

"Okay, let me face the music. The kind with no accompaniment." He got up and stubbed the butt out.

He walked to Jane Street in the warm sunshine. The working crowd had thinned out, and the restaurants and cafés were opening for the dinner hour. He wasn't a bit hungry, even though he hadn't eaten since breakfast. All he wanted to do was talk compromise with his wife.

He felt so small and insignificant, walking the streets of New York with all those working men who didn't give him a second glance. He was used to drawing a crowd, not being swallowed up in one.

****

She wasn't home. So he wrote her a note. Then he crumpled it up and wrote another. By the time he was finished, he'd poured his heart out over a three-page sentiment, pretending it was his journal. By seven, she still wasn't home, so he packed a few of his belongings, took the subway to the club, and went to work.

After the place closed at three a.m., he debated whether to go back to her, but wound up at his new penthouse. Just for the night, he told himself. Bright and early he'd go back to Pru.

But when he woke it was after noon. She was probably in one of her classes or visiting those galleries she always peddled her art in. He tried to go back to sleep, but he was too tense to relax, his nerves on edge. Rosie had ordered a shiny black Steinway concert grand delivered to the living room. Billy named it George, after Gershwin. Now he set the top fully open with the long prop stick and opened the fall board over the keys. The ivories felt cool and smooth under his fingertips. The tone rang out rich and clear; it was perfectly tuned and beautifully voiced. He played till his fingers hurt. That killed another two hours. Good thing it was Monday and the joint was closed. He didn't have to go to work.

He went to Jane Street one more time. She wasn't there, but his letter was gone, so she must've read it. He peeked in the trash can; it wasn't crumpled up or torn to shreds in there. That raised his hopes. He went back to Fink's. Buying new clothes always perked him up.

Susan was helping a customer and waved to him when he walked in. He nodded halfheartedly and buried himself in a rack of sporty tweed jackets.

She sidled up behind him a moment later. "Well, did you two work things out or what?"

"I didn't connect with her." He caressed a few lapels.

"Why not?" She grabbed his arm to turn him around.

"She wasn't home. Who the hell knows where she went. So I wrote her a letter. A damn good one, too." He shook his arm free and rifled through a display of shirts.

"Never mind a letter. You'd better go looking for her, Billy. She is your wife, you know." Her voice rang through the store.

He glanced around for customers. Thankfully, the place was empty. "I went back there. Twice. One of those nutsy jealous types I ain't," he argued.

"Billy, aren't you the least bit worried about her?" Susan followed him to a necktie carousel. "She might be in trouble."

"She was. But I married her." He slid a green striped tie between his fingers.

"This is no time for jokes, Billy," she shouted, staring him down. "Go find your wife."

"Maybe she don't want to be found right now," he countered, knowing how she liked to be alone.

"You haven't seen your wife in two days. You don't know where she is. Find her whether she wants to be found or not," Susan demanded.

"Hey, you got this in a thirty-eight?" He held up a black wool double-breasted jacket with lapels faced in satin and matching covered buttons. "I'll be the niftiest guy onstage in this. Very dramatic."

"Your bride is missing and you're shopping for

duds? Get your ass out there and find her!" She ripped the jacket from his hands, nearly tearing the sleeve off. "You never grow up, do you?" She turned on a heel and clacked off.

"Come on, Suze..." He stopped to think. *Hey, maybe I'd better go looking for her. Just to make sure she's okay.* But damn, if Pru had to do one of her vanishing acts, like she always did when she was upset over something...

She was one of those quiet, moody types who needed to be alone a lot, to just sit and think. That would drive him nuts; he couldn't stand to be idle for one second. This married stuff was already encroaching on his time, and it wasn't even two days yet.

He went to the studio she shared on West Tenth and rapped on the door. "Pru? Are you in there?" He hoped none of her fellow artists would be in, especially Franck LeJardin. His real name being Mort Horwitz, he was about as French as Gummo Marx, but Billy had to admit the shtick sold paintings. He dressed in the traditional artist's getup—the tam, the smock stained with color-coordinated paint, usually in hues of mauve on gray. A Van Dyke beard. A fake French accent that got better the more he drank. Irritating as it was, he had bearcats climbing all over him, and didn't refuse one. So if he was homosexual, maybe he didn't know it yet. In Franck's case, he'd probably be the last one to find out.

Sure enough, Franck opened the door, paintbrush in hand, palette in the other. "Willie! Do come in. I just brewed a pot of black tea. Will add fifty years to your life." The accent was missing; he usually didn't bring it out unless more than three people were present, his idea of an audience.

"Got anything that'll take fifty years off?" Billy mumbled as he walked in and glanced around the studio for Pru. No one else was there, not even one of Franck's models. It occurred to him that a peek of a firm thigh would've been nice.

"What's wrong, Willie?" Franck put down the palette and straightened Billy's collar.

"What's wrong? Number one: you calling me Willie. Number two: Pru's missing. You seen her?"

He clapped his hand to his mouth and gasped. "Missing! Goodness gracious! No, I haven't. I thought you'd be on your honeymoon."

"Nah, we haven't started it yet. From what I know, there's one requirement for a honeymoon—there's gotta be both a bride and a groom." Billy went to the window, looked out over the air shaft, and turned back to Franck.

Franck's brows shot up, the tam moving with them. He let out a sharp grunt, as if he'd just stepped in something that messed up his shoes. "She stood you up at the altar? Oh, I'm sorry, W—Billy. There, there, now." He reached out to draw Billy into an embrace. Billy leapt backwards, banging into a plaster bust of some ancient Greek.

"Nah, she didn't stand me up. We tied the knot. Then we had a tiff, and now I can't find her." He paced the loft in circles.

"Oh, what a shame." He tapped a steady staccato against his teeth with the end of his paintbrush. "Let me see, where would she have gone to?"

"My sister said she'd been to her store," Billy offered, as if that would help.

"Have you tried Hester Norton's flat? Or Percy Duprée or Dagmar Bluebottle? She could be with any of them."

"I never even heard of any of those people." Thank God for small favors, he thought.

"They're all artists," Franck informed him.

"I didn't have them figured for presidential candidates." Billy pulled out his cigarette pack.

"How about any relatives? Her parents, perhaps?" Franck prodded.

"That's the last place she'd go." Billy shook a cig from the pack and captured it with his lips.

"Maybe that's why she went there, if she didn't want to be found. She'd stay away from the obvious places." Franck shrugged.

"I guess I can try there." Billy lit his cig and puffed. "They live in the Bronx. It's a real long shot, though. They boycotted the wedding—well, you know why."

"If I know Pru, she might have just done that, gone back to make peace." Franck looked down at his buffed nails as he thought. "Or maybe checked herself into a hotel. She likes the Gotham. We have afternoon tea there a lot."

"Okay, I'll try those places. Thanks."

"And—uh, Billy—when you do find her, tell her she got a letter from a gallery in London. Unless you want to deliver it to her personally." He sidestepped over to a beat-up desk covered in paint cans and wine bottles, and retrieved a letter. "You know how badly she's been waiting to hear from some of them."

"Wow, yeah—of course I'll tell her. I'll take it." He took the letter and slipped it into his inside jacket pocket.

"You want to sneak a peek at it? Boiling water has more uses than just making tea, you know." He gave Billy a sly grin.

"You mean steam it open? Nah, I'd never do that. We respect each other's privacy. I'd never do somethin' like that." He slipped out before Franck had a chance to offer him anything else or come up with an even worse term of endearment for him.

Walking back toward their apartment, a twinge of worry niggled at him. Maybe some bum mugged her or something. His imagination started going wild, that ethereal songwriting mode he slid into when he wanted his thoughts to run free; "busy brain" he called it. It happened all the time when he had a fever. He wished he had something to write on. The perfect song was running through his head, about a man whose girl leaves and he doesn't know why. Before the words vanished, he got out his pen and a handful of dollar bills and scribbled his lyrics along the borders as he leaned against a storefront window. Tucking them back into his pocket, he continued walking. He didn't want to call on any of those queer birds Franck had mentioned; he knew them only by sight, but they didn't look like they knew where *they* were, much less Pru.

They did have one friend in common, Greta Schliessmayer. She was a dish, but she had brains. She lived in a ritzy brownstone on East Tenth, with an older gent she'd met gallivanting around Paris. She was a chorus girl and he sold stocks. They got married in a Paris courthouse, lived high on the hog for a while, penthouse overlooking Central Park, a car each, but lost everything in '29. While forced to live in an unheated garret, she wrote a novel about a woman who's rich one minute and poor the next and escapes poverty by writing a novel about the Great Depression. She titled it *There and Back Again* and sold it to Wm. Denton & Sons, made a name for herself, and really did escape poverty. She quit the kick line and now had a series of murder mysteries going, a real racket. She was known simply as G. J. Schliessmayer, for gender ambiguity, but Billy was convinced she'd sell more books if she shortened Schliessmayer to a more readable number of syllables. But she refused. Brandishing her Teutonic smugness, she declared she'd never hide behind a fake name. He admired her for that; he didn't believe in stage names or pen names either. They were showy and pretentious. So what if he called himself William Amadeus McGlory? That was no more than a joke anyway.

He rapped on Greta's door, a red lacquered job with a huge brass knocker. Door knockers set the elite apart from the rest of the poor slobs, who only had buzzers. But he found that as phony as holding a glass with the pinkie extended. So she was a bit like his sister, bent on giving that high-life appearance. But he couldn't take that away from her. She was a dedicated worker, and her books were real page-turners. He always kept the latest one next to the crapper.

A maid answered the door and led him upstairs into what Greta called her studio, with four typewriters lined up on a long table. She worked on more than one book at a time. Smoke hung in the air, and the last movement of Beethoven's Eighth Symphony floated out of the victrola. She sat at the farthest typewriter, her red lips clamped around a skinny cigar. "Be right there, Sheik."

She spoke, typed, and smoked, not missing a beat. The steady clackity-clack told him she knew exactly what she wanted to say, like Beethoven's purposeful melody. Her fingers finally rested. He turned from the pages of her novels that papered the walls and looked at her. She stood, put the cigar down, and blew out a stream of smoke. Tall as he was, but with curves in all the right places, she sported a wine-red silk dress with a V-neck just low enough to leave something to the imagination. "Sorry, just had to finish that thought. I can't stop in the middle of a sentence, no matter what those constipated college professors say. So, what's happening, Sheik?" She used her favorite nickname for him, after Valentino's famous movie role. It hadn't taken him long to get real comfortable with it.

"Pru's missing," he relayed the news.

"Since when?" She didn't act surprised, but she knew Pru. She slipped a cigarette from a gold case and handed it to him.

"We had a fight after the wedding." He shuffled his feet.

She huffed and puffed. "Jesus Christ on a camel, Billy, couldn't you wait till the ink was dry on the license?"

He could tell she was trying to hide a smile from that lipsticked mouth. She'd probably use this imbroglio in her next novel. What did he expect from someone who wore a silk dress and matching lipstick to sit all alone in a room and type? "What happened? Do you think she did something impetuous?" She was talking like a novelist now.

"Dunno. I thought I'd check here first before goin' to see those wacko artistes she pals around with."

"I'm an artiste!" she protested at once. "Oh, sorry. You did single out the wackos." She poured them each a whiskey.

"Yeah. As opposed to the ones who know what planet they're on," he countered.

She shook her head, chewing on a nail as red as the lipstick. It got him wondering if her unmentionables matched. "I don't know..." She shot him a quizzical glance. He looked away, hoping she didn't think he'd done anything to harm Pru and was just looking for cover. "Maybe you'd better go to the cops."

"Maybe you write too many crime novels. She's only been gone one day. She went into Susan's store yesterday, so she can't be far. She's not the type to jump on a train. I just thought maybe she stopped in for a drink—or something." He knew Greta occasionally smoked "or something," which Pru had tried a few times. But now, carrying the baby, he hoped she had the sense to avoid cannabis or opium or any of that other crazy junk he never touched.

"Tell me your whole side of the story." Eyes wide with interest, she sat back down and motioned for him to sit at a typewriter chair. Sometimes he thought she'd missed her calling and should've been a reporter. But the way he figured it, writers were writers.

He took a generous mouthful of whiskey. "My partner in the club, Rosie, bought us this gorgeous palace on the Upper East Side. She don't want nothin' to do with it. Thinks it's contaminated or something, just 'cause Rosie's kind of, well, you know—"

"A mobster," she finished his sentence, her tone flat.

"Well, not like that. They don't call them that in

real life. That's for those pulp novels and stuff. They're just—businessmen. For lack of a better word." He raised his glass and sipped.

"I know Rosario Ingovito, and there's no other way to put it. He's a machine gun-totin' cheek-kissin' cigar-chompin' spaghetti-twirlin' mobster." Her stern tone rattled him.

His eyes widened in surprise. "Yeah, that's Rosie. How do you know him?"

"Who doesn't?" she asked.

"I didn't." He shook his head. "Not till he came into the speak and told me my piano playing killed 'im."

"Well, he does appreciate music. He can dance up a storm. But he's not from around here. He's from Chicago, originally with Capone's gang. Only been in town about a year." She sipped her drink.

"Maybe that's why I never met him." He glanced around. "Susan knows him, though. He's one of her steady customers."

"That's the safest way to do it. Something I learned from experience. Keep it to business. But he is one of my biggest fans." She brandished a smug grin.

"Yeah?" He couldn't imagine Rosie sitting and reading anything that didn't have names of horses and odds on it. "How'd he ever find you? I mean, novelists and...his type of business don't cross paths very often."

"He didn't know I was a novelist till the next morning, when we exchanged small talk over joe and hotcakes at Zelli's," she said.

"The next morning? You mean—"

Now the smile widened and accompanied a wink. "I could never get serious with somebody like him. He goes through babes like I go through carbons. I didn't mind, though. He's not my type. I was kind of oiled at the time; it was after one of my signing parties. I was having dinner at the Waldorf with my publishers, he came into the place, walked right over to me, and—he was so charming, we danced together, talked—he offered to take me to Italy on the *Santa Pantaleone*, first class all the way. So how could I refuse?"

He blanched. "You went to Italy with him? Where was Stanton when this was going on?"

"In San Francisco, trying to set up that branch office of his. I know he's got a chippie out there. It doesn't bother me. Just because we're married doesn't mean he owns me. And I don't own him. Besides, when you're a continent apart—" She didn't need to finish.

"Yeah. Nice arrangement." He hoped he'd sufficiently kept anything resembling envy out of his voice. "So, you know Rosie. Hmm. Small world, ain't it?"

"Not really. This is New York. We all travel in pretty small circles, when you think of it. I know a lot of the Broadway people from my chorus line days. I've met a lot of the cats you play with in the nightclubs, and everybody knows who the bootleggers are. That's everybody who's not permanently on the wagon. So I would venture to guess that includes about ninety-nine percent of the adult population of the city."

"Yeah, lotsa entanglements in this city." He realized how many people knew his parents, for better or worse. "So can we put this intricate web to work and try to find Pru?"

"If I were you, I'd just stay at Jane Street," she advised him. "She's got to go back there sometime.

There's no sign she moved out, is there?"

"Nah." He shook his head. "Everything's just the way we left it. She just wants me to get worried sick about her."

"Come on, she knows you better than that." Their eyes met.

He gave her a knowing nod.

"What could she possibly do to make you worry?" Greta's tone challenged him to come up with a believable answer.

"Well, she is my wife now, Greta." He waved his hands around. "I'm s'posed to worry about her."

"Yeah, Sheik, and I must say, I do admire you for that. How you became the devoted family man." She voiced her approval, her gaze lingering, making it hard for him to turn away. Damn, if she wasn't a dish. He always figured she had a thing for him, but he'd brushed it off as another character study for her. She went out with fellas just to study their quirks and use them in her novels. So he'd never picked up on it; besides, he had Pru and never wanted anybody else. And with songs to write and clubs to play, who had time for alley-cattin'?

"I may be devoted, but I don't know if I'll be able to keep up the family-man bit," he admitted.

"You will," she said. "You've got it in you. I mean—you must. Sometimes you just have to force yourself."

"Yeah, I got my own self into this." He thumped his chest. "I guess, in a way, we do make more choices than we think, in some things."

"Of course." Greta bobbed her head. "I could have been Mrs. Ingovito if I wanted to. But like I said, he

69

just wasn't my type."

"He asked you to marry him, too? When? On the ship?" He poured himself a refill.

"That was the second sentence out of his mouth after 'What's your name, doll?' And he had a rock the size of Gibraltar ready to slide onto my finger if I'd said yes. I guess he carries it around with him, in case some gold digger does say yes. But I'm not the money-hungry type. I'm like you—I can live with money or without it."

They were a lot alike, come to think of it. "Didn't he know you were married?"

She licked her lips, and they glistened. "It just never came up in the conversation."

"I'm surprised he'd even think of marriage again. You're right—he couldn't stay faithful. He's got a different skirt in there every night, sometimes two—like an antipasto and a main course. Then he's prob'ly got dessert waiting at home."

"Oh, I wouldn't care about that. He just didn't have the right touch, if you know what I mean." She raised a plucked brow.

He knew she didn't mean it as a musical analogy. He felt his cheeks go hot—he'd never talked to a woman like this before. He didn't know if Greta was trying to get at something or was just leading the conversation to use it later as dialogue. After all, her books did get pretty steamy. "Yeah, I guess so. He doesn't turn me on, either." They shared a smile and when she offered him a refill, he took it.

They sat for a while longer and read the first chapter of her book out loud, each taking different characters' parts. The snappy dialogue had a steady rhythm. The conversation eventually returned to his reason for being there. "I'll take the night off and go find her, if I have to. Well—I guess at this point, I *do* have to."

"I'm really sorry, Sheik. I know how straight-laced she is. I could've told you she'd never go for accepting a gift like that from somebody like Rosie."

"She don't even want me in partners with him, but I couldn't pass that chance up. Besides, I've never told her what to do." The defiance crept back into his voice.

Her eyes kept looking him over, from left to right, like she was reading him. "I like that in a man. Don't ever become one of those Percy pants. I have no respect for Percies. Disgusting." She stuck out her pink tongue.

"Yeah?" He sat up from his slouching position and took another refill, though he knew he shouldn't. "Well, sometimes you have to compromise. And sometimes you have to give in. That's what defines a marriage, if it's gonna work." He tried some of his newfound wisdom on her.

"Depends on what you compromise or give in about. When your beliefs or principles are at stake, you don't give in. Giving in to 'okay, we'll go to Jack and Charlie's instead of Tony Soma's' is one thing. But don't let compromise or giving in chip away at who you are. Then you're no longer a spouse, you're a pet."

"So you think I should let her stay lost? I mean—you know—don't go looking for her?" He took a long pull of his drink.

"She knows where you are, Billy," she said in her matter-of-fact tone.

"You're the first person who's given me that advice." He put the glass down.

"That's because I'm the first person you've talked to who knows where she is," Greta said.

"You know—God dammit! Why the hell didn't you tell me when I walked in the damn door?" The amount of alcohol he'd consumed made that sentence come out just as he felt. "So she's just busting my balls. Well, let her find me!"

"She's just cooling her heels. She's pregnant and a little out of balance. How many times has she done this to you, Billy?" Greta asked.

"Since we've been married? Just this once." He went back for the drink, but on second thought he left it there.

"No, before that," she said.

"I dunno." He gave a one-shoulder shrug. "I lost count. When she's miffed, even if it's not at me, she goes someplace to think—a church, the library, someplace nobody bugs her."

"You know she's kind of—well, overemotional at times, bless her heart. But she's fine. She'll be home tomorrow, I promise."

"Are you gonna talk to her?" he asked. "When?"

"As soon as you leave," she now whispered. "Because she's—" She pointed upwards.

"Where? On the roof?"

"No, you dolt. Upstairs." She jabbed her pointer finger upwards. "In my spare bedroom."

"Oh, Jesus. Well, don't tell her I was here—no, tell her I was here, but I didn't want to bother her, and that I love her and that we can compromise, okay? I'm not gonna go storming up the stairs and demand she come home with me. Just let her be, and tell her I love her. I'm just relieved she's not lying in a ditch someplace."

He lit another of her cigarettes and took a long grateful drag.

"You can tell her all those things. She knows you love her. You're one of a kind, Sheik, you know that?" She smiled and winked, but there was nothing flirtatious about it.

So he left, after giving Greta the letter for Pru from the London gallery. He would have liked to give it to her himself, later, but he knew it would lift her spirits and get her home faster. Now he could go to work and not spend his evening scouring Manhattan for her. But first he had to get to a piano and some blank sheet music. If they kept this up, he'd have enough songs for a musical!

****

Billy was in his dressing room stripping off his play clothes after the club closed. He balanced a highball in one hand while he discarded his shirt with the other. Rosie knocked. "Hey, kiddo, got a minute?"

"Yeah, sure. Come on in." He was never modest in front of Rosie. He'd seen Billy in every stage of undress, and it didn't bother him. So he finished shucking off his clothes and drained his drink as Rosie entered.

"So how's married life?" He opened a bottle of Scotch, took the glass from Billy's hand, and refilled it.

"Haven't had enough of it to really say." Billy didn't want to go into detail. He took a sip of Scotch as he pulled his satin robe off its hanger. He liked to lounge in the robe for a while and unwind before leaving.

"How you mean? You two gettin' along? Geez, you're s'posed to be on your honeymoon, Chrissake."

Rosie settled into the chair.

Billy kept his mouth busy filling it with Scotch.

"C'mon, kiddo. You didn't seem yourself tonight. Like you weren't there. That's not like you. I know you love bein' at that piana more'n anything in the world. What's on your mind?" He slurped his drink.

Billy felt comfortable confiding in Rosie, and had, many times, about personal matters. But they were usually limited to bodily functions; never had they discussed anything to do with the mind or the heart, the way he talked to Susan. Maybe now was the time. "You wanna get a bite to eat, and I'll tell ya?"

"Sure." He nodded. "I'll get Tony to make us veal parmesan with your favorite fried calamari."

They chowed on that—and three bottles of different wines. The only light in the empty club came from the footlights lining the stage and a candle stuck into a Chianti bottle on their table.

"Pru's not happy with my—should I say—place of business. She thinks—well, she's afraid—ya know." Billy gestured with his hands full of garlic bread, crumbling the crust as he spoke. "I told you she's from one of those Midwest Baptist or Methodist or whatever-ist families, law and order, the whole bit. A bunch of Abe Lincolns. Would walk three miles to pay a three-cent library fine. So how does she like her husband involved in anything that's beneath the law of the land? Hell, she even gave Susan a lecture one time about the evils of alcohol consumption, quoted Lincoln, saying how intoxicating liquors came forth like the Egyptian angel of death, slaying the fairest in every family, some malarkey he probably lifted from the Old Testament."

"Good ol' Abe." Rosie chuckled. "Yeah, he was a

teetotaler. Good thing he ain't President now, huh? There'd be no chance of a Prohibition repeal. Unless somebody shot him, I guess. But look. She'll come around. She don't wanna be a starvin' artist forever, does she?"

"She'll never be anything but." He helped himself to some calamari. "She thinks she's gonna be another Michelangelo or something. She just got a letter from a London gallery. I hope that's an invitation to exhibit her stuff there, but she don't care if she's not famous till she's dead, like those other guys. Even if she makes it big it won't change her mind about liking what I do."

"Then maybe she'll like this." Rosie reached into his breast pocket and in one fluid gesture dumped a wad of bills onto Billy's empty bread plate, scattering crumbs all over the checkered tablecloth. "Tell her I threw ya a few crumbs." He refilled their wine glasses.

Billy eyed the new serving on his plate. "How much is this, Rosie?"

He shrugged. "I counted it, so it's more'n fifty bucks." He looked at Billy and flashed his gold tooth. "Tell her you earned it fair and square. And you did."

"I didn't earn this much tonight, did I?" He gestured at the wad.

"Sure you did. A few of the boys sent it over to my table, told me to give it to you. Just a token of their appreciation. Go out and buy a shiny new Packard or Nash roadster and take her for a romantic drive through the park, sit in the rumble seat and neck. That'll get her mind off the money." He swished his wine around in his glass like brandy. "There's much more where that came from. She'll want a summer home before too long. Try the Jersey shore. The wind ain't as high there as the Hamptons."

Billy had never asked Rosie to see one side of the books or the other, or the bottom line. After counting the take every night, he gave Billy his cut. Billy sat in on a few of these tallying-up sessions, so he knew Rosie gave him his fair share. Once in a while, he'd throw Billy a few extra bucks, usually on a weekend, or when another of his investments paid off. So he let the old boy indulge him. After all, where would this place be without its star piano player?

"Thanks, Rosie. I'll take good care of this—of her with this." They stood, and he shoved the roll into his pocket. It embarrassed him the way it bulged. "She'll sure think I'm happy to see her."

****

Billy went straight back to their Jane Street dive on a hunch she'd be there by now. She never stayed mad long. That's why he wasn't too worried when she first vamoosed.

He turned the key in the lock, and the door swung open. There she stood, in the red crepe-de-chine pyjama suit he'd bought her, with its low neckline and short bolero jacket, trimmed with chiffon. They stared at each other, drinking each other in. As she threw herself into his arms, her wide-flared trousers billowed around him. He'd stripped the outfit off the dummy in Susan's display window, leaving it naked, then started dancing with it, to the amusement of passersby, till Susan ordered him out of the window and decently re-draped the dummy. When he paid for the outfit, she wasn't mad anymore.

"I'm so sorry I acted that way, I never should have; I ruined our wedding night. I'm just not myself these days," she cried.

"It's all right, Honey Bear. You did what you had to do." He decided not to mention he'd been at Greta's when she was there. Somehow he knew Greta didn't mention it to her. He didn't tell her he'd gone to her studio looking for her, either. He didn't want her to think signing a piece of paper turned him into one of those jealous gorillas. So their wedding night was a bust. But he understood. He understood why she couldn't bring herself up to that Fifth Avenue place. He was so attuned to her, he felt her fear.

"But I hate that you're involved with those ruffians. It's so dangerous!" She shuddered, leading him toward the bedroom. She'd made the bed with satin sheets, the pillowcases monogrammed with their initials intertwined. He felt like a king about to bed the queen.

"It's nothing to worry about, Honey Bear," he assured her. "We're not doing anything worse than bootlegging."

They sat at the edge of the bed. He almost slid off. "But your father was the Chief of Police! How can he let his son and daughter get involved with that?" She ran her hand up his leg.

"He might've been the Chief of Police, but he's Irish," Billy said. "He likes a tipple as much as anybody and is just as anti-Prohibition as anybody. There's nothing to worry about with the speak or the club. There's plenty of money to pay everybody. So nobody complains. You have to learn the ways of the world, Pru." His tone sharpened. "This isn't Lincoln's frontier. And I'm living my big dream. My own nightclub. My own combo. This will lead to a better life. How 'bout a summer home at the Jersey shore?" He tried that on, but got no response. Just those two big eyes burning into his. Hell, he was burning, but not in his eyes. He looked down at the bulge in his pants. "Here." He extracted the wad of bills and tossed it into her lap. "Go on a shopping spree tomorrow."

She fingered the roll, and he knew she felt that same sensation he had when Rosie gave him his first cut. He'd never handled so much dough in his life. It was a new, thrilling, yet scary, experience, to be in control of all that lettuce. And to know much more was coming. "Like the way it feels in your hands, nice and thick, huh? You know what's better?" He took it from her, pulled the rubber band off, and fanned the bills out. A few fluttered to the bed and the floor. He scattered them onto the satin sheet and laid her down on top of them. He slipped her tiny feet out of her satin-trimmed velvet mules and wriggled out of his clothes. "Now you'll really know what it's like coming into money."

He peeled the pyjama suit off her and they finally consummated their marriage three times, making up for each night they were apart and once for good measure.

He got up to get a cigarette, and she started to giggle. "What's so funny?"

"You've got money stuck to your behind." She pointed at his bottom.

"Well, do I, now." He peeled the bill off and flicked it to the floor. "We can clean up later." He'd never cared about money before, and he didn't now. It was great to have it, though, to peel off his ass and make love in a bed of it and buy nice things with it. But to let it rule him the way it did Susan—he'd slash his wrists first. The biggest difference between him and his beloved sister was that his money got stuck *to* his ass, while her money got stuck *up* hers.

"So, we'll go shopping tomorrow?" He lit his cigarette. "I have the afternoon free. How about a Russian sable? You'd look gorgeous in one of those. Or those stripey gray things. What are they called, chinchilla? They import them from Canada or someplace, don't they?"

She tilted her head this way and that. "To be honest, baby doll, I'd rather check into the Plaza and have a nice honeymoon. Room service, sunken bathtubs, heated towel racks, whatever else they have there." Her sculptor's hands began playing him like clay, but at this minute he felt more like yeast. He moved closer. "I've always wanted to see what that place looks like on the inside. It's every artist's dream. I want to tell everybody I spent my honeymoon there."

He had all that in the penthouse, for what it was worth. "Sure, Honey Bear, if that's what you want."

"Now for my news." She sat up straight. "That letter, from the Royal National Gallery in London, they offered me a month-long exhibit there. But I want to go before the baby is born. It'll be easier that way."

He let an ash drop to the satin sheet, but brushing it made it worse. So what. They could get more. "Hey, that's swell. If only we could put music and art together instead of music and words, we'd make a great team."

"Can you go with me?" Her eyes brightened with hope.

He knew that was coming. He really didn't want to, or think he could take all that time off. "I'll have to see. I don't know if the club can do without me for that long. They need me."

"But I don't, is that it?" Her voice took on a

defensive edge.

"No, you know what I mean—I didn't mean it that way." He waved his cigarette through the air. "Look, I'll arrange for some time off. But the whole month— no matter what business I was in, it'd be hard to take that much time off."

She nodded.

"I'm glad you understand." He drew her to him in a hug. Hell, he didn't want to be jackassing around London, lost in all that fog, while he had a public here who adored him, willing to pay money for him to roll around in and stick to his ass.

****

"...only if it's all right with you, Rosie. I don't want to hurt the club in any way. I know you gotta strike while the iron's hot, and I—"

"Go! Go, have a good time already. What is it, a week goin', a week back? Do that, take a few days in London to take in the sights, turn around, come home. Everybody needs a break. You're workin' your *bajoles* off. You deserve some rest. Here." Once again Rosie opened the safe and gave Billy a generous bon voyage gift.

This wad would've choked the Tammany tiger. "Rosie, I don't need all this. I didn't make that much tonight or even all week—"

"Consider it an advance, then. Or vacation pay." He waved it off.

"We get paid for vacations in this business?" he marveled.

"And while you're sailin' the ocean blue, you can think of somethin' else." Rosie shut the safe and covered it with the Mona. "I've been talkin' to a few show biz people, Broadway and all that. I know how you always wanted to write the score to a musical."

"Hell, that's all I've ever dreamed about! Even before I knew Tin Pan Alley existed, I was dazzled by Broadway. To team up with a composer and write an original score, and see my name on a marquee in lights, all those tiny bulbs spelling out my name—" He closed his eyes and caught his breath, letting the dream carry him away.

"Well, now you got your chance. Any composers you wanna team up with?" Rosie sat back and propped his feet up.

"Jumpin' Jehoshaphat, there are at least half a dozen!" He knew all he had to do was say the names and Rosie would hunt them down. And Pru was so set against these guys! If they were patrons of the arts, what could be wrong with that?

"I'd love to work with Gershwin or Berlin, but they wouldn't be interested in working with a nobody like me. How about Lester Fontaine?" Fontaine had written one smash hit, *When Dreams Come True*, which ended its run in 1931. Billy loved that musical; he went to see it every time he had some spare money, and he knew all the songs by heart. It was his favorite musical after Gershwin's *Of Thee I Sing*. "Fontaine retired, and word got out that he'd become a recluse, but I wonder if he'd be willing to get back into the swing of things again. Can you contact him?"

"It's done." Rosie nodded. "You two ever met?"

"Once." Billy smiled at the memory. "At the Blue Horse, a club I was working down in the Village. He came in one night and sat almost right on top of me. Made me nervous as hell, but later I worked up the

81

nerve to introduce myself. He was a real nice guy. I seen his show a dozen times. I have a lot of his sheet music."

"I'll get him in here and introduce ya's." Rosie folded his hands across his chest.

Billy was so excited he couldn't even light his cigarette; he kept missing it. Rosie lit it for him. "I have an idea already. It can be about life in New York. About a couple who's living the good life, then the market crashes, and they're evicted from their fancy apartment, forced to live in a dumpy attic, then she starts writing a novel about being rich and losing it all, then the book gets published, and they make their money back, and she becomes a famous author."

"That story sounds familiar." Rosie smiled into his empty glass.

"That's 'cause you know who wrote it," Billy said.

"Yeah, what'sername." Rosie tapped his head. "The Schliessburger dame."

"Schliessmayer. Yeah, Greta. She's a good friend of mine—ours," he added. "Pru and me. I can write the lyrics and music with Fontaine. She can write the book. Well, the book's been written, but I mean the book for the musical. I think audiences'll love it—they can all identify with it, all right—and her novels have sold a zillion copies. *Headin' for Better Times* can be the title."

Rosie stopped chomping on his cigar. "Hmmm…sounds like a winner."

"I even kinda have some lyrics rolling around in my head already." Billy closed his eyes and released a long sigh. "I don't know how they came to me, they just did. Like my lyrics always do. Sometimes I don't even have to think. They just come to me, like a little voice speaking to me. Maybe 'cause of the crash, how everybody went broke. It's something that's part of all our lives now."

"Well, tell the little voice to join you on the voyage over the ocean. Good thing you don't have to book passage for little voices, huh?" Rosie smiled.

Billy went into the john and, while sitting there, took out his pen and began scribbling lyrics on the toilet paper.

A half hour later, Rosie knocked on the door. "Hey, what'cha doin' in there, takin' a swim?"

"Sorry, I'll be right out." Billy folded the paper. "I was writing lyrics."

"Nah, no hurry, I can use the can in your dressing room if I need it." He meant that literally; what passed as a john in Billy's dressing room *was* a paint can. "I found your guy—what's his name? Fontaine?"

Billy swung the door open, almost hitting himself in the face. "You got him on the phone?"

"Not him, his agent," Rosie said. "But he's gonna relay the message. And if he's smart, and knows there's lotsa dough to be made, he'll be standin' right here tomorrow puttin' your crapper paper to music."

"How—how did you manage to find him?" Billy knew how naïve that sounded; it was even kind of rude, like asking someone how much they paid for a gift. Rosie could've gotten President Hoover's wife to come here and sweep the floor if he wanted to. Nobody said no to Rosie Ingo. Something he'd have to teach his wife.

"It's a small town," was his answer.

Billy left it at that. "Hey, thanks, Rosie. I'll make

this the most entertaining show since Minsky's opened."

"Oh, it's gonna be that kind of a show?" He raised his brows.

"Well, no, I didn't have burlesque in mind. It'll be more highbrow than that, if it's gonna be based on Greta's book. You do want it to be more highbrow, don't ya?" Billy went to wash his hands.

Rosie nodded. "I thought it'd be nice to have some class. Not the same old vaudeville schvatzola. Go for the uptown crowd."

"That's exactly what I had in mind," Billy said. "And I'm sure Fontaine will, too."

"Now get back to your honeymoon. And make sure you don't use that paper for nothin' else!" He swatted Billy out.

Billy slipped the paper into his pocket. "I'll transfer it to good paper as soon as I get home. I just have my greatest bursts of inspiration at the oddest times."

"Then go home to your wife." Rosie gave him a one-shoulder hug. "You might get another burst of inspiration."

"Yeah, she always did inspire me," he stated reverently. And that was the truth. "I could've filled a vault with all the songs and poems I've written about her." Just like Rosie said, this was only the beginning!

When he got back to their Plaza suite, he nearly stumbled over a steamer trunk in the middle of the floor. Pru, dressed in an artist's smock that was way too short, just the way he liked it, greeted him with a long leisurely kiss.

"Why such a big trunk?" he asked when they came up for air.

"I want room for my clothes to breathe." He'd heard Susan say that a few times. He hoped nothing else would rub off.

"Well, I'd better get a normal-sized one myself," he said. "Looks like I'll be going with you for a while."

"Oh, Snuggles!" She jumped into his arms, wrapping her legs around his waist. They spun around the room and landed on the enormous bed.

"I'll be able to go over with you, stay a few days and come back. But that's not the real good news." He rolled on top of her.

"Well, to me it is!" She cupped his face and planted a kiss on his lips.

He supposed it was. He had some getting used to with this marriage thing. "Rosie's gonna finance a show I'm writing the music for, based on Greta's first novel. I'm gonna ask her to write the book, and guess who he got to be my collaborator? Lester Fontaine!"

Her expression turned from that of elation to disbelief to dread in the time it took her to push him off her. "What does Rosie know about show business?"

"He's bankrolling it—footing the bill. A backer, or an 'angel' as we say in the business, don't have to know show business. All he has to know is how to shell out dough. With his backing, we'll have a lavish production, get the top talent, the best theater, and this is the beginning of the career I've always dreamed of."

"I thought you always dreamed of what you're doing now—owning a club." She inched away as if he reeked of garlic.

"Well, yeah. But who said you gotta be confined to one dream? I've got at least a dozen. Owning a club is swell, but writing a Broadway musical—the whole world will know who I am now. That'll springboard into other things—the William Amadeus McGlory Theater, the William Amadeus McGlory Orchestra—you can be the set designer for the show, if you want."

She forced a smile and a nod. "I never thought that far ahead of the game. I only thought as far as will I sell my next painting or sculpture so I can eat, and can I stay in the studio I'm in or do I have to move into a smaller, dingier one at the end of the month."

And that's where they differed. "That's what I need to teach you—how to plan ahead. I'll have to let you in on my long-range plans. We can talk about it on the ship going over. But you always knew I didn't want to stop at New York, Honey Bear. Just like you're off to London now."

"But that was a fluke." Her voice rose. "The fella who came into the gallery and saw my work, he only ducked into there because it was raining. He was on his way to the Museum of Modern Art and didn't want to get his shoes wet. It was by the slimmest chance. I never planned on getting anywhere near London."

"Why not? You're good enough," he insisted.

"That doesn't mean I'll get anywhere." She bunched up the pillow and rested her head on it. "Plenty of artists a lot more talented than me are starving. Same goes for musicians. There might be better ones than you, but they're destitute. They didn't have your lucky break with a gangster."

"Now hold it. Hold it just a cake-eatin' minute." He got up and refilled his drink, glancing out the window at Central Park, realizing how well he had it already. "It's far from a lucky break. I busted my ass since I'm fifteen getting my songs out there. My meeting Rosie was no stroke of luck. He came into my speak and said my piano playing killed him. So he gave me a head start, but if my piano playing was crap, he wouldn'a gave me the time of day. What's lucky about that?"

"Yeah, you're right." She sat up cross-legged. "There's nothing lucky about getting hooked up with the mob. I'm surprised Greta is letting you drag her into this."

"Greta is going into this head first. Greta also knows who's backing it. She knows him better than you think." He grasped her shoulders. "Pru, everybody's hooked in with the mob, to some degree. Who do you think owns your studio? Prob'ly some gangster who owns the whole damn block."

"An old homosexual who attempted suicide when Valentino died owns the studio I work in," she informed him. "And he's the furthest thing from a mobster I've ever seen."

"Well, they do own a lot of property. They also own a lot of people. Cops, judges, politicians, you name it. They're here, Pru." He gestured around. "In the air we breathe! If you wanna get away from them, you'd have to move to Siberia, but they prob'ly run the vodka racket there, too."

"I'm afraid of them." She gave him her round-eyed raccoon look. "And afraid for you."

"It'd be nice if you'd say you're happy for me. For once." He sat hunched over.

"Of course I'm happy for you." She leaned over and slid his jacket off.

"Don't let me mess this up." He carefully extracted the toilet paper from his pocket and unraveled it. It was a good three feet long.

"This is the Plaza, Billy." She tilted her head. "They do have toilet paper here."

"It's not just any toilet paper." He smoothed it out on the floor and brought it over to drape across the bed. "It's got the opening song lyrics on it. This is the most valuable toilet paper in the world at this moment. Once I'm famous, I'll use it for its primary purpose, and it'll be worth a lot more!" He chuckled at his vulgarity, but she turned away, unamused. "I'm going to meet Lester Fontaine tomorrow for the initial meeting about the show, invite Greta to do the book, and when I get back from overseas, we're gonna hire a producer and a director and a cast and a crew and get to work. I might just send you home in our own yacht!"

"Oh, Billy, I don't want a mansion or a yacht or a string of polo ponies." She folded her arms across her chest. "I just want to share my talent with the world. I don't have to get rich from it."

"Well, I wanna do both. Audiences show their appreciation by coming back for more. And I plan to give 'em a lot more!" He began reading his lyrics to her. She listened, raptly, as she always did.

He only wished she were as driven as he was; he wanted them both to set the world on fire. Maybe once she was caught up in the excitement of the show her enthusiasm would catch. She'd hear the thundering applause, as he could now; she'd see his name on the marquee, as he did whenever he closed his eyes. Then she'd know how intoxicating fame could be.

He had a movie reel going in his mind at all times, and never an intermission. He just had to get her over her silly fear of this mob thing.

****

Interlude: Sunday Dinner at the House

After they finished singing happy birthday to Irv, which of course Billy had to play on the piano, Susan thrust a wrapped box at her husband. He pushed aside his half-eaten rum cake and methodically unwrapped it. "Here, save the bow." He handed the bow back to Susan. She deposited it into her purse.

"Wait, now, wait!" Susan set up the camera and focused on the birthday boy. "Okay, you can open it now."

The flash blinded everybody as Irv gushed, "Oh, Susan!" at the gleaming new adding machine. "Just what I wanted! How did you know?"

Susan blushed and beamed. "I know my Froggie!" They gave each other little pecks on the cheeks.

"It's lovely, Irving." Ma, barely concealing her envy, gave it a good once-over, pushing buttons and handling the lever expertly. "Tom, we ought to get a new one of these."

"Your birthday's not till March," Da replied, in all seriousness.

Tessie, uninterested, went back to shuffling her tarot cards. Pru looked on in bewilderment, and Billy just stayed at the piano and lost himself in Mozart's "Turkish March." It was his safe haven; he didn't have to fight to keep a straight face because nobody was looking at him.

If someone had told him about this, he would have thought they made the whole damn thing up, and applauded their imagination.

Chapter Three

"Within a half mile of my home I have run across more than twenty speakeasies wholly by accident. They operate under an engaging variety of disguises: a bakery where one may obtain a superb glass of lager, a dry cleaner and pressing establishment where a solid phalanx of garments in the window effectively conceals the festivities within, a dozen or so cigar shops where cigars are grudgingly sold, a vegetarian restaurant, and a real estate office."

—F. Smith, 'Look Behind the Front,'
Outlook, March 13, 1929

~*~

"Though people are entering Tony's by the dozen, they are being sharply scrutinized at the door. Those not being immediately recognized must produce membership cards in order to gain admittance. Technically, the place is a club with the right inherent in all clubs to exclude non-members from its premises."

—Harper's Monthly, April 1932

Billy went to Greta's the next day before work, with one long-stemmed red rose and Pru's blessing. Another reason he was thankful they didn't live in the traditional world—Pru didn't demand that all his friends be men. Pru and Greta were like sisters, and there was never any rivalry between them. Their taste in men was completely different, which cut down on complications. Greta was a knockout, but she had a roughness about her edges that he found somewhat unsettling. She was a hard worker, hard player, hard boozer. She shot pool. She played poker. She smoked cigars. He wouldn't be surprised if she one day expanded that G. in her pen name to George. But she was too original for that.

Once again Greta's maid answered the door and led him up the stairs to her studio. The door was closed this time, so he knocked. He was surprised she was still working at this hour—she was a morning person and never gave up her afternoons or evenings. She didn't even like to talk about work during her leisure time. He'd hoped she was already wondering what to do for dinner.

"Enter."

He opened the door but didn't see her at any of her typewriters. Then he peered around the room. There she sat, on the window seat, Indian style, in a shimmery dressing gown, smoking a cigarette with a long holder like a squaw puffing on a peace pipe. She gazed out the window, lost to the world.

"Greta? You busy?" By now he felt foolish holding the flower, like a delivery boy. So he stuck it in an empty whiskey bottle.

She turned to him and her holder almost tumbled from her mouth as she gaped in surprise. "Sheik! You're here! How did you know I was sending you a message?"

"Message?" He shrugged. "Uh—I don't think smoke signals would get very far in New York."

"No, I mean a mental message." She beamed. "I've

been meditating and sent you one. I hoped you'd get it."

"I thought it was my idea to come over here." He stepped in. "But you never know. My sister claims all that psychic stuff happens to her. But I do it the mortal way—with the telephone."

"I didn't want to call you on the blower." She slid off the window seat and placed the cig in a classy-looking black onyx ashtray, the kind that shouldn't have butts stubbed out in it. "It would seem too forward."

He shrugged. "I wouldn't a thought so. Why?"

"With Pru going overseas and all—and I didn't tell you about Stanton and me."

"Isn't he in Frisco?" he asked.

"Yes, and he's staying." She patted her hair and glanced in the mirror across the room.

"Are you going with him?" He fully expected her to say, "Yes, of course, I'd follow my husband to the edge of the universe."

"No. I don't know a soul there. My life is here, my family, my publisher, my home, my friends." She gave him a warm smile. "I don't want to give any of it up."

"Then—you're separated?"

"I'm here and he's there. I can't think of a better synonym." She gave a dismissing wave of her hand. "We have lawyers who get along better than he and I ever did, so I think the divorce'll be civil, if not amicable."

"I'm sorry." This got him wondering how Pru would take to his traveling, once he got his orchestra together and started booking dates all over the world. Would she stay behind so as not to abandon her fellow artistes?

"Me too. Oh, well, I tried. Maybe marriage just isn't in the cards for somebody like me." She picked up the rose and inhaled. "Smells pretty. Thanks." Then she looked up, as if she'd just realized something. "Are you having problems again? Pru's not here this time."

"Not at all. She's okay," he assured her. "She's lapping up luxury in a suite at the Plaza. I was just thinking—you wanna grab a bite to eat, chew the rag for a while? I'd like to talk to you about some—stuff goin' on."

"I'd love to eat. Or chew the rag. Or drink." She sighed. "Anything but write." She poured them each a whiskey, sat, hiked up her hem, and crossed her legs. They were stockingless, her feet bare, her toenails painted bright red, matching her fingernails and lips. He looked away and for an instant felt that he didn't belong here; it was like walking in on her in the bath.

"What's wrong with the writing?" He reached over, grabbed his glass, and went back to his standing position a safe ten feet away.

"I have writer's block." She sipped her drink.

"Oh." He took a gulp and nodded as if he understood all about it. "Er—what's writer's block?"

She looked him up and down, appraising him. He always took special care grooming himself, but now that she'd noticed it, he wished he hadn't combed his hair coming up the stairs. "It's when you can't write. You're blocked. Sit down, will you?"

But not next to her. He sat at her third typewriter. A blank page stared up at him from the machine, not so much as a word on it. That must be awful, he thought. He'd never had anything like writer's block. In fact, his problem was always the opposite, too many ideas clamoring to get out.

"This ever happen before?" He gestured at the empty page.

"Not till I realized my life with Stanton was over. I can't seem to come up with anything fictitious." She took another sip.

He turned to face her. "Maybe you don't have any more words left in you."

"Words left in me?" She cocked her head, urging him to explain himself.

"Yeah. Louie Armstrong said: 'Musicians retire when they have no more music in them.' And it's true. I s'pose I'll have to retire if I ever wake up one day and don't have any music in me anymore. So maybe you said everything you had to say in those other books. You got no more words in you, and it's time to do some other kind of work."

"Funny you mention that." She looked past him, focusing on a distant point. "I've felt like that for a while, that I want to do something else. But I was afraid to admit it. I thought I'd keel over at a typewriter, but not till I wrote 'The End' at the end of my final book. But now I would like to do something new, even though that means starting all over and pounding on doors."

"Any idea what you wanna do?" he asked.

"Perform." She nodded. "Do something on a stage again. Show biz."

He shot her a grin. "Hmm, what a coincidence. I have something you might like to do. And it is on a stage, in a way. But it's show biz, all right. And you sure won't have to pound on any doors."

He looked forward to springing this on her like a

Christmas gift. No one knew about the show; no one but Rosie and Pru. Rosie never discussed his business ventures with anybody on the outside. Billy hadn't told his family yet; he planned to surprise them with opening night tickets and watch them beam with pride. For once. "I wasn't talking about going back to the kick line," she said.

"Nope. Something a lot better." He clasped his fingers around his glass.

"Well, I would like to get back up there. But on a stage, not a runway." The look she gave him told him just what she meant.

"No, it's not burlesque. It's highbrow uptown stuff." He paused for effect. "Broadway, to be exact."

By the time he'd finished telling her about Rosie's fixing the meeting with him and Les Fontaine, and asking her if she'd like to do the book based on her novel, he'd drained his third drink. Now his feet were bare and propped up on her table. He sat next to her, his arm comfortably resting along the back of the couch, barely touching her shoulder, the dinner date forgotten.

"That's fantastic, Sheik! I know this is what you've always wanted. I'd be honored to be part of it." She squealed, jumping up and down.

As thrilled as he was that they'd be working together on this sure-fire hit, the whole thing saddened him, because of the one person he really wanted to share it all with. "I wish Pru could say that. She's dead set against anything to do with Rosie. She can't even be happy for me now, now that I'm on the brink of having a smash Broadway hit. She thinks I'm on my way to becoming a gangster. What an imagination."

"That's what makes us artistes, Billy." She got all

serious. "Imagination. We don't live in the real world, we're on the outside looking in. And we observe. How do you think we create music, or art, or fiction? By observing. And you can't observe effectively when you're part of it. You have to be outside of it, with a detached, sometimes cynical, eye."

"Yeah, you're right." He agreed. "Sometimes I feel like somebody left me on the doorstep after I was born. And whoever left me there is torturing themselves with what-ifs."

"That's just human nature." She drew in a long breath. "What might have been."

"Well, I never what-if. There's no what-if in my life. I'm doing what I was meant to do. There couldn't have been any other way." He slashed the air with his hand.

"Sometimes I wonder what if I'd gone with Stanton. I'd be a hausfrau in San Francisco, cooking and cleaning up after him and wondering what if I'd stayed here," she mused.

"Wow, there's no way out of that one, is there?" He looked into the depths of his glass. "Like a snake biting its tail."

"Well, I'm glad I stayed, now especially." A satisfied smile lingered on her lips. "This was meant to be, wasn't it? *There and Back Again*—even though it's fiction, it's so real, and right for the times."

"Yeah, that's why I think the show'll be a hit. Especially if it has a happy ending."

"Just make sure the music's good. I'll take care of the book." She gave him a sideways grin, her holder at the other corner of her mouth, as she lit the cigarette. He noticed the red lipstick ring around it when she placed it in the ashtray. He started noticing other things with red lip prints on them—pencils, glasses, tissues. It sounded like something he could write a song about— no matter how ravaging the Great Depression, there'd always be that red lipstick print on everything.

"All right, I'm gonna get going and meet up with Les, my, uh—my collaborator, for that initial meeting." He straightened his lapels, feeling like a real Broadway mogul now. Collaborator—that sounded so *show biz*. So legal, even. "I'll introduce you two after I feel him out and maybe when we've sat down for a few songs, once I get back from this London thing. But I'll be bringing your book for him to read. He's got some homework to do now."

She stood and plucked a book off a shelf that contained nothing but copies of *There and Back Again*. Opening it, she slid the pen from behind her ear and signed it with a flourish on the title page. "This is for Les. With my compliments."

"He'll love it. Thanks, Greta. I'll see you when I get back." He snapped his fingers. "Oh, drat, we never made it to a restaurant. Sorry 'bout that."

"That's okay. I'll catch you when you get back. There'll be plenty of restaurants. Well, have a bon voyage!" She gave him a friendly hug which he returned. He skipped out of her house, blowing a kiss to the heavens.

He hoped to be able to write songs about the Great Depression when he was feeling so happy.

****

When the club closed that night, Rosie invited Billy for fried calamari and to meet a friend. Fried tentacles hardly looked inviting at three a.m., but Billy knew he'd better sit and meet the important-looking guy sitting at Rosie's table. His black shirt and contrasting white tie said he meant business; not too many guys looked like they stepped out of a fitting room at that hour. He flashed a clean smile and stood to shake hands with Billy as Rosie introduced them. "Billy, this here's Jackie Harper."

Billy's jaw dropped.

Herbert John Harper, known as Jackie, was one of New York's biggest moguls: offices in Times Square, hotels in the Roaring Forties, breweries and distilleries. Billy also knew he'd already backed one Broadway hit. He was glad the handshake was over; now his palms were sweating like crazy.

"Mr. Harpo—er, Harper, uh—glad to meet you." He tried to stop stammering, but this man was every bit as much a New York legend as Teddy Roosevelt.

"Glad to meet you, Billy." Jackie gave him a smile. "Rosie here tells me you're ready for Broadway."

Rosie poured each of them a glass of wine, just to the rim, as always, without spilling any.

"It's always been a dream of mine. All my life." Billy spoke his words like a prayer.

"You're a gifted musician. I'll be happy to be one of your backers," Jackie offered.

Billy pinched himself. Yep, he was awake, all right. "I—er—hey, thanks!" He felt like Saint Anthony had just come down and handed him the world. Here was his future, his bankroll, his ticket to fame and immortality in the world of musical theater.

"Rosie told me a little about it. Based on that dame's book—what is it—" Jackie tapped his head, trying to remember.

"*There and Back Again.*" Billy gave him the title.

"Yeah. That's the one." He held up his finger. "I like them hard-luck stories. I come up the hard way, too, Billy, so we're all in the same boat here. You know I used to be a pickpocket on the Lower East Side? Started when I was nine years old. I hadda do it, see—it was the only way I could eat. I'd get caught sometimes on purpose so they'd throw me in the reformatory, so I could get three squares a day. Then I got too old for that. They wouldn't take me no more. So I was a slugger for a gang. Then I really got in trouble. I got tried for murder, but got released. I, uh"—he paused, took a sip of wine—"never murdered nobody, did I, Ro?"

"Wha'd ya say? Didn' hear ya," came Rosie's noncommittal reply as the calamari arrived.

Billy couldn't choke down a bite, so he stayed rapt, his gaze fixed on Jackie's piercing onyx eyes beneath the brows, connected in the middle, like two bass clefs.

"Ironically. That's the word, ain't it, ironically, when things happen like a surprise?" Jackie asked him.

"Yeah." Billy leaned forward. *Get on with it!* he wanted to urge.

"So then I get caught on a minor assault an' battery charge, and whadda they do, they throw me in Sing Sing!" Jackie laughed and picked up a squid.

"Whew." Billy whistled. "You really came up the hard way." He and Rosie exchanged appreciative glances.

"So then I decide I ain't cut out for this small-time piffle. I wanna be a beer salesman. Like my idol, Frank Costello. So now—here I am. But I ain't no thug. Well, not no more." He chewed on his squid. "I like the arts—ya know, art, opera, thee-ater. I have a few paintings in my house in Jersey."

Billy knew "a few" and "house" were both understatements. He was just being modest. Like so many of Rosie's friends were.

"You wanna come see us work any time, just drop in." Billy wouldn't mind if Jackie wanted to watch him every minute of his workday; that never bothered him. He liked to be watched, to be gawked at. "I'd enjoy having you as an audience."

"No." He waved a pinkie-ringed hand. "You just gaw'head, write the thing, with that other fella, what's his name—"

"Les Fontaine." Billy gave Jackie his collaborator's name.

"Yeah. I know it'll be great. I trust ya." He gave Billy a clap on the back that made him pitch forward.

Good God, Jackie Harper a backer of his show. Now he knew why they called backers angels. Was he dreaming, and would he wake up back in his Horatio Street basement dive, with nothing but his beat-up piano and his virginity still intact? Was all this really happening?

By the time they broke it up, Billy looked down at his plate. He'd eaten all his calamari without even realizing it, and now he was hungry.

****

Billy and Les, now official collaborators, started working together the night his ship got back in from London, after sandwiches with some small talk. They sat at facing grand pianos in the practice studio Jackie Harper had rented for them.

Billy named the grand piano Ira, after the other

Gershwin, and polished it twice a day. He explained to Les that by naming it and taking care of it, he knew it would become his friend and bring him lots of good music. Les just screwed up his face, uttered a "Hmmf," and moved on.

Billy soon realized he couldn't compose show tunes on a concert grand. The action was too stiff, and despite all the polishing, he was ruining it with cigarette burns and glass stains. So he brought his childhood Wurlitzer from his parents' house and bought them a new one to replace it.

Buried under reams of sheet music, they created what they hoped would be the smash hit of the century, working in shifts four days a week and together for the other three, till one of them dropped and the other was too tired to prop him up. Greta came up a few times, and they worked through her storyline.

When Billy wasn't in the studio composing, he was at the club playing. This gave him no time to socialize or read Pru's letters. But he wasn't a bit tired or hungry. He slept in twenty-minute spurts, then got back up to work. He'd never been so excited or energized or exhilarated in his life. As much as he missed Pru, truth was he wouldn't have had time for her if she were home. So maybe it was for the better that she was across the ocean, living her own dream. There'd be plenty of leisure time in their beach home.

"Where do you think we should have tryouts?" he asked Les as they put the finishing touches on the final song.

"I like Boston," Les said. "It's a good city for tryouts."

"Yeah?" Billy brightened at that. "I've never been

there."

"But that's getting a little ahead of ourselves," Les said. "We have to hire a producer yet. Besides, I don't feel the score is polished enough even to start rehearsals or casting or anything." Les sat at his piano, buffing the brass duck head on his walking stick. Even their short breaks were taken at the pianos; neither wanted to waste the time to walk across the room and sit on the sofa.

Billy tried to hide his amusement when Les showed up on the second day with a porcelain chamber pot, which he actually used. He didn't even want to get up to go to the john. "Those first coupla songs don't seem to set the tone."

"Yeah, I know what you mean," Billy agreed, blowing smoke rings. "They're too, uh—" He looked for the right word.

"Upbeat," they both said at the exact same second.

Since the moment they'd met, it was just as Billy had anticipated; their chemistry was like something a sorceress conjured up. They were born to work together. They liked the same music and books, and even dressed alike. Rosie called them the Tin Pan Twins, although Tin Pan Alley was far behind them now. Les loved Greta's book as much as Billy had, and felt it had great potential as a musical.

Les scribbled down a few notes. He broke his pencil, so Billy tossed him another one from a huge box of pencils sharpened by some flunkie Jackie had hired just to sharpen their pencils. Although they were painstakingly organized, with a servant borrowed from Jackie's household attending their every need, they managed to run out of staff paper one day and resorted to the old toilet tissue trick until their helper came back with another stack.

But work was where their chemistry ended. Their personal lives couldn't have been more different if Billy's blood had been made of oil and Les's of water. During their rare conversations, Les divulged that he was a homosexual who'd been living in the West Village with a companion for the last twenty years, that he'd joined the Jewish faith in deference to his companion, and that he didn't drink, smoke, gamble, curse, play cards, eat sweets or meat, go to ball games or horse races. Music was enough for Les; it ruled the man's soul. Billy had already seen him laugh hysterically and sob openly in response to a lyric or a particularly moving melody line. But Billy felt his own relationship with music was much healthier.

They'd drawn an invisible line down the center of their workspace, between the pianos, and Billy's side looked like Billy's side. There was never a glass of booze or a stick of gum or candy or a cigarette butt anywhere near Les's half of the studio while they worked. The only adornment was a framed photo of Les's companion on the piano lid. "Nice-looking fella—uh—I mean, looks like a nice fella," Billy stammered. Truth was, he was nice looking. Not to be outdone, Billy brought in a portrait of Pru and placed it on his own piano. But Les didn't comment on her looks.

****

"What's with that Fontaine guy? He's like a phantom," Rosie commented one night after the club closed. "I seen him that one time, then never again."

"He keeps to himself," Billy explained. "But I

think it contributes to his genius. Imagine if I never went out, except to work. Never smoked, never drank, never went to any shows, never had any diversions, just concentrated all my energy on music. I'd probably be as brilliant as he is."

"If you never went out or never did nothin' else for fun, what would you write about?" Rosie asked.

"You got a point there," Billy conceded.

"There's different kinds of genius, Billy. Don't go comparin' yourself to him or to Irving Berlin or nobody else," Rosie philosophized, which impressed Billy, even though the guy probably never finished third grade. He was smart in other ways, ways of the world, that Billy admired. "Doin' nothin' for fun might work for him, but it wouldn't work for the likes of you."

Billy returned his smile. "Maybe that's why we collaborate together so well." He wished he and Rosie had more time to just sit at a table after a good meal with a few bottles of wine and gab. "I'm me and he's him, but together we're us."

"Speakin' of us…" He gave Billy his cut for the week. Plus some extra, for Path Cutter, the racehorse they'd bought together with some other investors, which he kept forgetting to tell Pru about. "We got ourselves a winner. Belmont last Tuesday, third race, she came in first with six-to-one odds in the Trifecta."

"Hey, that's great. I wish I could'a seen it." But when did he have time to go to the racetrack these days?

****

Billy went to Piano's that night for the first time since he'd started working on the show. He'd told Susan he was busy making a record. Well, in a way he was. The music would be on records someday. It bothered him to stretch the truth like that, but it was more important to him to surprise them with opening night tickets.

When he went in the back to tell Susan he was there, a cable was waiting for him. "Boarding USS Constitution, arriving NY Harbor on 20th." He knew they charged by the word, and frugal as Pru was, she didn't want to pay for "Miss you" or "I love you." He didn't take it personally.

Two more weeks without her. His heart tripped. The time would fly by, and they'd be together again! As "together" as possible with his insane datebook.

Susan toasted him with his favorite contraband from Canada. She suggested they all go to his club to celebrate, tonight being their parents' anniversary, too.

He didn't want to refuse, though he dreaded another blowup with his father, this time over his going into business with Rosie. "What do you think he's gonna do?" he asked Susan. "Lock me in the hoosegow or disinherit me?"

"He knows all those fellas; he's worked with them," Susan said. "He's not holding it against you."

"Boy, he is getting old." Billy couldn't miss the humor in that.

"It's just the times, Billy." Susan sipped her drink. "Prohibition going on, cops and robbers working together. It's not 1900 anymore. He's finally seeing you as your own man and butting out of your affairs."

"Yeah? When did hell freeze over?"

"Billy—stop being so cynical." She lit a cigarette. "He's not on your back about this. Just be happy about it."

"I'll have the band play all Irish dancing and drinking songs. He won't have time to bust my horns if he's busy kickin' up his heels to 'Delaney's Donkey and Paddy McGinty's Goat.'"

Da didn't bust any horns. His parents had a blast at the club, with the best table in the house—Rosie's table, which he gave up for the evening. Billy and the band struck up "The Anniversary Waltz" after an entire set of Irish songs. If his father knew who any of Billy's business partners were, it didn't faze him.

Or maybe it was the Canadian whiskey.

****

With the club closed the following night, he and Les took a breather. So he had an entire day and night off. But instead of looking forward to his first good night's sleep in three weeks, he began wondering what he was going to do with himself for twenty-four hours. He didn't feel like cruising around in the Cadillac Sport Phaeton Rosie had given him. He craved company. Female company. So he went home, took a shower, put on some clothes he'd never worn, swiped an unopened wine bottle from the rack, and took a taxi to Greta's. He didn't wear cologne.

This time she let him in herself. Her hair was comfortably mussed, and her black satin belted robe puddled on the floor. One stockinged leg peeked out. Not that he noticed. "Sheik, you look half dead."

"Thanks. Compared to how I feel, that's a compliment." He handed her the bottle, which she promptly opened with a gold corkscrew.

"What the hell's wrong? You having trouble with Les?" She pulled the cork out.

"No, it's just—the letdown." He hung his head as

that empty, disheartened feeling came back. "We're finished, for all intents and purposes. We're just tinkering now. With chords and melody lines and stuff. I changed a few words here and there, added a few more vowel sounds, stuff like that. But otherwise, we're finished. It's over." He flopped down on her sofa and accepted the full glass she held out to him, tinkling with ice cubes.

"Over? Now that's not William Amadeus McGlory talking, the great musician who's got a stellar future. It hasn't even begun yet!" She sat on the sofa and tucked her legs under her. "When the show ends its run, it won't even be over then, because after that, we'll be selling records, and then the movie'll come out, and while that's still going on, you'll be writing another one. So don't say it's over. Jesus Christ in a bottle, Billy, what's gotten into you?"

"I'm just exhausted." He rested his head on the sofa back and closed his eyes. "I never crammed so much work into so little time in my life." He couldn't even see beyond getting out her door, and he didn't want to make that a habit. "This is the biggest thing I've ever done." He lifted his head and looked over at her. "Let's face it. I know opening night will be a big deal, when the lights go down, the curtain rises, and everybody holds their breath for that magic few seconds. But for now—that time in between wearing down the last pencil stub and curtain time—I'm in a hole." He reached for his wine. "That ever happen to you, Greta? You finish a book and sink real low, like you'll never write anything again?"

"Every time." She nodded her understanding, and he blew out a whistle of relief.

"So it's not just me." He sampled his wine. Although chilled with ice cubes, it warmed him.

"Absolutely not. All creators experience that letdown when they finish a major work. Or should I say abandon it. The best thing to do is plunge right into a new one." She made a diving gesture with her fingers straight out.

"Sheesh!" He shook his head. "I don't have the energy to jingle change in my pockets."

"I don't mean two minutes later," she said. "Give it a while. New ideas will start rolling around, and before you know it you'll be as absorbed in another story as you were in this one."

"The thing is, how can another musical ever measure up to this? How could it ever be as good? I might sit down and turn out the worst dreck the critics ever saw." He splayed his fingers.

"Now that's defeatist talk, not my Billy Amadeus. What if Irving Berlin said that?" She sipped her wine.

"I'm no Irving Berlin. My problem is I want to be a success so bad I can taste it. Sometimes it even takes away the joy of just being there, performing, the act of making music, when I go off thinking how much I want my name on a marquee and on records and—" He paused for breath. "Everything else."

"Let's just hire a producer and see how tryouts go, all right? Hell, nobody even knows this thing exists yet. The records and the marquee will all come in time. Be patient." She shook her head. "Shake the ants out of your pants already."

She poured him a refill after he'd drained only half of it. He started munching on the cashews from a gold nut dish that matched the corkscrew. It looked more like her husband's taste than hers. "I know I'm bein' a hard on. But it all happened so fast. Same with Pru and this London gallery thing—the big break for her could be right around the corner. I can't fail, for her sake, either. I want her to roll around in success like a pig in muck, and sit out and bake in the sun. Then maybe she'll get over this mob phobia she has."

Before he knew it, she'd poured his third refill. He made a feeble attempt to hold his hand over the glass, but she poured right through his fingers. "She'll be all right with it once she gets used to it. This is all new to her, and it's scary."

"Well, it's scary to me, too. But just take a peek out the window." He glanced over at her French windows, the curtains drawn. "What isn't scary? This is New York. Sometimes I think she wants to be back on the farm in Iowa, where the most dangerous thing that can happen is getting butted by a billy goat. She's just not a big city girl." But that's what he loved about her; city girls just didn't do it for him. They were all too much like him.

"She may never be," Greta said. "But you'll do all right. You're making pots of money already. Just think how much you'll make when the show opens. And I know it'll be a hit. That is, if you don't want to retire and live the good life." She gave him a subtle grin.

"Retire? Me? Nah. My idea of the good life is living my dreams. And you know I have big dreams. Big—" He tried to stifle a yawn, but didn't quite make it. "Biiiig dreeeeams." He kept his eyes averted to stay alert, afraid he'd fall all over her—fall asleep, that is. "Pru don't care about money." He laid his head back again. His eyes slid shut. "She actually likes being poor.

That whole Greenwich Village bohemian artiste thing, you know. Thinks it's real glamorous standing in a paint-stained smock and beret, freezin' her ass off in a garret on MacDougal, gnawing on a piece of stale bread while she shapes her clay. What's so glamorous about that?" He drew a long breath. "So you get a fancy tombstone in some cemetery in Paris, if you're famous enough to afford one." He shook his head and rubbed his eyes. "I don't know what's gonna happen, Greta. I never thought I'd admit this to anybody. We're just not—it was never like this before. She won't even come down to the club. She thinks it's gonna get raided."

"Well, you never know." Greta checked her manicure. "Something might go wrong, and it might get raided some day."

He looked over at her. "So what if it does? You spend a night in jail. Hell, that'd be a step up for her, the way she's used to living."

"She's a very moral girl, Billy. To be honest, I'm surprised you and she—I mean—you know—" She gestured back and forth, "before you were married."

"Yeah, well, the rock was just as good as on her hand. I always knew I was gonna marry her. We saved ourselves for each other—there was never anybody else. It's all this law-and-order crap—she won't do anything that even hints at anything unethical or illegal. Now that I'm in with Rosie, she thinks I'm one of them, too. Like I'm gonna get a gold tooth just for show."

She cast him a sideways glance. "Face it, Sheik. Like it or not, you are one of them."

"I am a musician, and that's that!" His voice cracked with fatigue, but he wasn't going to let this argument fester. "I go to the club, play, get my pay, come home."

She laughed, stood and stretched, then looked down at him and shook her head. He felt like her little brother.

"Sit down, will you?" He reached up to pull her back down. "You look like Susan, staring me down like that."

She straightened the seams of her stockings before sitting. "It can get very dangerous very fast. It can happen in the blink of an eye, Sheik. One minute you think you're only on the fringes. The next minute you're in so deep, you'll never get out alive."

"You're in it too, in case you haven't noticed," he reminded her. "Your name's goin' up there in lights right next to mine. Bankrolled with Jackie Harper's dough."

"But I'm not denying it," she said. "And I don't have a spouse telling me how much he hates it."

He stretched his legs straight out. "I'm gonna enjoy the ride, Greta. My being partners with Rosie and having him and Jackie Harper as angels for the show is just like—incidental. 'Cause, you know, when I'm up there on the stage playing, I'm so lost in the music, I don't even think that if it wasn't for Rosie and Jackie and their money, it would've taken me another ten years to get there, instead of in the blink of an eye."

"Other things can happen in the blink of an eye, too. Just don't blink too often." Her warning came with a smile.

"They're open at all times." *Especially now*, he wanted to say as he opened them.

She lowered her green-shadowed lids. He realized she had the longest lashes he'd ever seen. Maybe they were false; they did look a little dark. Now why was he noticing these things all of a sudden?

"I have to stay out of trouble for Pru's sake, too. God forbid she leaves me 'cause of this crap," he said over a yawn.

"If she really loves you, she'll overcome all the doubts and love you unconditionally," Greta said.

"Well, I sure miss her like hell. If it wasn't for the show, I'd still be over there with her—ah, no, I wouldn't. Who am I kiddin'? I couldn't get away."

"Couldn't or wouldn't?" she persisted.

He wished she didn't ask these loaded questions when he was just as loaded. "Both."

"So she's doing what she wants, and so are you. So she hates what you do. Hopefully, she loves you enough to look the other way. If not, you'll have a decision to make, as a married couple." She sipped her drink. "That's what Stanton and I were doing, very separate things, and unfortunately, unlike you and Pru, our relationship couldn't withstand the pressure. I love him with all my heart, and he loves me, but we're just too selfish and self-centered to put each other's needs before our own. So that's why we're getting divorced. I'm just glad there aren't any children involved."

He hadn't even thought of the baby; her mention of children triggered something in his mind. "Yeah, that too. If it wasn't for that, I'm sure she woulda left me as soon as I hooked up with Rosie."

"I have a feeling she'll come around." Her tone encouraged him. "I know Pru. She's wild about you. Besides, she's very adaptable. That's what's good about artistes. We can adapt to anything, because most of the time we have to. She could sleep on a bed of nails. She could get used to having a husband in the mob."

Now the conversation gave him a sour stomach. "I wish you'd stop calling it the mob. For the last time, I'm not in the—" Then he said what he'd been thinking and was afraid to admit it to himself. But it was the wine talking. "All right, I'll come clean, sometimes I think I've gone in over my head in this. I'll never admit this to Pru, 'cause the way she is. I don't want to be a gangster, I just want a successful career. But expecting that in a world like this without getting at least mildly involved is damn naive."

"Just be careful, like I said. And don't ever get greedy," she warned. "That's the real kiss of death."

He laughed and shook his head. "Greedy? Me? Nah. I might be ambitious, but not greedy. That's when it gets dangerous. When you want more than you know you can handle. Just for the sake of havin' it. Who the hell needs those kinds of headaches? That's when you start doin' what you ain't supposed to do."

"Well, it is dangerous, and I'm just telling you, Billy, keep your eyes open."

He put down his half-finished drink. "All the time? Like right now?"

"Except for right now," she said. "You need some sleep."

He was about to drop anyway. He began falling forward. His lids felt like lead. Her hands caught him and rested on his shoulders.

****

He opened his eyes to the dull glow of daybreak. She was snoring, one arm flung across his chest.

Whew, that was close! came to mind as he slid out from under her arm. She was a heavier sleeper and a louder snorer than he was. All he wanted to do was rinse out his mouth. It tasted like a rum hole in there. He made his way to her pink-tiled bathroom and cleaned himself up.

"Feel better?" she asked when he came down the stairs. Draped in a different dressing gown, she sat at the dining room table, a coffee cup and a bottle of anisette in front of her. She poured him a cup and slid the anisette bottle toward him.

"Much." He sat down and combed his fingers through his hair. "What happened after I fell asleep?"

"You'll read about it in my next book." She smiled and twisted a cigarette into her holder.

"That good, huh?" He splashed anisette into his coffee.

"Nothing happened for real, but it sure got my imagination going. I wrote five pages before you woke up, then came back to you and went back to sleep." She waved in the direction of her writing room at the top of the stairs.

"So, I helped you get over your writer's crack?" He sipped his coffee. The rich fragrance made his stomach growl.

"Writer's block!" She rolled her eyes.

"Oh." He fished out his cigarettes and lit a couple, one for each of them.

"I think you did, Sheik. Oh, it was so good to feel my fingers flying over those keys again." She threw her head back with a sigh.

"Yeah, I know what that's like. Magic, ain't it? So, does it have Broadway potential?" He took another deep breath of fresh coffee.

"I was hoping for Hollywood potential." She blew

out a stream of smoke.

"With music, maybe?" The caffeine jolt fortified him; gone was that fear of failure. He was Billy again, thank God.

She laughed, belting her gown tightly around her waist, squeezing her figure into an hourglass. "Right now it's a sloppy draft covered with coffee stains and cigarette ashes."

"Can I see it when it's cleaned up, all shined and spiffy?" he asked.

"Oh, I don't know if anything will come of it." She took a sip of coffee. "When I write, I throw away more than I actually use."

"Hell, that'd scare the crap outta me. I'd be afraid I was losing my marbles if I started throwing stuff away like that."

"Well, I'm not afraid of failure. Ask anybody who's survived '29. You get up and try again." She warmed her hands on her cup.

"Yeah, I guess the only way you can really fail is if you don't get up and try again." He dragged on his cig.

She smiled. "I'll never see you quit, Sheik. Your spirit's unbreakable."

"Hey, thanks. I like that shot in the arm first thing in the morning." The grin that spread over his face showed his boost of confidence.

She made them bacon, eggs, and toast, and after breakfast he went to the telegraph office to cable Pru: "Be waiting at the pier."

He spent the extra money to add "Miss you!" He missed her even more after spending an evening sleeping in another woman's arms. Maybe next time he felt like female companionship he should just go visit

Pru's buddy Franck.

****

Interlude: Sunday Dinner at the House

After lasagna, sausage and meatballs, dessert, and coffee, Tessie started making more wacky predictions with her tarot cards. Susan's husband, of all people, asked her for the reading. He wanted to know about his stocks and bonds, if business was going to improve, if they should open another store uptown before the economy recovered. Billy knew damn well Irv wouldn't get the answers he wanted. His questions were too specific. Who the hell asks tarot cards how much General Electric is going to increase their quarterly dividend by, for Chrissakes?

Then she did an unsolicited reading on Billy, and for the final result, got the King of Cups card upside down. "What's that s'posed to mean?" he asked, thinking of worse things than an upside-down cup.

"Artistic temperament, double-dealing, dishonesty, scandal, loss, ruin, injustice, a crafty person without virtue, and shifty dealings." She swept the cards into their wooden box and gave him her trademark worry-wart face.

"Artistic temperament?" he shouted theatrically, in his best Bela Lugosi impersonation, raising his arms like bat's wings and making a dive for her neck with his fangs bared. "Who's got artistic temperament? Who's dishonest? Who's shifty?"

She screamed and darted around the table. "Ma! He's doing a Dracula! Stop it, Billy! Get outta here!"

"Let me drrrink your blooood!" He pretended to bite her.

"Billy, you're scaring me!" She grabbed her tarot

116

box and fled up the stairs.

"Aah, buncha mumbo jumbo…" he mumbled, helping himself to another biscotti.

The only thing that scared him was when he first walked in. Tessie had asked him who he'd spent the night with. "You look guilty," she'd said.

"Get out! Do I look guilty?" he asked his mother, then Susan, then Irv, then looked in the mirror. "Me? Nah, I don't look guilty!" He managed to get out of it without revealing any female names.

He didn't miss the look Susan gave him, either. And she was no psychic.

She called him aside later when everyone settled in the living room for Jack Benny on The Jell-O Program.

"Billy, have you been in any female company since Pru's been away?" she asked right out.

"Well, of course. Every night at the club. It's not one of thossse"—he affected a lisp and a limp wrist—"men's clubs, you know."

"You know what I mean." She did the fist-on-hip pose.

"Okay, I'll come clean. I went to see Greta Schliessmayer last night. She just left her husband—well, he left her. But nothing happened, I tell you. It was as innocent as the driven snow. We're friends, and that's it."

Susan's brows shot up. "She's been hot for you since you had your first shave. And she didn't put the moves on you?"

"Of course not." He threw his arms up and dropped them to his sides. "She's Pru's friend, too, don't forget. We both love her like a sister."

She eyed him up and down like their father always

did—he called it the "eyeball frisk." "Don't slap the cuffs on me, Suze. I'm innocent." He raised his hands, palms out.

She finally smiled, and he relaxed. "All right, you already have one bundle of joy on the way…"

"Give me some credit. *Mama mia.*" He glanced into the hall mirror and saw himself blushing. She made him think of things he was afraid to think of. Now he couldn't get Greta off his brain—the way she flipped her shoes off and worked in her bare feet, her jangly earrings as she nodded in agreement, her red lipstick marks on glasses and cigarettes and pencils—he wished Pru would start wearing that stuff again. Since they got married, she never wore a drop of makeup anymore. "She'll be home in a week. I'll be okay then."

"All right, but behave yourself in the meantime," Susan warned, in the same tone their mother used.

"I think I'm handling adulthood very nicely, if I do say so myself," he jumped to his own defense. "Too bad nobody else does."

****

He made sure he had the afternoon free when Pru's ship pulled in at the pier. He waited and waited and waited. He finally spotted her, and did a double take. She waddled down the gangway, her enormous middle seeming to lead the way. He calculated as he ran to meet her—one month to go? Two?

He hesitated to hug her, or even go near her. "Will I crush him?" was the first thing he said to his wife as she smothered him with kisses. No lipstick.

He helped her into the Caddy and slid behind the wheel. She ran her eyes over the walnut dash as she sank into the leather seat. "This looks like a gangster's

118

car." No "Snuggles" this time, either.

"This old flivver? Nah, it's nothin' special." He rolled the window down.

"Flivver shmivver. It's brand new, and you know it. It must've cost at least five thousand dollars." She tried to face him, struggling to turn sideways.

It didn't cost me a dime, as a matter of fact, he wanted to say. "Honey Bear, I earned it, the honest way. I just want some of the finer things in life for me and my family. Please. Let's not argue, okay?"

"I'm sorry. I missed you." Her slender sculptress's fingers slid up his thigh, bringing new meaning to the phrase "driving to distraction." He gulped a mouthful of air to calm himself, but let her hand do what it pleased. Their bodies leaned toward each other, and his lips sought hers. He wanted to devour her right there, with blaring horns and roaring engines all around them. As they came up for air, their eyes connected once again, and he lost himself in her gaze. He realized how much he'd missed her, the relaxed cadence of her Midwest twang, gathering her hair in bunches. He forgot all about lipstick and jangly earrings. Pru didn't need those folderols.

"So what happened over there? How did your exhibit go? Are you world famous yet?" tumbled out of him.

Her hand slid up higher on his thigh as her thumb circled slowly. Without taking her eyes from his, she answered, "It went great. I got to do some more sculpting there, too. I got a cheap studio with a couple more artists, a German girl and a guy from Belgium who was as swishy as a pair of nylons. It was great, Snuggles. I had such a good time there, but it's so good to be home. I could smell New York about an hour before we pulled into port, you know the way New York smells? It was then I realized how homesick I was. Nothing smells like New York." Her hand splayed out and caressed him like a statue she'd just finished sculpting and was putting the final touches on.

With the little blood left in his brain, he agreed. "You're right about that." Her hand squeezed gently, and his desire surged. He started the engine, desperate to get her home and in bed. "My place or yours?" he said jokingly, but she didn't take it that way.

"I'm not going to that mob place," she stated flat out.

His desire ebbed, but it was a relief.

"Then we'll check into a nice hotel with a huge bed and an even huger bathtub. How's that?" He entered the stream of traffic.

Starving artist that she was, she liked first-class accommodation. So they checked into the brand new Waldorf for a few nights, although he would have loved to bring her up to his penthouse and make love on the terrace under the stars.

He wanted to take the whole night off, but they had a guest playing at the club, Chummy MacGregor, and expected the place to be more mobbed than usual.

And it was. They had to turn people away at the door all night. When Billy opened his dressing room door to leave, a crowd waited for him, and he spent a half hour signing autographs. He signed each one with a flourish, feeling like a king with his adoring subjects. *This is only the beginning,* as Rosie always said. He was busting to tell them all about the show he wrote— he'd never realized he had the willpower to keep his mouth shut, till now. He'd been dying to tell his family, customers at the club and at the speak. But he kept telling himself, "It will have more impact when they see my name on opening night tickets and on a Broadway marquee."

The crowd finally disbanded, and he stopped in to see Rosie before leaving.

He got up from his desk and gave Billy a bear hug that nearly crushed his ribs. "This was our best night ever. If the place was double the size, we'd need to turn 'em away. We gotta get a bigger place. We're goin' to look at some tomorrow. You wanna come?" He went back to the business at hand—counting the evening's take.

"You mind if I just sit this one out? I mean, with Pru back, and Les working alone this week, I thought I'd have a few afternoons off. Whatever you decide is fine with me."

"Yeah, sure." Rosie waved a hand as he lit a cigar. "Take the time off. We're lookin' at a place a little further uptown, on Central Park West. Classier neighborhood, too, ya know?"

"Whatever you want. I'm with you." He backed out of the room. "Now I'd better get with my wife."

The crisp morning still held the blackness of night in its sleeping arms. He decided to walk to the Waldorf in the peace and quiet. Half a block from the club, he heard the distinct clack of heels on the sidewalk behind him. He turned to look. A well-dressed woman was following him, now increasing her pace to catch up.

"William Amadeus McGlory! Your playing is hotter than July jam! Your music just melts me!" She fell into line with him and kept up pretty well, considering he wasn't exactly strolling.

"Gee, thanks." Much as he reveled in it, he still didn't know how to handle this kind of praise. He was just doing his job, after all. But to a non-musician, he supposed it was a big deal.

"I'm Gloria." She ran her hand down his sleeve. "Can we extend the evening a little longer? I have a penthouse on Park Avenue South, lots of good hooch. Name your poison."

He couldn't have been more surprised if she'd pulled a gun on him. He'd never been approached like this before, so directly. He'd had to fight off a few bearcats in high school, but that was kid stuff. "Sorry, Gloria, but right now my poison is sleep, 'cause I'm beat."

"You can sleep there, too. I've got twelve rooms." Her voice was awfully breathy, considering they were walking at a fast clip on a city street. It had that intimate quality of a secret telephone call.

"A persistent one, you are. You better go back to your twelve rooms, Gloria. I'm just not up to it." He hoped she'd get the meaning of that, at least.

"Come on…" She slid her hand around his arm and clasped it, like they were a couple on a date. "I can show you a good time. Good hooch, good food, anything else you want."

Was this a sign of things to come when he became famous? Gorgeous dames mobbing him with invitations to their penthouses and all the contraband he could hold down? He hoped not. He preferred being mobbed by a bunch of them, not just one.

"I really gotta go. I think you'd better, too. This is no place for a woman to be walking alone." How to get rid of her now? he wondered. There wasn't a cab in sight. He'd have to walk her all the way to the Waldorf and get her a cab there. It was barely two blocks away now.

"Please, Billy, just this once?" Her tone begged. "You're my idol. I adore you. I'm not like all those other flies swarming around you."

He didn't want to know what the hell she was like. He hoped she was just another of those flies and would leave him be. He didn't want to get rude, but how to shake her? "To tell you the truth, Gloria, I'm not what you think. I'm one of those." Once again he attempted a limp wrist. He was getting pretty good at it, he hated to admit.

"One night with me will straighten you out," was her rebuttal to that.

Oh, no. Now what? Tell her he was Jack the Ripper?

"Okay. I'll level with you. I'm married. And I'm sure you won't believe this, but unlike ninety-nine percent of musicians in this town, I don't cheat on my wife. So don't take this personally, but I really don't want nobody else. That's the truth. I'm not an Ethel, and I don't find you repulsive, I'm just married. Okay?"

"Well, I must say, I do admire you, you fool." She gazed at him with genuine admiration in her well-made-up eyes.

By now they'd approached the Waldorf, and the last thing he wanted was for her to know he was staying here. He grabbed the doorman, slipped him a twenty, and told him to put her in a taxi. "Anywhere she wants to go." The doorman knew him; he'd already given him an autograph. "She's got digs on Park Avenue South with twelve rooms and a load of hooch. Just for your information," he murmured out the side of his mouth. He didn't mind doing the fella a favor. The doorman dutifully tipped his hat, and Gloria blew Billy a kiss as a taxi pulled up. Billy gave her a mock salute and dashed through the revolving doors—to face his wife, standing in the lobby.

"Who was that, Billy?" She waddled up to him.

"Huh?" He halted in his tracks. "What are you doing out here?"

"I had some friends over. They just left. Who *was* that?" She gestured out the door.

"She followed me from the club. She—just kind of latched onto me." He brushed his sleeve off as he explained. Gloria's hand had wrinkled it.

"Oh, yeah?" Pru's gaze glared like a light shining in his eyes.

"I told her I was married and I don't sleep around."

She nodded like she believed him. "Okay, that's fine."

He thought he'd better keep trying anyway. "Look, Honey Bear, do you think I'd go for that chunk of lead even if I was single?" Maybe shifting the blame would prevent from this happening again. "If you'd come to the club with me once in a while, I wouldn't have Janes following me home."

"That's not necessary." She turned, and he followed her to the elevators. "I know you're handsome and talented and floozies have trouble keeping their hands off you."

Hmm, nice thought. He tried to keep his face straight. "I don't mean come to the club to check up on me. I mean, because it's part of my life, and I would like you there once in a while. Or every night, if you want."

"And if the place is raided, we all go to jail," she started in.

That deserved a serious eye roll. "It's not gonna get raided, for the love of Pete. Do you have any inkling how much protection we got?"

"If it was on the up and up, you wouldn't need protection." She raised her head and jutted out her chin.

"My sheltered little lamb, nothing in this town is on the up and up."

"I am," she declared.

"Well, I don't see you pullin' in two grand a night," he snapped, sick to death of her tirades.

"So that's what it means to you. Money." She walked ahead of him. "You're getting to be like those gangsters who'd sell their mother for a nickel."

They'd reached their room, and he was just too tired to argue. When would it ever stop?

"Without the money, you'd be in that Jane Street dive instead of a suite at the Waldorf. Ever think of that?" he pressed on.

"I can leave right now and it wouldn't kill me." She inserted the room key and opened the door. He followed her in. "This is nice," she gestured at the elegant suite, "but I don't need it. Not like you seem to. And you're consorting with gangsters to get it. You're turning into one of them, Billy. You're even starting to dress like them." She gestured toward his suit.

"I got this at Susan's store, for Chrissake!"

"Yeah, so do all the gangsters." She turned around and sneered. "I know a gangster suit when I see one."

"Yeah? You buy clothes there, too, don'tcha?" He

grabbed the whiskey bottle he'd left half full earlier and poured himself a neat one. He knocked it back in one shot.

"And I wish you'd stop drinking so much!" she nagged.

"When's the baby due?" He had to get off this subject.

"What?"

"When's it due?" he repeated. "Do you know the due date?"

"Late September. Why?"

"Because I hope he makes things a little more peaceful around here." He poured another shot. "Because I hope I can be a better father than I've been a husband."

She started weeping, and he wrapped her in his arms. If only he could make her understand his world.

He also hoped she'd have a girl, to dress up and do girly things with. He was glad she didn't like broccoli.

****

After closing the next night, Rosie caught him on the way to his dressing room. A few fellas stood next to him.

"This is Luigi Quintannaro, Billy." They shook hands, and Billy was afraid he'd never play another piano again after that grip. He didn't bother introducing the other guy, so Billy concluded he was either a soldier or a bodyguard. Luigi Quintannaro was important enough to have one around.

He knew who Louie Q was but had never been introduced. He saw him and Rosie gabbing occasionally, sharing cigars, a few hot patooties between them that Billy figured they shared too. The tall and muscular Louie Q was nearly as blond as him, but Billy figured he bleached it, because of the dark roots. A former prizefighter, he still had the bulk to show it. He didn't breathe; he wheezed. He'd graduated from longshoreman to one of New York's biggest magnates. He had a string of fancy offices from Times Square to Wall Street and was a partner in nightclubs, race tracks, and a hockey team. But he was best known for his rum-running syndicate. Rumor had it that Louie Q swung both ways, but nobody held that against him.

"He's gonna run the new club with us," Rosie announced. "And we're calling it Swing Street."

"Hey, swell!" Billy beamed. With Louie as a partner, the place couldn't lose. Everything the guy touched turned to gold. Rosie awed him enough, but compared to Louie—whew! He planned to watch the guy carefully, just to see how that magic wand of his worked.

****

Swing Street opened to a fanfare of mobbed sidewalks, flashing bulbs, a street clogged with Rolls Royces and Cadillac Tourers, and a back-door shipment of booze that Billy thought would last till Prohibition ended.

More than twice the size of the old club, the elegant five-story townhouse could accommodate up to two hundred patrons. The centerpiece was the twenty-foot-square walnut bar stocked mostly with their ninety-proof whiskey, better than the stuff sold in juice joints. Rosie's Aunt Nettie, of all people, did the decorating, in softer tones she thought would appeal to women. The carpet and wallpaper complemented each other in mauve and rose. Impressionist paintings covered the walls. Even the awning running from the curb to the entrance was a soft lilac, with the address in simple purple lettering.

Swing Street had a huge dance floor, two stages, and far more luxurious dressing rooms. He actually could turn around in this one.

It also had all the necessary equipment of a sophisticated speakeasy, including a warning buzzer and a button for the bartender to push to make the shelves collapse and the bottles fall into the sewer.

The closet was furnished with electrical wire that, when connected to two coat hooks, would create an electrical current, making the back door open to where the booze was hidden.

Swing Street boasted 5,000 bottles of wine in the cellar, which was also a private eating and watering hole for important people. Mayor Walker himself had his own booth in the wine cellar.

A half hour before opening, Billy lounged in his dressing room on the new sofa, sipping a whiskey and listening to the radio.

A light knock at the door told him it wasn't Rosie. "Come in." He knew it wouldn't be any autograph hounds. The police barricades outside the place prevented that. It might even be Louie Q, wishing him luck.

The door opened, and he had to strain to see who it was. Finally, his visitor peeked into the room, came in, and shut the door quickly behind him.

"Les!" He couldn't have been more surprised if Eleanor Roosevelt had slipped in.

"Really nice place here, Billy, lotsa luck with it." He held out his hand to shake.

"Hey, I didn't expect you here tonight." He sprang up off the sofa and they shook hands. "I have some smooth—well, I can offer you seltzer water—"

"Nothing for me. Thanks." He held up his hand. "Rosie let me in. Really nice guy, though a little rough around the edges."

"Yeah, a diamond in the rough is Rosie. I'll make sure you get a ringside table," he promised, and meant it.

"I wasn't planning to stay all night." Les remained standing. "I just was wondering if you'd care to make the announcement about our show opening. What with the press here and all."

"That's a great idea." Billy gave his collaborator a clap on the back. "I didn't think you'd want to make the announcement here, in person, though. Don't you prefer to stay behind the scenes?"

"I usually do, but not for this. To tell you the truth, Billy, I never planned on doing another show like that again. I'd kind of retired, planned to do some recordings, maybe some concerts, private parties, things like that. But this was a reawakening for me. I realized I'd been asleep all along, and this woke me up. So I want to revel in it while it lasts. Enjoy the lights, the crowds, everything. And I'm sure you do too."

"Oh, you know it!" He'd lived one of his biggest dreams with Les during those endless nights at the keyboards, scribbling on music scores and scratch pads. "Let's do that, you and me. Go up on stage before the band goes on, and I'll quiet the crowd. You want to announce it, or me?"

"You can if you want to," Les said. "I thought it'd be nice to play a few of the songs, like a sneak preview.

Is Miss Schliessmayer going to be here tonight?"

Billy hoped she would. He'd sent her a personal invitation, aside from the ones Rosie had sent out, telling her how much he'd be honored by her presence. Pru wouldn't show up, so having Greta there would give him a boost.

"Yeah, er—I think she'll be here." Billy kept picturing Greta all dolled up. "I sent—we sent invitations out to everybody."

"All right, then, she can make the announcement with us."

That sounded good to him. As soon as Les left, he dabbed some French cologne behind his ears.

The minute Billy walked onto the stage, the audience stood, clapped, whistled, and roared. Even the dames. Good God, he hadn't even played a note yet! His eyes swept over the crowd, a mass of humanity beyond the spots shining down on him. The applause washed over him like a tidal wave and roared in his ears like the ocean. *They're all yours, kiddo*, he heard Rosie's voice echoing in his mind. That's all he thought at that moment. *They're all mine*. Wow, what a feeling! *Imagine what the Broadway theater will be like, how deafening that roar will be.*

He grew more furious at Pru for deliberately staying away. He'd crossed the ocean and back for her damn art show; why couldn't she cross town to share this moment with him? That thought made him turn to his left, where Les and Greta waited in the wings. He clasped Greta's hand and brought her out. Les followed.

Billy adjusted the mike. "I have an announcement to make, ladies and gentlemen…"

While he spoke, the place could've been a tomb,

stone silent. His amplified voice carried to the far walls, bounced off the ceiling, then rushed back to him. He spoke slowly so as not to create too much echo. "It's called *Headin' for Better Times*, with music by Les Fontaine, lyrics by yours truly, and book by Greta Schliessmayer. After tryouts in Boston and two weeks of previews, it will be opening at the Majestic Theater."

After he introduced Les and Greta, his audience gave him another standing, roaring ovation. They nearly blew the roof off.

Playing, as much as he loved it, was almost anticlimactic after that announcement.

But at 3:00 a.m. he didn't feel like doing anything resembling resting. So at 3:01 a.m., when he entered his dressing room, Greta followed, bottle in hand. He cranked up his victrola and let Benny Goodman bounce off his walls.

Behind that closed door, they drank and tangoed and sang and drank some more.

"You wish she was here, don't you?" Greta asked as they flopped onto the sofa, exhausted.

"Don't even talk about her," he muttered.

"You have to see it her way, Billy. I know it's hard to imagine her upbringing, her family disowning her because she got pregnant, and now she's married to a guy who's business partners with a mob figure and all." She slid out of her shoes.

"That's such phonus bolonus." He scowled, stretching his legs. "This whole frigging city's run by the mob. She's in a dream world."

"She's a down-home, heartland-of-America kind of girl," Greta said.

"She don't even wanna come to see the show on

Broadway, much less to Boston for the tryouts. Sometimes I wonder about this 'compromise' hokum." Finding his glass empty, he took a swig from another bottle.

"Once the baby's here, you'll be fine. You'll both be parenting, things will get better," she assured him in that way of hers.

"I damn well hope so." It was just then he realized it was the middle of the night, the joint was deserted, and he was alone with a beautiful woman on a couch in his private dressing room, surrounded by booze and some potentially seductive music. Although he was sloshed to the gills, he still buzzed with energy. He knew he should get back to Jane Street and between the sheets with his wife. "Greta—you know what we should be doing right now?"

"Yes. Getting the hell out of here." But she didn't make a move to leave. Instead she slid down the couch till her thigh touched his. She leaned on him, closed her eyes, heaved a deep breath, and relaxed.

As she snuggled up to him, he savored her warmth, her scent, her company. The close human contact comforted him. Yet it felt wrong. Imagine if Pru walked in on this. He froze up, guilt nagging at him although it was as innocent as two puppies cuddling. "Uh—you wanna—help me stand up?" he asked her.

"You sick or something?" She drew away.

"No, I just need to sober up and get the hell home. I think you understand why." He struggled to sit up straight.

"Of course I understand." She stood, grasped his hands, and pulled him to his feet.

He stumbled toward the bathroom. "I'll call a cab."

He grabbed onto the wall for support.

She pointed at the door. "I have a car and a driver waiting outside."

"You better check and see if he's still there." He went into the bathroom, opened the tap in the basin and splashed cold water on his face.

Once she was gone, he peeled off his play clothes, staggered into the shower stall, turned on the cold water full force, and leapt under it. He stayed there until he froze himself into sobriety.

****

The show started to take up most of Billy's time. They hired the producer of Jackie Harper's last show, Hal Samuels, a no-nonsense buck-stops-here guy who looked more like a Wall Street banker than a Broadway producer. Tall, long-legged, with thick spectacles, he wore a double-breasted suit and spats to every meeting. Billy told him about Susan's store, and he became a steady customer.

After four hours' sleep, Billy would get up for the morning meetings with the director and crew. He wanted to be there to bang out the songs during the read-throughs. He sat in on the rehearsals in a studio Les had once used and liked because it had no windows—therefore, no distractions. Billy and Greta went to every audition and every callback. She wanted to see her creations in the flesh; he wanted to make sure they could sing his songs.

For the heroine, they cast a former stenographer from Astoria, Ethel Merman, who'd just made her Broadway debut in Gershwin's *Girl Crazy*. Big-boned, with bleached hair and too much lipstick, Billy didn't see her stage appeal till she belted that first song out.

She almost made the roof rattle. He sat there, mouth open in astonishment whenever she let go with those golden pipes. She was a dish with all her makeup on, but a little too brash for Billy's taste. He didn't go in for the theater types anyway. They talked about themselves and drank too much.

The night before boarding the train for Boston, he tried one more time to get Pru to join him. He'd already told his family they were steaming back to London for a combination honeymoon/art exhibit. So he'd covered that base.

"Billy, I'll be bored to death," she whined. "You'll be doing all that theater stuff, and I'll be sitting in a hotel all by myself."

"But you won't be. Boston has as many art galleries and museums and speaks—well, speaks don't matter to you, but—there's a lot to do there. Besides, if you don't go, I'll miss you like hell." Even though he wouldn't have time for her except in bed, at least he'd have that.

"Maybe I'll come up for a couple of days," she said in that wishy-washy tone.

"Please, won't you come now?" he begged.

She glanced out the window, then at her portrait-in-progress. "Can I bring my art supplies with me?"

"Of course! I'll hire a separate car on the train just for your stuff if you'll just come with me!" He clasped her hands, held them to his lips and kissed them.

She gave him the look that said, "Okay, why not?" without a word, and he twirled her around the room.

"It'll be just like the honeymoon we didn't have yet," he promised.

But it was far from a honeymoon, for him, anyway.

Pru broke her ankle getting off the train and spent the whole time in a cast. The show opened in Boston to a chilly reception. The applause sounded like marbles being scattered over the floor. The audiences got smaller and smaller every night. He and Les and Greta, and Hal and the director, and the cast and lighting designer and costumer all got together daily and changed everything that hadn't worked the night before. Different things didn't work the next night. The audience clapped loudly after the first act, but after the second—crickets. Nobody could figure it out.

Thank God Jackie Harper never showed up to check the return on his investment. The few letters Billy wrote him gushed with cheer and hope. Finally, he had Les write them, because he couldn't bring himself to lie any more.

"Maybe it's too realistic. Too much like the misery people are going through already, even though it has a happy ending. Maybe it should have wizards or something in it, like a fairy tale," Billy offered one daybreak, lying stretched out under the piano in the rehearsal studio as Les rewrote the show's first song, called "Can't Get Much Worse." "Maybe we should call it 'Each Night is Worse Than the One Before.' Only because it is."

"This is show biz, Billy," Les replied, then went back to humming the melody as he played it. "This isn't New York. That's what tryouts are for. You gotta take the bad with the good."

But he'd already fallen into an exhausted sleep, lyrics swirling through his dreams.

When he woke, he scribbled down the lyrics to a new song he called "You Gotta Take the Bad With the

Good." They inserted it into the second act, and it brought the house down, especially the way Ethel sang it.

****

"It needs a really catchy song for the finale, so they can walk away feeling inspired, knowing that things will get better. Something strong and determined, yet sentimental, reminiscent of the Tin Pan Alley tunes," Les said one late night as they polished off the corned beef sandwiches Greta had brought them from an all-night deli. The three of them were in the rehearsal studio, Les at the bench with his right foot on the sustaining pedal, Greta draped over the piano, Billy stretched out underneath.

"Well, I certainly had enough practice at that." Billy folded his hands behind his head. "You wanna just use one of my old songs?"

Les idly rolled a C chord. "I don't know—it's got to have that 'I'm not gonna let these hard times get me, I'm gonna come out fighting' angle. Something Ethel can sing at the very end, that the audience can take with them, with it ringing in their ears. You think you can come up with any ideas, Greta?"

"Yes, I can." Greta hadn't been involved too much in the music end of it. She'd been a creative consultant, making sure the songs followed her storyline closely enough. But either the late hour or the corned beef gave her a burst of inspiration, because she tore off a sheet of paper and started scribbling.

"What is that?" Billy got up and tried to read her scrawl upside down as they leaned over opposite sides of the piano.

"It's 'Yes, I Can.' That's the title of the song. Here.

See what you think of it so far." She slid the paper to him over the piano lid, and he scanned the lyrics.

"Hm. Sounds good." Billy had a few ideas himself now. He took a pencil from his pocket and jotted a second verse. He slid it back to her, and she wrote a third. Then Les took a look and started fitting a melody line to the words, in the key of G, to accommodate Ethel's vocal range. They gathered around Les and sang the first few bars.

Billy and Greta looked at each other over Les's head and something clicked—a solution that had always been there, yet never surfaced, for whatever reason, until this moment.

Greta held up her sheet of paper and waved it like a flag. "This is it, Billy! It works. It's perfect."

Les added chords to his melody line as Billy wrote another stanza.

"I can just hear Ethel singing it right before the curtain falls," Greta said as Les took a blank sheet of staff paper and started writing down the music notes. "Can't you, Les?"

"Yes, I can!"

Billy slid the now-finished song back to her. "Hit it, Greta."

"Years ago when I was small
I looked at those who had it all
And said I will be just like them someday.
Working 9 to 5's okay,
you punch the clock, you get your pay,
But dreams are not reality, they say.
Then a voice from deep within
Just brushed my ears and whispered
Three small words that somehow

changed the world for me:
Yes, I can!
Yes, I will be the very best someday.
Yes, I can touch and feel and see
because it's all so real to me,
I'll never stop and doubt myself again.
But hanging on me like a shroud
that ominous and darkened cloud
The negative self doubt I always bore,
Talent seemed to grow on trees,
performers were all trained like fleas
I had to show that I was worth much more.
I had to pass up all the rest,
and prove to them that I'm the best
And push through each and every single door.
Although I would reach out and clasp,
my dreams were just beyond my grasp
Determination flowing through my veins.
Yes, I can!
My worries are all part of yesterday.
Yes, I can have the moon and then
I can give it back again,
There's a star out there named after me.
I climbed the mountain steadily,
no one dared discourage me,
I showed them what I wanted them to see,
Not once did I stop to see
that others were in front of me,
My next goal was always just ahead.
Detours always staggered me,
but only temporarily,
I just found another path to tread.
Yes, I can!

Yes, I can write a novel in the sand.
There's no place that I can't go
especially if they say no,
They can't stop me if I know I can.
When times were bad I felt so small,
how easy just to end it all
And just live by the clock and drudgery,
When the feeling would subside,
the little voice from deep inside
Would sing those very special words to me:
Yes, I can!
Yes, I live and breathe my dreams, I can!
There is nothing I can't be,
these dreams I have inside of me
Will now make me what I was meant to be.
Yes, I can!
I know that I am very small,
yet somehow I've attained it all,
But there's no magic tricks, no sleight of hand.
There is nothing up my sleeve,
I simply made myself believe
What the masses just don't understand.
I am all I want to be and you can either envy me
Or say the words that master every plan:
Yes, I can!
Yes, I can reach the brightest star, I can!
Now I won't stop till I'm the best,
I'll simply pass up all the rest
I'll do it because I know I can.
Yes, I can!"

That summed it all up so well—the leading lady's struggle to make it, her determination to show the world what she had, despite all her hurdles, the crushing poverty just outside her door.

But it worked. Somehow the magic they created at 3:00 that morning seized that stodgy crowd by the heart. Ethel got her first standing ovation.

"Our song's a hit, Billy!" Greta jumped out of her seat and shrieked in delight.

He simply sat there, shaking his head in wonder at this other miracle of birth.

****

The show underwent numerous revisions during tryouts. But nothing could thaw the chill every time Billy looked out over that cold Boston audience. Les and Greta admired the revisions they made on the train back to New York, passing notes to cast members with new and improved lines of dialogue.

If it bombed on Broadway, Billy knew it meant he'd wanted too much too soon. Who the hell did he think he was, expecting to shoot from a Harlem speak right to Broadway?

"Billy, don't you have any faith in your collaborators? Or Hal? Or the cast? All the people who've been working so hard on this? If you go down, we all go down with you!" Greta told him off when he voiced his self-destructive thoughts, slumped in his seat in the rear car.

He nodded, mouth shut, but couldn't help feeling that some superior force was using this incident to slap him down. He mumbled an apology, sorry he'd shared it with her.

But she kept on at him. "You can't be all mopey in front of the cast members. They have a lot more to lose than you, you know." She got up and slammed out of the car. Pru sat across from him, her nose buried in a

Rodin biography, but he knew she'd been listening.

She lowered the book an inch and looked at him.

"Don't you start." He held up his hand, wondering if he could get a drink or if the train was dry.

"I wasn't going to say a word, Billy," Pru said. "But she's right. Wait till it opens in New York. What's the worst that can happen?"

He spoke the obvious. "It'll bomb."

"Yeah? And then what?" She put the book down.

"I'll be humiliated." Obvious again.

"Yeah? And then what?" she repeated.

"Oh, it's your Freud routine again. Nobody'll like me, that's what." He wasn't in the mood to be analyzed.

"Yeah? And then what?" Once again.

"Aw, hell." He knew what she was trying to say. She put it all in perspective with her wholesome Midwest logic. He went over and sat next to her, draped his arm around her shoulders, and realized what was really important.

By the time they pulled into Penn Station, he wasn't feeling so down anymore. If it wasn't because of the Scotch bottle Ethel had given him after he'd drained his flask, it was due to the quickie he and Pru had standing up in the phone-booth-sized lavatory.

The group disbanded at the train station, all hugging and kissing and well-wishing. Les wasn't there; he'd stayed in Boston to meet his companion and go to some place called Provincetown for the weekend.

Greta gave him one more pep talk. "It'll be fine, Billy. It was only tryouts. The New York audience is completely different. They'll love us. Trust me." She gave him a reassuring squeeze.

"I just wanna get loaded to the muzzle." He

grabbed his valise. "Not think about it till opening night."

So that's where he went, after taking Pru to the doctor to have her cast removed. He got her back home, and with her blessing he headed for the nearest gin mill, without the patience to travel uptown.

He came home, fell into bed, and the next thing he knew, Pru was shaking him awake. "Billy, come on, it's Sunday morning." He knew what that meant.

****

Interlude: Sunday Dinner at the House

Two Sundays later he sprang his news and held the tickets out like a hand of cards. He'd planned to wait till after dessert but just couldn't. He wanted to see the expression on his father's face so badly he'd have passed up manicotti altogether.

"Billy, my baby boy, with a Broadway show!" Ma ran up to him and hugged him, pulling his head down to her shoulder. He inhaled her warm vanilla scent.

"Yup. That's me. Two weeks of previews, then the twenty-eighth is opening night. At the Majestic, Broadway at Forty-Third. Right next to the theater where Noel Coward's *Design for Living* is playing."

His father stared at the ticket in his hand like it was printed in Yiddish.

"Well, Da?" Billy couldn't help blurting out. He held his breath.

"Well is right. You did it, my boy." Da smiled, showing all his white teeth, nodding. "What is it, a burlesque show?"

"No, it's a musical. It's Greta Schliessmayer's first book!"

"Oh…" They all nodded in unison. Da almost

looked disappointed.

"Next one'll be a burlesque show," Billy kidded, and Ma walked him to the table.

"So you didn't go to London. You went to Boston for tryouts." Tessie slid his chair out like he was the President at a state dinner.

"Yeah, well—I wanted to keep it to myself, so I could surprise you." He also wanted to keep to himself that it bombed in Boston.

Da held out the armed chair at the head of the table, his place. "He's sitting here, Tess. Today Billy's in the place of honor."

"Hey, thanks!" He walked around the table and let Da seat him. "But don't you think you should see it first? You might hate it."

"It'll be a hit, I'm sure. Greta's book was one of the best I've ever read," Da replied, and Billy felt his insides churn, but just then Pru's eyes caught his and told him to shut up.

Every once in a while, his wife knew best.

****

"You'll go with me? You mean it?" Billy knew his mouth was hanging open, but he wanted to show his astonishment. Opening night was less than a week away, and Pru agreed to accompany him. Turning water into wine couldn't have been more of a miracle. He didn't know what he'd said or done to change her mind, but every wound of the last six months had instantly mended.

"I know how important this is to you, Snuggles. Just like your family, I'm very proud of you. We're all very happy for you. And I hope the show becomes a classic. You deserve it."

"What made you—ah, never mind." He didn't want to know what made her change her mind. After all, it had been bankrolled with dirty money, just like those other ventures. "Honey Bear, it's only the beginning!" He borrowed from Rosie. "Go buy yourself a new dress, new shoes, new hat, new stole, new jewelry, whatever you want." He peeled off a few bills and realized how much like his bosses this looked. She noticed it, too, because she waved it away.

"I'll go to Susan's and buy a few things on account. I don't like the idea of carrying all that cash. Maybe because I never had any—oh, well, I just feel better charging it."

"Whatever you want." He couldn't get very close to her, as she was enormous by now. He wondered if she had triplets in there.

He found out sooner than he expected.

****

After two endless weeks of previews, during which they rewrote more songs and strings of dialogue, the day finally arrived. He got backstage first thing in the morning, going over his checklist of details—*Are all the lights in place? Is the curtain working? Do they have all the props?* But mostly he wanted to stand on the stage, stare out over the empty seats, and imagine what it would be like a few hours from now—the crowd on its feet in thundering applause. All for him, to thank him for his talent, his hard work, his gift to them. He took a low bow, swept off an imaginary hat, and blew a kiss out into the empty seats. Just then one of the stagehands came up and asked him if he was sick or something.

"Oh, no, just doing some calisthenics..." He

scurried off the stage to the orchestra pit and played a few tunes on the piano, listening to the tones recede and die within the soundboard's depths. Tonight his name would be recorded for newspapers, for entertainment magazines, and for history.

****

One hour before curtain time, their rented silver-trimmed Duesenberg pulled up to the stage entrance. The chauffeur opened the door for them. It took him a while to help Pru out, her bulk causing her to fall back a few times.

How a pressing mob of well-wishers got backstage, he didn't know. He and Pru got to their private box ten minutes before curtain time. Watching an usher lead his parents to their seats, a surge of pride thrilled him. Rosie winked up at him from the front row, sitting next to a bearcat who looked like she didn't know where she was. There sat Jackie Harper with a blonde bombshell in a box opposite. He looked over at Billy and gave a little salute. It made him feel like the most important person in the whole world. He saluted back.

He looked around at the ladies and gents in their finery, flipping through their programs or peeking through opera glasses, their jewels glittering under the crystal chandeliers. What a turnout, even in these hard times. He had the strangest feeling that it was all a dream, and he'd wake up and be a kid banging on the old Wurlitzer, his feet not touching the floor.

As the orchestra tuned up, the crowd's chatter nearly drowned them out. Then he heard a high-pitched screech. He thought it was one of the violins. But it was his wife.

"Billy! I'm—" She slid to the floor.

"What's the matter?" He knelt at her side. "You're not going into labor, are you?"

Oh, yes she was.

He started yelling for help, but no one heard him, it seemed. Finally an usher hustled in, and they got her back into the car. "Billy, aren't you coming with me?" she called out as her hand slid out of his. He made sure she was in safely and closed the door. "I'll be right along. I promise."

He rushed back in as the curtain began to rise. No, he wasn't going to miss this for anything. She probably wouldn't have the baby for a few hours yet. This was the happiest moment of his life, standing in the wings at his very first Broadway show. He had time to get out and experience his next happiest moment. "Billy!" he heard in a voice that nearly shattered his eardrums.

"What?" he turned around and there stood Greta, stunning in a low-cut lavender gown. It took him a second to notice that she was stunned herself, just to see him there.

"Didn't Pru just go into labor?" she shrieked.

"Yeah. It's all right—" He held up his hands. "I'll go join her in a minute. I can't miss this."

She gaped at him like he'd sprouted a third eye. The house lights faded and he peeked out at blackness beyond the footlights. But hundreds of bodies sat out there, waiting. Energy charged the air. The tension heightened. Billy thought he'd burst.

The orchestra struck up the opening chord. The chord he and Les had bickered over for an entire day.

"I'll go right after the overture," he vowed as he backed away, inching up to the door. "I'll get to the hospital on time." He wondered how long it would take to get a cab. Maybe he could bum a ride from one of those idle chauffeurs.

Following the overture, Ethel made her entrance and sang the opening song, which he had written in Boston, lying on the floor at four a.m., to replace the previous two openers nobody liked.

He tore himself away and ran out the stage door, heading for the nearest Rolls. Maybe he could get back during intermission and see the second act! Of course there was always tomorrow night, but it would never be the same. He knocked on the window and jolted the driver out of sleep.

"Can you take me to—" Holy Jesus! He slapped his forehead, nearly knocking himself over. He didn't know which hospital she'd gone to!

Chapter Four

"It means the increase in honky-tonk joints,
The blast of the radios from the amplifiers hanging over dance-hall doorways,
The peddlers and the barkers shouting at the top of their lungs:
'Buy a balloon an' act natural';
'Come in and see the great flea circus';
'This way for a good time, folks';
'No tights in this show';
'Plenty of seats in the first balcony; "She Kissed Him to Death" just starting';
'Magnificent love story; bring the children.' "
—*George M. Cohan,*
after a tour of Broadway, 1933

"What's the closest hospital to here?" Billy clamped his fingers onto the driver's shoulder, making terrible marks on the poor guy's uniform.

"Uh—Roosevelt, I guess."

Billy loosened his grip and flipped open his pocket watch, part of his formal attire. "Then shove in your clutch—my wife's gonna have a baby." He tumbled into the backseat. Ah, a well-stocked bar—just what he needed.

"Okay, buddy, we'll—" He turned and looked around, scratching his head under his small cap.

"Where is she?"

"They already took her, but she didn't tell me which hospital. So we gotta look till we find her. Start with Roosevelt. I'll pay you whatever you want."

On that note, the engine roared into life and the Rolls leapt into the street. He dug into his right pocket, and out came a wadded-up hankie instead of his billfold. "Damn!" He'd put his cash in Pru's purse because his formal attire didn't have deep pockets.

Billy grabbed the nearest bottle from the bar and took a swig. Whiskey. Not the best, but wood alcohol would've sufficed at this moment. As the driver yabbered on about some new skyscraper on 34th Street named the Empire State Building, Billy kept his eye on the watch like he was timing a horse race. Three minutes passed, then four, with no hospital in sight.

"Say, how long does it take to have a baby?" Billy knelt in the jumpseat, too nervous to sit back and savor more whiskey.

"Gosh, bub, I got no idea," the driver answered over his shoulder. "Why, I heard of some women givin' birth right there in a taxi, or elevator, or wherever."

"Oh, hell. I really needed to hear that. I thought it took more like a coupla days." He silently begged Pru not to have the baby before he got there. He'd envisioned it so many times—pacing the hospital floor, hearing the magic words—"Congratulations, Mr. McGlory, you may see your son now!"—and handing out cigars all over the place. He didn't want it to happen all wrong. The suspense had swelled over the months till it welled up like a dam waiting to burst. He didn't have any cigars, either. He rummaged around the clinking bottles and glasses in the bar. Nothing in there but booze. He didn't think handing out shots of whiskey was such a good idea. Oh, why did this have to be tonight? Any other night would've been perfect. At least this was one birthday he'd never forget.

When they arrived at Roosevelt Hospital, he slammed out of the car. "Just wait here, keep the motor running," he instructed the driver, and dashed in. The lobby was mobbed. He found the maternity ward and gave the desk nurse a description—"a short gal in a pink imitation dyed rabbit fur stole with a pink satin hat and purse and matching pink satin shoes. And an expensive gown from Bloomingdale's, cut in a V at the neck." He gestured at his chest with his hands. "And borrowed diamond jewelry. And she's gonna have a baby."

He got a nod and dropped to his knees before the front desk. "Oh, thank you, God, she's here! So am I a father yet?" He pulled himself back up, jumping from one foot to another, cracking his knuckles.

"And who are you?" the nurse asked in her crisp voice.

"The father of the baby who's being born here!" He spread his arms wide.

"Sir, there are dozens of babies being born here. Help me narrow it down by giving your name."

"Oh, uh—McGlory. But she doesn't use my name, she kept her own when we got married. See, she's an artist. She kept her own name. Muller. But we're married. Trust me on that. We really are married. See?" He held up his hand to display his wedding band, then realized he'd left it home. "Well, we are married. And the baby's last name is McGlory. 'Cause after all, I'm the father."

"You're sure of that, sir," the nurse chirped, flipping through some papers.

"Of course! And I'm Billy McGlory! My musical, *Headin' for Better Times*, just opened on Broadway!" He hopped from one foot to the other.

"Did it now?" A smile finally cracked that pancake veneer.

"Yeah, about twenty minutes ago. Tonight's opening night. In more ways than one, I guess," rushed out in one breath.

Just then another nurse, with a smile as white as the walls and floor, glided through the flapping doors and made the announcement he'd been waiting all this time for.

"Mr. McGlory?" She searched the room, her glasses reflecting the ceiling lights. The other men either shook their heads or didn't acknowledge her.

"That's me!" He rushed up to her, crushing his hat between sweaty hands.

"Congratulations, you're the father of a baby girl." She gave him a hospital-white smile.

"Me? You sure it's hers? I mean, mine?"

She nodded. "All yours, sir. You can go in and see them in just a minute."

He pumped her hand over and over, till she shook. "Thanks so much, I wish I had a cigar—thanks so much, Nurse! I'll be a good father, I swear to it!" He crossed his heart.

"Just have a seat, sir, and relax." She patted him on the arm.

Seat? Who the hell could sit? As for relaxing—forget it; every muscle in his body tensed, coiled like a mainspring. He found himself pacing the floor—and it was after the fact!

****

"Honey Bear, she's gorgeous. Looks just like you." He feasted his eyes on his newborn daughter.

"Oh, come on, Snuggles, how can you tell who she looks like?" Pru held their baby in her arms, rocking her gently.

"What did you name her?" He couldn't stop staring. This breathing, living child nestled in Pru's arms was his flesh and blood. And he thought his songs were a divine creation!

"Nothing yet." She looked up at him and smiled. "I thought I'd leave that to you."

"Jumpin' Jehoshaphat, I can't even think straight." He slapped the side of his head. "I might wind up calling her Zeppo or something. You better name her."

"Well, we don't have to decide right now." Pru gazed down lovingly at her newborn baby.

"No? You mean she won't have a name? She'd be nameless till we decide?" he yabbered.

"She'll be Baby Girl McGlory. She has a last name, of course." Pru's tone was too calm, too unruffled, considering what she'd just been through.

"Nah, that's not right. She deserves a really pretty first name." He thought of Ma, sitting there in the theater, watching his show, not yet aware she was a grandmother. "I'd love to name her Vita, but that's too old world. That name was okay back then, but now—" He stroked his chin. "I want her to have an American name. But a real good strong name, a name she'll be proud of."

"How about Victoria?" Pru suggested. "It's got all the letters in Vita. So she can still be named after your mother."

"Hey, that's a nifty idea! Victoria McGlory. Sounds kinda regal, doesn't it?" He reached out and hovered his hand over his daughter's head. "I'm afraid to touch her."

She softly sang to their baby as he said, "This is only the beginning."

****

So Victoria Anna McGlory and *Headin' For Better Times* were both born on the same night, to equal fanfare. He read the reviews the next morning, open-mouthed, dazed with amazement. Streams of visitors came through the Jane Street door all day, bringing flowers and cards for the baby, congratulatory notes for the show. Rosie sent over two of those flower horseshoes. They were so damn big, he had to put one on the fire escape and the other in the bathtub.

"See, you were worried about nothing!" Greta I-told-you-so'd him over the phone. "I knew our show would be a hit."

Susan brought some cooked meals or he would have starved. A nanny appeared out of nowhere; he'd had a feeling Rosie was going to do something like that. Even though Pru and the baby weren't home from the hospital yet, the nurse took a look around the place, and at him, and got to work immediately.

He escaped to his East Side penthouse for a little while and fell into a dead sleep. What seemed like a minute later, the jangling phone woke him up. He glanced at the clock. It was four p.m.

"Thanks for being home to greet your wife and new daughter."

"Aah, Honey Bear, I'm sorry—" He cleared his

throat. "I was so beat, people clumping in and out all day, the nurse—"

"She's gone." Pru's voice sounded more stern over the phone.

"What? Why?" He rubbed his eyes, his mind still fuzzy.

"I don't want a mob nurse here," she proclaimed.

"A mob nurse? Pru, she's not with the mob, for Pete's sake. She's just a gift." He sat up, leaned on his elbow.

"Ish kabibble. I don't want her or anybody that has anything to do with her."

"You'll appreciate help at two a.m. when the kid starts squalling and your eyeballs are hanging out of your head from lack of sleep." He rolled over and slid out of bed onto his knees.

"I don't want some stranger raising my baby. And it looks like there'll be another stranger around here if her father hardly comes home." She had to throw in that dig.

"I'll be right there. I just needed some peace and quiet." He stood and held onto the headboard for support.

He wondered how much peace and quiet he'd get with an infant in the apartment. Why'd she get rid of the damn nurse? He'd have to find a way to get her back. Maybe even hire a male nurse. Pru wouldn't balk so much at that. A nice-looking, young—well, maybe not so nice-looking. Or young.

The thought of seeing his new daughter chased away every other thing from his mind. He threw some clothes on and headed out.

****

Pru still wouldn't set foot in his Fifth Avenue palace.

"I want to bring my daughter up in the Village." She hung another washed diaper on a clothesline strung across their kitchen. Their own clothes hung from a line in the bedroom.

"With panhandlers and bread lines and garbage lining the streets?" He spoke in a high whisper, holding the fragile new life in his arms, rocking her. Never having held anything more delicate than his one-eyed teddy bear, he still feared he'd crush her.

"I want her surrounded by art and artists." Pru parted two diapers on the line so he could see her face.

"There are plenty of those on the East Side, only they ain't starving," he countered. "I want my daughter exposed to the arts, but I want her to have indoor plumbing, too."

"I want her to be an artist. Or maybe a writer." Pru went to the sink and began filling the baby bath.

"How about a musician?" He looked down into Victoria's sky-blue eyes.

Pru went on over the running water like she hadn't heard him. "She's going to be a woman ahead of her time. I'll make sure of that. She's going to grow up in the '50s and '60s—think what life will be like then. We'll probably have men on the moon, we'll be flying everywhere…imagine. Our daughter will grow up in an era when everybody'll have their own robot and maybe even go to the moon!"

He couldn't resist—he bent his head and rubbed noses with his baby daughter. "Well, even if you want her to be an artist, I want her college-educated. Like Susan's kids will be. But I have a hunch she'll be smarter."

"Let's hope so." She took the baby from his arms and placed her in the bath water.

Billy went to answer a knock at the door. It was the nurse again. He thought Pru'd given her the boot. "Uh, sorry, nurse, ma'am, but—well, my wife—"

"My employer told me to come back and ask you to reconsider." Her tone carried a pleading edge. Billy knew the Depression must've gotten to her, the poor soul. She bustled in, glanced around, spotted Pru bathing the baby, and nodded her approval.

"Your services are not required here," Pru replied over her shoulder, politely enough.

She walked past Billy and stood next to Pru, shoulder to shoulder. "But Mrs. Fink said she wouldn't take no for an answer. She said to reconsider. Please, Mrs. McGlory? I need the job."

"Mrs. Fink? That's your employer?" Billy closed the door and stood on the other side of Pru.

"Yes." The nurse nodded as if to say, *Who else would it be?*

"Uh—um—" He nudged Pru as she sponged the baby. "Honey? Want to reconsider?"

She glanced at him. "Well, if it's Susan who sent her over…"

He nodded. "Yeah, Susan sent her over."

So Frau Pertl, from Linz, Austria, stayed, and that was the last he saw of his cigarettes.

****

He had to get back to his nightclub job, although he wanted to watch his Broadway show every night, to sing along and bask in the glory of his creation. But he had an audience—the club audience. They'd already seen the show, didn't care to see it again, and wanted him back at the piano.

That first night back at the club was like a homecoming—they'd hooted and hollered and applauded—he finally had to start playing to shut them up. But he kept following the clock so he'd know what was going on at the theater—which song they were doing, what act it was.

His new role as a parent inspired an avalanche of songs, all about his little girl. Every night he rushed home and packed his journal with verse even more sentimental than his old Tin Pan Alley lyrics.

He finally had a whole day and evening off, and hovered around F.A.O. Schwarz's door, pacing and smoking, until they opened. He burst in and swept up and down the aisles, picking up armloads of toys. He dashed back to Jane Street with four bulging shopping bags of goodies. Pru sat at her easel painting when he let himself in. The nurse stood in the kitchen scrubbing out the baby's bassinet. It smelled like a hospital in there.

He glanced at Pru's canvas. "Hm. Nice." He didn't know squat about art; the only things he liked about paintings were bright colors. But this portrait of hers seemed darker than usual. Besides that, it wasn't one of her sweeping landscapes or cheery settings. It looked like an ocean churning or something. It made him seasick just looking at it. "Uh—what is it?"

"It's the interior of a vortex," came her answer, flat, dull, and lifeless as the painting itself.

"Why you painting that?" He tiptoed over to his baby girl, sleeping peacefully.

"Don't get too close, you're crawling with germs!"

Frau Pertl ordered from her corner.

"Aye aye, general!" He held his hands up in surrender, but moved closer anyway, and sat on the chair next to Victoria. He itched to wake her, sing to her, and present her with all her new toys, but he just sat and stared. This baby was a work of art. "Hey, beautiful," he whispered softly so as not to wake her. "I'm gonna write a song about you during every stage of your life, till you grow up to be a gorgeous woman."

"I needed a departure from the usual stuff I do," Pru remarked, but he was only half listening. He sat, captivated, as his baby slept. His mind wandered—what talents would she develop, would she take after him or Pru, what kind of world would it be when she grew up? Would the Depression be over? Would they really have all those modern marvels they dreamed about?

"I express the world as I see it. And this is how I'm seeing it right now," came Pru's voice from across the room.

"Okey-dokey." He knew she'd said something, but wasn't sure what. But all Pru ever needed was occasional praise for her work. She didn't crave the thundering applause of an adoring packed house every night like he did. A few browsers stopping to admire her work was good enough for her. She didn't need to hear how brilliant or talented or gifted she was every day of her life.

Which of those traits would Victoria inherit? he wondered.

"No, it's not okey-dokey, Billy," she raised her voice. "You haven't heard a word I said."

"Can I feed her when she wakes up?" He looked up, but the propped-up canvas blocked Pru out.

"I fed her before you came in," she chided him, like he should've known.

"Oh, right." She was nursing. He certainly couldn't compete with that.

"I said you weren't listening." She dipped her brush into some paint on the spattered palette.

"Sorry." He looked away from his sleeping angel and got up to observe his wife. Now that he noticed, she did look kind of dark, like the painting. "What—you don't like your painting?"

"This is called simply *Void*." She flicked the brush back and forth, smearing blue-gray paint onto the canvas. "It's how I feel. The state of my being. The expression of my visions from within. If you look closely, you'll see a figure in the vortex, right at the center here." She pointed with the tip of her brush.

He leaned over and looked closely at the painting. "Is that you?"

"Not me, but my being." She sounded like a sleepwalker.

"So why are you—uh, your being—caught up in a vortex?" He gestured at the canvas.

"It's the way I've felt lately. That one over there— I call it *The Edge*." She pointed her brush to another canvas he hadn't even seen, propped up against the wall. Maybe because it blended in with the curtains. It was just as bland.

"The edge of what?" He went over and knelt down to study it. It made as much sense to him as if she'd painted the Greek alphabet on there.

"The edge is a different place for everybody, depending on who and where you are," she enlightened him.

"Are you sure it ain't upside down?" He turned his head sideways. "What is it of?"

"Of? A painting doesn't have to be 'of' anything. It's not a song, or a book, which have to be 'about' something. It just—is," she lectured from her perch.

"Oh." He'd never understood art and, quite frankly, didn't care to. All he knew was that he couldn't sit at an easel with a handful of brushes and create something for people to 'interpret' and 'absorb.' So he took it for granted that she knew what she was doing. "It's nice."

"It's not supposed to be nice!" she snapped.

"Okay, it's not nice. It's ugly. What do you want me to say?" He came back to her, but kept his distance. He didn't want to crowd her.

"Nothing. Go stare at the baby some more." She began applying more dark brushstrokes to her vortex, humming a long, low tone with every stroke. He'd always wished they could create music together. She did have a nice humming voice.

But why the cold shoulder? And why the dark paintings? She had everything a woman could want; a new baby, a nurse, a penthouse she could move into anytime—but no, she preferred the poor artist bit. Maybe she didn't want to show up her penniless friends.

"Hey, she's waking up!" He rushed over to the baby. Making sure the nurse was busy, he gathered her in his arms and held her close.

"Don't you dare handle that baby without washing your hands! And don't breathe your filthy alcohol fumes on her!" the general ordered from her corner. "You have to wear a mask!"

He put her down as fast as he could without

dropping her and dashed to the sink for Nurse Pertl's brown cake of soap. "I haven't had a drink all day!" he protested to this stranger now changing the sheets on their bed, snapping them crisply before smoothing them out. "Why am I defending myself to a servant?" he muttered, returning to his daughter. "I'm taking her for a ride in her carriage," he stated, not waiting for a rebuttal but of course getting one anyway.

"Not without me, you aren't," came the answer from the bed, as Nurse Pertl tucked in a sheet corner. Now he knew what army cots looked like.

"I need a chaperone to take my own daughter for a walk?" He stomped up to her. "Who's working for who here?"

"I don't trust you not to escort her into any speakeasies." A sneer accompanied her snide tone.

He turned away from her unyielding bulk. "Pruuuu!"

"Do what she says, Snuggles," she said without missing a brushstroke.

"Yes, it's my job, and I'm escorting you on all your walks with the baby...*Snuggles*." Nurse Purtl brandished a smirk.

"Aah, crapola." He patted himself down for cigarettes, then remembered there was another kind of Prohibition going on here.

****

That night at Piano's he sat alone nursing a Scotch on the rocks and his first cigarette in twelve hours. His last visit here felt like a lifetime ago. So much had changed so fast. He now had a hit Broadway musical, already in its third week, with no end in sight. A new baby, who he longed to see more often. A business partner urging him to invest in lakefront real estate, more racehorses, and a printing company. When most people would've gone dizzy with it all, he wished he had more time for more wheeling and dealing.

Susan came over, sat down, and sipped her Pink Lady. "Nice of you to drop by," she remarked, although she beamed at him.

"Thanks. I wish I could have more nights to just come down here and wait on customers, but I see you hired some help."

"Well, I know how busy you are." She wiped the lipstick off her glass. "How's Frau Pertl working out?"

He rolled his eyes and expelled a puff of smoke, wanting to inhale the whole pack at once. "Kaiser Pertl has me living like a monk. I can't smoke. I can't breathe. I can't go near the baby without pasteurizing myself first. Anything I touch, she scrubs it down with this brown soap that smells like it came out the back end of a horse. God help me if she catches me takin' a leak!"

"I gave her a contract for six months, till Pru gets completely back on her feet." She sipped her drink. "You men have no idea what's involved with giving birth and everything that happens after."

He swirled the rocks in his Scotch. "Suze, this sounds strange, but does this happen to all women after they have a baby? She's just not herself." He looked over at her. "You should see these things she's painting. Bleak, dark stuff. Nothing like her other paintings. And her sculptures—they looked better as lumps of clay."

"Maybe the style is changing." She waved hello to a customer. "You know—art goes through fashions, just like music, clothes, everything. What do they call them—movements."

"Nah." He shook his head. "I don't think it's that. She said it's how she feels. I'll tell you, it's downright dreary. Nobody's gonna buy that stuff."

"Could just be a phase she's going through." She sat forward. "Or postpartum depression?"

His head snapped up. "What the hell's that?"

"Sometimes, after a woman gives birth, she's depressed," Susan explained.

"Did that happen to you?" he asked, the first personal question he'd ever asked his sister.

"No, fortunately. But it happened to a girlfriend of mine."

"What can you do for it?" His tone bordered on desperation. "I'll try anything."

"Well, the more extreme cases get institutionalized." She picked up her drink. "But I'm sure it's not like that with her. She'll be okay in a few months." She sipped.

"I wish I could be there more often, but, you know, I've got the club, I've been writing more songs, the show's going—" He waved his hands around.

"You don't have to answer to me, Billy." She captured his hand in a squeeze. "Maybe you can cut back."

"On what?"

"Club dates, maybe?" She gave him one of her steady stares, inherited from their mother.

"Hell, I can't do that." He shook his head. "We're thinking of buying another club, a bigger one. This one we've got now is even more jam-packed than the last one."

"It's up to you," she said, still staring. "Remember

what I said about compromise?"

"Yeah, but I can't give anything up. Not right now anyway." He gulped his drink and chewed on a cube.

"Just pretend you have six months to live." She pushed her chair out. "That makes you get your priorities in order. Think about it." She stood. "I have to scoot. It's getting busy."

She hadn't even asked him to help, as if he wasn't running the place with her anymore. It just occurred to him what she'd said. Six months to live! Who the hell wants to think like that? But, without realizing it, he started listing everything in his life—in order of importance. When he was finished, a shock shook him to the bones—that was exactly the way his father would've done it.

Chapter Five

"In 1925, $286,950,000 more of $10,000 bills were issued than in 1920 and $25,000,000 more of $5,000 bills were issued. What honest business man deals in $10,000 bills? Surely these bills were not used to pay the salaries of ministers. The bootlegging industry has created a demand for bills of large denominations, and the Treasury Department accommodates them."

—Fiorello LaGuardia,
Hearings before the Committee on the Judiciary,
U.S. Senate, 69th Congress, 1st Session

October 4, 1932, 4:10 a.m., 55 degrees under a clear, starry sky.

Everything good happened, but why did it all have to happen at once? Billy wrote in his journal, sipping a Scotch, lying in bed in his penthouse, alone. He felt like he was on a raft floating in the ocean, by himself, with no one to rescue him.

It'd be nice to savor it slowly, like this Scotch I'm sipping. All these adoring fans, the Janes in their bias-cut satin dresses groping me with their painted nails, they'd all be surprised to see me here sitting alone in a huge bed in the middle of the night with nothing on but the radio. He took another sip. *With only a journal for companionship. Half spifficated.* He wasn't, really. But he wanted to be.

Things would be a lot easier to handle if they'd happened one at a time, spaced out over three or four years, instead of— He stopped to think. When had he met Rosie? When had Pru hit him with the surprise? Six months ago? It seemed like six years, for all the growing up he'd done. He'd certainly aged six years since then.

Take last night, for instance. I come home—I mean to the Jane St. place—and she had those queer birds over. A few of them were smoking reefer. "Where the hell is the baby?" I demanded, looking around at the place. It's worse than that shabby old garret she used to live in. Paint smears all over the walls, empty glasses, bottles, overflowing ashtrays, paint brushes stuck in bottles of turpentine— It stunk, too. She assured me the baby was okay, Susan came to take her. Nurse Pertl went with them. Susan wanted her kids to get to know their cousin. Well, that's okay—they hadn't seen her since the christening. So that was a relief. But it looked and smelled like an opium den in there. Her buddy Franck came up to me and held my hand—rather than shook it, that is—but he's a harmless enough fella. I can't fault him for the way he is. After all, my collaborator, probably the most gifted genius this side of Gershwin, is that way, too. Pru actually looked half alive—she came up and gave me a big kiss. It stirred my juices. It's been a long time since we've been alone together that way.

"Can we sneak into the bedroom for a few minutes?" I asked her, but she playfully slapped me (that didn't exactly act as a deterrent either) and whispered "Later!" How much later? I wondered. What would it take to get those Ethels out of there? She

glowed around those queer birds more than when she was alone with me. But I chalked that up to pressure. She had the baby to feed and diapers to wash, and I had this glamorous life going on.

I poured myself a highball and went around the room looking at her paintings and sculptures. She'd finished two or three more pictures since that one with the swirling bowels of hell. These others were just as gloomy and surly. I had to admit, though, not knowing a watercolor from a bootleg Scotch label, they began to strike a chord in me.

I looked at one of them for a good five minutes, sipping my highball, letting my senses capture it. Breathing in reefer fumes didn't hurt, either. It seemed to talk to me, then it seemed to sing to me. Maybe it was the musician in me, but I actually heard a melody going through my head, time signature and all. It was in G minor, in three-quarter time, like a waltz, but it was slow and funereal, like the painting, every brush stroke a phrase. The closer I stood to it, the more defined it got. Kind of like something Chopin would've done if he'd been a painter instead of a composer, when he was freezing his stones off in Majorca. Was that happening to Pru, too? I wondered as I held out my finger and traced the brush strokes that swirled around in the sky, like a gathering storm in shades of gray and pewter. Did she feel like someone had let her down? Who? You, you idiot! *I yelled at myself, taking another mouthful so I wouldn't cough. I was neglecting her a lot. I wasn't even there when the baby was born. I had to stay and watch the curtain go up. I hope nobody told her that. No matter what the reason, I was now a negligent husband. Maybe that's why she painted all these dark portraits of forbidden worlds that resembled winter on Pluto.*

Needing to talk to her, I looked around. I had to tell her I'd made a list of what's important to me, and of course, she and the baby came first. I did it differently than Susan suggested: instead of pretending I had six months left, I pretended my life was being confiscated and I had to list what I'd be willing to part with, in order of importance. The car Rosie gave me was first. I didn't need that big fancy roadster. I hardly ever used it anyway. The penthouse was next, and my key to the safe came after that. The club and the show stood neck and neck, but the show won out. George the piano was close to the end, but hell, I'd need George even if I had to play her out on the street. My journal came right before the final item, Pru and the baby. I couldn't list them separately, of course. They went together. But they were the most important.

I wanted to tell her that she and the baby were number one in my life; I'd die for them. But she was busy talking and laughing with these three Ethels and one skag, smoking dope out of a pipe, emptying another bottle, yakking about whatever painters and sculptors talk about. It's like that with musicians, too. She'd never be interested in the stuff we talk about. Some of it's pretty dull, to be honest. If I wasn't a musician, I wouldn't want to listen to any of it. She can have her little soirée.

I vamoosed before I breathed in any more reefer. That stuff didn't like my system very much. The few times I smoked it, it made me dizzy, then hungry as hell. Like right now.

I went to Moriarty's and devoured a T-bone steak.

I didn't even ask for a drink. Then I headed down the street to Molly McGuire's, where Carl Sandburg played his guitar and sang old folk songs. Some of these poets really do have musical talent. I went up to say hello and we shook hands, but he'd never heard of me.

Then I dilly-dallied for a while, just enjoying being out in the world instead of on a stage. I hoofed it up to the Majestic, where intermission had just ended. I slipped in the stage door and watched the rest of the play from the wings. I thought of taking Greta out afterwards, but I didn't even see her there, and slapped myself across the face for even thinking of it. I should be with Pru!

I cabbed back. By then it was late, and I hoped the Rodin society had broken up by then. I was lucky. The place was dark, and they'd vamoosed. But she wasn't sleeping, like I'd expected her to be. The company alone would've put me to sleep. She just sat there, her head in her hands.

"Honey Bear? What's wrong?" I went up to her and knelt at her side.

She turned to me and looked just the same as the other day. Her eyes held all the sadness of the storm she'd painted on that canvas. Her hollow cheekbones showed she hadn't had a decent meal in ages. Her mouth dragged down at the ends like a drooping mustache. And where was that lustrous hair I loved to bury my face in? She'd pulled it back into a bun like an old Italian lady, all the waves and curls gone, just slicked back, but not with dressing. She just hadn't washed it. Then I noticed a few gray strands.

"What the hell's the matter?" I felt like an idiot asking. I should know what was the matter. "You

wanna talk?" I waited for her to tell me to beat it, but she just shook her head and sighed, ending it with a hacking cough that took a glass of water to calm down.

I knelt again, and told her I wished her hair was down, so I could play with it. It wasn't much in the way of a solution, but I found it very intimate, and maybe that'd open her up a little.

"Oh, I just haven't had time to fuss with my hair, or any of that stuff. I've been too busy with my art."

"Well, that's good. Isn't it? I mean, when I'm on a roll, I don't think about eating, or washing, or—" I shut up before I really put my foot in it. I didn't have time for her, either, and she knew it.

"But they haven't been selling." A scowl further darkened her features. "I had that one spurt of success in London, and that was it. I haven't sold a painting since I got back. I never expected to get rich from this, but getting ignored is very humiliating."

I wouldn't know. I'd never been ignored. Ever. "So everybody's got their ups and downs. In this business especially. Who knows, I might never have another hit show." Of course, that was the wrong thing to say. I could tell she really wanted to hear that. Oh, why couldn't I write these things down first, and polish them, like my damn lyrics? "I mean—it's not us. It's the public. You know how fickle they are. You're a hit one minute, gone the next. What's the alternative, though? Be like my sister and her husband Irving Bean Counter? You wanna live like that, with inventory control, debits and credits, payroll, all that crap? Ptui!"

She looked at me with those dark eyes. "I have to get a job, Snuggles."

I lit myself a cigarette. Finally, I got one over on Nurse Achtung. "You don't have to get a job. I make enough for the two of us." Hell, I don't want my wife out there punching a clock when I'm taking curtain calls on Broadway. But I know Pru. She feels useless unless she's laboring. "Besides, jobs are hard to come by these days. What would you do?"

"Anything." Another shrug. "Maybe paint murals on rich people's walls."

"Yeah, but you gotta paint what they want, not what you want," I argued.

"If it keeps me busy, I'll do it." She stared at the floor.

"Sure. That'll keep you busy. But you don't have to go out and work to bring money in. We've got plenty. Hey, you know what? I can even buy us another apartment somewhere, anywhere in New York you want. You can decorate it and it'll be your own little work of art." God, don't let her decorate it looking like those paintings, I prayed.

"It would still be with mob money." She cast me a sideways sneer. "Only you're making it yourself now."

"The hell I am! You think all the theatergoers are mob members? How about my audience at the club? Maybe a few wiseguys and their molls are scattered throughout the place, but the vast majority is just plain folk wanting to hear good music to forget their troubles for a while. Same with the theater audience. There's hard times out there, and they want to see a show with lively, gay music telling them that it's gonna get better, that the bad times won't last."

"The mobsters bankrolled it," she threw out.

I groaned. "And got paid back many times over.

171

Even if I got a loan from a bank, you think they're straight? Hell, they're as crooked as any racket, with those interest rates they charge. The money's just as filthy; so's the source. Come on, Pru. I couldn't have gotten the money from St. Andrew's Church!"

"I just don't feel like I'm in control anymore." Her voice dragged with despair.

"I know. I'm sorry. A lot of it is my fault. The way things happened, so fast—I know I've been neglecting you. But I'm going to take more time off from the club, slow down a bit, just to spend more time with you and Victoria." I draped my arm around her shoulders.

"You don't have to." She wiggled out of my grasp. "I know how much you're enjoying all this hoopla and all the attention and your adoring fans."

I had no argument there. "I'm not enjoying watching you paint pictures of hell and face a wall in the middle of the night."

"It's not you. It's me. Really. Enjoy what you're doing. While it lasts. I don't want to deprive you. Then you'd resent me." Eyes downcast, she lowered her head.

"No, I wouldn't. Look—it's not you. You were perfectly happy before. Now you're miserable. I'm never around. I know it's me." I grasped her hands and warmed them.

"Really. It isn't." Her voice sounded so convincing, I believed her.

"Then what the hell is it? That postmortem—what do you call it? After you give birth?"

"I don't know if it's that specifically," she said. "I'm in a slump I can't get out of. It doesn't make me feel any better that all my friends are selling and having

gallery exhibits. Franz is going to Brazil for a few months, Franck's going to Venice. They all got these good commissions, and I'm just stuck—nobody wants to buy my work anymore."

"Well, paint the stuff you used to, that did sell. Do some happy statues—of people spooning, like that Rodin 'Kiss' statue. Let's face it, this stuff is—" I waved my hands around at her efforts. "It's downright morose. Maybe people look at it and get depressed. Or scared. Go back to your other style—or whatever you call it. You know, the brighter stuff, the flowers, with the sun shining. Like that sunny painting you call "Bright Eyes." This stuff would depress a groundhog!" Come to think of it, I haven't seen "Bright Eyes" in a while. It always hung on the living room wall, a happy, peaceful blend of leafy greens and sky blues, with the sun peeking through the trees, looking like two smiling eyes. A bright, cheerful picture. I even wrote a song to it. Now a picture of hell's armpit hung in its place.

She looked at me. "So you think it's that easy? Just go back to the way I painted before, just like that? Do you? Well, you don't know much about self-expression, then."

"I don't know much about self-expression?" How many songs have I written in my short life?

"What do you know about art? I don't tell you how to write music." She narrowed her eyes and looked away.

"Well, if all of a sudden I was writing songs that made everybody wanna crawl under a rock, and couldn't get past the second measure, I'd reconsider." It fell out of my mouth too fast.

"Then you're nothing but a hack!" she shouted.

173

"Huh?" Why? 'Cause I have a smash Broadway hit and she hasn't made a dime in a year? But I didn't say that, of course. Even I know better than that. I just let her talk it out, and wisely shut my trap.

"If you don't write from the heart, you're a hack, a laborer for hire," she went on. "Well, I'm not a hack. I'm an artist. This is my soul projected on this canvas. My soul screaming for release. I need this release. I don't give a damn if nobody's willing to shell out money for it. It's their loss."

"All right, then keep doin' it, then. You just seem miserable, that's all. It don't help hangin' around with those losers and breathin' in all those reefer fumes, either."

"I should tell you, Billy. I smoke it, too." She folded her hands in her lap.

That explained a lot. "Aah, you don't need that junk." I wished she'd started drinking instead. Smoking was for hopheads, but drinking—everybody did that.

"I know it's illegal, but—" She shrugged. "Reefer makes me creative."

I flicked my hand. "Aah, illegal, shmegal. That stuff's junk. And you wind up creating crap, too. I know for a fact that any kind of mind-altering drug, including alcohol, does nothing for the creative process, nothing but makes it worse, makes the creator think he had a work of sublime genius on his hands, only to wake up the next day and realize he makes better sounds with his ass, to quote Mozart. I know. I've been there many a time, banging on the piano completely blotto, writing it down, then stumbling out of bed the next day, realizing my ass deserved better than to even be wiped with that stuff."

174

But she had to work this out for herself. I couldn't tell her not to smoke, just like she couldn't tell me not to drink. "You want some company tonight?" I at least made an attempt to be her husband.

She smiled and, without warning, reached up and pulled all the pins and combs out of her hair. I dragged her into the shower with me, and I shampooed it and rinsed it till it squeaked when I ran my hand through it.

"Come on, let's get the hell out of here. Let's buy our own place on the East Side, or the West Side, or wherever you want." I wrapped a towel around her and gently dried her off. I then powdered her and sprayed her with White Shoulders, a new perfume to come out of Paris, my first splurge when Rosie gave me my first roll of bills.

"I'll think about it..."

"Don't think about anything right now," I whispered as I led her to bed.

****

The rattling of the key in the door woke us. Bright daylight streamed through the window as Nurse Pertl marched in with Victoria in her shiny English carriage.

"Good morning," she declared. It sounded like an order: have a good morning or else.

I couldn't wait to see my daughter. I jumped out of bed and rushed up to her. The nurse took a sudden step back and stood there, staring, like I had two heads. "What, what?" I said. "What are you starin' at?"

She didn't say another word, until Pru came up from behind and wrapped a sheet around me. I'd been stark naked.

"You'd better go shower, Mr. McGlory." Nursie smirked. "And make it a cold one." She held her hand

175

over the baby's eyes. She'd kept her own wide open, though.

He closed the journal and turned out the light. He had to get Pru to go shopping for a place of their own—with the money earned from the show. He'd have to tell Rosie that Pru was afraid of heights, and find something lower than the eighteenth floor.

Chapter Six

"The drys seemingly are afraid of the truth. Why not take inventory and ascertain the true conditions. Let us not leave it to the charge of an antiprohibition organization, or to any other private association, let us have an official survey and let the American people know what is going on. A complete and honest and impartial survey would reveal incredible conditions, corruption, crime, and an organized system of illicit traffic such as the world has never seen."

—*Fiorello LaGuardia,*
Hearings before the Committee on the Judiciary,
U.S. Senate, 69th Congress, 1st Session

"Siddown, Billy, we're gonna talk some business." Rosie took him by the elbow and led him to the table reserved for the bosses. They were in between sets. After the usual bevy of babes finished mobbing him for autographs and various offers, which he turned down, he wiped his brow and took a sip of malt whiskey.

"Ooh, that feels good. My throat is in heaven." Billy lit himself a cigarette and Rosie's cigar. Then it occurred to him—Rosie never talked business until the club was closed. This must be a good one. Then Louie Q came over with one of his soldiers and complimented Billy on his musical talent. "A gift from God," he called it.

"Hey, thanks." Billy offered his hand, and they shook. "It means a lot, coming from you." And he meant that, too.

"We're goin' in business with Louie here," Rosie informed him as they sat. "We think we can help each other out."

"But we already are in business," Billy said, in all naiveté.

"I mean big business." Rosie raised his brows. "The rum-running business."

"Ah, I see." Would he dare refuse? He knew what a rum-running syndicate involved. No small-scale enterpriser with weak nerves could hope to head one of those. It took vision of the most unlimited kind. It was the biggest of the big time. It meant controlling cops, public prosecutors, magistrates, and judges. It meant dispatching fleets of speedboats and trucks manned by tough hoodlums. It meant warehouses with hidden sub-basements and doors that looked like walls, a cutting plant, a printing plant making fake labels, bottle factories able to duplicate foreign distillers' bottles. Bookkeepers, lawyers, bondsmen, pay-off men to bribe the Coast Guard—an enormous undertaking. The federal government itself wasn't that complicated.

"Sure, I'm in." Why the hell not? He'd amassed a nice chunk of change. Now he had to tell Susan he wanted to liquidate some of that capital. Liquidate? Capital? It amazed him that he was even thinking in language like this, like a big-time capitalist. Soon he'd be the owner of not only the club and a racehorse, but speedboats, trucks, and one of those warehouses with the fancy doors that disappeared into the wall.

Holy smoke, it was getting scary. He shivered, but

not with fear…with excitement.

But Rosie assured him, with a wink, "This is only the beginning."

****

As he walked into the Jane Street dive, the sweet earthy aroma made him gag. He wished she wouldn't smoke dope, but he understood why she had to. An Ethel swished by. "Hey, aren't you Pru's husband, the flute player?" he asked. Normally Billy would've flattened him, but it would've resulted in second-degree murder. Two more Ethels lounged on the couch, and a few skags sat cross-legged on the floor, sucking on a Turkish hookah. He noticed a new painting propped on an easel, half done. It was even bleaker than the other ones, if that was possible. Pru stood at the stove scrambling eggs. An early breakfast, he guessed. Real early, considering it was 3:40 a.m.

"Where's the baby?" he asked her back.

"At Susan's." She didn't turn around.

"Again? I thought you wanted to raise her yourself." He went up to her and peered at her profile.

"Susan asked to take her for the weekend. They're going to their house in Connecticut." Her eggs sizzled.

"Oh, they're going to Connecticut. Isn't that just the eel's hips. Thanks for asking me." He turned to leave.

"You wanted to go too?" She giggled, sliding eggs off the pan onto one of the china plates his parents had given them as a wedding present. Way too classy for this crew.

"You know what I mean." He didn't bother to keep his voice down. "Letting her go without asking me if it was okay."

"I didn't even know where you were, Snuggles." Her voice sounded high-pitched. "What's wrong with it? The baby needs to get out of the city and get some fresh air."

"You can say that again." He swept past her and threw open the window over the sink. It didn't help much. The air was muggy after a soaking downpour. "You can suffocate in here."

"You want some breakfast?" She cracked three more eggs into the pan.

"Nah, I'll eat when I get up. I guess you didn't look at apartments today." He tried to keep the sarcasm out of his tone.

"Oh, I did. But not on the East Side. I found one I really like on Washington Place." She slid more china dishes from the cabinet.

"The whole idea of moving out of here is to go to a better part of the city," he argued, wondering why he should bother.

"It's got eight rooms, Snuggles. And it's not an apartment, it's an eighty-year-old brownstone with hickory floors and high ceilings and three bathrooms and a garden. It costs thirty thousand dollars. You want me to try for better than that?" She flipped the eggs.

He knew the Village had some exclusive properties. But uptown was stylish, sophisticated. The Village was still the bohemian enclave of the shabby genteel, as far as he was concerned. Most of all, it was where his parents lived, and he preferred to dwell in his own upper corner of Manhattan.

"If that's what you want, take it." He waved the idea—and her—away. Anything was better than this hole in the wall.

Let her have her fancy-pants Washington Place brownstone. This was her way of staying in the artiste environment, pretending she was poor. The East Side was pretty snooty, he had to admit. He must have an extra thirty grand lying around by now.

"When's the party gonna break up so I can breathe in here?" He watched her carry the plates out to the living room like a waitress.

She answered over her shoulder, "Oh, Pete and Shirl and Rollie, they've been staying here."

"Staying? As in boarding?" He followed her out to the living room.

"Well, they don't pay me. I'm letting them stay here as guests till they find another place. They got evicted from their loft." She did a good balancing act with those plates.

In the living room, three of the "guests" grabbed the plates from her arms and began digging in like they hadn't eaten in a week.

"You can't fault them, Snuggles." She turned to him. "It's this Great Depression. They'd do the same for me."

What, invite you to share their piece of the curb? he wanted to ask. But he didn't want to start a war. These were her friends, and if she wanted to help them, he couldn't protest. At least she looked alive today. Happier than he'd seen her in weeks. She sat with them, all giggly and relaxed-looking. Of course it was the reefer. But maybe she needed the company, too. All she had was the baby and that rear admiral nurse, enough to drive anybody off their nut. So he didn't balk.

He didn't stay, either. He wasn't needed here. The icebox was well stocked, so he took a carton half filled with eggs, a loaf of bread, a hunk of cheese, and a bottle of milk and saw himself out. Nobody stocked the huge icebox in his Fifth Avenue palace.

****

He got up later that day and went straight to the Majestic to see the matinee. The only place in the world he wanted to be was in his private box at that dark theater.

The house was less than half full. It didn't look good, even for a matinee, a sign of the hard times. He always got mobbed when he came here, but for once he craved peace and quiet. *Is that a bad thing?* he wondered. No, he chalked it up to his mood, went up to his box, and sat back to enjoy the show.

As he watched the orchestra tuning up, someone brushed against his arm. "Now what do they want from me up here?" he mumbled, annoyed. He looked over and saw that rim of blonde hair bordering a kerchief. A sudden spurt of joy swelled his heart. "Hey, Greta. What a surprise! What are you doin' up here?"

"Same as you, looks like." She sat next to him. "Came up here for privacy. It's nice to see your show with no one around, isn't it? Like they're performing it just for you."

"Yeah, I'm in my own world here. Living out my fantasy." He patted himself down for his cigarettes. She whipped two out, along with a lighter, and lit both. "Take one," she said, with them both in her mouth. He plucked one from her lips and took a drag, not bothered by the red lipstick ring around it.

"How's Pru?" she asked.

"You mean today? Or yesterday, or last week? Sometimes I don't know who the hell I'm gonna meet coming through the door, and I don't mean the moochers she's got holed up there. I mean her." He took a drag. "It's like there's two of her, and more crawl out of the woodwork every day. It seems she's got all these different personalities."

"Oh, dear. That's not like her." Greta frowned. Her lipstick glowed.

"When I left her last, she was acting like a schoolgirl at a pyjama party." He hunched forward, his eyes fixed on the first violinist.

"Well, at least she was having a good day," Greta commented.

"Yeah, and you know why?" He turned to face her. "She's been smoking goof-butts with those deadbeats she hangs out with. Every time I go to that Jane Street dump, it's like an opium den in there. They're all sprawled out, sucking on one of them Turkish pipes, laughing at Christ knows what." He took a long drag of his cig.

"Where's the baby when all this is going on?" Concern crept into her voice.

"Either at my sister's or with the nurse. And she wanted to raise the kid herself!" He expelled his smoke in an exasperated breath.

"She doesn't drink, so she does reefer," Greta reasoned.

"That's no excuse. It'd be better if she did drink. And it's no substitute for drink. She's just turned queer on me. I don't know. Her pictures and her statues—have you seen any of them?" The orchestra got louder.

She shook her head. "When would I have seen any of them?"

He ground the butt out in the ashtray between their

chairs. "You ain't missin' nothin'. The pictures—
they're dark and morbid. Nothing like her bright, sunny
landscapes."

"Maybe that's what's selling now. I don't know
anything about art, but—"

He cut in. "They're not selling. That's the thing."

"Have you talked to her about it?" She flicked an
ash into the tray.

"Yeah, but every talk turns into an argument. I told
her to get a decent apartment. She found this
brownstone on Washington Place to the tune of thirty
G's, unfurnished, so I'm hoping that'll get her back to
earth."

Greta let out a low whistle. "Starving artist, huh?"

"She likes to play the part." He nodded.

Just then the orchestra hit the opening note to the
overture. He didn't want to talk anymore. They became
lost in their own thoughts, watching their creation in
living color before them. Once again, it was like
nothing he'd ever experienced. Her hand slid over and
rested on top of his. He turned his palm up and
squeezed her fingers. They sat this way, rapt,
throughout the whole performance, as if it were
opening night all over again.

Afterwards, they went to the Breevort to eat. It
wasn't a date, he kept telling himself. She confirmed
that when she insisted on paying her own way. He
heaved a relieved breath at that. She must've been
thinking the same thing.

She promised him she'd go see Pru tomorrow.

"Hey, thanks, that's a load off my mind. Pru needs
somebody level-headed to get her back on an even keel.
You can walk the baby in the park or go shopping or

something. Maybe see some bright colors, to get her painting cheery things again."

He had to get to the club, so he dashed uptown, able to concentrate on his job now.

By three a.m. he was too tired to think of anything but what kind of nightcap to have before hitting the sack. Too beat to go back to Jane Street, he went to his penthouse and crashed.

What seemed like a second later, a buzzer woke him. He didn't realize till he opened his eyes it was morning. Bright daylight streamed in. He stumbled over to the intercom, grabbing a cigarette along the way.

"It's Greta. I have someone here who'd like to see your place."

No! he meant to say, but his half-asleep brain produced, "Yeah, come on up." Who was so important they couldn't see the place a mess? He just hoped they had cigarettes, because he was down to his last two.

When he opened the door, the butt tumbled from his mouth. There stood Greta off to the side, and who stood next to her but his wife. She displayed a tentative smile—either trying to hide it or force it, he couldn't tell anymore these days. Then she sort of leaned in and glanced around. He stepped back, more in astonishment than courtesy. "Honey Bear! Come in!"

"Thanks." She entered slowly, the way she strolled through art museums, scrutinizing each item before moving on. Greta slipped past him, giving his arm an assuring squeeze.

"How'd you get her up here?" He didn't really have to whisper. Pru was already in the kitchen peering into cupboards and cabinets.

"Just some girl talk, and a promise that you'd let

her hang her paintings all over the walls here." Greta glanced around, nodding in approval.

Oh, no. Not *those* paintings. But he kept his trap shut on that. "Of course, she can hang her bloomers all over if she wants. I've been trying to get her up here since our wedding night!"

Pru came out of the kitchen, and he couldn't help but hug her. "Oh, it feels so good to hold you in my arms again. Did you hear from Susan? Is the baby okay up there in Connecticut?"

"She loves it there," Pru gushed. "Everything couldn't be better."

"Thank you for coming up here," he said, and meant it. "This is your home, too, you know."

"I'll disappear now." Greta's voice came from far away, followed by a polite closing of the door. He had to send her some nice flowers—nah, booze or a box of cigars was more her type of thank-you gift.

"So—" He gestured at their comfortable surroundings. "We're alone. At last. Or are some of your star boarders coming to join us? It won't do them any good. The icebox is bare."

"No, Snuggles, just me and you." Still looking all over the place—the velvet drapes, the papered walls, the burgundy carpet—she wandered around the living room till she found a chair she liked the looks of and sat down.

"You uh—wanna see the bedroom?" He jerked his head in that direction. He couldn't believe it; he actually felt shy with his own wife! The girl he'd loved all his life and never kept anything from. She gave him that genuine smile he knew better than his own body. He took her hand and led her to the bed.

"It looks kind of bare without money strewn all over it," she joked.

"You want some?" he breathed, now barely able to keep his brain under control, as they rolled around on that huge bed, and rolled and rolled...

"No, just you," she whispered. How long had it been? He couldn't even remember. But it sure as hell wasn't recently, or he would have remembered.

Afterwards, "Oh, I wish I had a joint," were the first words out of her mouth.

"That's all you can think of?" He leaned over and lit his last cigarette.

"How about you? It's still half erect and you need a cigarette. That's all *you* can think of," she shot back.

"No, I'm also thinking it'd be nice to have a pepperoni pizza and a bottle of Giacomo Conterno Barolo Monfortino, too." He took a drag and handed it to her.

"I don't like tobacco in the morning." She wrinkled her nose.

"Smoke's smoke, ain't it?" He offered it to her. "Pretend it's a joint."

She refused it. "It's not the same."

He sat up straight. "What's with you, Pru? You getting hooked or something? The last three times I went over to Jane Street, you're smoking goof-butts with those dopeheads. Why?"

"'Cause I enjoy it." She played with the embroidery on the pillowcase, a huge M, another gift from Rosie that came with the place.

"You never did before. You only smoked to impress your friends. Now it's like you need it." He tried not to shout.

"So what if I do?" She wouldn't look him in the eye.

"Well—what for? Drinking's just as good."

She let out a sad laugh. "Oh, come on, Snuggles. There's no comparison."

He wouldn't know; the few times he'd smoked dope, it made his brain feel like a burnt-out light bulb. Then he ate like a gorilla. "How can anything like that junk be enjoyable?"

Maybe it was better she didn't like booze. "Reefer is a lot worse," he lectured her. "I'd prefer that you tied one on every night instead of loading your head up with dope. I see what it does to people—I don't even want to think about it, much less write about it. That shit's really bad, and I wish you wouldn't do it."

"Oh, now look who's throwing orders around." She got huffy. "The second lieutenant in the Fifth Avenue Mafia."

He raked his fingers through his hair. "Honey Bear, it's hardly an order. Just my opinion." He cupped her cheek with his hand. "Look, let's not argue. Come on, we just made wild passionate love, and I'm still feeling aftershocks. I'm also still shocked that you're here."

"Greta talked me into it." A smile teased her lips. "She told me all about how Stan left her. It just—struck a chord in me."

"I know all about how certain things strike chords." He nodded. "Now can I talk you into staying here permanently? You can still buy that gaudy brownstone, but spend the nights here with me."

"I'll think about it. I'm still afraid to be up here." She looked around and shuddered as if she'd been dragged into the chamber of horrors.

"There's nothing to be afraid of. Sheesh!" Oh, how she drove him round the bend sometimes!

"I said I'll think about it." Her voice carried an irritated edge.

"Yeah, but—all right. I won't push it." It was a miracle getting her up here at all.

The buzzer went. "Who can that be?"

"Oh, it must be the delivery." She slid off the bed.

"What delivery?"

"I'm having the art store deliver some supplies up here. I didn't think you'd mind." She went into his closet.

"Of course I don't mind." That gave him some hope. She'd be here more often now.

She wrapped herself in one of his shirts and left the room. As he was washing up, she called him into the living room.

She stood next to a sketch pad and a big lump of grayish brown clay.

"What's all this?" he asked her.

"I want you to model for me." She sported a sassy grin.

"Huh?" He eyed the clay. "Model what?"

She sauntered up to him and flicked the towel from around his waist. He stood in the middle of the living room in his birthday suit.

"I want to make a statue out of you," she informed him.

"You mean cover me with that stuff?" He pointed to the blob.

"No, silly. I mean have you pose for me, while I sculpt you."

"Cripes, that'll take forever." The clay was at least

three feet high.

"No, I'm going to sketch you first, then do the statue from memory. I might have you pose a few more times, though." If he'd been dressed, she'd have undressed him with her roving eyes, up and down, lingering here and there.

"I don't think it'll get very far. With the posing, I mean." Standing there exposed to her made his blood rush from his head to other places.

"That's okay. Just stand there just like that. Or—how about putting your foot up on that pedestal there?" She pointed to the Venetian vase in the corner.

He took it off its marble base and propped his foot up on it. "How's that?"

"Now put your hand on your hip." She struck the pose she wanted from him.

"How long's this gonna take?" He placed his left hand on his left hip. She removed it and placed his right hand on his right hip.

"There, that's better." She stood back and admired his form. "I don't like to rush through my works of art. You know that."

She walked around him in circles, drinking him in slowly and deliberately, emitting little moans of pleasure, raw desire in her eyes. It drove him insane.

"You're a work of art, Billy. A glorious sculpture in marble. Like Michelangelo's *David*," she cooed.

"I was hoping you'd say Gary Cooper."

"No, Billy. A work of art beyond human." She stood back and stared some more.

She finally approached him and began working her magic with those long sculpting fingers, caressing his bare body with torturingly light strokes, like he was a statue in the making. "Your cheekbones are so chiseled, like a work of art," she whispered. Her hands slid down his arms. "You're so muscular, I can feel the firm sinew under your skin." Her fingers slipped down to his thighs. He was ready to burst into flames. "I love the rippling of your muscles, so lean, so—so rigid. So hard." She slid her hands around to his buttocks and kneaded them. His breath quickened until he was panting for her. "Such beautiful, rock-hard muscles. Like a statue."

Then she stepped back, took up the pad, and started sketching.

"How much longer?" Blood rushed to his lower region, engorging him there.

"It's only been two minutes." She kept sketching.

"Pru, this ain't gonna work," he groaned, and she put the pad down, smiling.

"Okay, come here."

He practically attacked her, and they tumbled to the couch. He drove into her furiously until they were both exhausted.

"Sorry, but I think you'd better get one of your queer friends to model naked for you," he said afterwards.

"That's okay, Snuggles. I'll get you to model for me again when you're less, uh—" She gestured at his virile manhood. "Energetic."

They spent the rest of their time together at the piano. He played his show tunes, some songs he'd written for the baby, and their favorite from a few years ago, "Embraceable You." She gazed out the window, marveling at the view. "The glowing golden sunset makes the park look like a painting."

He could get her used to this.

"Please be here when I get back from work tonight," he implored while he got dressed, which was difficult in itself, the way she kept distracting him, unzipping his pants after he zipped them up, unbuttoning his shirt after he buttoned it.

So he was a little late for work. But his audience showed him that he was worth the wait.

****

That warm cuddly body he found sleeping in his bed when he got back at three-thirty that morning meant more to him than the applauding audience or the week's pay he tossed into the safe. He didn't disturb her, just held her close and fought sleep because he cherished these moments lying here next to her.

As usual he slept like a rock, and when he woke at noon, her side of the bed was empty. But when he stumbled into the bathroom he saw a good sign: her toothbrush in the holder next to his. He gave himself a huge grin and a wink in the mirror.

Maybe it was a good thing she wasn't there after all, so she wouldn't see him doing the chore he'd been putting off: dragging the mattress aside to gather all the dough he'd stashed under there. When he counted it all, it was well over ten grand. He always put half in the safe he shared with Rosie and took half home when he got paid. Now he realized it was time to do the sensible thing.

He tossed the bills into a brown bag and took a cab downtown to Chase Manhattan Bank. He'd never done any banking in his life. He might've gone to a bank with his mother when he was a kid, but all he remembered was a big cavernous lobby with bars all over the place, like a prison. Feeling like a eunuch in a whorehouse, he went up to a teller and asked how he could open a savings account. He looked down at his new passbook and hoped a repeat of '29 wouldn't happen for a long time.

****

That afternoon, Rosie and Louie Q took him down to the docks to see the speedboats. One of them said 'LIL BILLY Mc' in big letters on the back. The other one said 'BIG LOU Q.' He knew people named boats, but these kinds of boats? The old boys got a charge out of the names, but Billy couldn't care less. Boats weren't his thing. Then they visited one of the drops, the warehouse where they stored the contraband, somewhere on First Avenue. They went down to the sub-basement in what looked like a grain elevator. But damned if the doors didn't disappear into the walls when they closed. "These elevators can hold ten-ton trucks," Louie boasted.

Billy was still shaking his head in wonder as they piled back into Louie's new Rolls Royce 20 Open Tourer. Louie ordered the driver to take them to his Central Park West residence.

His penthouse could've made Lady Astor ask for decorating tips. In fact, it was only a few doors down from her mansion. It made Billy's Fifth Avenue digs look like the Ninth Street subway station between cleanings. He let out a low whistle as he took in the sights. The sprawling penthouse sang decadence and opulence like an opera diva. Paintings hung everywhere in those fancy gilded frames like a Paris art museum. Velvet curtains, thick carpets—and a bar the length of Central Park West itself was stocked with every kind of hooch under the sun.

They retired to the terrace with their anisette-laced coffees. Billy clammed up while he listened to them talk turkey.

"I'm having a few Tammany boys to the club tonight." Louie toyed with his tie clip, a gold-and-diamond-studded number in the shape of Italy.

"Yeah, I seen Al Marinelli in there the other night." Rosie slurped his coffee. "Told me we got a real classy joint."

"Monahan and Hines, and maybe Farley, are comin' tonight," Louie added.

"Hey, why not, after all, they own the place, indirectly," said Rosie.

Billy knew about these Tammany heavy-hitters. They were bought politicians. Their power procured people like Louie a high degree of immunity and kept the civil government of New York at bay. So let them into the club for free music and free booze. They earned their keep.

"Why not give them a few show tickets?" Billy offered. The show was still doing well, but that opening night hoopla had died out. If the Depression hadn't been going on, they'd have packed the house every night. But in the last few weeks, the house wasn't so packed.

"Yeah, good idea. Hey, why don't you tell 'em yourself, Billy, tonight, when you go on break. I'll introduce youse. They'd like to meet the genius behind this whole musical thing." Louie shot him a cap-toothed grin.

"Genius?" Billy's eyed bugged out. No one ever called him a genius before. Not even Jackie

Harper, who knew his show biz. But, like Rosie, all these guys had some musical ability, they all sang or played a horn or accordion, and danced up a storm, so they recognized good musicianship when they saw it. One of Billy's most memorable nights was when Louie stepped in for the ailing saxophonist and backed the band for the entire gig—he blew a pretty damn mean sax, at that. "Nah, I'm no genius." He shook his head and stared at his new shoes that would've cost the common man a month's pay.

"Who you kiddin'?" Louie leaned forward, flashed all his caps, and jabbed his index finger at Billy as he spoke. "That show is the best thing I ever seen. And I ain't just talkin' out the back of my neck. You're headin' for a great career, Billy. You're right up there in Berlin's league. You're every bit as good as him."

"Me? Nah!" He felt his cheeks grow hot. Irving Berlin was a genius all right, but Billy hadn't half his talent. Berlin churned out songs like nothing. Billy sweated through every line, agonizing over a word here, the right vowel sound there. He wasn't exactly sure what genius was, but he knew it was some otherworldly ability that only a few had. "I'm just another mortal with a passion for song. I got a knack for knowing what audiences like—that's all it takes. Hard work, too."

"Well, kiddo, you heard it from the horse's mouth this time," Rosie said. "See, I tell him how great he is, he don't believe me." He turned to Louie, his gold toothpick gleaming.

Billy basked in warmth, and even love, at that moment. What was there to fear anyway? Most of the time.

"Yeah, well, he's humble. Maybe he oughta stay

that way, then. I like it in these whippersnappers."

Louie rang for another round, and an authentic French maid showed up, complete with black stockings, white apron, and frilly cap. She served them refills and pastries, her derriére sticking out provocatively as she leaned over. Billy sucked in his breath. He needed his wife again. He was feeling "energetic."

****

It was still early, so he figured she'd be at the Jane Street dive. But when he let himself in, only the moochers were there, flaked out on the couch and rooting through the icebox. Another one was asleep in the bathtub.

"Where's Pru?" he asked no one in particular.

"Who? Oh! She's over at the other place," one of them answered.

He hadn't even gotten the damn house number of the Washington Street place. He didn't waste time trying to find it out from these hopheads. So he went over to Susan's store. She'd know the address. She and Pru were pretty tight these days. He felt like buying some new duds anyway.

"HEADS UP! HAIR BACK! BRIMS DIPPING INTO THE RIGHT EYE! WEAR YOUR NEW EUGENIE HAT WITH A 'MANNER,' EITHER MADCAP OR MARQUISE!" shouted a display of the new Empress Eugenie hats. He picked up a red one for Pru.

Susan gave him a warm greeting, but she was busy with customers. It was a good half hour before she could talk to him. By then, he'd tried on a few jackets and trousers. He couldn't decide between a trio of shirts, so he took all three.

"I can go in the back now. The floor's pretty well covered," Susan said. They went to her office door, and she opened the three separate locks.

"I thought you didn't work the floor anymore." He made himself at home on her couch and helped himself to a monogrammed glass of whiskey.

"I had to let two of the girls go. Have to cut back." She sat behind her desk.

"Oh. Sorry 'bout that." He found that ironic. His businesswoman sister cutting back as he set the world on fire with music. "How's the speak doin' these days?"

"All right. Irv comes in and helps out now. He's been keeping the books and doing some of the purchasing." She lit a cigarette.

"Santa Maria." They all knew Irv was tighter than a crab's ass.

"It's all right, Billy. He's cut down on a lot of expenses. Like those potted plants I was renting. He returned them and bought his own plants, and keeps them really nice," she boasted, blowing out a stream of smoke.

So now he was Fink the plant pruner. "Come to think of it, I got a nice terrace at my place. It can use a few plants. Maybe some roses and vegetables and stuff, I dunno. Ask him to come over and plant some seeds, if he's got nothin' better to do." He poured himself a whiskey.

"I'll see." She swiveled in her chair. "He's pretty busy with the kids, too. Speaking of kids—Victoria's getting to be a lovely child. The twins adore her."

"Good. Hey, you know the number of that brownstone on Washington Place Pru bought? I never got around to asking her." He took a pull of his drink.

Susan looked at him with knitted brows. "She's not buying it. Didn't she tell you?"

"Huh?" This was news to him. "She was all gung-ho on it. It was gonna be her castle, her refuge, her—"

"Well, she changed her mind. I just saw her this morning, when I brought the baby back. She didn't tell you?" Susan shook her head, her eyes wide with bafflement. She just didn't know Pru.

"Well, she must've changed her mind pretty fast." Then it dawned on him: maybe she was going to move in to Fifth Avenue with him! "Greta talked her into coming up to the penthouse yesterday, and—oh, wow, I hope that means she changed her mind and is moving in there!"

"Well, don't you want to go find out? Or would you rather do more clothes shopping?" She gave him a wink and he turned to dash out the door.

"Have that stuff delivered to me, okay? And throw in some sexy lingerie for her." He closed the door after him.

He stopped in Bloomingdale's to buy some cologne and splashed it on in the elevator on the way up to his penthouse. He combed his hair, using the chrome on the buttons as a mirror.

When he entered the apartment, a pleasant surprise lightened his step. There sat Pru, in a pure white negligee, a cigarette dangling from her long fingers, waiting for him. So that's what the hophead meant by "the other place" after all.

"The baby is in another bedroom, sleeping in her bassinet." She answered his unspoken question.

Another shot of delight sent his blood rushing. That

was the bassinet he'd brought here, hoping she'd move in someday.

She twirled around and, losing her balance, fell onto a huge Fink's box on the couch. "This was just delivered, along with those other clothes," she said, and he blew his sister a kiss for the fast service.

"Come here," he growled. He rushed up to her, snatched the cigarette away, which turned out to be a goof-butt, and swept her up into his arms. Without missing a beat, he whisked her into the bedroom. He figured she was hopped up out of her mind. But she was so wild and responsive he didn't mind this time. Except for feeding the baby and playing with her till she fell asleep again, they didn't get out of bed till dark, and he needed to get ready for work. "You gonna be here when I get back?" Hope energized his voice.

"Yeah, we'll be here. I thought some more about what Greta said, and—I just felt so bad about her husband leaving her here and staying in California. She really loved him, just like—just like the way I love you. I thought about it a long time, and—I just got really sad."

"But you know Greta. She'll bounce back. Always does. Don't be sad for her." In a strange way, he was glad her husband had gone his own way. He wasn't good enough for her anyway, the creep.

"Well, I think she's right," Pru said. "We don't see enough of each other, and it isn't all your fault."

"Then my hat's off to Greta." He reminded himself to thank her—again. "Hey, is that why you changed your mind about the digs on Washington Place?"

She paused, then explained, "Well—it wasn't exactly what I was looking for, after all."

"That means you'll get rid of the Jane Street flophouse and move in here?" He was almost giddy as he zipped up his pants, forgetting to tuck in his shirt.

"I can if you want me to. Can I paint and sculpt here, too?"

He embraced her, wishing he could stay here all night, but his audience awaited his magic on the keyboard. "Of course. This is your home, too. This was supposed to be our love nest. Never mind Rosie paid for it. It's ours now. I made enough money to make it ours. You can decorate it, do whatever you want. Just please stay here," he whispered into her hair, smelling reefer smoke. "And please hang 'Bright Eyes' over the mantel."

"Of course."

He headed for work, whistling the whole way.

****

He phoned Greta between sets, to thank her for getting Pru to make that monumental step. She sounded surprised that he was taking the time to thank her.

"You practically brought us back together, Greta. I don't know how to thank you. Hey—how 'bout comin' down here for the rest of the show? Then, if you're not too tired, we can grab a bite somewhere."

When she showed up a half hour later, he brought her up on the stage and she sang a few numbers, canarying like a pro. It was one of the best nights he'd ever had.

But when they went out to grab at bite at three a.m. they had company. Louie Q had his eye on her since the minute she walked into the room, and wouldn't let her out of his sight. She seemed pretty smitten, too. The fella didn't have much going for him in the looks department, but he was built like a rock, dressed to the teeth, and was as charming as the proverbial prince.

He took them out in his new Lincoln V-12 to an uptown juice joint, then to the Waldorf Astoria for breakfast. Although Louie had eyes for Greta and she'd picked up on his signals, Billy didn't feel like a third wheel. He belonged, very comfortable with the company. The rum syndicate, and Billy's involvement, came up in the conversation, but Greta didn't even flinch. Not having told Pru yet, he didn't want that to get around this soon. Jokingly Greta asked him when he was going to acquire the obligatory summer home. Louie jumped right in with, "I know of three properties for sale in my area. I'll set up an appointment for you to look at them." It was just as good as a done deal.

At daybreak the new lovebirds went their own way, and Billy went home. He looked in on his daughter and slipped into bed next to his wife, feeling like the luckiest guy in the whole world.

Chapter Seven

"At least one million dollars a year is lost to the National Government and the several States and counties in excise taxes. The liquor traffic is going on just the same. This amount goes into the pockets of bootleggers and in the pockets of the public officials in the shape of graft."

—Fiorello LaGuardia,
Hearings before the Committee on the Judiciary,
U.S. Senate, 69th Congress, 1st Session

Rosie wore plain black, no pinstripes, when Billy stepped into the office the next day. That meant one of two things: An Italian wedding or an Italian wake.

"So who bit the dust?" Billy closed the door and locked it.

Rosie blew out a long stream of cigar smoke. "It was the God-dammest thing. A real shame, too. Damn shame. *La Madre di Dio.*" He blessed himself and clasped his hands together in a praying gesture.

"Why? You missed?" It was a feeble attempt at humor, but he knew Rosie wasn't a hit man. He sat in one of the leather chairs facing Rosie's desk. With the bosses dropping in all the time, Rosie made sure these chairs were nicer than the one he used.

"Nah. You know Bruno Izzoli, who comes in and takes the numbers?" Rosie asked.

"Bruno Chicken Body? Yeah. Hey, that's too bad. He wasn't that old, was he?" A stab of fear twisted his insides. Bruno Chicken Body, only a numbers runner, hadn't been any older than Billy. "Gunned down in his prime. Must've ratted somebody out, right?"

His stomach churned too much to ask about details. "I'll send some flowers to the funeral parlor. Where's he laid out? You sending something to his widow?"

"That's it." Rosie fiddled with his tie. "There ain't no widow. It wasn't him. It was his wife. She came out on the stoop to get the morning paper and they was waiting for Bruno. Got her instead. Blood spattered all over from the door to the curb. Spattered Bruno's car, spattered somebody walkin' their dog, spattered the streetla—"

"Okay, I get the picture, and how!" Billy felt like he'd been hit. He almost doubled over. "That's sickening. Gunning the guy down would've been bad enough, but his poor wife?" A mishmash of hideous thoughts ran through his brain like a film at high speed. He stood and leaned against the wall, convinced he was going to lose his breakfast right there in the garbage pail. "Lousy rotten rat-bastard pricks." He took a few deep breaths and, with a trembling hand, managed to unscrew his flask and take a mouthful. He swished it around like mouthwash before swallowing it.

"You okay?" Rosie got up and went over to him. "Wanna go lay down in your room there?"

"Nah. It's just—Christ Almighty, what a sin." He took another swig from his flask.

"Yeah, now Bruno Chicken Body knows he's next. I feel sorry for his kids. They'll be orphans before the week's out. But—hey, whatcha gonna do? *Se la guerre*." Rosie went back to his desk and his ledgers.

Billy felt so helpless at that moment. Helpless and sad. Sad for the wife who died for no good reason. Helpless to do anything for poor Bruno Chicken Body. Why bother sending flowers now?

"So—when's the wake?" Billy asked. "I ought to go, too."

"Tonight." Rosie gestured at his dark duds. "That's why I'm dressed in my wake suit. It's the suit I wear to all the wakes. And it's the suit I'll wear to my own. Why bother buyin' a new suit to plant me in? Might as well wear this. Ish kabibble. It's gonna get dirty anyway."

"Christ, you're morbid." Billy hated himself for the grin that crossed his face. But sometimes gallows humor was the only way to survive this racket.

****

He went to Susan's store during a rehearsal break and started pawing through black suits. He needed a wake suit, too. But he tried not to let that stark fact get to him.

She sat in her office typing a letter, and Irv hunched over sweating over a ledger. She got up, greeted him, and poured him a Scotch.

"A black suit?" Irv looked up. "Who died?" Leave it to him.

"Somebody I kinda know from work," was all he could bear to repeat.

"This'll be the first of many, Billy," Susan warned, in that impending-doom tone of hers. Now he knew where Tessie got it from.

"Aah, quit it, willya?" He waved her off. "It was an accident."

"Oh? What kind of accident?" Susan poured herself one.

As he tried to string together the right words, Irv fretted, "I've been trying to balance these books for three days now. I'm only a nickel out. I just can't find that damn nickel!"

Billy fished around in his pocket, came up with a nickel, and tossed it on Irv's desk. "Here. There's your nickel. Now you're even."

"That's not the way you balance a ledger, Billy. You have to find it in the accounts here!" He gestured at his endless columns of numbers.

"All right, so keep the damn nickel. Off the books."

Irv promptly swept the nickel off the desk and into his pocket.

"So, what happened, Billy?" Susan repeated, adding water to her whiskey.

"Some—" He sighed and took a long gulp of his drink. "Some wife of a numbers runner."

"Oh, I'm sorry." Susan's quiet voice barely reached his ears. She paled.

"Yeah, but not half as sorry as I am. She was gunned down. They meant to get him, but got her instead." He hadn't planned to tell her. But he couldn't keep it in any longer. It ate away at him like a festering wound. They hadn't had one of their heart-to-hearts in a long time, and he needed one. "Damn shame, hah?"

"Shame isn't the word. It's an atrocity. Billy, you know what can happen to you? Or Pru?" She stood over him.

He held up a hand. "Don't start. I've been through the 'what ifs' a thousand times already. Pru don't have to know."

"She'll see that black suit and assume it's not for playing in the band." She stood rooted to the spot, glaring down at him.

"What's the big deal?" He forced a guffaw. "Everybody has a black suit."

"I don't." Irv punched the buttons on his adding machine.

"I figured you'd have a dozen of 'em. Especially since you can get 'em wholesale." Billy turned his back and drained his drink.

"That's enough, Billy." Susan gave him the once-over. "You look pretty sick, if you don't mind my telling you. Irv brought in some chicken soup he made last night. You want some?"

"Nah. I'll see ya later." He really wanted to stay and talk to his sister—alone. Just to get this out of his system.

"Come on, we'll go get some lunch. You look like you haven't eaten in a few days." She lifted her coat off its satin hanger, and he wanted to kick up his heels, so grateful they'd spend some time together. She called over to her husband, "Irv, I'll be back in an hour or so," as she placed her hat on. He was equally grateful she hadn't invited Irv to join them. But he knew his sister, and she read him like a book, as usual.

"Have a nice time, Sadie my Lady." That was Irv's pet name for her—the extent of his romantic abilities.

They walked down 14th Street and into The Purple Pup, a quaint basement tearoom like all the other quaint basement tearooms going bankrupt these days. This wasn't a juice joint; it was a real restaurant. That was all right by him. He didn't feel like boozing anyway.

He needed to spill his guts, since he didn't know when they'd have another private time. He told her about the rum-running syndicate, how it worked, how much money he was making, how he was now afraid for his life, and those of his wife and daughter.

"Oh, Billy." She rubbed her forehead as if he'd given her a splitting headache. "What have you gotten into? My baby brother—"

"Don't say it, Suze." He held his hands up. "I need you to listen, not talk."

"All right, I won't say anything." She put her fork down. "But that doesn't mean I'm not worried about you."

"It's only till Prohibition is over," he assured her. "Then everything'll be legit."

"Then you'll get involved with something else," she shot back.

"Let's not look that far ahead, okay? I figure five years with this, then I'll have enough to retire." He convinced himself.

"If you last that long."

He didn't have an answer to that, so she went on: "Christ, Billy, when you met Rosie I thought you'd just play in his club once or twice, I didn't know he would suck you under like this."

"He didn't suck me under. He said my playing killed him, and it all snowballed from that. He became—he's like a big brother to me."

"But I should've told you who he was." She looked down, lips in a tight line, plainly mad at herself.

"That wouldn't have made a difference. I ain't a little kid anymore, Suze. I got a handle on the whole thing." He took a forkful of his omelet.

She sipped her eggcream. "What does Pru say about the rum-running syndicate?"

"She don't know yet." He chewed on his eggs, not really tasting anything.

Susan shook her head. She was miffed, he could tell, because she finally stopped talking.

After a pregnant silence, he explained, "I'll tell her, when the timing's right. Look, we just got back together—she actually moved into the penthouse, with the baby—and I feel like I got a second chance."

"You're lucky. Most people don't even get a first chance. Somebody's looking after you," she said, her tone somber.

"Yeah, I know," he whispered, taking another small bite of his omelette, not even wanting to eat that. He remembered his mother telling him about the beautiful angel painted in a dark corner of the Church of the Transfiguration, with dreamy blue eyes that seemed to be looking right at her. She'd pretended that angel was her mother, and a warm comfort always came over her. She showed it to him when he was a little kid, and he never forgot it. Maybe that mother-angel was watching over him with those heavenly blue eyes, too.

Or maybe it was just his supreme creator.

"Lately I've been having a love/hate relationship with my life." He let it all out. "One minute it's finally coming together, then this death, so close—I know it could be Pru, like Bruno Chicken Body's wife. Don't think it doesn't scare the crap out of me. I love what I'm doing one day, hate it the next."

"Life does throw you unexpected curves, Billy," Susan said. "But most aren't as terrifying as the ones you've created for yourself."

"Don't blame me. I didn't plug Bruno Chicken Body's wife full of holes." He pushed his omelet around on the plate.

"Oh, don't start that! I'm not blaming you, it's just part of the life you chose." She ate her soup.

"There we go with that choosing crap again." He put down his fork with a clang. "Who the hell chooses something like this, Susan?"

"You're in your situation because of a series of choices you made, little brother. Nobody else—just you. We all are. Not always directly, but here we are. Face it, Billy, death is part of life, but it's a bigger part of yours, because of the—business you're in now. I don't want to sound crass, but you'll get used to it. Like they all do."

He remembered Rosie's "whatcha gonna do?" and realized he'd said it not out of crassness but out of resignation. Sure, the rewards were staggering, but so were the risks.

"I ain't gonna ask, 'How'd I get inna this?' anymore. I'm in and I can't get out." He propped his chin in his palm.

"That's my brother the grown man talking. Finally you've stopped asking me, 'How did I get inna this?' and, 'How do I get outta this?' and you're doing it yourself. Now you're truly a mature adult."

"Yeah, and this is what it took." He gave an ironic laugh. "For the first time, I realize there's no way out, and I accept it the way any responsible adult would. It's a bittersweet victory. You notice the worse things get, the better I get at rolling with the punches?"

"You just never realized how many punches you

can take. You're stronger than you think, kid." She took a compact out of her purse and powdered her nose. "I have to get back to the store." She checked her hair in her mirror. "By the way, make any plans for your birthday yet?"

"My birthday?" He flinched. "Jeez, I haven't even thought about it."

"Of course the folks will expect you at the house, *on* your birthday," she warned

"When is it?"

She rolled her eyes heavenwards and applied lipstick. "A week from Wednesday, of course!"

"Oh, yeah." There was a time in his life when he'd counted the hours till his birthday. Now the days, weeks, and months whizzed by in a blur. "I'll be there." He hoped he wouldn't forget.

****

The sun peeked through wispy clouds, and it was warm, so Billy strolled up to Broadway. He loved the energy up and down Broadway, the pushcart peddlers selling whiskey candies, three for five cents, the peepshows, the flea circuses and cheap chow-meineries, one dance hall after another, an auction sale of gewgaws blocking the sidewalk. Stepping into the street to skirt the crowd, he breathed in the old Chinatown bus fumes, the pungent aroma of roasting nuts. He approached the Majestic's box office, but sitting through another performance wouldn't excite him so much. He knew every line, every note. He could lie in bed and run through the entire performance in his head or play it on George in the privacy of his own home. He also admitted to himself that it was no fun seeing the show without Greta by his side.

****

He took an hour off that night to attend Mrs. Chicken Body's wake. The funeral parlor was a sea of black suits just like his. He fit right in, and that was even scarier than dying.

He hadn't wanted Pru to know any of this, but just his luck she chose that night of all nights to come to the club to surprise him—and he wasn't there. Some blabbermouth told her he was at a wake and would be back later. So she sat there all dolled up, drank tonic, fended off a few advances, and waited.

When he returned at eight o'clock and saw her there, he thought he'd died and gone to heaven. His beloved Honey Bear, finally coming to see him play, after all that begging. She stood to greet him and he embraced her, fighting back tears. She was so beautiful, so precious to him, all gussied up in a ruffly turquoise chiffon dress with bows on the sleeves and a matching cloche hat. Her hair curled around it like she'd taken great care fixing it. She even said hello to Rosie. He kissed her hand and bowed to her like royalty.

"Whose wake did you go to?" she asked just when he thought he'd escaped it.

"Oh—uh—the wife of one of the boys. It was an accident." He got up to change into his playing clothes.

Of course she wanted to know all the details. What kind of accident? Car? Train? Drowning? Nope, none of those. He owed his wife the truth. So he told her.

She did just what he'd expected: turned white as a ghost, and got up to leave. "I—I—I have to go—have to get outta here—"

He clutched her arm and pulled her close till he felt her heart pounding next to him. "No, don't go, Pru, please. Honey Bear, stay here. Please. It's okay, it's safe, calm down…"

He finally talked her into staying. He sat her at a ringside table and promised to sit out a few numbers so they could dance together. But she hardly said another word all night. He knew what she was thinking; words weren't necessary. But when he took her home, they clung to each other all night.

She even went to the funeral with him, and he kept his black suit out. He knew he'd wear it again.

And he did, three days later, at Bruno Chicken Body's funeral.

****

The casket wasn't even open, it was such a mess. Pru gaped at Billy, sheer horror darkening her eyes when he put the suit on for the second time in a week.

He sat her down to explain. "The guy talked too much. That's what happens when you forget where your allegiance lies."

Still, he wasn't convincing enough. She sat there and shuddered.

He held her. "Look, Pru, people die. I mean, that's the way it is."

"But not like this." Her voice shook. "These are murder victims. These people aren't dying in their nineties of heart failure."

"Aah, come on, who wants to live to their nineties?" He tried to lighten the moment.

"You know what I mean." She started putting some of her paints away, and he thought she was packing up to leave him.

"No, don't go, please!" Just when he'd finally gotten her up here, he couldn't bear to see her move out because of a few deaths, one purely accidental.

"Huh? I wasn't—"

He gathered his most precious possession in his arms, and didn't fight tears when those sickening thoughts returned. "Pru, you know how much I love you—I can't live without you. Please, don't ever leave me, I'm begging you."

"You don't have to beg, Billy," she whispered into his black fabric. He glanced at himself in the mirror, clinging to her for dear life, in that dreary suit that turned his complexion sallow and made him feel like a walking corpse. It reminded him of how he danced with death almost daily now, putting his family in danger. If she didn't turn around and walk out on him, it'd be a miracle. "I love you too, Billy, and God help me, but I can't live without you, either." She began to weep.

The moment was just too intense for him. He wished he could make love to her and play the piano at the same time, to indulge both his passions at once. Instead, he found a Caruso record in the storage side of the victrola, cranked it up, and put the record on. He turned and approached her with naked longing. Watching him, she picked up his cue and began removing his black jacket, black tie, and black trousers. "I hate this suit on you, it's dreadful." She flung the jacket to the floor and pulled his pants down to his ankles. "I want it all off you." He let her remove every stitch, even his socks, until he stood before her naked. "That suit looks like death!"

Like your paintings, he wanted to say, but bit his tongue. Maybe this would snap her out of it, and she'd start painting cheery things again, if he kept the suit around for contrast. Urgent desperation filled him as she slowly tormented him with a feathery paintbrush. She could've been covering him with tar for all he cared; he ached with the need for release. "Pru, please, now." Finally, she lowered him to the sofa and laid him down on his back, shrugging out of her artist's smock. She was naked underneath. She worked better that way, she said.

She covered him with her slim body, and a dizzying array of sensations shot through his network of nerves as she stroked him. She drew him into her and covered his mouth with hers. Their gasps and cries of passion drowned out Caruso, and as his aria came to a shuddering climax, Billy exploded.

Oh, making love to music! He lay there for a long time, catching his breath, his fingers tangled in her hair, growing cold as his sweat evaporated. The record ended, and the needle went over and over a scratch. The room grew dark except for the faint glow of his piano lamp.

"I'll go with you, Billy." She got up and started putting on black stockings and a black dress. She fitted a black hat with a black net veil over her head. She pulled on long black gloves and stepped into black shoes.

"Why'd you get all that black stuff?" he asked, but halfway through the sentence, he reached the stunning conclusion. She'd bought a wake suit, too.

Then he realized they were widow's weeds.

****

The next day was his birthday, and they went to the traditional dinner and birthday cake affair at his parents' house. Going from facing death to celebrating life wasn't easy, especially his life. Never had he experienced such extremes, back to back like that. But he kept the smile pasted on as they feasted on the salad and ham and ravioli and sausage and meatballs and sauce and rum cake his mother made from scratch. They sang an off-key Happy Birthday and he blew out his candles. He opened his presents, a huge book about composers from his parents, a shirt and tie from Susan and Irv, a shaving kit from Tessie.

Pru had kept closemouthed all day about what she was giving him, although he badgered and hounded her, but she wouldn't give in. She was still shaken up about the murders anyway. He'd poked around all their closets and cupboards, finding nothing. Where the hell could she be hiding it? he wondered, baffled. But when they got to his parents' house and she still wouldn't give him a hint, he began to wonder if she'd gotten him anything at all.

As Ma began divvying up the rum cake, the doorbell rang, and Da came back with a long box. "This thing's heavy. What's in here, Pru? Billy's tombstone?"

In light of the events up to this point, Billy didn't savor his father's weak attempt at black humor.

Pru shot Billy an anticipatory glance.

"That's my present?" He walked around the goofy-looking box.

"Yes, but it has to be stood upright, like this." She stood the box up longways on the dining room table, with the lid facing him. "Now you can open it."

He cut the ribbon with the cake knife and slid the lid off. Wads of tissue paper filled the box. Everyone gathered around and stood holding their breath as he unwrapped the tissue paper, layer after layer. As he removed the last layer of covering and revealed what was inside, they all gasped—a sculpture of a naked man, in all his masculine glory—and fully aroused. He had one hand on his hip and one foot upon a pedestal on which was inscribed in bold letters, "BILLY."

"Oh, crap." His face turned red hot.

"Billy, is that supposta be you?" Tessie, the only one to approach the statue, fastened her gaze to the generous male anatomy. Everyone else's eyes purposely avoided that area, being past Tessie's age of zealous curiosity.

"Yes, it's him." Pru proudly beamed with adoration for both her work of art and its model. "He posed nude for me. My Billy is a work of art. Like Michelangelo's *David*. He's even more gorgeous in the flesh." She sauntered over to him and nuzzled his neck as her sculptor's fingers caressed his chest.

"Not now, Pru," he warned through clenched teeth.

"Well, son, I'm glad to see you resemble your old man in all the right places." Da clapped him on the back with a nudge and wink.

Ma discreetly draped a linen napkin over the statue's private area—and it stayed.

****

November 28, 1932, 4:15 p.m., 45 degrees under partly cloudy skies.

She thinks I'm next.

That's what I told Rosie as we sat in the empty club after closing. The staff cleaned around us and stacked the chairs upside down on the tables. Except for the front center table, which was ours. I poured the last of the wine and shook my head when Rosie gestured to the unopened bottle next to him.

"She'll get used to it," he replied, but it wasn't

comforting. I couldn't even get used to it.

"How in God's name do other guys do it?" I raised my eyes to heaven. "I mean, handle their wives worrying about them getting bumped off?"

"Other wives butt out, sit back and enjoy the money." Rosie opened the bottle anyway, and poured himself a glass.

"Pru don't care about money. She's always been poor, so she can live with it. Me, I've never really been poor, but I see what it's like to be rich, and I like it. I ain't willing to sell my soul for it, but it's nice having dough. But, Rosie, ya know what? Sometimes I get ascared. This racket's scary sometimes."

"Well, I'll tell ya a secret." He leaned forward. "Sometimes I get ascared too."

"Yeah?" I was surprised to hear my friend admit such a weakness, even in private.

"Sure I do. And these other fellas, they crap their pants and don't tell nobody, either. No matter how high up they are. It's human to be ascared. Don't be ashamed about it." He wagged his finger at me.

"I wouldn't spill this to anybody except you," I admitted.

"Well, I don' think no less of ya for it. Salut.*" He held up his wine glass and imbibed.*

But I didn't feel like drinking any more. Now that Pru is at the penthouse with me, I can't wait to get home to her every night, even if it is just to slip into bed next to her sleeping body. I don't even think she smokes reefer in the penthouse. If she goes back to Jane Street at all, she never tells me, and I don't want to know. All her paints and easels and stuff are at the penthouse now, so maybe she don't even want to go back to that dump. I hope. Lord, I hope.

"I need ya to do me a favor." Rosie lit a cigar. He *offered me one, but I wasn't in the mood to indulge in any vices, I was just too beat. It'd been a long day and a longer night. I only had this meal 'cause I was starving, not having eaten since breakfast.*

"What?"

"Can you run a payment down to somebody?"Rosie drained the last of his drink. "I'm s'posed to do it, but it's my Aunt Nettie's birthday, and I promised to take her to Coney Island."

"I gotta go now?"I asked him.

"Nah, tomorrow." He shook his head. "Business hours."

"Yeah, sure." I nodded, eager to please, even if it meant running go-fer errands. "Where's the money?"

"In the safe." He jerked his thumb in that direction. "Louie come down and gave it to me tonight. We gotta pay off a few of the boys downtown."

I didn't ask how much. I didn't want to know. Just give me the dough and I'll do my errand, no questions asked.

Under cover of night, we took two briefcases stuffed with lettuce and deposited them in the trunk of my car.

"Do you want the briefcases back?" I asked.

All he did was laugh, and I kinda felt like a jackass. Well, briefcases must cost money. I never had one, but I always see those stuffed shirts trudging back and forth to their offices toting them. I figured they were status symbols, flashing the gold locks and initials and gewgaws.

I shit bricks walking the two blocks to the

penthouse from the closest parking space I could find. I kept looking over my shoulder, convinced I'd be mugged or killed. How many guys walk down East 72nd Street at 3:30 in the morning carrying two briefcases stuffed with cabbage? But not a soul was in sight, and I nearly keeled over with relief when I got inside my locked apartment.

I put them in the hall closet, feeling guilty as hell for hiding them from Pru. But I didn't want to explain I was doing Rosie a favor, especially something like delivering graft. Better she didn't know.

I usually slept till the crack of noon, but I woke up at eight and couldn't go back to sleep. Probably 'cause hiding that stash in the house all night scared the deuce out of me. She wasn't up yet, so I looked in on the baby, also slumbering peacefully, took the briefcases, and slipped out the door. I didn't feel as scared walking back to the car, 'cause it was rush hour and pedestrians jammed the sidewalks. I'd worn a suit and tie to blend in with the masses. Nobody looked at me twice, with a briefcase in each hand. I slipped into the car, glanced at the address, and took off.

Heading south on Madison Avenue, I heard a blaring siren. I glanced into the rearview mirror and saw the unmistakable Greyhound radiator ornament of the Lincoln behind me. Cop car. All the gangsters drive Lincolns, which have a top speed of 80, so the cops had to get Lincolns to keep up with them. I tried to get the hell out of his way—he must've been going to a robbery or a diner or something. I pulled over, and he pulled over behind me. What luck. It was me he was after.

I rolled down the window and asked sweetly, "Yes, sir, what can I do for you, sir?"

"License and registration, please."

"Uh—what's wrong, officer? Did I commit a traffic violation?" As the son of the ex-Chief of Police, I should feel real cool around cops, but to tell the truth, they scare the bejesus out of me. The cops my father knows aren't the crooked ones. They're the straight-assed ones, just like him, who fought Tammany and made a career out of busting crooks. They don't have a price, like the rest of them. Hardnosed bastards, some are frustrated politicians and not smart enough to get into law school, so they enforce the laws from behind their badges. Hell, I am all for law and order, but these guys sometimes take it too far. "Your back license plate is missing."

Oh, merciful Jesus. I threw my head back and closed my eyes, drunk with relief. As I released a warm breath, my bladder released a warm stream. "Oh, drat. It musta got stolen. You know this city—just crawlin' with thieves."

"License and registration, please," he repeated, in what passed for a more menacing cop voice. Now he assumed his cop stance, pudgy fists on meaty hips, waiting while I dug through the glove compartment, yanking out all the crumpled sheet music and junk crammed in there. Oh, there's my emergency pack of cigs and that old box of prophylactics! But damned if I could find the registration.

"Uh—I can't find it, but it's my car, honest. I mean, it was a gift to me, but it's been paid for, it's not stolen or anything. I can probably find it in my penthouse. You wanna follow me there? It's only two blocks aw—"

"Step out of the car," he ordered.

Uh-oh. My bowels started burning. I silently prayed, my lips moving: "Please don't let him find those briefcases bulging with shitloads of cabbage in the back seat."

He poked his head into the car. "What's in the briefcases?"

I stiffened, paralyzed. My breath caught. "Uh—I dunno. I'm doing an errand for somebody."

"Yeah, I'll bet you dunno. Step aside, please."

Now he pissed me off. "Hey, you got a search warrant?" I demanded.

But demanding a search warrant from a New York City cop was like demanding a shot of Scotch from Satan in the middle of Hell.

I didn't want to look. I turned my head and flattened my palms on the roof of the car, like I was being searched. I heard the clicks as he sprang the latches and his not-so-surprised "mm-hmmm" as he checked out the contents.

"Who you doing this errand for, sonny boy?" He turned to me.

What was the "sonny boy" bit? He wasn't much older than me. I knew he just wanted to humiliate me. Screw that. I've been called a lot worse by much better cops than him. He obviously didn't know who I was. "Uh—I'd better get a lawyer or something."

His "You'd better come with me" didn't sound like a suggestion.

"Look, uh—you wanna just take a few bills outta there and forget it?" I asked, real generously. "I mean, uh—we're all in this mess together, ya know—"

"Bribing an officer of the law is a very serious offense, sonny boy," he scolded me, shaking his finger

in my face. "Park your car there, please."

"There?" I gestured at the curb. "But there's a hydrant there. I'll get a ticket."

So I wound up going with the lug. And didn't the dirtbag slap a pair of cuffs on me and push my head down into the back seat like a common thug. He also closed my jacket in the door. "Hey, watch it, will ya? I paid two hundred bucks for this suit!" At least he opened the door again and let me pull my jacket in.

Then the slimeball tore down Madison Avenue with the siren blasting, like he was racing to a murder scene, almost running people over in the street. Traffic cleared the way for him like the parting of the Red Sea. But I wasn't impressed. He was just showing off.

It sent me back to the last time I got in trouble with a cop...

One night when we were about fourteen, Pru and I got caught in Central Park. We were lying on a blanket and I was kinda on top of her; it was getting pretty hot and heavy. A cop shone his flashlight in our eyes and pretty much killed the moment. He started reading us the riot act, and I felt I could throw my weight around, so I challenged him, "Do you know who my father is, copper?"

He said, "No, do you?"

I retorted, still panting from my previous exertion, "My father is Thomas McGlory, the Chief of Police and your boss! So I suggest you vamoose outta here and leave us alone, or your ass'll be pounding a beat in Alphabet City!"

He stalked off, mumbling, with his tail between his legs. Pru was impressed, which meant more to me than telling a cop off. So she let me finish what we'd started...

I didn't think that would work now. My father is retired and no longer has any pull with the force. I didn't even know if this cop ever heard of my father. The bonehead probably never even heard of Teddy Roosevelt. So I kept my trap shut until I could get Rosie or a lawyer or somebody to spring me.

He parked in front of the 20th Precinct. He grabbed the briefcases and went in with them, leaving me in the back seat. I tried to get the door open, but it was locked. I was trapped inside.

He came out about ten minutes later and escorted me to the basement, down a long corridor with frosted glass doors on both sides, and into a tight interrogation room. I figured the window was a two-way mirror and I was being watched. He started questioning me. After writing down all my credentials, he frisked me, a little too slowly for my taste, and emptied my pants pockets. I had a matchbook and about a hundred fifty bucks and change in there. He pocketed all of it. Then he started asking the good stuff: Whose money was in the briefcases? Where was I bringing it?

First I tried pleading the Fifth. But he said it wasn't a courtroom. Nah, it was a Goddamned hotbed of corruption. For the first time in about ten years, I wished my father was there. Maybe he could straighten this mess out. But that meant I'd have to tell him everything. This sonofabitch wasn't even letting me make a phone call. But even if he did, I wouldn't know who the hell to call.

So I kept denying I knew whose money it was; I was just running an errand for somebody.

"Who are ya running this errand for, sonny boy?"

he inquired like he was the commish.

"Uh—nobody. Just a friend." I knew my rights and didn't have to answer to this schmuck.

"A friend, huh?" He sneered. "After I'm through with you, you won't have no friends."

"Okay, then you can tell me what it's like." The retort dripped from my tongue.

"Oh, a wiseguy, hah?" He smacked me on the side of the head.

"Look, I was just doing an errand. I'm an errand boy. Not important enough to be wastin' time on."

"You ain't important enough to waste time on. But that pile of dough is. So—ya don't know whose it is, do ya? Maybe this'll make ya remember." His fist connected with my jaw. It happened so fast, I was blinded with shock. I just sat there, stunned, struck numb. I couldn't believe he clocked me like that. I didn't dare fight back; he'd probably throw me into Sing Sing or something. Then he grabbed my lapels in his fists and yanked me to my feet. This time I didn't complain about the jacket—hell, I could get another one. I didn't think I'd want to wear this one again anyhow. He opened his palm and slapped my face on one side, then backhanded the other side. "Ya still don' know whose it is?"

"No, I don't! And even if I did, I wouldn't tell you, ya bum, ya. Go to hell," I spat, glad I didn't spit out a few teeth.

I knew I wasn't dealing with a decent cop who was above taking bribes. He's one of those crooked dirtbags who give cops everywhere a bad name. I got no respect for his ilk, and I didn't mind showing it. My cheeks stung like hell and my jaw throbbed, but I was ready to put up a fight. I wanted to wipe up the floor with the slimebag.

I raised my fists, because at that moment I coulda took him apart. Murdering somebody like him would be a heroic thing, the kind of deed I'd go to jail for, but honorably. And I'd spit on his corpse on the way to Sing Sing.

I aimed a blow at his jaw, but he was too fast for me. His sockdollager to the side of my head dizzied me. I clutched at the table, but he kicked me in the shins and knocked my feet out from under me. I went down, bit my tongue, and tasted blood. He kicked me in the ribs, then his shiny black shoes moved around to my middle. "No, not there!" I pleaded, my voice a weak croak. I cupped my crotch and lay there on my side as he kicked me repeatedly in the ribs and stomach. "Don' know whose it is, huh? Don' wanna tell the law where you got two cases filled with two hunnerd grand, huh?"

Out of all that, only the "two hunnerd grand" registered. Holy cow, had it been that much? No wonder he was making sure he'd flatten me.

"No, no..." was all I could utter as the blood trickled from my mouth onto the floor. He yanked me back to my feet with one meaty fist—he was built like the Flatiron Building—and rammed his other fist into my jaw again. I half-collapsed onto the table. He shoved me to the floor again, yelling and accusing and snarling.

"Maybe you'll tell me after ya cool off for a while." He then drug me down the corridor, up some stairs, and down another corridor. Next thing I knew he hurled me into a cell and threw me against the wall. A door with a tiny barred window clanged shut. It was

pitch dark except for a weak shaft of light though the bars. Senseless with pain, I crumbled to the floor against the wall and lay there crumpled on my side, clutching my gut, trying to cradle my throbbing head in my other arm. I must've blacked out, 'cause a split second later, it seemed, the door opened again and another cop, a rookie-looking youth, helped me up.

"You okay, sir?"

"Whadda hell d'ya think?" came out garbled.

"Come on, let's getcha outta here." He got me to stand on wobbly legs.

I could barely walk. I must've looked like hell, too. And I had to piss the length of the Mississippi River. "Can I go to the head?" I felt like a school kid asking that.

He led me to the men's room, and I stumbled over to a urinal, unzipped my fly, and barely had the strength to pull it out of my pants. I got my pants wet putting it back in. That mortified me more than my shiner, my swollen jaw, and my kneecaps, which must've been shattered, making me walk like a crippled Neanderthal.

I sat in some other stinking holding room for about an hour, a wet rag pressed to my face and in my other hand the cup of water he'd given me. Then the dirtbag who'd beat me up came in and told me to shove off.

"Uh—where's the money?" I didn't have much more to lose at that point, so what was the harm in asking?

"We'll just keep it here till the rightful owner shows up, since you seem to have a memory blackout when it comes to that." He gave me his practiced sneer.

"That effin' figures." I knew this would happen.

Two hundred thousand clams, gone. Lining the filthy pockets of this lowdown shamus.

I instantly had a new appreciation for everything my old man went through. I even missed him at this moment, and very badly wanted him there next to me. Not to pull my nuts out of the fire, just to be there. For the first time in my entire life, I respected my father.

I held back tears and wasn't ashamed to admit it.

Not only that, my entire body felt like a loose sack of fertilizer. I just wanted to lay down and shrivel up. But I had to get myself out of there somehow.

He shoved me out the door, and if I was lucky, I'd seen the last of him.

One or two people looked at me kinda funny, with that familiar New York expression that said, "Here's another screwball," or "Another skid row bum," and gave me wide berth on the sidewalk. After what seemed like ages, I finally flagged down a cab.

"Where to, mac?"

"Uh—" Where the hell could I go? Not to the penthouse. Pru would be there. Rosie was squiring his aunt around the Iron Pier. "Uh—"

"Where to? The meter's runnin'."

The only place I could think of to go was Louie Q's. Thankfully, I remembered the address.

I had some dough in my jacket pocket—I was surprised the shamus didn't empty that out too. He was too stupid to look there. So I gave it all to the cabbie.

Louie's doorman recognized me—barely. "Uh, I just got mugged," I offered, which was true enough, although it was really none of his damn business.

He got really solicitous. "Oh, you poor kid! Are you all right? You want me to call an ambulance? You want me to call the police?"

"No! Christ almighty, don't call the cops." I held up my hands to halt him. "Just please let me up to Mr. Quintannaro's."

I got buzzed in, and when the butler opened the door, I pitched forward onto the thick pile carpet.

I came to on a velvet fainting couch, draped in a blanket. I felt my ribs. They were wrapped. My arm was bandaged, too. And so was my head. I felt around some more and realized I was naked beneath the blanket. Somebody, a nurse or something, must've attended to me when I was out. Now a servant brought me a tray with something that smelled like garlic. Ah, sweet garlic! It was heaven. My mouth watered. All of a sudden I was ravenous. My stomach growled and rumbled. It didn't dawn on me till much later that the servant was a very attractive blond fella, pretty almost. I hoped he wasn't the one who'd stripped me when I was knocked out. But at the time, all I wanted to do was dig into the cavatelli and slurp the minestrone like a bum on a soup line. I didn't care; nobody was in the room anyway. The pretty boy servant asked me if I wanted anything else. I gave an emphatic no, and he flounced out.

A little later, Louie Q came in with a sharp-looking brunette dame. She served me a bottle of brandy and a snifter. Louie dismissed her with a wave of his cigar. "That's it for now, Toots."

"Hey, she's a good looker, got a nice pair a headlights on her," I remarked, giving him an approving thumbs-up. "I never seen her before. Where you been hidin' her?"

"She's my wife."

Oops. Gulp. "Oh. Uh—I didn't know—" *I wanted to crawl into that bottle.* "Sorry, if I knew, I woulda—" *Woulda what?* "Uh—"

"Fugget it." *He knelt beside me, cupped my cheek tenderly, and asked me what happened.*

So I told him. I told him the money was gone—well, it wasn't gone; I knew where it was. At the 20th Precinct. I described the cop, right down to the lisp caused by his missing front tooth.

"Do you know him?" *I asked.* "Can you get the money back?"

"I don't know him, but I'm sure I can get the money back. Don't worry about it." *He gave my shoulder an assuring pat.*

"Hell, Louie, it was two hundred grand that gavone took off me!" *I held my ribs together. A sharp pain stabbed me.*

"Awright, I said don't worry about it. And get some new plates on your damn car, will ya?"

I slapped my bandaged head. "Damn it to hell, the car! It's still parked in front of the hydrant on Madison Avenue."

"I'll get somebody to move it," *he said. But that was the least of my worries. I was in the deepest shit of my life, letting a crooked cop rob almost a quarter of a million clams from me.*

"Are you—uh—are you gonna kill me now?" *I asked in a very small voice. But I had to know. I had a family to think about. A picture of Pru in those black widow's weeds flashed into my mind.*

"Nah, 'course not." *He laughed, and I laughed back. I didn't know the rules of this game well enough to know what was a serious offense worthy of the death penalty and what was a mere felony, deserving a mere roughing up. "I'll get the money back," he said. "Just take it easy."*

I finally felt strong enough to stand up and get out of there. He put me in one of his chauffeur-driven Caddoos, and this time I had to go home—I had no choice. Thank God Pru was out. I cleaned myself up, changed, threw the suit down the incinerator, and went to the club.

One of Louie's boys, another girly-looking type (hey, maybe the rumors were true), drove my car to the club, came in, and gave me back the keys, with the parking ticket I'd got for blocking a hydrant. I was tempted to have it squashed or just rip it up and send in the pieces, but I didn't want to sink to their level. I'd pay it.

That night, on stage, I got lost in my music. Mercifully, I'd done a good job forgetting what happened. After closing, Louie and one of his goons, Bruno "Piggy Balls" Rizzo, came to my dressing room. I almost dropped my whiskey when I saw who they dragged between them, holding him up by the elbows. None other than the shamus cop who'd beat the crap out of me. I barely recognized him. His face had been beaten to a bloody pulp. But I could see, through all the swelling and bruising and bloodiness, he desperately tried to make eye contact with me.

"Billy, we'd like ya to meet somebody," Piggy Balls said, deliberately faking congeniality. "This here's Officer Sid Cunningham. Officer Cunningham, this here's Mr. McGlory. Say hello, Officer Cunningham." Piggy Balls jerked him upright.

"Hwmpfh," he managed through broken teeth and

swollen lips.

"By any chance, is he the member of New York's finest gave you a little trouble today, Billy?" Piggy Balls sounded like a waiter asking me how I wanted my steak done.

"Uh—yeah." I nodded. "That's him, all right." I didn't look the dirtbag in the eye. Didn't need to.

"Well, we gonna finish him off." He sneered at the cop. "But Mr. Quintannaro aksed me only if it was all right with you."

"You mean—finish him off? Like—you mean—" I ran a finger across my throat.

"Only if you say so, my friend." Piggy Balls jerked the cop upright again. He grunted in agony.

Louie, looking like a kid about to get a lollipop, looked at me and winked. "It's up to you, kiddo. You want him taken care of, we take care of him. We got the garotte in the car."

I shuddered. Now I know why power corrupts. "Did you get the dough back?"

"Oh, yeah, we got it back, all right. With interest. See?" He yanked on the cop's arm, eliciting a howl of pain.

I couldn't watch. "Nah, don't whack him. I just never wanna see his ugly mug again. But you know what he can do? Here." And out of my pocket I slid that parking ticket I got on Madison Avenue. "He can pay this." I tossed it at his feet, which were missing a shoe. Piggy Balls bent down, picked it up, and stuffed it into the cop's pocket. "And I want a new Enrico Rosati suit. Size thirty-eight."

"You're all heart," Sid Cunningham mumbled through his swollen lips and broken teeth as his escorts

dragged him away.

Billy read over what he'd written. "Truth really is stranger than fiction," he muttered as he closed the journal.

Chapter Eight

"It is common talk in my part of the country that from $7.50 to $12 a case is paid in graft from the time the liquor leaves the twelve-mile limit until it reaches the ultimate consumer. There seems to be a varying market price for this service created by the degree of vigilance or the degree of greed of the public officials in charge. It is my calculation that at least a million dollars a day is paid in graft and corruption to Federal, State, and local officers. Such a condition is not only intolerable, but it is demoralizing and dangerous to organized government. The Government even goes to the trouble to facilitate the financing end of the bootlegging industry."

—Fiorello LaGuardia,
Hearings before the Committee on the Judiciary,
U.S. Senate, 69th Congress, 1st Session

Sooner or later he had to face Pru. He'd rather it be sooner. So he came home that night like nothing had happened, and went in to kiss the baby. He found Pru sitting up with her when he went into the nursery. The color drained from her face as she looked him up and down, and not like she wanted to sculpt him naked this time.

"What happened?" came out as a whisper. She put the baby in her crib without taking an eye off him.

"God, Billy, what happened? Who did this to you?"

"Look, it's nothin' to worry about. It's over, and I'm fine. Just a minor brawl, that's all." He turned to look out the window.

"Minor? You're a mess!" She followed him. "You went to work like that?" she shouted in his ear.

"Well, yeah, I had to. But I wore my hat and dark glasses the whole time. And one of Rosie's dames who's in a chorus line put all this stage makeup on me. I think I got it all off." He walked over to the mirror to check himself out.

She trailed him there, too. "Never mind checking yourself for makeup! What the hell happened to you?" Her voice rose to a screech.

"Shhh!" He pointed toward the baby's room.

"What happened?" she wailed, and started crying.

"It's okay, just a misunderstanding with a cop, but they took care of it, the boys, they found the cop and— er, straightened out the misunderstanding." He leaned into the mirror and checked out his wounds.

"Billy, you're being very vague here, and I know you're leaving out a lot of details, and probably the real truth is hidden away somewhere. I just don't want to know. I also don't know if I can take any more." She raised the back of her hand to her forehead like a Victorian damsel about to swoon.

"I said it was okay, didn't I?" He headed for the kitchen.

"You really look okay!" She followed on his heels. "You scared me to death when you came in the room, because I didn't recognize you!"

"Hey, I could give Boris Karloff a run for his money, couldn't I?" He couldn't help smiling. A glance at his reflection in the toaster brought back the whole scene, and he suppressed a shudder. "Come on, it's okay." He wrapped his arms around her. Putting her through this hurt more than his wounds. But how could he explain that he had a powerful force protecting him? If Sid Cunningham had known who Billy was, none of that would've happened. It was the cop's ill fortune that he took Billy for some schmo. Stupid greedy cop, that's all he was. Billy was busting to tell Pru he'd actually saved the pig's life; it had been his decision alone whether the slob would live to see another day. That's the kind of clout he had now. But why gloat? It was over with and time to move on.

"Come on, let's change the subject. What did you do today?" He began to strip slowly. She always loved to watch him, but not tonight. He wouldn't be able to get her into the mood now. Who would want to make love with Frankenstein?

"I had lunch with Greta."

"Hey, how's she doin'?" He tried to keep the interest out of his voice.

"She finished her last novel and delivered it to the publisher. I went with her to their offices on Park Avenue. Pretty posh place." She glanced around their kitchen brandishing a smug smile that said, "But this place is posher."

"So she's over that writer's bar or whatever it was."

"Writer's block," she corrected.

"Yeah." He nodded. "That was it."

"Did you ever have anything like that?" she asked.

"Nah, not me. I can write songs in my sleep. Sometimes I wish my brain'd slow down."

"Well, I have artist's block." She got a milk bottle from the fridge. "I haven't been able to paint anything in two weeks."

Why hadn't he noticed? "Not even those—er, well, maybe that's good." He figured no paintings were better than those visions of hell she'd been smearing on canvas.

"What's good about it?" she pressed him, pouring herself a glass.

He lit a cigarette. "Well, sometimes you need a rest. That's how the creative process is. I'm always creating songs, but I'll admit, some of 'em are crap, like when I'm tired. I ought to give it a rest, but I don't. I like the act of scribbling down words too much, even if it is dreck."

"You don't have to tell me about the creative process, Billy. I always thought I was a born artist. But now I'm wondering if I'm an artist at all. Maybe it's not really my divine calling, like it is with my other friends, or with you, or with Greta. Lately I haven't felt like an artist. Or like an anything. Even when I smoke reefer, I don't get creative anymore. I just sit there." She sipped her milk, focusing on something in the distance.

"I'd take that as a hint to stop smoking reefer," he stated plainly.

"I don't want to. I like it." She took another sip.

"What?" He grabbed the bottle and took a swig. "Sitting there like a kumquat?"

"It's relaxing." They went into the living room. "It's the only way I can relax anymore. Especially since I've been living up here." She gestured around the huge, thick-carpeted, expensively furnished room, with the sweeping view of Central Park.

"Well, what's wrong with being here? This place is darb! I told you to get your own house, and you didn't want to. What else can you possibly want?" He raised his arms and they fell at his sides. He bit back a groan at the stabbing pain in his ribs.

"A husband who's straight," she stated.

"Straight?" he repeated. What the hell kind of rumors was she hearing now?

"You know, I mean—on the straight and narrow," she explained. "Legit. Not in the rackets."

"Aah, hell. Don't let that bother you. Just sit back and enjoy the money." He repeated Rosie's words of wisdom, for what they were worth.

Her answer was exactly what he'd expected: "I'd rather live in a Hooverville shack than like this, worried sick that you'll get killed, or I'll get killed, if you make one false move. It worries me sick, Billy!"

He heaved a deep sigh. His eyelids felt like sacks of sand. All he wanted was to fall into a dead sleep. "Look, can't we talk about this later? It's four o'clock in the morning. I didn't have the most jolly of days myself. Let's just go to bed, okay? I've been meaning to ask you this, but—would you like to have another baby?" He couldn't think of any other possible way to calm her down, get her mind off this rackets thing, and just get her into bed so he could get some sleep.

She beamed at that. "Well, yes, I'd love to have a houseful, but—"

"Okay, then, let's just concentrate on that. Just that and nothing else. All right? Please? Let's go to bed now? Please?" His voice cracked with fatigue. Forget starting a baby tonight; he couldn't get anything up if he'd dipped it in a bucket of ice.

"I'd love to give you a son, Snuggles." She sidled up to him and tucked her arm into his.

"That'd be nice." He yawned as she led him to bed.

She removed the rest of his clothes and laid him down, fluffing his pillow. Then she went out and came back with something she placed on the bed. He was too tired to care what it was. But she must've read his mind, because what she did next made him jump in shock.

"Holy hell, what's that?" He rubbed his eyes to see more clearly.

It was a bucket of ice.

"My word, Pru, you're a mind reader."

She sucked on an ice cube and slid down his body. She took him in her mouth and his weariness faded into instant numbness, which didn't last long: in five ecstatic minutes, he was as stiff as if he'd just woken from a fourteen-hour nap.

He felt a small ice cube rolling around as she flicked her freezing tongue and lips over him. At the point of exploding, he lifted her head away. She slid up and straddled him, bringing him inside her. He warmed instantly, yet the shock from the cold stayed with him in a wild combination.

"Where'd you learn that trick?" he whispered, now too exhausted to even remember if he'd said it.

"Something to do with the creative process," she replied, but in all his tiredness he realized there were certain things a man shouldn't ask his wife about, and that was one of them.

****

Interlude: Sunday Dinner at the House

He couldn't stay away, just because of a few

bruises. They'd get even more suspicious and probably come see him. He'd taken off the bandages and now sported only half a black eye and a bump on the forehead. The other bruises he could hide, even though he still walked with a limp. For a fleeting moment, he wondered if Sid Cunningham could walk at all. By the looks of him the other night, it'd be a while before the slob could wipe his own rear end.

Of course they wanted all the gory details.

His mother and sisters couldn't take their eyes off him. Ma couldn't even finish cooking dinner, so Susan had to take over at the stove. He couldn't convince them enough that he looked a lot better than he had yesterday.

"Can you help me in the kitchen, please, Billy?" Susan called from the doorway.

"Why? I don't know how to make pasta," was his immediate response.

"Billy—"

"Billy, go and help Susan," came from Pru, with one of her looks, and then he realized.

"Okay, Suze, what is it?" he asked when they stood alone in front of a simmering pot of meatballs and sausage.

She gave him one of those hugs—not simply a warm "I'm glad you're my brother" hug, but a nearly rib-cracking, head-to-the-breast embrace with the rocking back and forth and the whole bit. "Billy, my God, what did they do to you?"

"It's okay, really. Guys get into fights all the time." He tried to calm her.

"Who did this to you?" she insisted. He expected her to grab the rolling pin and aim it at his head.

"Suze, not here, please? It's nothing. Case closed." He turned to leave, but not before snatching a meatball and dripping gravy onto his shirt.

"It was just a bar room brawl," he must've said a hundred times at dinner before they realized he wasn't going to spill any gory details and switched the subject to Governor Roosevelt's recent nomination for President.

But the subject wasn't closed as far as his father was concerned. He took Billy aside—upstairs, actually, where he closed the bedroom door.

"All right, what happened to you?" he demanded in his don't-mess-with-me-or-else tone.

"It was a bar room brawl." For the skatey-eighth time. He turned to look out the window, knowing that turning his back on his father was the wrong thing to do. But it wasn't out of disrespect; he just couldn't face him.

"Look, I wouldn't say this to your mother, but it's obvious to me what happened." Da spoke over Billy's shoulder. "You don't have to tell me. I'm not a Goddamned idiot. So don't tell me if you don't want to. It's entirely up to you. If you do tell me, it's only because you want to. I'm here for you, son. If you want me."

His father's footsteps faded.

"Da, wait." He didn't want him to go.

Rather than exert his hard-won independence and tell his father it was none of his damn business, he decided to tell him what happened. Maybe it was because his father had given him the choice and had actually treated him like an adult. But somehow it was a catharsis for him, and afterwards he felt a strange bonding with his father that he'd never felt before. Neither Pru nor Susan nor his mother nor his uncles Butchie and Dominic would have understood. But his father had been on the streets all his life. He'd fought Tammany and the worst of New York's finest and simply understood.

Da sat for a long time in his leather reading chair, hands clasped between his knees, staring at the floor. Billy nearly mimicked his position, sitting on the edge of the bed. They sat in silence, each thinking his own thoughts.

"Do you regret telling me this?" he finally asked.

Billy let out a relieved sigh. "Nope."

"I never want this to happen again, Billy." Da looked him in the eye. "You're my only son."

"I'll be okay. Don't start anything with the cops or the boys. Just forget it. It's over with. I can handle it."

A slice of a smile curved Da's lips. "Now where have I heard that before?"

****

A few nights later, in Tony Mazza's, a hangout for cops, Rosie overheard that Sid Cunningham got transferred to some cushy desk job in Brooklyn. Apparently the captain of the 20th Precinct wasn't impressed with the way his deputies went about cutting him out of the action. After a few drinks, Rosie forgot about it. Too much was going on these days to dwell on one crooked cop out of a million.

****

Tom McGlory never wanted his career on the police force to end. But when his retirement came, he knew it was time to hang up that old hat. He also enjoyed his newly found leisure time. He'd become a great tennis player. He read voraciously and kept up with his journals. He and Vita had a little catering business going. Now with a grandchild, life was good.

But he couldn't stand the life his son was living; it was tearing him apart. He could no longer watch the boy inch closer to a violent death. He had to do something with the little pull he had left. So he went to the son of his departed old friend Frankie Munn. Frankie Jr. was now Chief of Police. Tom explained that Billy was in over his head. Could they keep an eye on him? Maybe get a cop to befriend him, protect him if any heavies came after him.

Frankie Jr. got right on it. He knew of a cop who'd just been relegated to a desk job in Brooklyn. He could keep an eye on Billy.

****

Sid Cunningham hung up his phone and shook his head in disbelief. He'd been out of the hospital a week, looking at only another two weeks in the wheelchair if he was lucky, and then it was off to Brooklyn for the mind-numbing desk job. But now he had a much more interesting assignment.

Keeping an eye on Billy McGlory. The snot who screwed him out of two hundred grand.

"Oh, yeah, I'll keep an eye on little Billy McGlory, awright. I'll take real good care a him," he snarled as he wriggled his ass over his bedpan.

Chapter Nine

"I will concede that the saloon was odious but now we have delicatessen stores, pool rooms, drug stores, millinery shops, private parlors, and 57 other varieties of speak-easies selling liquor and flourishing. I have heard of $2,000 a year Prohibition agents who run their own cars with liveried chauffeurs."

—*Fiorello LaGuardia,*
Hearings before the Committee on the Judiciary,
U.S. Senate, 69th Congress, 1st Session

"Billy, we don't need all this." He and Pru stood on the back terrace of their 5,000-square-foot five-bedroom architectural marvel overlooking the Atlantic Ocean.

"Who ever does?" He gazed at the waves crashing on the beach, *his* beach, then looked up at the magnificent structure. Windows jutted out in every direction. Doors opened into rooms leading into more rooms. Their master bedroom with its private bath and sitting room was bigger than the entire Jane Street flat. What a place. "You get a house like this because you can afford it. Nobody needs a mansion on the beach."

"But, Billy, it's so far away!" she half whined, half wailed.

"From what? It's the Jersey shore. It's what, forty, fifty miles from New York? Just think, no more sweltering in the city. You can come down here and enjoy your own private stretch of beach. I can set up the piano in the octagon room, you can paint in the room with the terrace, that room at the other end will be a great nursery."

"Swell," she muttered, but he knew once she spent her first summer here she'd never want to sweat away another day anywhere near the city. This was for her and Victoria, after all.

He still hadn't told her about the rum syndicate, the reason they could afford this house in the first place. He was waiting for the perfect time to spring it on her.

But someone did it for him.

****

He brought her to the club, without telling her where they were going. It was their first wedding anniversary, and he wanted the night to be special. So he hired a Rolls Phantom, had an orchid corsage delivered to her, and a red carpet laid out from the curb to the door. Greta and Louie Q shared their table, and best of all, he had the night off. They'd hired another pianist, Lefty Banks, to fill in for him. Billy played a few numbers, though; he couldn't resist.

Then the inevitable happened.

One scream was all it took. The music stopped dead in its tracks. Cops poured into the place like it was on fire, shoved men and women alike up against the walls, dragged them out, and herded them into paddy wagons.

It was so sudden, the doormen didn't have a chance to ring the warning bell. The bartenders didn't have time to dump bottles and glasses through the trapdoors. They were on the right side of almost all the Prohibition agents; some were even patrons. How the hell could this have happened?

Billy turned to Louie, pleading in his eyes. "Louie—what the hell is going on here?" he croaked in disbelief. "Is this a raid?"

"I'll get ya's for this, ya *figli di puttane! Fidente!*" Louie shook his fist in the air as two cops dragged him out like a common criminal.

Billy didn't even want to look at Pru. "Just stick by me," he kept saying as he forced himself to look into her big terrified eyes. She clutched his arm with cold shaky hands, too petrified even to speak.

The cops hauled them off to a jail on First Avenue. All night long, they herded men and women into separate cells. Pru and Greta huddled together with some dames of Louie's cohorts, and some Tammany molls. During the inevitable hen session, one of the broads opened her trap about the rum syndicate, and that was that.

They got sprung the next day on bail, but Billy had a haunting hunch that nothing would ever be the same. The stark reality hit him: *no one is immune, no matter how well connected.*

What would it take to get Pru to trust him again?

She packed her bags, set them in the hall, bundled up the baby, and headed out the door.

He begged her with tears stinging his eyes. "C'mon, Pru, I was gonna tell you. Honest. I never lied to you. I was just waiting for the right time."

She turned her back on him and ignored him.

"C'mon, get back in here, God dammit!" He slammed the wall with his fist.

She turned halfway around, not looking him in the

eye. "I'm not staying married to you, Billy McGlory, if you're involved in this. I'm seeing a lawyer in the morning and serving you with divorce papers. I took as much of this as I could take. This is the end." Without facing him, she entered the elevator. The doors closed on her, his baby, and his life.

"Son of a bitch!" He'd fought tears all his life, but this time there was no need. His life was as good as over. He sat down at the piano with his head in his hands and sobbed his heart out.

What to do now, two hours later, full of Scotch, but without so much as a buzz to make him forget it all? "Can't even get Goddamn tanked," he muttered as he grabbed the phone cord and tugged on it till the phone came to him. He dialed Greta's number out of habit more than anything else. Wanting her company in particular, he would've been happy just to hear her voice.

She answered on the first ring, all bright and cheery like nothing happened. Louie Q must've taken good care of her after they got sprung.

"Greta—she left me—" His voice shook.

"Billy, oh, God, I'm so sorry! Look, come on over. I'm all alone here. Louie's tied up for a few days. It'll be okay. I'll talk to her. Meanwhile, let her cool off. Just come over. We'll have a nice dinner."

With no word as to when the club would open again, if at all, he had evenings to himself. Which meant he could sleep during normal hours, something he hadn't done since grade school. He couldn't spend every evening with Greta; he had to find something else to do at night.

As he drove his Sport Phaeton across town and

looked for a parking space, he wondered, *What can I do? Do I have it in me to write another musical? Get a gig in another club?* He could always go back to Piano's, but Susan and Irv had that tied up between them now. Get to work on his next dream—the William Amadeus McGlory Orchestra. Things were starting to look up already. But glancing down at his wedding band brought all the pain back. Should he wear it after Pru divorced him?

Greta opened the door and gave him a warm hug, which he returned. In fact, he didn't want it to end. He craved warmth, the feel of another human body against him. Especially a soft, feminine body clad in a burgundy satin dressing gown. One of Rosie's Italian bear hugs just wouldn't cut it this time.

"Oh, Christ, what have I done?" he finally spoke, inhaling her perfume. It was so unlike anything Pru would wear, it repelled and excited him at the same time. "She found out about the syndicate. How do I get her back?"

"You'll be fine," she soothed. "I'll talk to her. She's just upset you didn't tell her about it."

"When the hell could I've told her? Every time I tell her anything she gets the fantods." He broke away, dying for a cigarette. He patted himself down. She produced a lighter and her holder. They sat on her couch and smoked as she poured them drink after drink. He didn't even know what the hell he was drinking. It could've been Scotch, it could've been gin, it could've been White Lightning for all he cared. He'd never felt so empty.

"I knew she was going through a bad time, 'cause she smokes reefer like it's going outta style, and then this happens." He stared at a gold pen lying on her table. "I shoulda—I don't know what I shoulda did. I'm too deep in this thing already, I couldn't say no when they asked me—no, *told* me, about this rum-running thing. I shoulda known it was the next step. Go into business with Louie Q and not go for broke? If you're in for a penny, you're in for a pound with him." Just then he noticed a diamond doorknob on her third finger. So she was in just as deep. "That looks like an engagement ring."

"No, it's just a token." She held up her hand for the gems to catch the light. "He's already married. These guys don't leave their wives."

From somewhere deep inside, he felt greatly relieved that she wasn't going to be the second Mrs. Louie Q.

"Now come on, let's go somewhere—" She stood. "Anywhere. Let's go see our show. Come on. Curtain's up in twenty minutes."

"I don't feel like it," he droned.

"Then let's go see Fred and Adele Astaire dance at The Trocadero. Or Ruby Keeler at Texas Guinan's place. Or that new Mae West movie, what's it called— *Night After Night*? Or we can go see Jimmy Durante. We can use a few laughs."

"You call that humor?" He looked up at her. "He's too insane even for you."

"I saw some real talent at a hole in the wall in Hoboken last night." She walked over and halted in front of him. "A singing group called the Hoboken Four. This skinny kid can croon better than anybody in the business. What was his name again?" She shut her eyes and snapped her fingers. "Oh, yeah. Sinatra."

Billy nodded. "I saw them a few times. Yeah, the kid's good. He might get somewhere someday." He still made no move to get up.

"So you want to sit here all night and mope?" She tilted her head and crossed her arms over her ample chest.

He perked up. "Hey. You wanna see my new house?"

"The beach house?"

"Yeah." He nodded, smiling for the first time in ages. "Ten rooms…or is it eleven? A game room with a bar, an exercise room, a movie theater, fireplaces in every room, a sweeping view of the ocean, servants' quarters, not that I have any servants…"

She pulled him to his feet. "Why not? You got the car?"

"Yeah, just throw a few things in a bag, and we'll vamoose." His heart tripped. He tingled all over.

If she'd refused, he'd have gone himself. So it was a big gaudy house, just like other capitalists owned. But, hell, it was his. Bought with his money, with his risks, with his sweat. He wasn't going to sell it, even if Pru never came back. It was his escape, his sanctuary. Nobody in the whole damn world would know where he was. It was like letting Greta in on a secret, taking her there. He felt like a little kid again, but a little kid with real big toys.

****

"This place is darb, Sheik," she remarked as they stood on the deck overlooking the ocean. The foamy waves crashed up on the shore, surrounded by blackness. A sprinkling of stars glittered in the moonless sky. He breathed in the salty sea air. "It's nicer than any of the gangster houses I've seen, much more elegant."

"Gee, thanks a lump," he uttered.

She had a blanket wrapped around her, and opened it to let him inside. They huddled together, standing there, staring out into infinity. Warmth and exotic perfume enveloped him.

"You want a drink?" he offered. "There ain't a crumb of food in the house, but I have enough booze to flood the place."

"No, thanks, nothing right now."

They stood, enjoying each other's closeness, for a while longer.

She broke the silence with, "You know, Sheik, I always liked you."

"Yeah, I like you, too." Aww, how cute, he thought.

"I mean, not just that way, I sometimes had romantic thoughts about you, like me and you just like this," she admitted, her voice now sultry.

A surge of excitement shot through him. He moved closer, inhaling her sweet powdery scent. "I guess it is kinda romantic. Being on the beach and all. At night."

"Alone. Just the two of us," she purred. "But I always knew it wasn't right. We could never start something. For one thing, I love Pru. She's like a sister to me. I could never hurt her. Another thing, you always loved Pru, so I'd never interfere. And of course I always had some heartthrob stringing along. But—if it wasn't for that—if I hadn't known you so long, or if you didn't have Pru, or if we'd just met in a nightclub or something—I'd flirt with you."

"Me too," he confessed, baring his soul. "But if we

let something happen now, it'd spoil it, wouldn't it? It'd be kinda awkward after, too."

"Of course," she agreed. "I value our friendship too much to dishonor it. I'm glad we're both mature enough to realize that."

"And I'd never mess with Louie Q's babe, not on your life!" What would Louie do if he saw them here together? he wondered. Probably plug him full of holes with a Chicago typewriter. But tonight, nothing mattered. He had nothing left to lose at this point. But that didn't mean he could take advantage of Greta.

"Oh, he's not like that. You'd be surprised. He encourages me to flirt with other guys. He even suggested a *ménage à trois*. With another guy," she added after a beat.

"Yeah, I heard he sometimes went that way." Billy nodded. He didn't need to affect a limp wrist this time.

"He wouldn't participate," she said. "He'd just want to watch."

"Watch you with another guy?" He looked at her, puzzled. "Most men want to watch two women at it. So what'd you say?"

"I said I'd let him know. I've never done anything like that before. Maybe if I was drunk enough I would," she said over a chuckle.

"Yeah, I would, too, but not with another guy, not on your life. It'd have to be two women. And I don't mean just me sitting watching. I mean, I'd wanna be right in the middle of it all!" He pumped his fist.

She laughed. "Well, he asked me more than once. One night he was pretty insistent. But he couldn't locate the other guy."

"He had somebody special in mind?" Billy asked.

"Ooooh, yeah," she drew it out.

"Who?"

She turned to face him, her red lipstick glowing like black ice in the darkness. "I'm looking at him."

"Nah! Me?" The blanket slipped off his shoulder. "He wants to watch me and you—do it?"

"Yup." A smile curled her lips. "But I told him you'd never go for it. I wouldn't either. No, I couldn't. There's Pru to consider—you know."

"Yeah, I know. After tomorrow—who knows?" His eyes met hers and held.

"I said, don't worry about that," she said.

It was really making him think now. His imagination ran wild, and he indulged in the fantasy. But he still couldn't believe it. "Why the hell would he want to watch me and you knocking boots?"

"He likes to watch. He's a voyeur. He has all sizes of binoculars in his front window. He peeks at the women across the way. He has a two-way mirror in his guest room so he can spy on guests in bed. He has me wear all these outfits, he has me spank him sometimes, he likes to whimper like he's being tortured—" She stopped to take a breath.

"You don't have to tell me all this." But it fascinated him at the same time.

"I want to tell you. You're one of my best friends. Why, am I making you uncomfortable?" She nudged herself closer. They now stood leg to leg.

"Well, in a way," he said. "I mean, why, I *am* a healthy fella, you know, with healthy appetites, and we're here all alone, and you're talking about this stuff—Pru hasn't been too attentive to me lately, if you know what I mean."

"Oh, I'm sorry." She gathered the blanket around her. "I'll change the subject."

"No, don't," he insisted too fast. "You can keep talking about it. It's kinda like—sweet agony."

"Oh, Billy…" She touched her fingertips to his cheek, turned his face to hers, and those red lips met his. His arms wound around her in a desperate embrace. The blanket fell away. They stood there, clinging to each other for dear life, swaying together in the seaswept wind.

They had to come up for air, and she spoke, very calmly, as if she'd given him nothing more than a pat on the head. "You really do love Pru, don't you?"

"Of course. She's my whole life, her and the baby." He took a deep breath to calm himself down. "I'm sorry this happened, Greta. I'm sorry I took you here. I didn't expect this to happen." He took a step away, not trusting himself. How easy it would be to sweep her into his arms again.

"Sure you did," she corrected him. "We've known each other, what, twelve, fourteen years? And you never wondered what it would be like to kiss me?"

"Yeah, well, the thought might've crossed my mind once or twice. Especially when you're wearing that damn lipstick. I wish you wouldn't wear so much of it. You know what I wanna do sometimes? I wanna eat it right off you," he growled. "And that damn perfume. Christ, it drives me nuts. I can taste that stuff when you wear it. I can taste it on my damn tongue."

"Yeah, well, it'd help me if you were a little fatter and uglier, too, you know. And shorter and balder. And stupider. And couldn't play the piano." She laughed, and he joined her, now two friends sharing some long-kept secrets. "You lose that golden mane and get fat, and I'll stop bathing and shaving, okay?"

"No how," he said. "I mean, don't do anything just for me. If Louie wants you to—"

"No, he's not that bent," she jumped to his defense. "He's never indicated he wants a gorilla. But I must say I do enjoy doing some of that stuff with him."

"Good. At least he's not forcing it on you. So do you love him?" he had to ask.

She fished out a couple of cigarettes. "I guess so, yeah. My feelings for him are growing. I think someday I can say I love him."

"Good for you. I'm glad you found somebody. And aside from being one of the most notorious, dangerous, richest magnates in the country, he's a pretty neat fella."

"I see him as a man first, Billy. Aside from what he does for a living. But you have to understand where he came from. He came from the streets—literally. He was one of those street arabs. When he's alone with me, he's the sweetest guy you'd ever want to meet. He'd make a great dad."

"I always say a fella who's a great dad is okay in my book." He lit and dragged on his cigarette.

"He really is a teddy bear. I do care about him a lot. It's hard not to. He'd give a stranger the shirt off his back, and I've seen him do that. He has a heart of gold." Her voice lilted.

"Then I'm happy for you," he said, and meant it.

"And we'll get you fixed up, too. What you and Pru have is too special to throw away."

"Tell her that," he said. "Tomorrow. Please." He added, "I need her."

"I will. After breakfast." She glanced at her watch. "Want to get some shuteye?"

"You go on ahead. Take your pick of bedrooms. There's five of 'em, I think. I can just stay here and watch the waves come and go, come and go, forever and ever." He propped his elbows on the deck railing and gazed out into infinity.

"All right, I'll stay here with you." She picked the blanket up and wrapped it around them again. They sat down together in the porch swing and swung the night away.

Chapter Ten

"When the Eighteenth Amendment was passed I earnestly hoped that it would be generally supported by public opinion... That this has not been the result, but rather that drinking generally has increased; that the speakeasy has replaced the saloon, not only unit for unit, but probably twofold if not threefold; that a vast army of lawbreakers has been recruited and financed on a colossal scale; that many of our best citizens...have open and unabashed disregard for the Eighteenth Amendment; that crime has increased to an unprecedented degree—I have slowly and reluctantly come to believe..."

—John D. Rockefeller Jr., 1932

Billy couldn't function, waiting for Greta to talk to Pru and report back to him. But he didn't lose hope—women had a way of talking each other out of all kinds of decisions, especially those dealing with men. So he prayed—for the first time in years, he went to church and really prayed, not just dropping to his knees, pressing his palms together and going through the motions. He had a long talk with God, and did a lot of apologizing.

"I'm sorry, God, I'm sorry I haven't been here in so long." He spoke into his folded hands, crouched on the kneeler, hunched over the pew in front of him. He felt comfortable talking aloud; he was alone but for two nuns on the other side of the aisle and a bum sleeping in a back pew.

"I've been so busy, you know—I—I shouldn't even be here." He knew he had a lot of nerve, coming to a house of God, asking for absolution at this late date. He had to face it: he was a gangster. No matter how he looked at it, he wasn't even on the fringes anymore—that was *his* club that got raided, and he took it as a personal violation. Gallons of sweat went into running that joint, and those self-righteous bastards had to balls it all up. "I'll quit, please, God, just bring Pru back to me." But he knew damn well he couldn't live up to that promise. And he knew God knew, too. Who was he kidding? He couldn't get out of it if he wanted to. That's what hit him now, and he began to tremble. Now he felt alone, truly alone, in the dark. Covering his face with his hands, he pleaded, "God, I'm ascared, I'm really ascared now. Them guys, they can kill me!" He wrapped his jacket tighter around him, shuddering. He trusted Rosie more than any of them, but—he wouldn't dare cross the guy. A long talk was in order, whenever they got together again. He hadn't seen any of them since the raid. He figured they were laying low, and he wanted to do the same. Hell, he wanted to crawl into the sewer and hide.

For what it was worth, he recited ten Hail Marys and stuffed a wad of bills in the poor box, blessed himself with holy water, and stepped back out into the cold.

Nothing had changed; the world was as ugly and dirty as before. He'd hoped going to church would've somehow made it all look cleaner. Nothing doing; New

York still looked like a rat hole, but his soul felt cleansed.

So he took his cleansed soul to see the new Loretta Young/Jean Harlow movie, *Platinum Blonde*. That made the world look a little brighter.

After the movie, too anxious to sit down and produce anything that resembled music, he went over to Susan's. At least he wouldn't get the third degree or a raking over the coals there. The store was closed today for some Jewish holiday, and luckily she was home by herself.

"Da told me about the raid. Why didn't you tell me? I would rather have heard it from you." She badgered him without wasting a second.

"Aah, screw the raid." He ran his hand over his brow. "That's the least of my worries."

"What now?" The color drained from her face. Now her makeup looked like makeup.

"Pru left me after we got sprung." He looked down and shuffled his feet.

"Oh, no." She pulled off an earring and rubbed her ear as he paced back and forth across her foyer. She ushered him into the sitting room.

"I'm in no mood to sit, Suze." He paced back and forth, biting the inside of his cheek.

She headed straight for the liquor cabinet, opened it with a key, and took out a bottle. "So what happened? You want to get it off your chest?"

He sat at the edge of her sofa, his face in his hands, as he had in church. "Couldn't take any more, she said. Greta's talking to her right now, trying to talk her out of it." He spoke into his hands.

She poured him a much-welcome drink. He gulped

it down without even tasting it. She nursed hers like she always did. Even though she was home, it was business hours for her.

"You have a serious problem on your hands, Billy." She stated the obvious.

"Yeah. And it'd take a genius to get out of it. Hey, Louie Q said I was a genius the other day." It seemed that was all he had left in the world, his talent. Without music, he'd be empty, with no reason to live.

"So what is that worth?" Hostility sharpened her voice.

He'd hoped she'd champion him on, but he should've known better. "What do you mean what is it worth? Like somewhere between five and ten grand?" Why the hell did everything translate to net worth for her? "It's worth a lot to me! So he's a thug. But he knows talent when he sees it. And he doesn't throw compliments around."

"We all know you're extremely talented, Billy. Okay, so you are a genius. We're very proud of your accomplishments. It's just this—" She waved her hands. Her bracelets jangled. "This life you've gotten yourself into. It's ruining your entire future. Don't you realize that?"

"I do now," he admitted.

"It took Pru walking out on you?" She leaned into him.

"I pushed my luck, and it ran out." He splayed his fingers.

"No, luck's got nothing to do with it. You just jump in without thinking of the consequences. Ever since you're a little kid. I remember the time when you—"

"Hey, cut it out, okay?" He held up a hand to halt her. "Don't start throwing childhood tales at me. I didn't come here for a history lesson. What's important is now, not some mess I made twenty years ago."

"All right, so *I'll* ask *you* the famous question this time." She stared down at him. "How are you going to get out of this?"

"Well, golly, Suze, I was hopin' you'd tell me." His tone dripped with sarcasm. "You always do." He got up and poured himself another drink. He tasted it this time. Real smooth whiskey.

"Not any more. You're not a ten-year-old brat anymore. You're an adult, remember? And I think you ought to go see Ma and Da before dinner this Sunday. They've been trying to contact you." She sipped her drink.

"Oh, yeah? How, with Tessie's crystal ball? The ex-Chief of Police's son's joint gets raided, and he's nowhere to be found. You'd think he woulda showed up and sprang me." But knowing he got through it without his father's help gave him a spark of self-satisfaction.

"He didn't find out till yesterday, when he told me. He's not on the force anymore, Billy, and even if he were, I don't know if he could've got you off the hook."

He waved a hand. "Never mind. I didn't need his help then, and I don't need it now."

"Just go see them," she urged. "Don't wait till Sunday."

"So I guess Pru hasn't come by here or the store or called or anything," he supposed out loud.

She shook her head, re-clipping her earring on.

"No, not this time. But if she does stop by, I'll make sure and let you know. I want to see you two back together, but frankly, Billy, not under the present circumstances. I don't blame Pru if she doesn't go back to you."

"Hey, thanks for the vote of confidence. Now you're against me. The whole damn world, and now you." He turned his back on her and plodded out, never having felt so alone and abandoned in his life.

"I'm not against you, Billy—all right, act like a spoiled six-year-old again!"

He halted, leaning his forehead on her door frame. "I can't do it, Suze. I can't get out of the rackets like you step out of the bathtub when the water's cold. It's like marriage vows. Till death do you part. It's easier to leave this world in a box than it is to quit them. I know that now. I'm not that green behind the gills." He kicked at the baseboard, determined to kill the spider in the corner, minding its own business. "Maybe I was before, but not now."

"Oh, God, Billy. I wish there was something I could do." He felt her hands around his waist and her head on his shoulder. "Yes, you're all grown up. But you'll always be my baby brother."

"Just don't turn on me now, like my wife did," he pleaded. "I need you more than I ever did."

"I'll never do that. But I'm also thinking about the safety of your family. Face it, Pru and the baby are safer if she goes her own way. As long as you stay involved with—those people."

He had a sudden urge to be alone. "I'll get back to ya." He walked out, and she knew him well enough to let him go.

****

With no place else to go, and no one else to turn to, he went back to his penthouse, where George waited for him like a faithful lover. That piano was his Rock of Gibraltar, always there when he felt sad, or lonely, or happy even. It responded to his touch, brought him back into harmony with himself. Even more than that talk with God did. But music came from God, so he wasn't disrespecting God by feeling that way.

The phone rang as he was halfway though playing Beethoven's "Sonata Pathetique." He finished the movement anyway; whoever it was could wait. Even if it was Pru. She could wait ten more measures. One thing he could never do was stop playing a piece before the end. Even if the damn house was on fire, he'd keep playing. Like those poor souls in the Titanic band, playing "Nearer My God To Thee" as the doomed vessel slipped into the ocean depths.

Or like Greta, who couldn't stop writing till she finished her sentence. Great minds thunk alike, he always believed.

He finished playing and swept the phone up. "Yeah?"

"Hey, kiddo." Rosie. Apologizing for what happened, and for not getting in touch sooner.

"Wasn't your fault. Forget it." What else was there to say?

"You okay?" Rosie asked.

"Yeah, I'm okay." He didn't care to share that he felt like he was standing on the Empire State Building's observation deck wondering whether to jump. Saying he was okay was sufficient. After all, he was okay.

"You want to come over tonight? We're planning

to talk about other avenues to look into next," Rosie said.

"Avenues?" That was a good way to put it. "Yeah, where?" Swing Street had been like home to the both of them. They'd never met anywhere else.

"My place."

"Where do you live?" All this time, and it just occurred to him that he didn't even know where Rosie lived. It just never came up in the conversation.

"Eleven-forty-nine Park. Ask the doorman to let you up to Penthouse A. Ten tonight."

He'd hoped it would be earlier. Now he had the entire afternoon to languish aimlessly, like a bum. What the hell would he do with himself for all those empty hours?

"Yeah. I'll be there." He thought of asking if they could meet right now; he was lonely as hell. In a strange way, he wanted Rosie to comfort him. He needed that, despite all that happened, and knowing how much danger the guy represented. But Rosie had hung up already. He never said goodbye over the blower; just stated his business and that was that. A man of few words.

Knowing he shouldn't, he dialed Greta's number. She was his lifeline at this moment. No answer. Maybe she was with Pru. Maybe they were out shopping. Maybe they were on their way over here!

He started cleaning the place up, picking up dirty clothes and towels, washing dishes. He even scrubbed the kitchen floor, on the hopeless hope that she'd come by and tell him she couldn't live without him. He downed a few bourbons, smoked half a pack of cigarettes, waxed the piano, sat down and played some more, then looked out the window for about an hour, craning his neck to see if she was coming up the street. He didn't want to leave; that'd be when she'd call. So he stayed put, polished off the bourbon, smoked the rest of the pack. Finally, at a quarter to ten, he gave up and headed over to Park Avenue.

The doorman let him pass with a tip of his hat. An elevator operator brought him to Penthouse A. The butler led him to a room down the hall. It was like walking into an Italian wake, with one less dead Italian. There they sat at a round table like King Arthur's knights, all ruddy-faced cigar-chompers. Venetian crystal ashtrays and wine glasses covered the dark red tablecloth. Their fedoras stood in a row on the sideboard. There wasn't a suit or tie or haircut in the room that cost less than a hundred bucks. An accordionist stood in the corner playing "O Sole Mio." A wave of grief swept over Billy, like at those funerals. The end of Swing Street was another death to him.

They all greeted him like he was their long-lost son. He felt that way, too. They were more than *paisans*, this old bunch of creeps, although they scared the bejesus out of him.

He saw a few guys he didn't know. He figured they were bodyguards, or enforcers.

"This here's Girolamo D'Alessio." Rosie stood and gestured to the man on his left. "He's one of the D'Alessio brothers. The oldest."

"Nice meeting you, Billy. Call me Jimmy." They shook hands, and Billy swallowed a golf ball. This was one of the capos. The head of the Upper Manhattan family. He'd heard the name plenty of times. And he'd thought the guy was a bodyguard!

"Likewise—Jimmy."

"Hey, your play's real good, kid. I really enjoyed it. I seen it twicet, ya know. And that singer, Ethel Mermaid!" He kissed his fingertips. *"Bellissimo!"*

He swallowed what felt like a football this time, and blinked in surprise. "Why, thanks! I—really appreciate it. I'm glad you liked it. It was a lot of hard work, but it's worth it when people like it and get their money's worth. Uh—if you wanna see it again, let me know and I'll have a couple tickets waiting at the Will Call." He knew he was babbling, but what else could he say to a don?

After a suspenseful pause, Jimmy finally threw up his hands. "Siddown, all of youse, willya? I ain't the king of Prussia."

The others chuckled, and it lightened the moment. Billy had him figured for a down-to-earth guy, even though he was who he was. Probably came from dirt just like the rest of them.

The guy at his left was Jimmy's *consigliere*, Billy found out. He sat and—to Billy's surprise—took out a notepad and started scribbling shorthand.

He'd waited all these agonizing hours for this meeting; he hoped for a divine solution, something that'd get him back into a club every night, behind a piano, with protection all around him, and a way to get his wife back.

He still had his lofty dreams.

"It ain't the end of the world, kiddo," Rosie assured him as a servant placed a drink in front of him. "You hungry? We got lasagna and my calamari inna kitchen."

"Nah, I ain't hungry at all." He hadn't even thought of eating. He clammed up to hear what they planned for their next "avenue."

One of them brought up union protection rackets. Prostitution was a lucrative enterprise, all right, but they didn't want to mar their reputations; after all, they were good Catholic boys. They left that one hanging.

Jimmy slid his poker chips aside and lit a cigar. The others followed suit. Billy found this a good time to speak up. "Uh—can I say something?" He raised his hand like a kid in a classroom.

Jimmy nodded. "Yeah, gaw'head."

"Well, uh—the club, I know it's small potatoes compared to the rum and all that, but it did bring in a good amount of cash. I mean—people came to see m— the band. It was a big draw. You fellas mind if I open a club, but keep it quiet? You know, an out-of-the-way place, with a low profile."

Nobody laughed at him or threw him out, two possibilities he'd half expected.

The others engaged in a combination of shrugging and grunting. "We'll talk about it later," Jimmy mumbled.

Then he changed the subject so fast, Billy's head spun. Did that mean yes, or maybe, or did he need them to vote on it—did he need a two-thirds majority? He still didn't know how this goombah government ran things on the inside.

The next item on the agenda made Billy's stomach turn. He didn't want to listen to it, so he excused himself, took his drink into one of Rosie's bathrooms, and stayed in there for a believable amount of time.

When he got back they'd finished talking business, had started a poker game, and dealt him in, although poker wasn't his game. He just stayed because he had nowhere else to go.

They broke it up around 7:00 a.m. Only he and Rosie sat at the table now, facing each other.

"Why the hell do they need to get tied up with that junk for?" Billy asked when he was sure even the butler was out of earshot. He didn't want any part of their new venture. He had enough money; they all did. It was bad enough Pru was smoking reefer; he didn't even want that around the house.

"What junk?"

"You know." Billy huffed. "What they were talking about. Heroin."

"Oh, that." Rosie dismissed it with a swat of his hand. "It's business, kiddo."

"That's all it is, isn't it?" He poured himself a cup of joe from the pot on the sideboard and spiked it with a healthy dose of anisette.

"There's riches beyond your wildest imagination." Rosie filled his coffee cup. "What you make in a month running a speak, you can make in a day with that, what you call junk. You wanna keep writing shows for Broadway? You can buy a thee-ater. You wanna make a movie? You can buy a studio. You want your music on radio? You can buy a radio station."

"I don't want all those things." But of course he did. "I'd rather have my dreams go unfulfilled than buy them with drug money." He swore to that.

"The hell you don't," Rosie argued. "You even told me—your name on the marquee. 'The William Whoozis McGlory Thee-ater.' "

"Rum-running ain't profitable enough?" Billy challenged.

"You can't depend on one or two things. You gotta

diversify." He spread his fingers on the tabletop. "You want a movie studio? You need jack for that—big, big jackola, kiddo. More than you can stuff in them safes of ours a hunnerd times over. You think you got it good now, 'cause of what you had before, an' it is a lot. But I'm talkin' four, five figures—a week. Think about it."

"I've been thinking about it since I'm six years old, and yeah, I want all those things, but not that way," he retorted. "Heroin? No, that's way too dangerous— deadly, even. I knew some guys killed themselves on that stuff. Younger than me. Couple colored guys from Harlem. Good musicians, too. A damn waste. I couldn't sleep with myself knowing I'm responsible for more wasted lives."

"You don't think booze wastes lives?" Rosie's voice loudened. "You don't think booze kills nobody?"

"Well, yeah, but it's not a drug," Billy shot back.

"Alcohol ain't a drug?" Rosie laughed, and Billy felt like he was being patronized. "If it ain't a drug, why's it illegal, just like cocaine and heroin are now? Why we got this Prohibition hooey goin' on? You ain't seen nobody kill himself with coffin varnish or jackass brandy or some other rotgut? You never heard of bootleggers adding iodine to the whiskey? A few drops of that is poison. Some load their hooch with as much as two ounces to the quart. Not to mention the embalming fluid some of them add. I guess you didn't see the D. W. Griffith movie last year, *The Struggle*, about a mill worker who drinks bad bathtub gin. You never seen anybody with Jake paralysis?" Rosie badgered him, his face red.

"No." Billy shook his head, his tone flat.

"Jake is extract of Jamaica ginger, almost pure

alcohol. The victims of that get Jake paralysis. First they lose control of their fingers." He wiggled his fingers in the air. "Then the feet. The feet drop forward from the ankle so the toes point downward. He got no control of the muscles that point the toes upward. When he tries to walk, his feet touch the ground first at the toes, then the heels go down. That's how he walks, toes first." He got up, stood in front of Billy and gave a graphic demonstration. "Then the calves hang down. Then the muscles between the thumb and pointer finger shrivel away. Then there's the wood alcohol, that makes people go blind or die in the street. The stuff that's 'Gilletted,' cut too much. And it ain't a drug?" He pointed a finger at Billy like a gun. "*Shit* ain't a drug!"

"All right, so hooch can kill, too," Billy admitted, just before he drained his laced coffee. "I get your point. But heroin—I don't want to get into that racket. It's too—too destructive. Either you're hooked or you ain't. You can't go to a juice joint and have a heroin cocktail. I've seen what it does to people's minds." His thoughts returned to Pru, smoking a goof-butt, knowing she wasn't enjoying it.

"And you never seen nobody piped from a good soakin' of rotgut?" Rosie challenged.

"But come on, H is a lot worse," he rebutted, refusing to lose this argument.

"You don't gotta take it, Billy." Rosie slurped his coffee.

"I don't gotta push it, either."

"Why so moral all of a sudden?" He gave Billy a quizzical eye.

"It's got nothing to do with morals." He lit a

cigarette, stood and walked in a circle. "Okay, I'll level with you." He stopped and looked at Rosie. "Pru smokes reefer. She said she's been doing it for a while now. She smokes reefer to get creative, but she hasn't been much of that lately, either. I just hope to hell she didn't smoke it when she was pregnant. But I hate that she does that crap. She don't need to do it."

Rosie shooed his words away. "So what? Reefer's chicken shit. Everybody smokes reefer. Well, I don't—it gives me the runs. But it's still chicken shit. It ain't exactly H, ya know."

"Reefer can lead people like her to worse drugs, like H, Rosie. So she's a sitting duck already. And if I got involved with H, then what kind of example would that set for her?" He still had every intention of getting her back—and soon.

"Who says you have to tell her?" Rosie quizzed.

"I've kept enough stuff from her, the rum-running—" He cut himself short. "I want her back, so I ain't getting involved with anything like H. I have to draw the line someplace. It's gotta be there."

Rosie sat and ran a hand over his slicked-down hair. He started to suck his teeth, and Billy could tell he was deep in thought.

Finally he nodded. "All right. I don't want to see your wife go down the tubes. Tell ya what. I happen to think hooch's just as bad as any drug, but since you got a personal stake in it—I'll tell them to deal me out of this one." He looked Billy in the eye with an unblinking stare. Rosie had never looked at him this intensely before.

"Hey, I appreciate that like I can't tell you." A wave of appreciation came over him. He rubbed his eyes to stop the tears falling.

"You're family to me," Rosie went on, "and even though your wife's not crazy about me, I know how much ya love her, so…we'll both stay out of it. Louie don't need to know nothin'—I'll tell him we ain't got time to spend on it." He twirled his cup around. "I really don't. I got the syndicate, the numbers, the horses—I don't need to dick around with heroin. But he don't need to know the real reason. Besides, I got enough money for my own needs. I don't need to buy a thee-ater or a radio station or any of the stuff you want. I just thought you wanted big bucks like that."

"Not from pushing heroin." He shook his head.

"Then don't. We both won't."

"Thanks, Rosie. I appreciate it." Truth was, he really did appreciate it. Rosie was giving up a hell of a lot of lettuce here, just to protect Pru from destruction. "That's the kind of thing family would do."

"Well, I feel like you're one of my own, ya crazy half-Mick, ya." He stood and gave Billy a bear hug.

"Yeah, let them other creeps deal in H, import it from wherever the hell it comes from." He pictured Pru sucking on that pipe, getting glassier-eyed by the minute. "I wish she'd just take up the sauce." He dragged on his cigarette.

"Hey, maybe she will. Never say never," Rosie pumped him with his pep talk.

"You know, Rosie, sometimes I thought about grabbing Pru and the kid and maybe moving to Europe where nobody knows who we are," Billy mused.

Rosie shook his head. "You wouldn't wanna live on the lam like that."

"I know I'd never do it, but I think about it, ya

know? Just to get away from all the…" He trailed off.

Rosie nodded, silently, like he knew too well.

"But I don't have balls of that quality brass to leave," Billy admitted.

"You have the balls of brass to stay. To leave would be what a coward would do. Don't sell your balls short, kid. I can hear 'em clangin' sometimes."

They shared a laugh.

"The possibility of Pru turning to H is too horrific to think about. I'd give pig slop to the starving masses out there before I'd sell that poison."

After a few minutes of comfortable silence, his stomach told him to change the subject. "Rosie, you think I can get somethin' to eat? This anisette just put a hole in my gut."

"Yeah, sure." He chuckled, pulling on the bell cord. "You're itchin' to get back into a nightclub, ain't you?"

"Well, yeah, I'm kind of—lost now. I can't just go to the Majestic and watch the show every night. I need to be part of the action. I guess I can play with the orchestra there, but I don't want to put the piano player out of a job." He stubbed out his cigarette butt, missing the club more than ever now. He just wanted to lose himself in music.

"Don't worry, we'll get you playin' in another joint."

"When Jimmy said, 'We'll talk about it later,' how much later do you think he meant?" Billy asked.

"Not long," was his answer.

That wasn't much more specific. He wanted a calendar date. "Well, since I won't be playing at a club every night, to stop getting bored, maybe I can hire a booking agent and a band and do bookings, like Carnegie Hall and places like that."

Rosie nodded. "You got a name for yourself now. You'd draw crowds."

"Yeah. I gotta keep busy, or I'll go off my nut." He pulled off his cufflinks and rolled up his sleeves.

The butler came in to take their breakfast order. "What you want? Eggs over easy, sausage, what?" Rosie asked.

"Whatever you're having is fine with me."

He ordered eggs, sausage and peppers, and toast for the both of them. Billy got himself another coffee, straight this time. "That was a shitty thing to happen, that raid."

"Yeah, well." Rosie shrugged. "It was a payback thing."

"How?" Billy asked.

"Seems there's a pissing contest between the D.A. and Louie Q. So we got busted. Whatcha gonna do?" He splayed his fingers and shrugged again, the universal Italian gesture.

Billy's blood began to boil. "Oh, for Chrissakes, that kid stuff?" Only now it hit him. If it weren't for grown men acting like eight-year-olds, the club wouldn't have been raided, Pru never would've learned about the syndicate, and he'd be in bed with her right now.

"Yeah, some of 'em are like overgrown kids sometimes with their payback and vendettas. Like overgrown kids in dirty nappies." Rosie gave him an ironic smile.

As the butler served breakfast, Billy didn't want to talk about drugs or booze or raids any more. He just wanted to enjoy his sausage and peppers. Besides, he hoped by tonight he and Pru would be back together. Even if he had to beg her on his knees. He appreciated what Greta was doing for him, but he couldn't rely on her forever.

So he went back home, cleaned himself up, and headed to Jane Street.

****

He let himself in with his key and sniffed the air. No trace of reefer or even tobacco hung around. But the loafers did, two of them, one sprawled on the couch, the other engrossed in a ball of yarn and some long needles.

"Where's my wife?" he asked, not caring who answered.

"In the bedroom with the baby," the knitter replied, not looking up.

He went straight in and there she sat, nursing Victoria. She looked up at him with those eyes that implored, "Why did it come to this?"

He felt a stab through his heart. "Please, Honey Bear, don't let it end this way. You know how much I love you." He approached her and dropped to his knees.

"I told you before and I'll say it again: I can't take any more. Not only that, it's too dangerous. I don't want to get gunned down or get thrown in jail again." She spoke barely above a whisper. "When I heard about that syndicate, that was the last straw."

He ventured closer, still on his knees. "The rum-running isn't all that dangerous. You're safe, I swear on the Holy Bible. The raid, it wasn't a typical raid. The D.A. and Louie Q, they have some kinda feud going, and it was a payback thing. So I'm going to get my own orchestra together, and play legit places like Carnegie

Hall. Do bookings, make records, nothing to break the law, so they won't come near us again." The idea sounded even better to him as he relayed it to Pru. A schedule without the nightly grind of headlining a club appealed to him.

Without responding, she rose to put Victoria down in her cradle, but stood guard like a sentinel when Billy held his arms out to hold the baby. She didn't even want him holding his own kid.

Maybe she hadn't heard him, nursing and all. "Uh—Pru, did you hear me? I'm getting my own orchestra together to play concert halls. Strictly legit. Without them other guys."

"How about all your other business—*with* 'them other guys'?" She balled a fist on her hip, looking like Susan. Now she sounded like her, too. "The speedboats, the factories, the cops, the judges, and God knows who else is being paid off with that?"

"I'm not high up enough to get hurt." He hoped she was naïve enough to believe that.

"No? How about the night you came home looking like The Mummy? You didn't get hurt?"

"That was a frigging cop who beat m—who I had the run-in with," he corrected himself fast.

"Oh, you're so self-centered, Billy!" she ranted in disgust. "You don't even think of me. Now I have a police record. And I have you to thank for it!"

He scowled. "That don't mean squat."

"Says you! I didn't ask for all this, Billy. You betrayed me, that's what you did. You went ahead and got involved in all this, when all I thought you were doing was running a speak. You lied to me, broke all our marriage vows." Tears shone in her eyes.

275

"Then just about every married guy in New York has broken marriage vows, 'cause more people are in bootlegging than not right now, in case you don't know! And you have the damn government to blame for that!" He struggled to keep his voice down.

"Oh, it's always this one's fault or that one's fault." She waved her hands, looking ready to slap him. "Never your own. Now the government got you into this mess."

"Well, yeah." He nodded. "They did."

"Just grow up, Billy." She pushed past him out the door.

"I did grow up, I did a damn lotta growin' up, but you're so hopped up all the time, you never noticed!" he shouted after her. The baby started to wail. "Aah, dammit!" He rushed over to her and started to sing. She quieted almost immediately, then opened those starry blue eyes of hers and smiled up at him.

He damn near melted into a puddle. "I'm so sorry, kid. How can I ever make it up to you and your mother? How can I make her believe I'm only doing all this for you and her?" Wiping away a tear, he felt the strongest bond with his daughter he'd ever felt since she was born. Here was someone who loved him unconditionally, in all her innocence, who'd never judge him or force him to make a gut-wrenching decision. She loved him no matter what. "I love you, little tyke, you know that? I'll always love you." He sang to her again, one of the Italian lullabies his mother sang to him, and the eyes slid shut. She slept peacefully as he tucked the blanket around her.

He sensed Pru standing behind him, looking over his shoulder. He didn't want to turn around, though; he just wanted to keep watching his daughter sleep. How many moments did he have like this? The hardest part of his life wasn't going to be how to handle Louie Q or how to get another club opened. His greatest challenge would be keeping this innocent life innocent, especially in a rotten world like this.

Finally he stood and faced his wife. "Now keep quiet. I sang her to sleep. She's asleep." They stared into each other's eyes for a long time. She made a move closer, but they didn't touch. "Hey, can you get rid of those scroungers out there, give us some privacy for once?" He gestured in that direction.

With agreement in her eyes, she turned and left the room. He sat back down to watch Victoria sleep. A few moments later he heard the front door close and Pru come back in. This time she approached him and wrapped her arms around him, kissing and nuzzling the back of his neck. Taking a ragged breath, he turned and held onto her like a drowning man. After a long desperate embrace, he swept her up and carried her to the bed.

"I don't know why, but I still love you, Billy. I love you to death, you crazy bastard." Her moans turned to impassioned wails; she cried his name, over and over, as he drove into her.

Afterwards, he lay atop her, their calming breaths in perfect synch.

"Then stay with me, please, don't leave me…"

"I can't," she sobbed. "I need a normal life."

"Normal? You call this normal?" He propped himself up on an elbow. "What's normal about your life?"

"I don't want to argue, Billy. You'd better go

now." She turned over.

"Go where?"

"Back to your place on Fifth Avenue," came her muffled answer.

"It's our place," he corrected her.

"Not any more," she retorted.

"Dammit, what does it take to get you back?" he exploded, nudging her shoulder.

"I can't stay married to a mobster." She slid to the edge of the bed.

"I'm a businessman, Pru," he corrected her.

She wrapped the sheet around her, sat up and lit a reefer.

He pulled his pants on. "Look, we'll talk tomorrow." He didn't want to stay if she was going to start smoking. As much as it hurt to tear himself away, he didn't want to see her like that.

Without another word, he kissed his daughter, brushed his pinkie finger over her cheek, and let himself out.

****

Interlude: Sunday Dinner at the House

"Where's Pru?" they all asked together as if prompted by a director.

"Uh—we, uh—" Oh, what the hell, they'd blame him anyway. "We had a misunderstanding, and she's home sulking. Nothing personal against your cooking, Ma."

"What happened?" Ma, wooden spoon in hand, actually let some sauce drip onto the plastic runner at her feet. "Misunderstanding about what?"

"She's just in one of her moods. We'll work it out." He realized he was trying to convince himself too.

"Did she disappear again, Billy?" Tessie stood behind their mother, holding an enormous mixing bowl full of cake batter, powdered sugar all over her mouth.

"I figured you'd already know and would tell me how it's gonna turn out," he muttered, going past them into the living room. He sat at the radio and fiddled with the dials.

They followed him. "Now Billy, don't be sarcastic to her," Ma said over the static on the radio. "And what's this about her disappearing *again*?"

"Well, it's kinda—personal, you know." He hoped they'd get the hint and sweep it under the rug with every other McGlory scandal and cardinal sin throughout history.

"If you want to talk about it, I'm here for you. So is your father." Ma squeezed his hand, and he squeezed back, with no intention of discussing this with her—or especially with Da.

They both disappeared into the kitchen. Their anxious voices carried, but he couldn't make out any distinct words. He really didn't care. All he wanted was a hot homecooked Italian meal. Then he'd go back to wondering where his life was headed. But for now he just wanted to be the McGlory kid again, in the warm bosom of home. So he went into the kitchen, grabbed the cake batter from Tessie, and licked the spoon till his mother shooed him out.

Chapter Eleven

"I went on board the five-master in the morning and met Captain Rockwell—as I shall call him—a man responsible for running more than 1,000,000 cases of liquor into the States."

—*R. Frisbie, American Mercury, May 1932*

Booking venues like Carnegie Hall during this Depression was harder than pulling a band together. So to keep from going off his nut with boredom, in between visits with the baby and begging Pru to come back, he threw himself into the rum-running syndicate. Its intricate inner workings fascinated him. To keep busy, he started delivering truckloads of hooch from the warehouse, which was also partly his, to their best customers. Once in a while, he'd go into a speakeasy and play a few numbers, or call on some of the cats from the old club or his Tin Pan Alley days and headline for the evening. The nightclub owners started calling him, and before he knew it, he was booked every weekend till next year.

His old following started coming back, and his loyal bearcats mobbed him. So he hadn't lost his touch, musical or otherwise. On his first Saturday night playing with a trio at The Montmarte, a line to get in snaked around the block. Gloria, the dame who'd trailed him back to the Waldorf that night, sashayed in on the arm of a dead ringer for Al Capone. She waved to him on stage, but he pretended he didn't see her.

After closing, he lounged in his robe smoking and reading Winchell's column. Rosie's distinct knock came loud and clear.

"Yeah, c'mon in," he called out, not bothering to pull his robe closed. It was just Rosie, after all.

The door opened. It wasn't just Rosie but the Gloria dame and the Capone lookalike. Only this close up, he wasn't a mere lookalike. The canary yellow suit contrasted with his dark olive coloring. His diamond tie tack and belt buckle glittered. The slash across his cheek stood out like another accessory. Built like a locomotive, he nearly filled the doorway.

Billy wrapped the robe shut and belted it. Winchell's column slid to the floor.

"Meet an old friend of mine from Chicago, Billy. Mr. Alphonse Capone." Rosie confirmed it. "You mighta heard of him. "He, uh—kinda runs Chicago. Al, meet the musical legend Billy McGlory."

Holy Mother McCree. Billy stood and walked toward his guests, not just at a loss for words but at a loss for even a mumble. They stood face to face. Billy's jaw dropped. *Jesus Roosevelt Christ, it really is him, Al Capone, in the living scarred flesh.*

"Uh—um—" he stammered, the cig still in his right hand as he held it out to Capone. "Yikes, I'm sorry!" He dropped the cig and ground it out, forgetting he was barefoot. "Oh, shit! Owww! Dammit!" He hopped around on one foot in front of the most powerful don alive. Capone simply smiled and extended his hand. "Pleased to meet you, Billy. You're about the best pianist around. But I think you already know that." His deep baritone carried a faint Midwest twang.

Billy finally finished his hotfoot dance and held his hand out—and blinked in surprise at Capone's limp handshake. "Why, thank you! Uh—pleased to meet you. Thanks for the compliment. I appreciate it. But I'm no legend yet," he blathered on. "I'm sorry I'm not dressed—uh—you want to come in? I have some Canadian whiskey and some fresh walnuts—"

"Nah, thanks just the same. Oh, this here's Gloria." He jerked a thumb in the dame's direction.

"We've already met." She tittered.

Billy wanted to crawl through the trapdoor and slide down the chute into the sewer, a good place to void his suddenly bursting bladder.

"Uh—no, you must be mistaken, we never met." He turned to Capone, flailing his hands like he was conducting an orchestra. "Never saw her before, I swear!" Without realizing it, he started backing away.

"It's okay, Billy. I told Alphonse you're a perfect gentleman." She turned to Capone and smoothed down his lapel. "I was walking down the street by myself one night, and Billy hailed a cab for me. He even paid for it. Wasn't that gallant of him?" She batted her lashes at Billy. He didn't dare return her saucy wink.

When he imagined the tale she could've spun about their chance encounter, he nearly wet himself with relief. "Oh, yeah, that time." He waved his hand, hoping they didn't notice how much it trembled. "Gee, I hardly remember what I did yesterday, he-he… You folks sure you don't want a drink?"

Capone shook his head. "No, thanks. I'm throwing a party for Rosie tonight at my place and would be honored if you'd join us and play a few tunes."

"A—a party? For Rosie?" He looked at Rosie with questioning eyes. Rosie beaming as if FDR had just invited him to Hyde Park.

"Yeah, it's my birthday today. The big three-nine." And only a one-inch bald spot so far. See?" Rosie bent over and pointed to the top of his head.

"Why, happy birthday. You never said a word." Billy went up and clapped his friend on the back. "Well, it is kinda late—" He shut his trap. What was he thinking? Nobody refused Al Capone, either his party invitations or his commands to kneel on the ground and get shot. Billy bit his tongue for being so shit-stupid as to even consider refusing. "I just need to get some clothes on." He turned and gestured toward his closet stuffed with both stage and street clothes.

"No, you don't. It ain't a formal affair. Come on." Capone tugged his sleeve. "We'll just slip out to my car and nobody'll even see you. Let's go." Billy had no choice but to follow, draped in his robe with nothing underneath. At least his host let him slide into his slippers.

He slid into the leather back seat of an armor-plated Cadillac between Gloria and another hot patootie, Capone in front with the driver. *Where's the birthday boy?* he wondered as the car pulled away from the curb and glided uptown.

"My name's Gloria, too," purred the dish on the right, her curvy body leaning into him. She noticed his informal attire and started working the belt loose. "Whatcha got under that robe, sugar lips?"

"Uh—not much. I mean—just me." He tried to pull it closed but fought a losing battle—with her hands and with his own body. Gloria Number One joined in, and before he knew it, five long slender fingers were working their way up each thigh.

Another hand slipped him a glass of much-needed Scotch from the backseat bar. He belted it down and held the glass out for another. Gloria Number One promptly refilled it. He refused to be responsible for his actions from that moment on. There was no way out, with the biggest mob boss in the world up front, heading to some party where he hoped to black out and wake up alone, preferably locked in the john.

"Uh—two Glorias, how 'bout that." He tried to make small talk to ease the tension. "At least it'll be easy to remember your names." He hoped to get so squiffed he wouldn't even remember his own name.

After his third Scotch, the Caddy pulled up to a swanky highrise with an awning and carpet leading to the door. The two Glorias clung to him as they passed the hat-doffing doorman into the gleaming lobby. Capone must've had his own private elevator, because Billy and his pair of patooties rode up to the penthouse without him. He didn't see Capone again until they entered the lavishly furnished penthouse. A combo played "Stardust" in front of the floor-to-ceiling window. Wall-to-wall dames, all scantily dressed, far outnumbered the fellas prancing around like Valentino, barechested in pyjama bottoms. Billy felt overdressed compared to these guys. A few of them recognized Billy and approached him. This attracted more admirers. Before he knew it, he'd drawn a crowd. Dames stroked his cheeks, men pumped his hand. He gave out autographs. Ah, yeah, he was back in his element. He basked in it.

The two Glorias finally eased him away from his fans and up to the polished wooden bar, staffed by three bartenders. Although champagne flutes and bottles covered the bar, he ordered another neat Scotch and belted that down. He didn't even sample the array of nuts and snacks. The faster he got snockered, the better. The Glorias walked him over to the combo. The piano player saw him and promptly gave up his bench. Billy looked at him, a colored fella with a big gap in his white smile. "Where have I seen you bef—by gosh, you're Jelly Roll Morton." He'd once flashed a diamond in that now-missing tooth—having fallen on hard times, he'd had to hock it.

"It's all yours, sir." Jelly Roll stood aside.

He nodded his thanks, sat on the bench, and picked up playing "Stardust" as if they hadn't missed a beat. Another Scotch appeared before him. He kept playing with one hand as he drank with the other. By now he was officially corked. He started to sing. The band had no trouble keeping up with him through the new hits "April in Paris," "Forty-Second Street," and the older favorites, "Let's Do It" and "You Do Something to Me." He had the band and audience completely under his control. He'd forgotten that the infamous Al Capone was his host. He just kept drinking and playing, drinking and playing, with the express purpose of passing out.

After playing "Happy Days are Here Again" he heard the usual round of applause as Capone came over and stuffed a wad of bills into his empty glass. Then Gloria Number One, Capone's date, her headlights spilling out of a gauzy negligee, settled next to him. Moving to the edge of the bench, he broke into "Happy

Birthday" for Rosie, then segued into the tunes from his own musical. She began working her hand up his thigh. It hardly distracted him, he knew his material that well. By now he was desperate to relieve himself. "Hey, I gotta find the men's room." They stood together, and as if joined at the hip she walked him down a hallway to a bathroom. He spent what seemed like an hour emptying his bladder. He had the wherewithal to close his robe again, and she led him not back to the party but to a huge bedroom. She lowered him onto a satin-sheeted bed. The room promptly started to spin.

"Uh—can I 'ave 'nother Scotch?" On the verge of passing out, he kept trying to prop himself up on his elbows. But he didn't fight it—if his brain ceased to function, so would another body part that threatened to betray him.

She opened his robe, her hands all over him. He lay sprawled out, slipping out of consciousness. It didn't even matter if somebody saw him in bed with Capone's moll and plugged him full of holes. He couldn't get up and leave, even if he were able to walk straight and remember his address. Leave a party hosted by Al Capone? He'd never get out alive. So he let the skillful long fingers do their work as distant music floated in, with the clinking of glasses and laughter. He took a deep breath of heady perfume and let it out with a moan. She slid down his body, caressing him with her tongue. "Forgive me, Pru," he managed to slur as a soft mouth closed on him.

****

He went limp with relief when he woke up in broad daylight, wrapped in a satin sheet, remembering nothing except the ride there in Al Capone's Caddoo, meeting Jelly Roll Morton, playing the piano, falling into bed with some dame, and passing out. He held his pounding head and looked around. He was alone, thank God. The room looked like a sheik's tent, decorated in animal prints and rugs. His robe lay next to him, about to slide to the floor.

"Mother McCree," he groaned, wondering what happened after he passed out, if anything. He pulled the robe on, stumbled into the adjacent bathroom, cleaned himself up, and stuck his head under the faucet to drink a gallon of water. Unable to find his slippers, he wandered down the hallway barefoot, looking for a way out. He didn't care to see his host again, but made a mental note to return the invitation. How the hell would he entertain Al Capone at his place? That made him laugh.

He found a maid sweeping in the deserted living area. "Uh—pardon me…" He tapped her on the shoulder. "Is anybody home here?"

"Oh, hello." She looked surprised to see him. "No, no one is in residence, but—"

"Never mind!" Just then he spotted the door. "I'll let myself out, thanks." He got himself the hell out of there, found the elevator, and pressed the down button with a trembling finger.

Still barefoot and hardly dressed for daytime in the city, he approached the doorman. "Can I get a taxi?" He had no money for a cab, so he hoped Rosie would be home.

After a bored glance, like he saw this kind of thing every day, the doorman stepped outside. A minute later, Billy sat in the back of a taxi heading for Rosie's.

Rosie was home. Thank God for small favors.

He greeted Billy with a knowing smirk.

"Don't say a word, just send a five-spot to the cabbie waiting downstairs and get me some clothes and a few bucks to get home. I don't wanna know what happened last night." He walked past Rosie into the living room and stood at the window overlooking Central Park.

"Too bad. It was a good party. Not the kind every guy gets for his birthday. Makes me look forward to forty." He dug into his pocket, pulled out a billfold, and sent his butler down with the cab fare.

"I was too plastered to remember anything, and I'm glad of it," Billy said as Rosie went to fetch him some street clothes. "Is Scarface gonna be in town long?" he called out as he helped himself to the bar.

"Nah, he's just here on business, keeps a few broads in the penthouse up there, has parties there when he's in town," he answered from another room. "He likes to come back to his roots once in a while. He come up the hard way, too, ya know."

Sloshing orange juice around his mouth, Billy threw off the robe and pulled on the too-big, too-short pants and jacket Rosie gave him. "You got any shoes?"

"Hey, you want everything!" Rosie kidded as he got out a pair of shoes. Again, way too big.

"I look like the Little Tramp," Billy remarked as he walked toward the door, the shoes flopping on and off his feet.

"Nah, you ain't waddlin' enough. Still, it's better than what you looked like when you showed up." Rosie grinned as he gave him cab fare home.

"I don't ever want to hear nothing about last night again." Billy held his hands up. "I wasn't there."

Rosie gave him a definite nod. "You got it. I won't ever mention it again. Just make believe it was one of them dreams, ya know, nocturnal whaddayacallit."

"Yeah. Good idea." He let himself out and asked the doorman to hail him a cab. *Now do I write about this in my journal or not?* he asked himself as the taxi took him home.

****

"I'm a gambler. I play the horses. I never was a bootlegger in my life."

—Al Capone

~*~

"They call Capone a bootlegger. Yes... What's Al done, then? He's supplied a legitimate demand. Some call it bootlegging. Some call it racketeering. I call it business. They say I violate the Prohibition law. Who doesn't?"

—Al Capone

****

When Billy got home, he made himself respectable again, with decent clothes and the usual roll of bills in his pocket. He went to Bloomingdale's and picked up a birthday present for Rosie—a pair of high-powered binoculars to view their racehorse at the track. He had the leather case engraved in gold with "Happy Birthday to the only brother I ever had. Billy." So it was hokey. But Rosie was a softie underneath, after all. Unlike some of those other dirtbags.

****

A week after he started running the hooch delivery truck, he was at the warehouse, taking a pee, waiting for them to load up. The phone rang in the office.

Billy zipped up and was walking by just as the

student who managed the office stuck his head out the door and said, "Telephone for you, Mr. McGlory."

"I wish you'd ditch the 'Mr. McGlory' bit. Makes me feel like my old man." He swept up the phone. "Yeah?"

"I'm gonna get your wife, McGlory," a gritty voice with a streetwise Brooklyn accent rasped into the phone. "I'm gonna rape her and kill her and feed her to the pigeons in the park."

"Who the hell is this?" It had to be some drunk who saw him play in a club. It couldn't be anybody he hung out with.

"Never mind." The voice grated on his ears like sandpaper. "I'm on my way over there now."

"Yeah? Well, she moved out on me, dickface. You don't even know where she is!" he retorted in his snidest wiseass tone.

"The hell I don't. And she looks pretty tasty in that blue coat with the polka dots and the pink collar today, goin' to Ferrara's with the kid in the baby carriage."

It dawned on him now this creep might be serious. "You scumbag." He slammed the phone down and high-tailed it to Jane Street with the truck half loaded. This time he wished a cop *would* stop him; he'd get there a lot faster in one of their souped-up Lincolns.

He fretted and fumed in agony all the way there. "Come on, son of a bitch, come on!" He pounded the steering wheel at every red light. The way he wove in and out of traffic put the most jaded cabbie to shame.

Not even remembering if he'd turned the engine off, he double-parked, tore up the stairs, and burst through the door. Pru screamed and flattened herself against the wall, knocking over her painting. This one wasn't as dreary as the others, just weird. It looked like somebody's brain that had turned to mush and been run through an eggbeater.

"You all right?" he panted, heart hammering. "Where's the baby?"

"What's the matter with you?" she shrieked, dropping her paintbrush.

"You and her are coming with me. Where you'll be safe." He poked his head out the windows, checked the flimsy locks.

"Safe? With you? You must be joshing. I'd be safer going over Niagara Falls in a barrel full of holes." Her tone oozed cynicism.

"I have to get you outta here." But he stopped short. His Fifth Avenue address was well enough known. If they could find her here, they could sure as hell find her there. "Come on, pack a few things and let's go." He went into the bedroom, dragged out a valise from under the bed and started flinging her unmentionables into it.

"Billy, have you really gone nuts this time?" She stood in the doorway.

"Pru, I was so worried about you—" He couldn't even finish. He rushed up to her and wrapped her in his arms. "I got a call—" Then he thought twice. Telling her about that phone call would make her turn around and run back to Iowa.

She broke the embrace and looked up at him, tears blurring her intense gaze. "Oh, no. Are you in trouble again?"

"No. But I'm worried. Especially after Bruno and his wife..." He took a ragged breath. "Please—come back with me. We'll go to the beach house with the baby, and it'll be real nice. Please? Let's get outta here. I'll come back to the city just for work. Let's go."

She finally agreed to go to the beach house for a few days, if he promised to take time off to spend with her and the baby. He got ready to load her easels and stuff into the truck, went downstairs, looked into the street, and realized there was no truck.

It was gone.

"Goddamn it! Goddamn it to hell!" He flung his hat into the street and stomped all over it. "Those filthy rat bastards!"

Pedestrians didn't dare make eye contact. They gave him wide berth as they slipped by him and a stunned Pru standing in the doorway with the baby in her arms.

He deposited her and the baby at the beach house with his own car. After having dinner delivered, he told her he had to go back to Manhattan.

"But we just got here!" She stomped her foot on the plush carpet.

"It's just for a little while. I'll be home by midnight, I promise." He moved to kiss her, but she turned her head away.

"I've heard too many of your empty promises. You'd better tell me what's going on now. I won't put up with your leaving me in the dark about all this. It's exactly this kind of stuff that drove me out, this crazy stuff." Her red-rimmed eyes looked frazzled, tired. He guessed it wasn't the baby wearing her out.

"All right, I'll level with you. I'm gonna go see Louie Q."

"What for?" She placed fist on hip, Susan-style.

"He asked to see me. He'll probably ask me to help

open another club." He glanced at the clock. It was getting late, and he grew more antsy by the minute. Now that his family was safe and out of the way, he had to get out of there and explain to Louie that the truck got hijacked. "I'll be back tonight, I swear."

"Don't bother to swear and don't bother to come back tonight." She turned and climbed the curved staircase, the carpet muffling her footsteps; such a difference from Jane Street, where he could hear the mice scurrying up and down the rickety stairwell.

"Aah, hell." He could argue with her later. Now all he had time for was to hightail it back to the city and explain how he let a new truck containing thousands in contraband get stolen off the street.

****

With his new fedora in his hands and his stomach in his throat, he followed the butler to Louie's sitting room.

Louie sat in his leather lounger smoking a cigar, studying the racing form. "Sit, Billy. Want a drink?"

"Yeah," he accepted in a grateful tone. "The stiffest one you got."

A waiter, who Billy swore was wearing eye makeup, served him a neat whiskey. He took a few gulps, telling himself over and over, *These guys trust me. I made an honest mistake.* The drink reassured him. He helped himself to another from the silver tray.

"So, what's goin' on?" Louie put the racing form on his side table and took off his specs.

"Uh—Louie, there was an accident today." He gulped his drink. "With the truck. The one I've been driving. Well, not an accident, but—it was stolen." He took another gulp.

"Where from?" he asked, his voice flat. Billy took that as a good sign.

"From outside my apartment on Jane Street." He took a sip this time.

"It have anything in it?"

"Yeah, a delivery, but it was half empty." For once, being half empty was a good thing.

"You mean it was half full." It figured. He'd find a way to twist it around.

"Well, yeah, but it could've been worse. It could've been all the way full," he ventured, his stomach in knots.

"How the *fongool* did ya let that happen?" He stubbed his cigar out in a crystal ashtray in the shape of Italy.

Billy choked. "Uh—I left it on the street with the engine on, 'cause I got a call from somebody who said he was going to rape and kill my wife. I went to get her out of the apartment, left the truck outside, and when I got back out, it was gone. So it makes me think it wasn't random. Somebody set me up," he rambled, without taking a breath. He gulped—for air this time.

"Never mind somebody set you up. Ya don't go leavin' trucks with their engine running in the middle of the friggin' street. Ya stupid shitforbrains!" He pounded his fist on the chair arm. His pinkie ring probably dented the wood. "What are you anyways, a *strunad*? I thought you was smarter than that."

"I am, sir," he assured Louie with a repeated nod. "But I was frantic with worry over my wife and baby. Certainly you can understand that. I'm sorry. I'll buy another one at my expense."

"Ya goof, it could've been a fed, for all you

know!" he thundered.

"Don't we have them all paid off?" he asked in all seriousness.

"Not the entire U.S. government, ya dumb shit!" He reached forward and smacked Billy on the side of the head. He didn't flinch; he knew he deserved a lot worse.

"I'm sorry! What do you want me to do?" He considered dropping to his knees and kissing Louie's ring.

"Just sit there and shut up." Louie got on the horn and called somebody named Dirty Neck Bruiso. Then he slammed out of the room without another word, leaving Billy there alone, to drain his whiskey and peek out to see if he could jump. It wouldn't be a pleasant fall down from the 24th floor, and there was no place to make a soft landing. So he paced the room. He thanked his lucky stars he found a nearby bathroom, because he spent a good amount of time in there evacuating.

He paced some more, telling himself it was no big deal. What's one lousy truck to these guys? Finally, after what seemed like half the night, the door opened, and a big sonofabitch with a nose broken two ways filled the doorway. If he wasn't Dirty Neck Bruiso, nobody was. He entered the room like a batter stepping up to the plate. "Let's go," was all he said, tossing his head. No "Good evening, how's it hangin'?" or anything like that. Another goon dutifully followed a few paces behind.

Together they led him out of the penthouse by the elbows, making him feel like Sid Cunningham. He didn't see Louie again. It wasn't like him not to come out and say goodnight.

He didn't dare ask where they were taking him. They escorted him into the back seat of a Packard Boattail Speedster that reeked of cigar smoke and garlic, and took off.

He tried to calm himself by praying to every Italian saint he knew, plus a few Irish ones. Nobody said a word. He wished one of them would say something, talk about the weather, Mayor Walker's resignation, anything. Then he realized they were about to cross the newly built George Washington Bridge, which he hadn't driven over yet. What the hell were they going to Jersey for? Did they think they'd find the truck there? But as he looked out over the blackness of the Hudson River below, it dawned on him that it might be a one-way trip.

They drove down some pitch black roads, and he guessed they were in the Hackensack Meadows. Nothing but wilderness stretched for miles around. They turned left and rode down a bumpy dirt lane. He clasped his hands to keep from trembling. He prayed some more, to God this time.

Bruiso cut the engine, and the car's interior went completely dark. He turned to face Billy. "You know where we are?"

"Uh—New Jersey?" He swallowed, but had no spit left to swallow.

Bruiso shook his head. "It's a graveyard." Like he should've known all along.

"Yeah?" He glanced outside. "I don't see any headstones."

"Ya won't."

"Oh." Billy got it. "It's that kind of graveyard."

The other goon, still nameless, got out and opened

Billy's door. "Get outta the car."

This is it, he thought. He looked up at the sky for what he supposed was the last time. The stars twinkled and glittered like diamonds, surrounding a sliver of a moon. Oh, eternity.

Bruiso came around and lit a flashlight. "Over here."

He had no choice but to follow, stumbling over rocks and weeds. It was so quiet, he could hear his heart thumping. He was hyperventilating now. He shook so much, he couldn't keep his footing. He prayed like he never prayed before, but this time he prayed for a quick death and a merciful release from whatever torture they'd inflict on him.

Bruiso shoved Billy ahead of him and shone the beam on the ground, illuminating what looked like a pile of clothes. "Look."

He looked. It was more than a pile of clothes, but not much more. It was a badly decomposed corpse. All that remained was part of the skull and the macabre grin where the skin had rotted away. A putrid stench rose from the ground. He gagged, turned, and vomited into the dirt.

Bruiso grabbed Billy's elbow, led him farther on, and once again steadied the beam down on a crumpled figure. Another corpse, this one dismembered, not much more than a torso.

"You seen enough?" He shone the light in Billy's eyes.

Blinded, he shielded his eyes and nodded, unable to speak.

"And you know what?" He lashed out at Billy before he had a chance to duck or even realize he was getting hit. "This is where your stinkin' corpse'll be"—his second fist connected with the side of Billy's head. The other goon grabbed him from behind and hurled him against the car—"if you ever do anything that stupid again"—Bruiso wrapped his fingers around Billy's throat—"like leave a runnin' truck out in the middle of the street!" His grip closed in on Billy's windpipe. He choked, clawing at Bruiso, gasping for his life's air. "You hear it?"

Just before he blacked out, Bruiso landed another punch on his jaw, knocking him to the ground. Blood poured from his head. He fell on top of the rotted corpse and felt a jutting bone dig into his ribs. With the little strength he had left, he crawled over the ground. Throat throbbing, he took a deep breath and let it out, retching. He didn't even know if they'd gone and left him there. At this point he didn't care. He was still alive and wanted to stay alive, just long enough to say one last prayer.

But they hauled him up and flung him into the back seat of the car. The engine started, and they took off—back through the meadows, over the G.W. Bridge, and into Manhattan.

So it was only a warning? He peed his pants in relief when they turned onto Park Avenue. The warmth instantly turned to cold. He shivered.

He hunched over in the backseat with his head between his wet pants legs and his hands cradling his bruised neck, trying not to pass out, or even worse, void his bowels in the flashy Packard. But the relief of being spared made him giddy. He wanted to kiss their feet for letting him live.

They screeched to a halt in front of Louie Q's

building, and Bruiso's goon opened the door for him again. This time he got out faster than he thought his legs could take him.

In Italian, Bruiso muttered what Billy could do to himself that was physically impossible. His thug added, "Now scram," with such authority Billy figured he'd spent the last two years rehearsing it.

Too shaken to drive, he watched their tail lights trail away down Central Park West, and started walking. He couldn't get the gruesome sight out of his mind or the stench out of his nose. He'd puked up everything inside him; he had nothing left. Oh, if only he could find the rat bastard who'd stolen the truck, would he get his!

He stumbled down the block like a drunk, trying to stop the bleeding with his gloves. Still gasping for air, he remembered what it felt like to struggle for breath, on the verge of suffocation.

A sudden anger and rage turned him into a lunatic. He ducked into a dark alley and started smashing up garbage cans. He kicked at them, hurled them against the walls, bellowed incoherent noises from deep within his chest and the depths of his soul. A bum sat up and slurred, "Wha's all the noise about?"

Billy stood there grunting from deep within his throat, like a wild beast on the attack. Now he believed humans had evolved from apes; he never felt more like an animal than at that moment. But the sight of the bum seemed to calm him somehow, and he slowly regained his senses.

"I—I'm sorry, I just went screwy there for a minute. Here." He caught his breath some more and handed the bum all the money he had in his pockets, probably a few hundred. Dollar bills fell out and fluttered to the ground. The bum didn't even scramble to pick them up; he must've been stunned. Billy didn't need any money that night; he could sleep in his car if he had to. But the bum didn't even have that. And there were countless more like him these days. "Get yourself something decent to eat. And I don't mean drink, I mean eat." Billy slipped his raccoon coat off and handed it to him, too. "And take this."

"Hah?" He just stood there, swaying slightly, too shocked to talk.

"It's okay. Just do me a favor—share some of that dough with your friends, so's you don't go hungry. Who knows what this Roosevelt guy's gonna do; it might be a long haul. Well—" He took another deep breath and felt human again, able to function in the real world. "See ya."

The bum held up a hand, covered with a fingerless glove. Billy kept that picture in his mind to block out the scene in the meadows.

Shivering now, he tossed his bloody gloves down the sewer, thrust his hands into his empty pockets, and strode back to his car. He sat there for a long time, his head resting against the wheel, thinking about everything that happened today. He was in way too deep. He knew it. But he'd been damn lucky Louie showed mercy; Greta must've been real good to him last night. If Louie'd been in a bad mood, the rats of Hackensack would've had a fresh corpse to feast on.

He needed to find the truck, but more than that, he wanted to catch the *cazzo* who stole it and make *strufoli* out of his nuts.

But he left the dirty city behind and, as he'd sworn

to Pru, got back by midnight.

Of course she gasped when she saw his bruised jaw. "Uh—I fell," was the only thing he could bring himself to tell her, and she turned away without a word.

He had to get to work the next day. So, after an early morning walk on the beach with Pru and the baby, after not sleeping more than fifteen minutes, he left them both playing with lumps of clay and drove back to the warehouse.

Punchy from lack of sleep, all he could think of was how to find that stolen truck. He racked his brain all the way into Manhattan. It could be anywhere. He kept an eye out for it, but there were thousands of trucks just like it, and it was probably repainted by now, with new plates. If only he could find the thief. Now he knew what vendettas were all about.

His last dying wish would be to find that bastard and make sure he rotted in hell. Nobody threatened his wife and stole his booze and got away with it.

****

Interlude: Sunday Dinner at the House

It was Susan's twins' sixth birthday, so the parents threw one of their festive birthday parties. They wore party hats, lit birthday candles, and blew into noisemakers. A million toys and yards of crumpled wrapping paper lay strewn on the floor. Ferrara's Bakery delivered enough Italian rum cake to sink Sicily. Billy hated that cake; it reminded him of a dirty sponge. He would only eat the buttercream frosting and the sugary flowers on top. But this time the kids got to that first.

They sang "Happy Birthday" with Billy accompanying them on the piano. Then he lost himself in a string of Chopin études and some tunes from his show. Nobody bothered him when he played. But they all clapped when he finished.

Da didn't take him aside for another talk. Nobody brought up the raid. Neither he nor Pru gave any hint how strained everything was between them. "Billy, I'm gonna do a tarot reading," Tessie announced when Ma finally cleared the table and served "grownup" pastries and coffee.

"Not again." Although he hated to admit it, though, he was curious. There might be something useful among all the malarkey. She was sure good at it, so far.

She led him to the table. "Just sit here. I feel uneven energy waves emanating from your being."

"I felt that too," Pru chimed in, and went on to describe the astrology chart she'd done on him the other day. "Billy, when Mars moves into Libra, you'll be entering a new phase. Between now and the twenty-first, carefully consider your actions."

"Only for a week? Then what? Go back to the way I usually am?" he mumbled as Tessie began turning over cards.

"Hmm—the Chariot." Tessie's eyes widened at that.

"What's that mean?" he asked. "I'm the reincarnation of Ben Hur?"

Ignoring him, she continued: "This is your present position, the atmosphere in which you're currently living and working. The area of influence in which you presently exist. And it means trouble, adversity, turmoil, vengeance, possible voyage or journey, rushing to a decision, urgency to gain control over one's emotions."

"So what am I supposed to do about it?" he asked the oracle.

"Wait till I do the whole reading, then we'll see which card shows the final result." She studied the cards with the intensity of a brain surgeon at work.

He didn't pay much attention to the rest of the reading, as he went over a melody in his head and tried to fit a set of lyrics to it. It sounded like the germ of a new musical, set in the near future—after the Great Depression and Prohibition ended. A time of prosperity, like President Roosevelt promised.

"…the beginning of spiritual enlightenment and understanding."

"Huh? What was that?" The positive tone caught his ear.

"It's your final result, brought about from all the influences as revealed by the other cards. The Devil upside down." Tessie pointed.

"Damn good thing it's upside down." He grabbed a cannoli.

"Well, that's the way it was when you chose it," she explained. "I mean, when the spirits guided you to choose it."

"Well, lucky me. Or, thanks to my spirit guides. So when's all this enlightenment gonna happen? Tomorrow? Or after Mars moves into Libra?" He shot Pru a sideways glance, but she was busy playing with Rachael's new doll. His nephew climbed onto his lap, and Billy held him back from messing up the cards.

"It's all around you now. And watch out for what that reverse King of Cups said about dishonesty, scandal, loss, ruin, and a crafty person shifty in dealings," Tessie warned.

"Now she tells me," he said, glad Pru didn't hear him.

His nephew scrambled off his lap and skipped into the parlor to start banging on the piano. The victrola was already on, so it got really noisy. He was used to noise, but not this early. This was his sleeping time, the middle of the night to him. The discordant tones were making him ill. He knew it was the aftereffects of the horror he'd seen the other night. Try as he might, he couldn't get it out of his mind. Those corpses had once been living, breathing human beings. The scene flashed before his eyes at the damndest times, like when he was trying to eat. He'd have to jump up and lose everything in the bathroom. Pru noticed, and told him he'd better go to a doctor. But how could he tell a doctor any of that? So he slurped bicarb and stayed away from booze till his mind recovered.

"Thanks, Tess. I'll heed that advice." He gestured toward the cards as Irv looked on, anxious to be read next.

Tessie looked up at Billy, puzzled. He knew it was because he'd never shown so much interest.

If he had to face dishonesty, scandal, loss, ruin, and shifty slimebags in order to reach spiritual enlightenment, he was probably almost there already.

****

The next day he got a call from the theater manager. After two hundred performances, his show was ending its run. "It was a good run," was all he could say, with mixed emotions. He knew the ending of the show meant bigger things were to come, and he still hadn't given up on his other dreams. Maybe they'd even have a revival of it someday. He couldn't be too sad to see it end.

He phoned Les and then Greta, asking them to attend the last performance with him. Les begged off; his companion had fallen off a ladder and couldn't walk.

"Hey, I'm sorry to hear that, buddy. I'll say a prayer for him," Billy tried to console Les. "He's young, he'll make a fast recovery. You know you were as close to me as anybody during that time we created our masterpiece. We made magic together. I'll make sure we work together again, and that's a promise."

Greta agreed to go with him. But as they sat in their private box during the last curtain call, a crushing emptiness tore him up like nothing he'd ever experienced. It didn't even come close to the loss he suffered when Pru said she was leaving him, or when Swing Street shut down. This was the public turning their backs on him; the show was ending simply because nobody wanted to come see it anymore. Now he knew how hopeless a politician felt after losing an election. "They snubbed me," he muttered as they exited the stage door.

"That's not true, Billy," Greta assured him. "No play goes on forever."

"Mr. McGlory!" He turned to see one of the ushers racing toward him. "Telegram just came for you."

"Thanks." He gave the kid a buck and unfolded the paper. "Congratulations on a great run. Look forward to working with your talented team again. Jackie Harper." He sported his first smile all day.

"That was nice of him," Greta said, a cheery lilt in her voice.

Billy folded the telegram and slid it into his pocket.

"I thought he'd be pissed."

"Why?" she asked. "He can't fault you for the Depression. It was good while it lasted, he got a great return on his investment, and he's thanking you for it."

"Yeah, well, I appreciate his offer and all, but I hope by the time I'm ready to do Broadway again, I won't need any backers." They headed north on Broadway. Honking horns, roaring engines, and the sweeping crowd swallowed them up.

"You never know, Billy." She curled her hand around his arm. "Just buy the guy a drink next time you run into him."

"Meanwhile, I feel like I've just been to a funeral." He fished out two cigs, lit them, and gave her one.

"Don't be silly. All shows have to end sometime." She squeezed his arm as she took the cig with her free hand. "It's the Depression. But this is for now. It can always open in Chicago, or Cleveland, or some another city, when times get better."

"Nah, it won't be the same." The wind whipped his cigarette smoke away. Those places aren't home. This is a New York story. It's about home, and they kicked me out of my home town."

"Applesauce. You're just not thinking straight. Hey, where are we going anyway?" They approached Columbus Circle.

"How about going to my penthouse, do some singing?" he asked as they stopped for a red light. "I need to get some music out of my system."

"Sure, that sounds swell."

Neither mentioned Pru until they got inside and Greta browsed the paintings all over the walls. "Bright Eyes," still above the mantel, offered the only relief from the gloom that undermined the decor.

"Hey, you're right, these are kind of, uh—downbeat," she commented as Billy mixed her a Scotch and water.

"Downbeat is an understatement." He handed her the drink. "They're downright dreary. The inside of a coffin is brighter than this stuff."

"So then what happened when you went back to the flat?" She took a sip. "She's not here, so I assume our talks didn't do much good in the end."

"She's at the beach house, staying there for a while." He mixed himself a stiff one. "I got a threatening phone call, so I brought her and the kid there."

"Uh-oh." She didn't ask for details. She didn't have to.

"Nothin' happened." He drained his drink in two gulps. "But it's still strained between us. She's real scared, still. I can't blame her. We're not where we were before—not yet. But thank you. I appreciate all you did."

"Yet? I like your optimism, Sheik. You're a true die-hard." She sipped her drink.

"When did you know me to give up on anything that meant anything to me?" He started for a refill but nixed the idea.

"Never. I feel the same way. She'll come around. She loves you like crazy. She'd be certifiably insane to let you go. You're one in a million." She smiled and winked at him. He smiled back, toasting her with his empty glass, not taking the compliment as anything more than just that—a compliment from a friend, fashioned to lift his spirits.

She slipped her shoes off and tossed them aside as she headed for the picture window. "I tried to use myself as an example. I told her I've been going around with Louie, and I don't feel my life's threatened in any way. But she said we're two different kinds of people. I'm a Taurus, and since she's a Libra, we'd never handle things the same way."

"Yeah, she relies on a bunch of planets to decide our fate. I wish she'd be a little more earthy." He poured himself another drink—plain water this time.

"No, it's not just astrology, she's going by personality types. Libras wouldn't do this, Virgos wouldn't act that way. Some signs are more compatible than others. It can be pretty accurate, you know," she said.

He gazed out over the park. "I gotta admit there must be something to Tessie's predictions with those kooky cards. Maybe it really is a talent. My step-grandmother was like that, too. She had a crystal ball and cards, and everything she predicted always seemed to come true. But I'd feel like a real jabeep paying money to somebody who gazed cockeyed into crystal balls. These days, with times so hard, some people skip meals to pay for that stuff. It's criminal." He paused to take a breath. "But Pru's judgment's clouded a lot these days, pardon the pun."

"She still smoking reefer?" Greta asked.

"Of course. With those damn scroungers, lying around smoking goof-butts. I want to crack their heads together when I see them all there, like they own the dump." He clenched his fingers around his glass.

"It's her life, Billy. Just like you have yours."

"She was just about moved in here, and we were

almost leading a normal life like a happy married couple. I let her hang these damn pictures—" He waved his hand at the sorry-looking things. "I gotta get these damn things off the walls. She brought clothes over, stuff for the kid, and then that damned raid happened, and some blabbermouth told her I run a syndicate." He took a long, thoughtful sip of his water. Ah, the clean taste of New York City tap water. He didn't seem to taste, or feel, or hear, anything since the raid. He hadn't even listened to music—really listened—since the raid.

"Hey, let's stop talking and start singing." She went to the piano and flipped through his sheet music.

"Good idea." He sat at George and she joined him. They sang some standards, and their favorites from "Of Thee I Sing." He started to come alive again. That familiar rush went through him whenever he played. It felt like a rebirth.

They called it a night around one a.m.; she had Louie picking her up early to go to the racetrack.

"Hey, thanks, Greta. I needed that." He released a contented sigh.

"I know, Sheik. Anytime." With a brush on the lips, she took off down the elevator and into the cab he'd called for her.

He sat back down and played and sang till daybreak; he couldn't get enough. He may have wrecked his marriage, but he still had his music. And a good friend to console him. So what if he was falling in love with her? He could handle it. Compared to everything else going on, that was hardly a turd in a punchbowl.

****

After he bought another truck with his own money,

the hijacking incident faded like a minor inconvenience. But he still couldn't get that graveyard scene out of his mind. He told Rosie about the whole thing one night when they met at the Salisbury Hotel for dinner. It helped to get it off his chest. When he got to the graphic part, he shivered, as if he still stood there over that rotting corpse.

"Sorry, kiddo." Rosie shook his head and twirled his gold toothpick. "Any more of them phone calls?"

"Nope." He shook his head.

"Prob'ly just some punk wanted to steal the truck, set you up."

"Well, now Pru's gone back to Jane Street, and I'm scared shitless for her and the baby's lives." Billy toyed with his cake fork.

"It's safe as anyplace else." Rosie poured the last of their wine into Billy's glass.

"And you can as easily say it's as dangerous as anyplace else. I'm resigned to that now. No place is safe anymore. Even if I hired fifty goons, they'd nab me if they wanted to." Louie Q had bodyguards, but Rosie didn't. Billy figured if he hired some for himself and Pru, he'd look like he was getting too big for his breeches. So he took his chances, but packed a rod in a holster, just in case.

"So you like driving the truck?" Rosie finished the last of his own wine.

"Yeah," he said. "Gives me a purpose, till I can get an orchestra together, but it's tough, with everybody broke and all. If the show ended because of the Depression, it's even harder to get people to blow a wad of dough to see a concert at Carnegie Hall. I never put much stock in politicians, but I hope this FDR'll turn things around."

"Yeah, him and his great plans. A chicken in every pot, he says. Don't he realize some people ain't even got the pot?" Rosie signaled the waiter for the check.

"They're talking about repealing Prohibition, too, soon," Billy added. "About time they repeal it. It's a royal pain in my ass, if you ask me. It'd be nice to have a club that's legit. Keep me out of trouble." He grinned for the first time since he forgot when.

"I dunno, kiddo. Trouble seems to be your hobby." Rosie peeled off some bills from a bankroll.

He shrugged. "Everybody ought to have one."

"Lucky for you it's been the kind you can get out of." Rosie tossed some bills on the table.

"Well, I believe in fate." Billy twirled his fork. "And somebody's watching over me. I can just feel it sometimes. All planned out. Like a script. And whoever it is has one hell of a sense of humor."

****

When Billy went back to Jane Street to convince Pru yet again to come back to Fifth Avenue, she wasn't there. Neither was the baby. No freeloaders, either. No note, no nothing. The place was colder than a witch's tit in Wisconsin.

He called Susan, figuring the baby was with her. Yup, she was. "Where did Pru say she was going when she dropped the baby off?"

"With some friends to hear Stephen Vincent Benét read from his book about the Civil War. She's going to pick the baby back up tomorrow afternoon."

"Oh," he muttered. "Nice of her to tell me."

"Don't worry, Billy, the baby's fine. You want to spend the night here?"

He glanced at his watch. It was after midnight. "Nah, I'll be by tomorrow to see her. G'night."

So he went back to Fifth Avenue, played George for a few hours, and fell asleep sitting at the bench. He finally went to bed at his regular time.

****

The phone call from St. Vincent's Hospital came in the middle of the night, like those kinds of calls always do. Pru had been rushed there and was listed in "fair" condition. One of her freeloading friends had the sense to call an ambulance and list him as the emergency contact.

Without putting any clothes on, he threw on a beaver coat, jammed his feet into a pair of shoes that didn't match, and tore out the door, not even knowing if he'd closed it or not. Somehow he got a cab. He burst through the hospital doors and up to the desk in tears, begging to see her.

He got some strange stares, even for the middle of the night in Greenwich Village. He gulped air, pacing the floor, remembering the last time he'd done this: the night Victoria was born. That had been a joyous occasion, the celebration of a new life. Now, he didn't even know what Pru was in there for. An accident? Did she get sick? "What the hell's going on?" he demanded, banging his fist on the desk. "Where's my wife?"

Without looking up, the desk nurse replied, "Sir, if you continue to behave in this manner, we're going to have to ask you to leave. That's if you don't get arrested for indecent exposure first."

He looked down at his open coat, and there he was. How the hell had she noticed? "Oh. Sorry." He buttoned his coat over his birthday suit, finally got a pass, and went up to her room.

A nurse barred his entrance. "She's sleeping."

"What happened?" he asked for what seemed like the millionth time, in what was left of his voice. "Will you please tell me what happened to her?"

"She took a drug overdose."

"Huh?" It didn't register. He stood there for the longest time, like a dummy. It just didn't make sense. "Of what?"

"Sleeping pills, sir. She just had her stomach pumped. But she's a very lucky girl. I'd say it's a miracle she's alive." The nurse gave him a frosty once-over, like he had something to do with it.

He peeked into the dark room and saw the outline of her thin form hooked up to an I.V. drip. Without asking, he rushed in and knelt at the bedside.

"Sir!"

"Shh!" He shooed the nurse away, and she reluctantly backed off.

"You have five minutes," she allowed, in that nursy Frau Pertl voice he despised.

"Pru—" he whispered, his mouth dry as cotton. "Honey Bear, what happened, why did you do it?"

She lay there, breathing but unresponsive. He clasped her hand. It was freezing cold. His first thought was to get some blankets, but he couldn't bear to leave her side. He knelt there for he didn't know how long, her icy hand in his, praying his heart out.

If she goes, I want to go, too, was his only thought.

Two nurses finally kicked him out. He didn't even know what time it was. He also didn't realize how cold it was outside until he looked down at his open coat and saw himself dangling in the wind. He buttoned the coat again, shivering, and chased a cab.

Once he was in, and the driver asked the inevitable, "Where to, mac?" he was at a loss. He didn't want to go back to his empty penthouse. Who would be up for company at this hour? He thought of the only person who would be.

Rosie answered the door himself, in his chef's apron, holding a wooden spoon, reeking of garlic. He sure picked odd hours to practice the art of Sicilian cuisine.

One look at Billy's face and his cigar nearly tumbled to the floor. "What the hell's wrong with you?" He pulled Billy inside and led him over to a warm cheery fire blazing in his Carrara marble fireplace. No *scagliola* here.

"Holy shit, what are you, nuts?" He stared wide-eyed as Billy opened his coat before the fire to let some warmth seep into his naked body. "Running around in nothin' but a coat, with nothin' underneath?" Rosie took off down the hallway, and Billy hoped he'd get a blanket or a drink. He crouched before the fire, still shivering. Rosie came back with some pants, a shirt, and what looked like an afghan. Billy wrapped it around himself as Rosie thrust a brandy snifter into his trembling hand.

"Now tell me what the hell happened."

"Pru's in the hospital. She overdosed. On sleeping pills." He rubbed his hands together and flexed his frozen fingers. He couldn't have played "Chopsticks" on a piano, his fingers were so stiff with cold.

Rosie bowed his head. "Oh, Jesus. How is she now?"

"They think she'll recover." His teeth chattered.

"Oh, God, I'm praying."

"Hey, I'm sorry, kiddo."

"She never did any kind of pills before." He sipped his brandy. "She smoked reefer on a regular basis, and then painted these dark, haunting pictures that made you feel you were descending into the bowels of hell. Of course nobody was buying them. She just started to sink deeper and deeper. This was a suicide attempt, that's what it was, you can't call it anything else, and it's all my fault."

"Why?"

"For neglecting her. I'm always either here or there, doing this or that—" He took a ragged breath. "I'm just a shit. I barely made it to the hospital when the baby was born on opening night. I had to see the curtain go up before I left the theater. What the hell kind of a jerk does something like that?"

"So, a few minutes, wouldn't've mattered." Rosie tossed another log onto the fire. "You got there, didn't you?"

"Yeah, but—hell, I know it's all my fault." He rubbed his aching head. "I'm goin' on almost an entire day on a few hours' sleep. I've done that before, but it never caught up with me like this. I'm exhausted in every way possible." He yawned. The comforting warmth almost knocked him out.

"I'm frying some calamari." Rosie held up the spoon. "You hungry?"

"Why are you cooking at this hour anyway?" Billy asked.

"Calamari don't wait for the dinner hour. The stuff'll be the death of me, but I'll die happy." Rosie rubbed his middle.

"Nah, thanks just the same." He took another sip. "I just want to know how I can stop feeling like rat shit."

"She'll recover, like they said." Rosie's low rumble seemed to comfort him. "And it ain't your fault. You're trying to make a living just like the rest of us. Providing for your family. Why is being a hard worker a mortal sin? She'd rather you be down on skid row, lining up for a tin cup of soup?"

"I don't know what the hell is right anymore. All I know is something is going to kill her." He indulged in another yawn. "Even if I was around all day and night, I couldn't stop her doing what she wants. She wants to smoke reefer, she'll smoke it. Me forbidding her to do something, that will just make her do it more. I'm no dummy. Cracking a whip won't make her obey me. Hell, I wouldn't want her to obey me anyway, like that line in the marriage vows. That sounds like you're marrying a French poodle." He wagged a finger. "Obey! Obey! Sounds like hooey to me."

"Yeah, but that's the church. It's just to make it sanctified, in the eyes of God, ya know. Damned if I'd obey some broad." Rosie snickered. "But hey, if she's one of those broads with a mind of her own, she's gonna use it."

"So how can I get her to stop swallowing pills before she kills herself?" he asked his wise older friend.

"You can't force her, like you said. Suggest it, real subtle-like. Have her talk to somebody who almost kicked over from O.D.'ing on something and will put the fear a God in her. But if that don't work, there's really nothing ya can do, Billy. Sickness and health, richer or poorer, I forget how the rest of it goes."

"She left me, you know," he finally divulged. "Walked out on me."

"Again?" Rosie crossed the room and came back with the brandy bottle and poured some more into Billy's snifter.

"Yeah, but she hasn't been back." He took another sip. It warmed him inside. "Said she couldn't take it anymore. Took the baby and left. After the raid she heard about the syndicate and that was the last straw."

"Hey, I'm sorry. *Madonna mia*." Rosie shook his head, blowing a long breath from between his teeth.

"What started out with us facing the same direction, it's us facing opposite directions. I guess you get different kinds of sights set when you're adults than when you're lovestruck kids, and lovestruck kids is all we ever were. We didn't become adults till after the wedding. Then I took off in my own direction. I still love her like hell, and she loves me, but—" He shook his head, at a loss for what to follow up with.

"Hey, it happens. Thing is, most wives ain' got the balls to leave." Rosie let out a sad laugh. "Or they stay out of spite."

"I want everything the way it was before we got married. We were madly in love, we did everything together. Now we hardly do anything together. I want to come home to my wife and baby and never argue, or defend what I do for a living, just be a happy family." Billy gazed into the dancing flames. "Is that too much to ask?"

"Well—yeah." Rosie stabbed at the logs with a brass poker. "Sounds like a fairy tale."

Billy thought about that for a moment, letting the warmth and the drink comfort him. "So what if I want

317

everything? Since when is that news to somebody who knows me as well as you do?"

"It don't work that way in this world, kiddo." He put the poker down. "Remember, you can have anything you want, but you can't have everything you want."

"Why not?"

"Simple. There's only so much of everything to go around. Houses, cars, clothes, racehorses, happiness, love, all them things, whether money can buy them or not. Not enough for everybody. I think because God wants to keep us humble. So we don't get too greedy, like the devil. Just think, even if you had everything— what the hell would you do with it all anyway?"

Another of Rosie's pearls of wisdom he began to wonder about. He imagined he had everything he'd always wanted—the theater, the orchestra, the catalog of published songs, the hit Broadway shows, the houses, the loving marriage, the happy kids. Hell, he barely had half of all that, and look at how he was handling it.

"You don't think it's possible, having everything you've ever wished for?" Billy asked him.

Rosie shook his head. "No. And it ain't worth trying. The ones who do try, they prob'ly die trying. I ain't never seen nobody who has everything."

"I've been trying." Billy's hands felt comfortably warm now. He sat on the floor and stuck his feet out to warm them.

"Yeah, I seen you in action." Rosie laughed. "Let me give you a hint. Just try for one thing at a time. Your wife moved out, let her stay out. Concentrate on something else for a while, and before you know it, she'll be back."

It didn't sound likely, but it was better than the way he'd been doing things. "Yeah, maybe once she's out of the hospital I'll make sure she's okay, but I won't beg and plead no more."

"There's nothing turns a dame off more than a guy groveling at her feet," Rosie said. "Loses all respect. And we got to damn well command respect. Makes me want to puke, things I learnt the hard way. Another hint: There are two theories for arguing with women, and neither of them work." He ruffled Billy's hair.

"Only two?" They exchanged grins. "You know, you're really smart, Rosie. Always coming up with these words of wisdom."

"That ain't mine, that's Will Rogers."

"I feel like I just gained back more than half my strength from this talk alone." But his other half, still weak and feeble, needed to stay here by a warm fire and be served brandies and told he'd be all right just by following some sage advice. He couldn't imagine his father having this talk with him now, leading him to a fire and giving him a drink, warm clothes and comforting words. The career law enforcer only knew how to keep the peace, not make it. That's why his only son was with Rosie and not with him.

He wouldn't even tell Ma and Da about Pru's being in the hospital. What could they do? Bring her a box of cannolis and say a novena on Sunday?

"Thanks, Rosie. I don't know where I'd be now if you weren't home. I guess I just woulda wandered the streets with my pecker waving in the breeze. I'm"—he stopped as another yawn took over—"a lost soul right now. I don't even want to go back to my folks. They'd just give me one of those lectures where they finish each other's sentences."

"You can always find me, if I ain't home," Rosie said. "You know my usual haunts."

Billy stood to go to the bathroom, and all of a sudden the room spun.

"Whoa!" Rosie caught him just in time before he crashed back to the floor. "Easy does it. You better sit and eat before you keel over." But Billy didn't want to eat, and he didn't want to let go. He just clamped his arms around his dear friend and held tight. He needed to be held up at this moment, physically and emotionally.

"Hold onto me, Rosie, just for a minute," he pleaded, feeling like a little kid, but right now he didn't care. Nobody had to know that the successful, gifted musician/businessman/husband/father needed a strong, warm hug. "Being grown up is just too damn hard sometimes, and that little boy still inside me needs somebody. You're all I got."

"It's all right, kiddo," Rosie whispered, his big hand stroking Billy's back reassuringly, like their prized Path Cutter.

Billy finally pulled free and saw the old boy's eyes glistening. "Hey. Holy Christ, don't get all gushy on me." Something about a man crying in his presence made him squirm, but seeing Rosie show this much emotion downright embarrassed him.

"It ain't often when somebody lets me know I'm worth something in this world. Kinda gets me right here." Rosie made a fist and jabbed it at his heart. "We're supposed to be the tough guys, never show our feelings, like machines. But I say shit on that. I never had a family, Billy. I mean parents or brothers and sisters." He focused on the fire. "My father vamoosed back to Italy right after we got here and never came back. Then my mother died when I was eight or nine, and my aunt took me in. She had seven kids of her own, but somehow managed to take care of me. Fed me, clothed me with my cousins' castoffs because we was poor, but there was no affection. So, you and"—he waved his hand—"them other guys, you're my family. But none of them ever gave me a reason to believe they need me around—like you do. Sorry—just a weak moment..." He turned away.

But he didn't need to finish. Billy nodded in full understanding.

Rosie cleared his throat and turned back to stare him down. "Listen, Billy, don't let what we just talked about go past these four walls. Don't ever tell anybody I showed any feelings or that I shed a single tear." Now he pleaded. "Because I didn't shed a tear. They were in my eyes but never shed. Got it?" His voice returned to the order-giving tone Billy was used to.

"Of course. This was strictly between us. But I'll level with you now—I gotta pee real bad." Billy wandered off down the hall, more surefooted than he thought he'd be.

"Can you find it in the dark?" Rosie called out after him.

"Huh?" He cupped his crotch. "Yeah, course I can."

"Nah, I mean the john!"

****

Interlude: Sunday Dinner at the House

They all asked, first Ma and Da when he walked in

the door, then Tessie in the living room, then Susan in the kitchen: "Where's Pru?"

"She's not feeling good," was all he answered as they took their turns fussing over the baby. No one asked how he was. It seemed they actually respected his privacy. But instead of being thankful for their consideration, it drove him nuts. He found himself busting to tell his parents that his wife left him and it was the damn government's fault; they had to impose these inane laws that went against the very grain of human nature. They had police records now, and it drove Pru over the brink. He had to tell them. But the dinnertime Roosevelt discussion got so intense he had to wait till after they put the baby to sleep in Billy's old crib and sat down to coffee and *cannoli*.

"I meant to tell you, Pru left me. She's in the hospital, but she's okay—" He spoke over his mother's gasp and looked away from his father's accusing glare. "She took some sleeping pills, see, and, well, she's been hanging with these good-for-nothings, these artists on skid row," he rattled on. "She let them move in, they sit around all day and smoke reefer, so they must've got her using that. I think it's the raid that started it all. After the raid, she left me. Then she took these sleeping pills—"

"Good God, Billy, why didn't you tell us sooner?" Da broke in. "She and the baby ought to stay here with us. We'll take care of them."

He should've known his father would pull something like that. But he didn't need his subtle put-downs right now. "She'll be okay. And I'm capable of taking care of my own family, thank you very much." Although he knew damn well the old fella was probably right this time.

"You just got finished saying she left you!" Da's voice rose to near window-rattling volume.

"Tom, shh." His mother butted in, and for once he was thankful. "Where was the baby when all this was going on?" she wanted to know. He explained it all away, how Nurse Pertl took care of the baby, and the rest of the time she stayed at Susan's.

Susan finally rose to his defense. "The baby is just fine. She loves being with her cousins."

"You'd better leave the baby here, for now, anyway," Ma demanded, standing and looking out the window, then coming back to stare him down. "That's no place to bring up a child. Even if the nurse is there."

"Pru says she only smokes when the baby's out with the nurse and never gets gowed up with the kid around." But he knew that wasn't true.

"You want me to go talk to her?" Ma offered, and for half a second it made sense. She was so convincing and persuasive, she'd probably have Pru feasting on kale and carrot juice by the time she was finished. But the effect wouldn't last long. A week, tops. He knew Pru.

"No, just wait till she's better. They said she'll be released in a few days. Then I'll take her back to the beach house, just to get her out of the city."

"What about the baby?" Ma insisted, going back to the window.

"We'll take her with us. We'll have a nice vacation together, the three of us." It sounded like a pipe dream, considering where they currently stood. But still he hoped.

"Where are those loafers now?" Da asked.

Billy was glad he didn't know. "She was letting them stay at the Jane Street place. I threw them out, and they haven't been back since."

"Maybe it's about time you move her out of that place," Da said, and Billy's wheels started turning. If she got released from the hospital and the place was rented to somebody else, she'd have to move in with him! But that went against his principles and everything he'd decided with Rosie; leave her alone to do what she wanted with her own life. To give the apartment away without even telling her smacked of just the thing his father would do. He was ashamed he'd even consider it.

"It's hers, the way the Fifth Avenue place is mine. I can't force her out." He stood his ground.

"What kind of a marriage do you two have? Don't you ever, you know"—Da gestured helplessly with his hands—"get together, and do what married couples...do?" Of course Billy knew his father didn't really expect an answer to that, but for once his old man deserved an explanation, for no other reason than to keep him from judging them.

"I'll tell you what kind of a marriage." Billy sat up straight and threw his shoulders back. "A marriage where we respect each other's space and time and right to lead our lives the way we want. A marriage where we're equals, and she don't have to obey me like a puppy dog. And yes, we do 'get together' probably more than couples who sleep in the same bed every night, and when we do, it's damn earth-shattering!"

"Yeah? Then why doesn't she want to sleep in the same bed with you, Casanova? Or even the same house?" His father's eyes met his and glared.

"What matters is that we love each other, not how

many residences we keep," he shot back.

"A woman's place is with her husband!" his father thundered. "At all times. Taking care of him, and that means in his bed, too. You both belong under one roof together!"

"The hell with that." Billy swept his hand through the air. "I can't stand the smell of reefer."

"And you let her smoke cannabis! You should never let her go anywhere near it again!" Now Da was really off and running. Billy knew he hadn't arrested anybody in ages and was just itching to be a cop again.

Besides, his father was a true product of Victorian times, when wives were their husbands' property. God help any chump who even looked at his mother when Da was around. The creep who'd been courting his mother nearly had his teeth knocked down his throat, so the story went.

"Let her?" He had to laugh at that one. "Da, this is a marriage we're in, not the army. I cannot and will not give my wife orders, 'cause you know what? She'll just turn around and tell me to go screw myself. She left home at fourteen, for Chrissake. She's a free spirit."

"Then I think you married the wrong girl, Charlie." Da gave him a full-face sneer. "Wives are supposed to be dutiful. Love, honor, and obey."

Ma shot him a glare that would've made Teddy Roosevelt's big stick shrivel up.

Da looked at her. "Well—you know what I mean, dear." Maybe during his diatribe, Da had forgotten who he was married to.

"No, I don't...*dear*." Ma leaned forward, nearly plopping herself into her pastries. "Dutiful? So the girl refuses to obey commands. He's her husband, not a prison warden. He's self-sufficient. I raised him to take care of himself."

Da's eyes bugged out. "Like I can't?"

"Do you know how to iron a shirt without burning the house down?" Ma challenged.

Christ in a bottle, what did I start? Billy looked around for Tessie, but she was long gone.

Da puffed out his chest. "Look, Vita—"

"No, you look!" Ma cut him off. "First of all, it's none of your business the way they want to run their marriage. They're adults. Second, you knew damn well from the start I wasn't going to take orders from you. You're telling your son he ought to—"

"Vita, lay off, will ya?" Da turned his back, hands over ears.

Billy slipped out the door before they started throwing dishes and stuff. His mother had a strong arm, and that brass bunny alone could put a respectable dent in a human skull—even one as hard as his father's.

Chapter Twelve

"The majorities in Congress were annoyed by several test votes. They complained that valuable time was being taken up by the extreme wets while the nation was waiting for action on the depression."
—The American Scene, 1932

Billy paced the hospital lobby like an expectant father. He finally saw an orderly walk Pru out. He wanted to melt into a pool of tears when their eyes met. He kissed her and clasped her hands. Nice and warm for a change. "How do you feel?"

"Better than I did when I got here." She gave him a shaky smile.

He gave her a cautious hug, afraid to hold her too tight. It was like hugging a bird. He needed to get her eating again. Oh, no, he was turning into his mother!

"Where do you want to go?" He couldn't insist she go with him to the penthouse and start another feud. "Back to Jane Street or—my place?" He phrased it that way to leave no question about him forcing things.

"Your place would be better. It's warmer."

Thank you! He wanted to shout to the heavens. She was coming home! The baby was with Susan, so they'd be all alone. Maybe, just maybe—he kept his fingers crossed as he helped her into the car he'd bought with Rosie's Phaeton as a trade-in, a gleaming 1926 Diana, named after the moon goddess. The Rolls-Royce lookalike grille was what sold him.

"Is this your car?" was her only comment.

"She sure is. Bought with my own money. I just love her. Her name's Diana. Well, actually, that's the name of the model, but you know how I like to name things." He went around and opened his side.

"Yeah. Always after a gorgeous woman," she said as he slid into the cushy driver's seat.

He checked his mirror. "Well, it's the name of the model, and you know how everybody refers to cars as females, and—"

"It's fine, Snuggles!"

They looked at each other. A surge of love captured him. He leaned over to her. She leaned over to him. They met in the middle and began necking furiously.

They finally came up for air. "Let's go," he panted. "Darb as the car is, I'd rather do it in bed." He listened to the purr of the engine for a few seconds. It was like music.

"You cold?" He ran his free hand up and down her arm.

"No," she replied. "But I'd like a cigarette."

"Cigarette? You don't smoke. Cigarettes, I mean." Somebody let him in and he pulled into the stream of traffic.

"I've decided to quit smoking reefer," she stated with the most conviction he'd ever heard from her. "I'm taking up cigarettes instead."

"Hey, that's great. I'm so relieved!" He fished out a pack from his shirt pocket. "Oh, God, you don't know how happy that makes me. I hope you never take any kind of pills again."

"I'm hoping I'll never need to," she said.

"That mean you'll move back in with me?" He glanced at her profile. "We'll be a couple again?"

"I don't know yet, Billy." She looked down at her hands in her lap. "I did some serious thinking in the hospital, and I know I can't live with you, but I can't live without you, either."

"Well, that sounds like a real solution." His voice dragged, his hopes dashed. "So what are you going to do, cut yourself in halfs?"

"Let's just take one day at a time for now and stop jumping ahead. Right now I want to get clean and healthy."

"But you'll stay with me till you decide what you want?" he pressed on.

"Yes, I'll stay with you." Her tone assured him. "And the baby, too."

"Thank you, Saint Jude!" He drummed on the steering wheel and bopped up and down in the seat. "Let's celebrate. You name a place, anywhere in the world, and we'll go tonight."

"I just want to go to bed." She reached over and tickled his earlobe. "With you."

So he took her home.

****

June 30, 1933, 3:22 a.m., rain

Maybe now after this she'll learn her lesson like I learned mine—well, hell, I never learned mine, but I always lock the truck now—I hope she'll realize how dangerous pills are. But I didn't bust her horns about it, though I could've asked her if that really was Stephen Vincent Benét she went to see that night. Sounded more like Edgar Allan Poe, for Chrissakes. But I didn't give her a hard time. I just want to be a family again. I want her with me where she belongs, away from that dingy dive. I don't have to hide her at the beach house, 'cause I didn't get any more crazy threats, either. Life is almost normal—for me, anyway. I keep busy with the rum syndicate during the day, and play clubs at night. I'm a regular at The Montmartre, where I first started playing way in the beginning, but not every night. My nights off, I'm home with Pru and the baby. It's a dull routine, but I need some dullness after all that drama.

Louie Q saw me at the warehouse and nodded hello. I apologized again for the stolen truck and offered to pay for the pilfered booze, but he waved me away like a fly. I took that as a good sign. He looked preoccupied anyway. Then right before he left, he invited me to a meeting at his place the next night. They were planning to discuss opening another business. I said, yeah, so happy he'd thought enough of me to ask me, I practically skipped out of there. I got flowers and chocolates for Pru, went to Susan's store and bought myself some new clothes. She was too busy to talk, but we hugged nice and warm, and I felt good about everything. "Hey, up there," I said to my guardian angel, or whoever was looking after me, "Nice going. You want to spice it up a little now?" But of course I was only kidding.

****

Now what to tell the recuperating Pru about the meeting at Louie Q's? He didn't want to lie, not after all that had happened. He started by saying he had a "business meeting."

To his surprise, she didn't even question him. "I'll

be all right. I just want to start painting and sculpting again," was her reply. He'd have dashed out and bought her an entire art supply store if she hadn't announced that Franck was coming over with all her supplies from their studio. "He moved out of the studio when he got the commission in Venice. Well, he's back, and is looking for another one. Meanwhile, he's living with his brother."

"Uh—is that a hint that you want him to move in here?" He tried to read her for some clues. But at times she was just plain unreadable. "Because I don't want this place turning into a starving artist's colony, like that Jane Street flophouse."

"Of course not." She went back to her folding; she refused to let the maid touch her laundry. "He and his brother are twins. They get along great. He'll probably stay with him a while."

"Twins?" He whistled. "Jesus, there's two of him? What does the other one do, I'm afraid to ask?"

"He's a pile driver," she answered.

"It figures, it figures."

"He visited me in the hospital and said when I got out he'd come over, cook a gourmet meal, and we'd do some painting." She looked up at him from her pile of undies. "Can you stay for dinner? He's a fabulous cook. Specializes in French cuisine."

"Yeah." He shrugged. "I guess so. The meeting's not till ten tonight."

Franck showed up looking right out of Delmonico's kitchen, floppy chef's hat and all. He didn't bring any other queer birds or twin brothers, just himself, with ingredients for what Billy admitted was a delicious dinner complete with Grand Marnier for the *crêpes suzette*. He also brought all Pru's art supplies in a rented truck. It took them three trips to get the stuff inside.

He trotted off to his business meeting with a full stomach, a clear conscience, and a wife safe from sexual harm.

At Louie's place, a bevy of butlers, doormen, footmen, and the majordomo greeted Billy in Italian and English. The butler relieved him of his hat and coat and led him down the corridor to the boardroom. The goombahs sat around the table gabbing, chomping cigars, and drinking wine. Louie himself greeted Billy and showed him to a seat next to Rosie.

"How is she?" were the first words out of Rosie's mouth.

"She's swell. Got released yesterday. She came back to my place with me. Said she's turning a new leaf. Not even smoking reefer anymore. I'm hoping." Billy crossed his fingers.

Rosie gave him a big smile. "See, I told you so."

"I got the baby from Susan's and brought her over, too. It's the first time in I forget how long we're a family again." A waiter served Billy a glass of red wine.

"Good for you, kid." Rosie nodded.

"I'm hoping she'll stay now. God, I hope." Billy clasped his hands together. "*Salut*." He raised the glass and imbibed.

"I knew you'd land on your feet." Rosie pinched his cheek, and it didn't even bother him, in front of all these old fellas.

The meeting didn't last all that long, considering what they'd accomplished, besides polishing off a few dozen bottles of Santa Anastasia Nero d'Avola. A parade of waiters brought in about a hundred pounds of *bruschetta, aglio olio*, and the piles of shellfish must've depleted the whole eastern seaboard. He wasn't hungry after Franck's *coq au vin*, but he ate anyway. Once he started eating, it didn't matter so much that he wasn't hungry; it just tasted so damn good. Even the fried tentacles.

They'd decided on a venture Billy didn't mind dipping his toes into—offshore gambling boats. Congress's impending repeal of Prohibition by year's end numbered the lucrative bootlegging days. What was the next biggest human vice, after sex and booze? Gambling, of course. Prostitution was still taboo. When someone brought it up, Louie actually got up to turn the Blessed Mother statue around. "Our Madonna can't hear none of this," he muttered as he sat back down and poured himself another shot of bootleg Scotch.

Although he wasn't a gambler, the whole concept of odds and probability excited and amazed Billy. But what unsettled him was the barbaric effect it had on human behavior. A smug grin spread his lips. He'd never get hooked on that lowbrow sport. It had one redeeming quality: there were no drugs involved.

Even Pru couldn't disapprove of this.

****

He rushed home to his wife and baby. Leaving his engine running, he slipped the doorman a ten-spot. "Just park it someplace safe. Thanks, pal."

He whistled all the way up in the elevator and did his usual routine of closing the door softly so as not to disturb them. He peeked in on the baby first. She wasn't there. Maybe Pru had her in their bedroom. He tiptoed down the hall to their room and looked in. "Pru?" Silence. He flipped on the light. No sign of her or the baby. She wasn't here.

He went back into the living room and flipped all the lights on, looking for a note. She wasn't one to leave notes, though. "Oh, no, what now?" As if to answer him, the phone rang, and he swept it up.

"Yeah?"

It was Susan. "It's about time you got home. Pru and the baby are here. I insisted they come over here when she told me what happened."

"What? What happened?" His voice rose to an alarmed shriek. His heart pumped.

"Some guy terrorized her. I don't want to talk about it over the phone. Just get over here."

"Are they all right?" rushed out in a breathless plea.

"She's fine, the baby's fine. But something happened that scared the hell out of her. Not knowing how to contact you"—she paused for effect—"she came here, and you should be here, too."

"I'll be right over." He didn't even hang the phone up. All he wanted to do was hold his wife and child in his arms—and tie somebody's nuts around his neck.

A maid let him in. The baby was asleep, but Pru sat in Susan's lounge munching cookies. Red rims hung under her eyes like two overfried eggs in a greasy pan. Susan and Irv hovered over her like eagles protecting their nest.

"I'm here now, everything's fine." He held her close, but she stiffened up. So she wasn't too keen to return the warm embrace. He couldn't blame her. "What the hell happened? Somebody threatened you?

What did he look like? I'll find him and tear him a new one." His fists and his teeth clenched.

"Don't you dare, Billy." She gave him a narrow-eyed glare. "Not after all that's happened. Don't you ever learn?"

"Nobody messes with my wife! Nobody, God dammit!" He struck the papered wall.

"Shhh!" Susan put her finger to her lips. "Have your tantrum during daylight hours, will you?"

"Aah, Chrissake." He threw his hands up and paced around the color-coordinated room. He halted before Pru. "Will you please tell me what happened? What he said this time?"

"If you stay calm." She nibbled on her cookie.

"I will," he promised.

Susan placed a drink in his hand. He took a sip. Neat whiskey. He needed that.

"This shabby-looking guy started following me when I ran errands. I didn't think much of it at first, then after he followed me to the third store in a row, and followed me to your apartment building, I told the doorman. But by then he was gone, so the doorman never saw him. Then when I let myself in, somebody phoned up, and—" She took a breath and let out a sob.

"What? Phoned up and what?" he probed, wanting to shake it out of her.

"He told me—" She could barely speak between sobs. "He told me you were dead, and to identify your body at the morgue before they put you in a wooden kimono and buried you."

"Son of a bitch." He looked at Susan and Irv. They stood there nodding, their faces long and ashen.

"I tried to dial the phone, but I was shaking too

much," Pru went on. "I don't even remember who I was trying to dial, it might've been Susan or the police, I don't remember. So I ran down and told the doorman. He called the police. They said they didn't have any reports of any murders of anybody of your description, but I kept screaming to take me to the morgue. They did, and you weren't there—" She broke down again. He dropped to his knees and clasped her hands.

"No, I'm alive and well, see? It was a prank, that's all—just a sick joke. I'm not in any kind of danger, none at all." He tried to convince her, but he couldn't blame her if she never believed another word out of his mouth.

"I don't remember how I got here, either." Her voice shook. "I think the cops brought me here."

"That's right, a cop car brought her," Susan verified. "Billy, you'd better get some police protection. Lord knows you pay them enough already."

"Yeah—I'll see what I can do." But police protection was out. Those lunkheads were as useful as tits on a bull. He'd have to hire an army of brick shithouse bodyguards. "We'll be all right, Honey Bear, I promise."

He sensed her mixed emotions as she sat there, quieted down now, staring at the flowered rug. She probably wanted to wring his neck for getting her into all this but at the same time wanted to jump for joy to see him alive and not stiff on a slab.

The widow's weeds flashed through his mind.

Then the scene in the Hackensack meadows.

Fighting the usual rise of bile to his throat, he shivered, then swallowed a generous mouthful of his whiskey. "Hey, what did he look like?"

"I—I don't—" She shook her head, obviously not wanting to talk about it.

"Pru, it's very important," he pressed her. "I might know who this creep is."

"Well—" She hiccuped a few times. "He was big, and with a stocky build, ruddy complexion, Irish-looking. Dressed shabby. That's all I remember. He didn't come that close."

That was close enough. "Let's get some rest. We'll talk more in the morning. Come on. All right if we stay here?" he asked Susan. She nodded, gesturing up the stairs.

This was even worse than the truck heist. He had a hunch the two incidents were connected. Somebody had it in for him, all right. But who? He never pissed anybody off. He didn't have one enemy in all of New York. He was the nicest damn fella anybody could meet, a real sweetie pie. He racked his brain into the night, sitting at a silent piano as his family slept upstairs, thinking of every single soul he knew. Who could possibly loathe him this much?

****

A few blocks away, Tom McGlory slept tight, knowing a diligent cop was keeping an eye on his son. The cop must be doing his job, because Billy hadn't gotten into any scrapes in a few weeks, a record for him.

****

The next day Billy felt like he'd hit a grand slam home run. He convinced Pru to get rid of the Jane Street dump. She agreed to live with him permanently if he sold the Fifth Avenue penthouse and moved them to the other side of town. For a bonus, he had two corns removed from his left foot.

They went looking at exclusive residences, this time on the West Side. She didn't want a penthouse, just a nice roomy brownstone. That was dandy with him, as long as the windows had bars on them.

He'd also begun poking around record labels. He wanted to get the music to his show recorded. Cutting a few records would be fun, too.

****

Their new residence, on West 71st Street between Central Park West and Columbus, had more rooms than he knew what to do with, three stories, with servants' quarters on the top floor, a garage, and a private roof garden where he planned to sunbathe naked and maybe get Irv to plant some flowers. Pru fell in love with the place and had all this art deco furniture delivered—a world of difference from the Italian provincial museum pieces he'd grown up with. And not a plastic slipcover in sight!

The first thing that went in that house, even before the furniture, was "Bright Eyes," right over the mantel.

On moving day, he used the truck to haul their other stuff, and he went on a delivery with a new kid they were breaking in. When Billy drove past the Automat, he realized he was starving. So he asked the kid, barely sixteen, to look after the truck while he double parked and ran in to grab them a couple sandwiches. His mouth watered for a hunk of their cheesecake, too.

Sticking his hand into his pocket to get some change, he ran in and looked over the choices. It couldn't have been two minutes later when he came back out. The truck was gone.

"Now where the hell did that runt go?" He wasn't bothered; maybe the kid got hassled by a cop and had to drive around the block. He'd been double-parked, after all. He didn't even think about cops anymore. Something about that ride to Jersey turned his balls to stone, and he feared nothing these days. After literally staring death in the decomposed face, he could handle any shamus cop.

He stood there on Sixth Avenue holding two sandwiches and a hunk of cheesecake. Five minutes later, still no truck. Now teetering between being worried and pissed off, he went back into the Automat, sat down, wolfed down his sandwich—and the kid's— and devoured his cheesecake. He even took another minute for a cup of joe and a cigarette.

He'd grown up, all right. Shit didn't scare him anymore. Still turned his stomach, but didn't scare him.

Cynical as he was, he didn't suspect foul play this time.

But if something was wrong, for once he wished he *could* call the cops, like a normal law-abiding citizen.

He let out a whoosh of relief when he saw the truck nosing down the street. He ran up to it and jumped in on the driver's side as the kid slid over.

"What happened?" He pulled the door shut.

"Cop told me to move on, we was double-parked," the kid said.

Something made him ask, "What did he look like?"

"I dunno. Big ugly-lookin' dope. Called me 'sonny boy.' Hell, nobody called me that since pre-one-A."

Sonny boy, huh? The penny dropped. Nobody called him "sonny boy" since pre-one-A either. Except Sidney Cunningham.

He finally did it: hired two bodyguards for Pru. He described Sidney Cunningham and instructed them to shoot first and ask questions later if he or anybody suspicious started following her. He brought his family to the beach house on weekends. He put burglar bars on all forty-six of those windows.

He also kept an eye out for Sidney Cunningham's mug, and packed his piece at all times. It had to be him terrorizing Pru—no two people were that ugly. That ass-wipe was messing with the wrong guy. And after he spared the pig's life. Nobody appreciated nothing no more.

****

Sid Cunningham appreciated the well-paying job of tailing the wayward Billy McGlory, but it bored the hell out of him. He wanted to get back out on the street, busting people. He decided to relocate to another part of the country, where nobody knew him, and he'd have his true talents put to good use.

But first he wanted to finish off the snot-nosed punk who'd lost him his job and got him into this mess in the first place.

Chapter Thirteen

"Mrs. Sallie Glasgow, sixty-two years old, who stood trial for selling one pint of liquor and four quarts of beer. Convicted...Mrs. P. Ridley, seventy-two years old, who confessed she had sold a quart of blackberry wine...Clyde Cox, eleven years old, who pleaded guilty to selling liquor. His father had run a barbecue stand, and Clyde made the deliveries...Such absurd trials go on daily throughout the country with preliminary hearings being conducted even on Sunday in New York in futile efforts to clear up congested calendars."

—*Outlook*

Louie Q's eighty-year-old grandmother backswung the champagne bottle and smashed it against the yacht's stern. "I christen thee *Mala Femmina! Saluti per cent'anni!*"

They all cheered.

The first of their fleet was officially in business.

Billy had been on one boat in his life—the Staten Island Ferry. So when he strode up the gangway to the *Mala Femmina* and looked around, he thought he'd boarded a floating Buckingham Palace. He walked through the restaurant, the theater, the bar with dance floor, and and the casino lined with rows of one-armed bandits, roulette wheels, and craps tables.

"I can't believe I'm on a boat," he said to Rosie

and Louie as they strolled toward the stage of the two-hundred-seat theater. He sat at the Steinway concert grand and played a few scales. Of course it was perfectly tuned.

"It ain't exactly a boat, Billy, it's a yacht," Louie corrected him, and Billy nodded his appreciation. "You wanna see your stateroom?"

"I have my own stateroom here?" All this and rooms too?

"Yeah, we all do. You can't gamble all the time, you know." Louie nudged Billy, but he was still too filled with wonder to guess what Louie was nudging about.

"Got the keys, Lou?" Rosie asked. Louie fished a keyring out of his pocket and handed it to Billy.

"Cabin Seven. If you need anything more in there, just let one of the cabin crew know. I hope the bed's big enough." He gave Billy a wry smirk.

"Uh—yeah, it should be. I don't need a lot of room to sleep."

"That's not why you get a big bed, my boy." Louie patted his cheek.

It finally registered. "Oh. Yeah, I'm kinda slow sometimes." So, the boat—oops—yacht—was for that, too.

Louie pointed him in the direction of the cabin deck and left him alone.

His 'stateroom' was every bit as classy as the Waldorf. Panelled walls, a sitting area with a leather couch and recliner, a tiled bathroom with a tub and shower. He glanced out the porthole at New York Harbor and saw Lady Liberty in the distance. "God bless America," he said out loud.

He helped himself to a whiskey from his fully stocked bar. "Eat your heart out, Bugsy," he gloated, as he sat and propped his feet up on his new coffee table.

****

Billy came home to a blaring victrola. Even with the windows wide open, it smelled like an opium den.

Pru bustled around serving sandwiches in their new living room, waiting on the same deadbeats he'd turfed out of the Jane Street dump. This time he stumbled over more of them. They didn't even acknowledge his presence. One of them lay stretched out on the floor in nothing but shorts and sunglasses, like he was sunbathing on Duke Kahanamoku Beach.

"What in the name of Jesus Roosevelt Christ goes on here?" He swiped the arm off the record with a sharp *zzzip* of the needle.

"Oh, hi, Snuggles." Pru looked surprised to see him. "We're having a picnic."

"In the middle of our living room?" He gestured at the mess.

"Well, the park's full of ants. Want to join us?" She handed a full plate to a floozy in a strappy nightgown.

"No, I sure as hell don't." He stomped up to her and clutched her elbow, causing the last plate of sandwiches to slide to the floor. The freeloaders dived around and began to gobble them up. "Look at them. Like a herd of piranhas." He couldn't watch the pathetic sight. He saw enough of it on the street. He didn't want to witness it in his own house. He turned back to Pru. "I thought you weren't hanging with these have-nots anymore," he hissed.

"I never said that," she stage-whispered.

"You said you wouldn't let them in here." He didn't give a damn how loud his voice got.

"Times are tough, Billy." Her sharp glare matched her scolding tone. "They have no place else to go."

"Why don't you invite every other bum in Manhattan to move in here?" he shouted.

"I would, if you didn't hide all your mob money from me." She set her fists on her hips.

"Shhh!" He stamped his foot. "For Christ's sakes, keep it down, will ya?"

"What are you worried about? You have all that protection. And a bodyguard." She peered over his shoulder. His bruiser was out in the car.

"I thought you quit reefer." He grabbed her elbow again.

"I haven't been smoking reefer." She jerked his hand away.

"Then why are your eyes glazed over and you're talking like your head is stuck in some cloud on Mount Olympus?" He waved away the sickly sweet stench of smoke. "You can't be squiffed."

"Nothing." She shook her head and began cackling hysterically. Then she started singing "I Got Rhythm" as she two-stepped back into the kitchen.

He turned and saw one of the deadbeats coming down the stairs, wrapped in a towel like he just got out of the bath. What were they, permanent residents now?

"Pru, I'm not finished!" Of course she ignored him. He decided against storming in there after her. She was obviously fried to the hat. What was the sense of screaming and yelling? Besides, he couldn't stick around; he had a delivery to make and a meeting with a record label executive. He'd only come home for lunch, but he wasn't hungry anymore.

He slammed out of there, with no one the wiser that he'd even been there.

But something dawned on him as he stepped out into the street: that's why she'd wanted a place with three floors and a self-contained flat on the top. Those damn scroungers *were* living there!

****

He had to celebrate, and would have done so with his wife, if things were different. But after crashing her deadbeat party, he didn't even want to be with her. So he called Greta, asked her to meet him at the Plaza for dinner, and, unable to contain the good news, spilled it all out. He'd gotten an offer from RCA to record the songs from *Headin' for Better Times* with the original cast. The recording companies were finally recovering and looking to sign new artists.

He got to the Plaza a little late; he'd spent extra time grooming himself and getting a shave and a haircut. He figured he had time for a manicure, too. "Billy! Over here!" Already settled at a cozy candlelit table for two, she looked stunning. Her hair was a new shade of blonde, shiny and wavy. It looked better on her than it did on Garbo. Diamonds glittered at her ears, throat, and wrists, but even without them she'd have dazzled. The red lipstick just begged to be kissed off. "Hiya, Sheik," she drawled softly, like the idling engine of a Duesenberg. It got his blood flowing to long-dormant places.

"Hey, Greta, long time no see." They exchanged appropriate cheek pecks, and he sat across from her. A waiter handed him a leather menu and the wine list and vanished.

"Congratulations!" She shook her platinum curls. "I'm going to buy a hundred of your albums and paper the walls with them!"

"Yeah, that's a lollapalooza, ain't it?" He gave her a wide grin. "It's a brand new studio, too. I can't wait to get in there and learn all about recording."

After exhausting the music topic, she asked about Pru. He didn't even want to tell her what he'd walked in on that day. "She's fine," was all he said.

"If you want to talk about anything, I'm here." She reached over to touch his hand.

Billy figured she knew something was on the rocks when he called her to celebrate instead of his wife.

But the subject died a prompt death, and she told him about her recent breakup with Louie Q.

"So what happened?" he asked after they ordered.

"I found him in bed with another man. Not just any bed." She jabbed a finger at her chest. "My bed. I don't mind what he does on his own time, but this was *my* bed. Enough to turn your stomach, huh? Sorry to bring it up right before dinner."

"That's okay, I've seen worse." He sipped from his crystal water goblet.

"So I'm a free woman again, Sheik." Those long lashes fluttered a bit more than protocol dictated, and her baby blues raked him up and down. Protocol be damned.

"Uh—not for long. I mean—I'm sure you'll meet the right fella. You're gorgeous, talented—" He didn't want to overdo it and slide into flirting territory. "You've got everything going for ya."

"So do you," she returned with a heart-melting smile. "I'm sorry about you and Pru."

"You don't look too sorry to me," he tossed back, with a cocky grin.

"What do you want me to say, Billy? I've known the both of you for years. I love you both dearly. But let's face it." She grew serious. The smile vanished. "There is something between us. Let's stop pretending."

"Well, uh—" It wasn't easy, but he broke eye contact. Where was that damn waiter? "Look, Greta, not at a table in the Plaza, okay?"

"If you're truly beyond reconciliation, do you think we can make a go of it?" she pushed on. Her soft diamond-ringed hand clamped onto his, her red nails gleaming in the candlelight. Not too forward, but just enough to make him respond in kind. So he turned his palm up and clasped back.

"We're not beyond reconciliation yet," he spoke the truth. "We just got that new brownstone, she's living there with me, we're together."

"No, you're not. You're here, and she's—" She waved her hands around. "Wherever she is."

At this point, he didn't know where Pru was, and finally admitted he didn't exactly care. All he cared about was that the baby was safely at Susan's for the weekend. "It looks like she's using reefer again, or who knows what else, with those vagrant hopheads. She's got them permanently installed at our new place now, on the third floor. Getting mail and milk delivered there and everything. Now I know why she passed up that house on Washington Place. Eight rooms weren't enough for her growing entourage of bums."

"Did you talk to her about it?" she asked him.

"I couldn't talk to her about anything." He didn't

hide his disgust. "She was too busy doing her Ethel Merman imitation."

"Oh, dear." Greta let out a low hum.

"I still love her, but I'm at the end of my rope, and that's that." Billy cut the air with his hand.

"Billy…will you come home with me tonight?" Her voice caressed his ears. She really cut to the chase. Didn't even offer to talk to Pru, like last time. She must figure it was beyond repair, too, so move in for the kill while the going was good. "For all intents and purposes, you *are* separated."

He took a deep breath, then another, till he realized he was almost panting. And aroused. "No. No, Greta. Separated or not, no matter how bad things are, I'm still married to her. Please. No more about this. Let's just change the subject." The waiter's arrival was a relief, but he had butterflies, and the tension between them thickened when she fed him oysters, one by one.

Intimate and sensual as it was, he assured himself: *I'm not cheating.*

****

On the ride back to the brownstone that night, he fantasized about what it would be like to sleep with Greta. He saw no harm in making the fantasy last until he walked up the steps. Pru was there, all right, sprawled on the sofa, hopped up out of her mind. None of the other deadbeats were in sight.

"What the hell's the matter with you?" He leaned over and shook her, a little too hard, but so what? Her eyes opened, glassy and unfocused. He didn't even know if she could see him. A goofball smile was pasted to her lips. "Hey, you in there?"

All he got in response was a giggle as she turned

her head away from him. Rejecting him. Mocking him.

"All right, be a gong-kicker, but—" Wait a minute. He smelled no trace of reefer smoke, saw no goof-butts in the ashtray, not even an ashtray in sight. So what the hell was she using? More of those sleeping pills that landed her in the hospital? Panic squeezed him. He grabbed her purse, determined to find the stash and flush it into the sewage system where it belonged. But what he saw on the floor made him halt dead in his tracks. He stared, unblinking, unthinking—for how long, he didn't know. There, at his feet, was a hypodermic syringe.

"Oh, no." Finally, the moment he'd dreaded had dared to happen, the beginning of the road to hell. His wife was a heroin addict.

"I'll get help. I'll get her into one of those hospitals," he muttered. "Then I'll find out who's selling her this junk and blow their sorry brains out." He talked all the way to the *Mala Femmina,* where he spent the night in his new stateroom.

****

The next morning he got up, at the time he usually went to bed, and went straight to Louie Q's.

When the butler showed him into the morning room, Louie sat reading the *Daily Mirror,* a half-filled glass and bottle of Scotch next to him. Their own label. "Hey, kid, look who made Winchell's column."

"Who?" Distracted, Billy had other things on his mind. He helped himself to the bar.

"You!"

"Huh? Where?" He dashed over to the open newspaper and fell to his knees. His eyes swept over the column till they halted at his name. He read aloud,

"'Billy McGlory, better known as William Amadeus McGlory, signed a contract with RCA Records,' blah, blah, blah. Wow." Six months ago he would've done cartwheels over a mention by Walter Winchell. Now it fetched a nod and a half-smile.

"Hey, kid, I'm cutting this out and putting it on the wall there, right when you walk in. You're a big shot now." Louie reached over and gave Billy's cheek the traditional pinch and pat.

Billy stood and took a gulp of Scotch, forgetting it was straight. They sure manufactured good stuff, but it was a little rough on an empty stomach. "Uh—Louie, I got a problem, and I need to address it. A personal problem. With my wife. I need to take care of her for a while. I need to devote all my time to her."

"What?" Louie asked. "She sick or somethin'?"

"I would say so, yes. She's a heroin addict, and I need to get her off it."

Louie shook his head and lit a cigar, offering Billy one. He declined. "Too bad. Gets the best of 'em sometimes. Can be worse than booze."

"It *is* worse than booze." Did this bootlegger need to be told that?

"You want to put her in Bellevue?" Louie asked. "I can get her in there."

"No. Not yet. I want to see if I can take care of her first. Take her to the beach house with the baby and just get her mind off it. She took all those sleeping pills, you know. She won't admit it, but I think she tried to commit suicide. Maybe without even realizing it."

Louie puffed away for what seemed like a long time, flipping newspaper pages. "Yeah," he finally said. "Do what you gotta do."

"Thanks. I'll take a few days to wrap things up, so I won't leave you in the lurch. Then I'll get back to you when things are better, and pick up where I left off." He sighed in relief.

"You won't play the clubs no more neither?" Louie asked.

"I—just can't right now, Louie." He held his hands up. "I have to save my wife first."

"I don't know whether to be pissed at you or proud of you." Louie gave him a crooked smile.

"Why can't you be both?" Billy asked. "Like my father."

"You want me to be like your father?"

Billy flinched as if poked from behind. "Christ, no!"

Louie gave Billy a spank on the bottom with the folded-up newspaper. "Next time you come in here, this column'll be hanging in my foy-a there."

"Yeah, thanks." He nodded, but right now having his name in the paper or up on the wall wasn't important. Neither was his new recording contract. He didn't even feel like a musician at the moment—he only felt like a husband who had a wife to save.

****

"Pru, we have to talk. Now."

She looked up from her sculpture. It was a winged angel. Really beautiful, he had to admit.

Yup, her down-and-outer chums were official residents, all right. She finally admitted it.

"Why the hell couldn't you have told me? I know there's a Depression going on. I'm not a coldhearted rock, cruel enough to deny a bunch of starving artistes a roof over their heads. Sometimes you have to freeload.

I guess." He shrugged and lit a cigarette. "There but for the grace of God goes I, or however it goes."

"I'm sorry, Snuggles. I thought you'd object." She went up to him and nibbled his earlobe.

"Never mind that." He didn't let her impulsive act of affection get to him. "We have something more important to talk about. You doing heroin."

"Oh, it's no big deal." Her mocking tone irked him as she placed her fists on her hips. "Just like your famous last words when I came to you all those times, worried sick you'd get your guts splattered on the sidewalk or get fished out of the Hudson River in a net like a tuna. I do this for recreation. Along with my friends. We share our hopes and dreams. More than I've been sharing with you lately."

"Can't argue with you there." He turned away, unable to look her in the eye, but couldn't have seen her eyes if he wanted to, through her blue glasses. "Why do you have to do drugs?" he badgered her. "Why can't you just drink, like everybody else?"

"Getting gowed up is fun, and getting drunk isn't," she answered as if he should've known that simple fact.

"That's fun? Lying here in cloud kookoo land?" He waved at the couch. "Getting hauled to the hospital on the brink of death? That's fun?" He did a good imitation of his father with the bellowing.

"Well, that went wrong." She gave him a lazy smile that spread into a smirk. "Like you never made a mistake. Listen to Mr. Perfect here. He never makes mistakes! Hah!" She put a Bing Crosby record on the victrola and started dancing. For the love of Pete, she was losing it.

"Look, I didn't say I'm perfect. But I don't do

Goddamn heroin. Where are you getting this junk from anyway?" He grabbed her arm and tried to pull her back down to earth.

"Oh, no. I'm not telling you." She wriggled out of his grasp. "You'll get them busted."

"Busted?" He clenched his fists and seethed. "I'll murder the bastards!"

"Then you think I'm gonna tell you?" She twirled around the room like a hopped-up ballerina.

"I'll find out," he vowed to her and himself. "And when I do, God help them."

She giggled and went back to her sculpting.

"Okay, ignore me." He walked out—out of the sumptuous brownstone where he now had a gang of junkies sucking off him.

"I'll be back, and I want this place cleaned up," he called over his shoulder, wondering if he should hire a detective or find out himself.

****

Officer Sid Cunningham sat in McGill's, a gin mill at the edge of Hell's Kitchen. Two unemployed teamsters, Benito Iannini and Dario Tizzoli, sat across from him. He called them Stan and Ollie, because Benito was tall and skinny and Dario was fat and had a brush moustache. "This is what I want you to do…"

They eagerly awaited their assignment and the ten simoleons apiece they'd get for it.

"You want us to take him out now?" Stan held his sweaty palm out, fingers wiggling, waiting for Sid to slap the tenspot into it.

"Nah, give him another week to live." He sneered into his beer. "I can be all heart too."

****

Billy heard a siren and glanced in his sideview mirror. No, they weren't after him this time. It didn't matter anyway; the truck was nearly empty. He had one final delivery to make, to Maison Felix on West 75th Street. Then he'd start handing his duties over to the underlings.

He didn't expect this to take long—a week, two weeks, tops, to get Pru back to her straitlaced ways. Bellevue was a last resort. God forbid.

Eureka—a parking space right in front of the joint! He locked the truck and went in.

In their car half a block away, Stan and Ollie waited. "Look at these rich bastards' houses!" Stan gawked at the elegant brownstones and their scrubbed porches. "How come there ain't no bread lines up here?"

"You just said it. They're rich bastards," Ollie muttered. "Just keep an eye out for that McGlory punk."

With traffic blocking their view, they couldn't see who was coming in or out of Maison Felix. They saw the back of McGlory's parked truck, though, and knew he was still inside.

They waited and waited. They got fidgety. The sun sank and the street grew dark.

"I could use some moonshine." Stan licked his dry lips.

"Yeah, me too," Ollie agreed. They broke open a bottle of whiskey and passed it back and forth.

"Still see the truck?" Ollie asked.

"Yeah." Stan got out and peered up the street. "Barely. It ain't moved yet."

"What's he doin' in there?" Ollie groused. "Is that

joint a speak or a friggin' whorehouse?"

****

While Stan and Ollie waited to do their job on Billy, he sat inside playing the piano for the early evening group.

Sid Cunningham headed for his favorite speak, Tony Mazza's across the street. He spotted the familiar license plate on the truck in front of the fancy Maison Felix. He rubbed his hands together—*hey, maybe the truck's full again this time*. That was damn good hooch from the last hijacking, and he'd made out like a bandit selling what he didn't drink. He glanced around to make sure the coast was clear, schlumfed down the street, and broke into the truck. He flipped the magneto switch, then got back out and cranked the handle till the engine turned over.

"Damn! He's goin'!" The whiskey bottle was a dead soldier now, empty. Stan and Ollie, half squiffed, almost forgot what they were supposed to be doing there.

"Then follow him, palooka!" Stan gave Ollie's arm a shove.

Sid made a right on Second Avenue and got on the Queensboro Bridge. Stan and Ollie, thinking they were tailing Billy McGlory, followed a respectable distance behind.

When Sid started heading south, Stan and Ollie knew just where he was going—Brownsville-East New York, an area notorious for nurturing hoodlums, like Al Capone. It was convenient for the overland liquor routes from Long Island and the barge landings in Jamaica Bay. The hijackers and smugglers loved it.

When Sid reached the deserted parking lot of the

warehouse where the Brownsville mob stored their contraband, he caught sight of headlights in the sideview mirror. Who's those assholes following me? he thought as a sharp crack shattered the cab's side window. "What the…"

A second later, another shot splattered his brains all over the inside of the cab.

"Good job, Jackson! You got him." Stan tumbled out of the car and ran up to the truck's cab. "Oh, no! Holy mother of Christ!"

"What?" Ollie rushed up to the horrific scene.

Stan stood, too shaken to speak. He pointed a trembling finger at the figure slumped over the wheel.

"Huh?" Ollie peered into the cab. "Oh, no."

****

After playing another set and nursing a smooth Scotch on the rocks, Billy asked the owner, his "cousin" he called him, as their mothers had the same maiden name, for some help unloading the truck.

"Where's it parked, Billy?"

"Right in front." They went out the door. "Right…" He looked up and down the street, trying to remember where he'd parked it. "I coulda swore I got a spot right in front of the place." An old flivver was now parked where the truck had been. "Oh, no, not again—" He took a deep breath through clenched teeth. "That bald-headed prick," he muttered.

This time he'd keep his mouth shut and just replace the truck. It had been registered to him, so in effect it was his truck, but he just didn't want anybody to know it'd been swiped. After the last fiasco, nobody would believe he'd actually locked it.

Meanwhile, he took Susan up on her invitation to

stay there for a day or so and spend some time with the baby before taking her and Pru to the beach house. It would be nice to have some home cooking for a change, before babysitting Pru full-time.

****

He dumped his overnight bag on Susan's spare bed while he gave her the explanation due her. "Pru's doing heroin, Susan."

"Oh, dear God. No." Her manicured hand went to her heart.

"I all but quit my job—jobs—for the time being, so I can spend all my time with her. I just need a day or so to myself, and I think she does, too." He pulled a few shirts from his bag. "Can you get your laundress to iron these?"

"Of course. Oh, Billy, that's wonderful, I'm so proud of you! I knew you'd do the right thing in the end." She went over and gave him a sister-love hug.

"Don't say 'in the end' like that." His voice carried a note of fear and doom.

"I didn't mean it that way. You know what I meant." Her hands fluttered around her diamond necklace.

"Yeah, now you sound like me, always saying the wrong words." He laughed, trying to lighten the moment.

"God forbid!" She looked up to heaven.

Brother and sister shared another warm embrace. "Oh, it's great to have you here, Billy. The kids'll love having you here. And I'm so glad you decided to take care of Pru yourself. You're true blue!"

"Don't throw rosebuds at my feet yet." He sat on the bed. "I don't know exactly how I'm going to do this. First I want to get a doctor up there to lecture her, or some nuns from the church, or another hophead who almost died—well, first I'll find the lugs pushing the junk on her and put a contract out on them."

"Oh, Billy, no." She sat next to him. "Now you're talking like one of those gangsters. I won't have my brother talking that way."

"I don't mean take them out personally." He waved his hands around. "I'm above that."

"You're not above anything if you're even considering murder. Billy, you're scaring me." Her body tensed.

"Don't be ascared." He turned around to unpack his toiletry bag. He took out his toothbrush, cologne, shaving soap and brush, flask, and a part of his past—his mechanical clown bank, with a hand in front that took a coin and popped it into the mouth. He'd never used the silly-looking thing to save money, just to watch it go through the motions. He always broke into it afterwards and spent the pennies.

"You've still got that?" Susan marveled as he lifted the bank by its pointed hat and placed it on the nightstand.

"'Course I still got it." He turned it to face the bed. "It's a collector's item."

"At least you graduated from the wind-up ducky on the string." She gave him a poke in the side.

"That's still at Ma's."

"Pushing thirty and still playing with your toys." She tousled his hair.

"I'm married to a woman who prefers heroin to me." His voice dragged. "What would you suggest I play with?"

****

He asked around, at the clubs he played at, the favorite mob hangouts, the neighborhood gin mills: Who supplies heroin to individuals, not the rich or famous, just plain folk who happen to have the money to pay for it?

He got one lead after another, which led him to a source on the Upper East Side. When he found out who his wife's dealer was, he turned around and lost his dinner.

****

Susan opened the door to a surprise—her father stood there, looking like he hadn't slept.

"Da! Come in!" They hugged, and he stepped inside.

"Is Billy here?" Da glanced around the entry hall.

"Yeah, he's—" Susan extended her hand.

"Upstairs?" Da pointed up the carpeted staircase.

"Taking a nap," she said. "He's in the guest room. The baby's asleep in Rachael's room, so try not to wake her."

Without another word, he took the steps two at a time with his long legs and barged in on the snoring Billy, sprawled out in only his shorts, on top of the chenille bedspread.

He watched his sleeping child for a moment, remembering what it was like to hold him as a baby, how close they'd been as he grew up. I did my very best as a parent, he thought. So what the hell happened? *Please God*, he prayed silently, *watch over this kid and don't let him be another New York statistic*. As the ex-Chief of Police he could only do so much.

He finally leaned over and shook his son by the

shoulder.

"Huh? I ain't in the mood, Pru," Billy mumbled, not fully awake.

"Wake up, Billy."

He opened one eye and, seeing his father's imposing figure, sat straight up. "What's the matter? Something happen to somebody?"

"No." Da sat at the edge of the bed. "But I found something out, Billy."

"What?" He still couldn't think straight. "What time is it?" A peek through the curtains told him it was daytime.

"I'm going to ask you one simple question, and I want you to think long and hard about whether to tell me the truth or not." His father drew out the words like he always did when he wanted them to sink in.

"Ask away." He looked away from Da's steady, accusing gaze, grabbed his flask and took a nip.

"Sidney Cunningham of the New York Police Department was killed, gunned down, found dead in a truck in Brownsville. The truck was registered to Virgilio McGlory." His father's eyes bored into him.

"What?" It was hard to take in all at once. "How'd you find that out?"

"Frankie Munn Jr. told me."

"So that's where the truck wound up," he mumbled. He saw a slight pleading in his father's eyes now, behind the rage. "No," he answered his wordless question. "I didn't kill him. I figured he was the one terrorizing Pru, but I didn't kill him. I'm no murderer."

"Did you hire a hit man?" Da continued his line of questioning.

"Of course not!"

"I hope to God you're telling me the truth, Billy." Da leaned over, their arms touching.

"Da, this is the God's honest truth—I was in Maison Felix till—" He blinked and rubbed his eyes. "Hell, it hadda be nine o'clock when I stopped playing, and then me and Vince Caputo came out and found the truck gone."

"That alibi better be airtight, son. And you'd better have a lot of witnesses to back it up. Because if you're found guilty of murdering a police officer in the line of duty, your life is over," he recited in his city-cop voice.

"No, I didn't—I wouldn't have killed the bastard!" Christ almighty, was somebody else trying to set him up now?

"Good thing your mother hasn't heard any of this." Da looked away. His gaze landed on the clown bank. A smile cut through the grave stony-face.

"Yeah. Damn good thing." Billy took another swig from his flask. "And I'm surprised at you, Da— thinking I'd kill a cop. Even a cheap shamus like him."

"With this life you've gotten yourself into, I don't even know you any more, Billy." Da's eyes fixed on him again.

"You never did." Billy stayed focused on his father.

"I tried my best, Billy, tried my damndest to raise my only son the best way I could. But you went in a direction nobody wants their kid to go in. This is the last thing I'd wish for you." He shook his finger. "I'd rather see you begging on skid row than mixed up with the rackets. Can you blame me for jumping to that conclusion when I heard this? Especially since the truck's registered to you? That can't do your sterling reputation much good."

"Yeah, so, it's one of my trucks." Billy pretended it didn't scare the crap out of him. "That don't put me at the scene of the crime. Hell, I've never been to Brownsville in my life."

"I want to believe you. God knows I want to." He brought Billy to him in a sudden embrace. After a moment they pulled apart.

"Well?" Billy insisted. "Do you or don't you?" They sat face to face, eye to eye, unmoving, unblinking.

Finally Da took a slow breath. "Yes, Billy, I believe you. I also believe in you. I'd hate myself forever if I didn't." He closed his eyes and lowered his head. For the first time, Billy could see his father was aging. His hair had grayed. There were creases around his eyes he'd never noticed before.

"Good. Because I'm innocent. And when they question me, I'll prove it," Billy declared, praying if there was ever a shred of justice in the world, it would serve him now.

"Oh, Christ, Billy." Da shook his lowered head. "I did something I shouldn't have done."

"What?"

"I asked Frankie Munn Jr. to put a cop on a special detail, just keeping an eye on you, to make sure you didn't get into trouble." Da now looked at the ceiling and let out a ragged breath.

"Keep an eye on me?" Billy's eyes widened. "And it turned out to be Cunningham?"

"Munn told me he knew a cop who'd just been relegated to a desk job, who could keep an eye on you," Da said.

"Yeah? Well, you know what? Remember I came

to dinner with all those bandages? He's the one who beat me up." He jerked his thumb in the direction of outside. "He was a rotten, no-good, stinking, corrupt shamus. Tried to…" He didn't want to go into that whole story. "Tried to steal some money from the back of my car when he pulled me over. Some of the boys found out and roughed him up a little." No sense going into gory detail. "Then somebody started making my life a living hell. Stole my truck. Kept terrorizing Pru. Called her and told her I was dead and go to the morgue and I.D. me on a slab. Just real sick gags like that. I had a hunch it was him. So I hired some bodyguards."

Da shook his head. "I feel terrible, Billy. I'd hired him to look out for you. How was I supposed to know he'd caused you all that trouble? Oh, Jesus. That never would have happened if it wasn't for my interfering. I'm so sorry," he wailed. "Parents make mistakes, too, you know. I was only looking after your welfare, son."

"Da, when are you going to realize I'm grown up now, and I can take care of myself? For Christ's sakes already!" Billy blew out a long breath, shaking his head side to side.

"You're my son, Billy. Somebody has to look after you!"

"Somebody is," he answered.

"Who?" Da's eyes bored into his.

"This is going to sound like Tessie now, but I believe an angel's looking after me. If they weren't, I'd have been dead and long gone by now. Don't scoff at it, say I'm off my nut—it's just something I believe. It's called faith."

"An angel." Da looked past Billy out the window. "How can any son of mine believe that applesauce?"

"I'm half Ma's, too," Billy reminded him. "Maybe I get it from her side."

"Yeah, the Italians." Da rolled his eyes. "With their evil eye and their exorcisms and their saints."

"Hey, it must be working. Like I said, I'm still here." Billy took another nip from his flask. "It might be a saint, even. Maybe Anthony. Ma always conjured him up when I was a kid. Maybe he stuck around."

A long silence followed. Billy finally lit the cigarette he was dying for. "You don't have to worry about me, Da. You don't have to hire any more cops or watchdogs or pull my nuts out of the fire. When our joint was raided, I thought it'd be nice to get sprung, but I didn't, and it all worked out. When was the last time I asked for your help anyway?" He took a drag. "When I was about sixteen? All the trouble I've gotten in, I've gotten myself out of it. You need to start realizing that Susan's not the only one in the family with a brain." He blew out a stream of smoke.

"I'm sorry about all this, Billy." Da's voice sounded defeated. "Sorry I ever got that cop involved in your life. I feel responsible for his death, and that's something I have to live with, too. Can you forgive me?"

"Yeah, sure." He couldn't fault his father. Maybe five years ago he would have. But that was before he became a parent. And an adult.

"Thank you, son." He put his hand on Billy's shoulder like the Bishop at Confirmation. "They'll be calling you in for questioning, because, after all, it was your vehicle. You'll need an attorney present."

"Why do I need a lawyer if I'm innocent?"

"Everybody who's questioned in connection with a

homicide, innocent or not, needs a lawyer present. You want me to call you one?" he offered.

Billy said, "Nah, I'll get one of the—some of the people I know are lawyers."

"Oh." He nodded. "Yeah, of course."

"This'll be straightened out, and to tell you the truth, I'm not worried about it. I've got other things on my mind." He took another drag of his cig.

"I'd ask what they are, but after this incident, I realize I've got to butt out. But, listen—you come to me first, anything you need, you hear? Sometimes the fire's just too hot to pull your own nuts out." He tugged on Billy's ear.

After his father left, Billy lay back down on the bed, smoking his cigarette. Somebody whacked that Cunningham lug after he stole the truck. But who?

Whoever it was, Billy owed him one. "Here's to you, whoever you are, pal. *Salut.*" He poured himself a long one and took his first leisurely sip of the day.

****

He was called in for questioning, all right. But not the kind of questioning he expected.

The law tracked him down later that day at Susan's house. Thank God nobody but the nanny was home. He went down to the 20th Precinct in the back of a police car, trying to forget his last ride downtown in a police car.

This time he was politely escorted into an interrogation room, offered coffee and cigarettes, and didn't get his pockets emptied or his head bashed in or his ribs cracked.

All he got was a second-rate good cop/bad cop routine.

"Think you're pretty slick, hah, McGlory, blowin' poor Officer Cunningham away?" Bad Cop started in on him.

"Come on, Larry, there's no evidence," Good Cop countered.

"Nah. Just his truck with Cunningham's corpse slumped over the wheel."

"That ain't evidence," Good Cop insisted.

Billy *tsk*'d at these amateurish hijinks, blew out swooshing breaths and played with the ash on his cigarette. He felt like saying, "May I be dismissed now?" and leaving them to it. Seems it was their amusement for the week.

"The word on the street is that you did it, McGlory." Bad Cop addressed him.

"Thanks for remembering I'm in the room, Officer whoever-you-are. But you know what? I don't give a tinker's damn what 'the word on the street' is. You think I care what you jokers think? I had nothing to do with this latest brains-and-guts-splattering homicide on the streets paved with gold. I have a roomful of witnesses that'll come down here and vouch for me. The bum was hijacking my truck—again."

Bad Cop shook his head, but Good Cop just looked at Billy with respect and awe on his face. "Well, with no evidence linking you to the crime, we can't charge you with anything."

"Then I'll see myself out, if it's all right with you and the rest of New York's Finest." He stubbed his cigarette out on the floor even though there was an ashtray on the table, and stood up to leave. He put on his hat.

"Thank you for coming in," Good Cop said as

Billy got up to leave.

"Sure. And, uh—you can keep the truck."

****

He let a day go by for it to sink in. Then he went up to Park Avenue South unannounced.

Louie Q greeted Billy in boxing trunks and gloves. "C'mon in." He waved Billy past the butler and led him into the gym. A recently beat punching bag swung from a meathook. "Wanna have a go at the bag, give it the ol' one-two?" he offered, taking his gloves off and heading for the bar next to a treadmill.

"Nah, I've seen enough one-twos for a lifetime."

"So, ready to get back to business now?" Louie patted his cheek.

"Not yet. Listen, I need to—"

"By the way, kid, attaboy! You're learnin'!" He thrust a glass of whiskey into Billy's hand.

"What?" He blinked.

"Good job, givin' Sid Cunningham the business. The *strunz* deserved what he got, and then some. So, why'd you change your mind and take him out?" Louie's grin could've spanned the East River.

"Oh—oh! That! Uh—" He scrambled for a believable story. "He was up my ass, terrorizing Pru, stealing my truck. I just reached the end of my rope, and you know me, I got a long rope."

Louie beamed at him with the same awe and admiration the 'good cop' had. Billy enjoyed taking the credit; it was the best way to get respect from these thugs and show what kind of brass his balls were made of.

"I always knew you had it in you, Billy." He held up his glass and clinked it against Billy's.

"Yeah. Well, now that I've earned this new-found respect, I'd like you to do me one simple favor."

"What's that?"

Billy took a long pull of his whiskey. "Please tell your goons to stop selling heroin to my wife."

He looked at Billy like he'd sprouted a third eye. Like nobody ever asked him a favor before. "You tellin' me what to do?"

No, you half-witted hothead! Billy wanted to bellow. Why did they always get so touchy once they got to run things?

"Hah? Who works for who here?" Louie took a step closer, and Billy backed away. Even without boxing gloves, this guy could probably flatten him with one hand.

"No, I ain't telling you, I'm asking you. Real nice. I even said please. I respectfully request that you request of your associates to stop selling heroin to my wife. It's for her, not me," Billy explained in the politest voice he could fake, since he itched to blow this crud's brains out.

"Listen, *cazzone*. I don't take no requests from nobody or nobody's wife or nobody else. Much less a punk like you. Hear it?" He gave Billy a shove. But that he could handle. "Besides, I don't know who the hell they sell it to."

Billy counted to five, too furious to count to ten— or even five and a half. "I'm not trying to breach protocol here or go against the code or whatever. This is my wife I'm talking about. The mother of my child. She's a heroin addict, and it's killing her. Our marriage is just as good as over, but she's still the love of my life. Just ask them to stop, will you? That's all."

Louie shook his head and scratched his bristly chin. "Let me explain something to you. And I ain't gonna explain it again. This is a business, see? I don't personally go to nobody's door and hand them drugs. And because it's a business, I don't give a shit who gets hurt, or who drops dead, 'cause if they're stupid enough to do dope, they deserve whatever they get. So don't go pissin' in my ears. Now all I want to see of you is your ass goin' out that door." He jabbed a finger into Billy's chest before turning his back and fitting his gloves back on.

Billy headed for the door. "Well, thanks for nothing, Louie. I'm sorry I took up your time."

"Putz," he muttered on the way out, and at this point he didn't care who heard it.

But Louie heard it. "He lets his wife go out and get hooked on the worst dope in the world. Who's the putz?" He snickered and went back to his punching bag.

Chapter Fourteen

"Three ruffians arrested in Philadelphia for threatened assault and battery told the police that the underworld had adopted a sort of blanket code. Under the code, $25 is fixed as the standard price for swinging a sandbag against a head marked for assault, $15 for wielding a blackjack, and $5 for a slap on the jaw. Payment must be made in cash, and must be handed over as soon as the client's victim lands in the hospital."

—Literary Digest, November 4, 1933

Billy moved his family to the beach house the next day and took them for a long stroll at low tide. Then they went to a nice restaurant for dinner, came home, and listened to the radio.

Not the kind of life he would have chosen, cozy as it was, but it was only temporary. As much as he itched to get back to the city, the crowded clubs and the breakneck pace of the business, he loved his family more, so he stayed put.

Pru sat facing the ocean and started a new painting, a masterpiece in the making—the horizon at sunrise, the promise of a beautiful day, and many more to come. He was thrilled to see her painting like that again.

"It's heavenly, Honey Bear." He couldn't remember the last time he'd called her that.

"Can I sculpt you again?" She turned to him, and how could he refuse a smile like that?

"Uh—yeah, sure, of course. But in another pose, maybe?" He picked up a plate and used it as a discus as he took an Olympic stance.

"No, not that. Lying on your side."

"With clothes on?" He hoped.

"No chance, Billy. Nudes are the best. Especially with a model like you." Her voice lowered to a purr.

"Come 'ere." He took her in his arms.

With the baby sleeping upstairs, he brought her outside, and they made love in the moonlight.

She never mentioned drugs, and he began to think she didn't need any doctors or nuns after all.

The next day, he helped Pru hang curtains, and after dinner they played with the baby.

The day after that, they went shopping for silverware, and after dinner they played with the baby.

By the third day, he was pacing the floor like a caged lion. She sat happily painting a portrait of Big Ben from memory, and the sun was shining, even in London.

"Billy, why don't you go for a drive or something?"

"You sure you'll be all right here?" He inched toward the door.

"Of course." She swept a bright yellow streak over the canvas with her brush.

"You sure?" He had to be sure.

"Billy, I'm not a child! Go, get some fresh air. Take the car out." She waved her free hand.

He'd just bought a new Stutz touring car, the safest-built car around, for the benefit of his family. But it was great to cruise around in. "See ya later, alligator!" He couldn't have left that house faster if it was on fire. "Just one set in The Montmartre, just one, then I'll come straight home..." He swore it up and down as he leapt into the Stutz and tore ass to Manhattan like a kid on his way to a candy shop.

His appearance at The Montmartre, even after only a four-night absence, drove the crowd wild. It felt so good to be back here, if only for one night, he savored every second, not knowing when he'd be back.

Rosie invited Billy to stay at his place so he wouldn't have to drive home at three a.m., but he insisted, "Nope, I said I'd be back home, and that's where I'm going. I only said I was going for a drive anyway." He thought it'd be nice to borrow Rosie's driver, collapse in the back seat of his Stutz, and enjoy the chauffeured ride back to the shore.

But Rosie's driver was off that night, giving Billy another idea. "Come home with me, then," he returned the invitation as they sipped some of their smooth Canadian hooch. "You've never even seen my beach house. We can have a game of cards, a few drinks. You're welcome to stay over. We have four bedrooms. Or is it five?"

"You sure it won't disturb Pru?" Caution crept into his tone. "I know how she feels about your play pals."

"Nah, she's probably dead to the world by now." He handed over his car keys. "Here. You never rode a real lady till you rode a Stutz."

Rosie, who loved to drive fancy cars, eagerly took the keys, and they headed out.

It all happened in a blur after he got home at four a.m. and saw her sprawled out on the living room floor.

"Pru, my God!" He rushed up to her and shook her, frantic for a response. "Pru, speak to me!"

"You got smelling salts, Billy?" Rosie knelt over her, smoothed her hair back, cradled her head lovingly, like she was his own child. He pulled the afghan from the couch and tucked it around her. The sight made Billy burst into tears. He backed off and stumbled up the stairs.

After checking on the peacefully sleeping Victoria, he rifled through all the medicine cabinets, Pru's bureau drawers, her nightstand. "No, nothin'!"

He came back down to Rosie checking her pulse. "Get me a cold damp rag."

Billy soaked a towel he found in the kitchen and almost broke his leg getting back to them.

Rosie took the towel and wiped Pru's brow. "The baby okay?"

"Yeah."

"She's breathing, but her pulse is weak," Rosie reported. "We gotta get her to the hospital, pronto. Where's the blower?"

As calmly as if he were ordering dinner, Rosie phoned the police to get directions to the hospital.

"Shouldn't we get an ambulance?" Billy's voice quivered as he dropped to his knees and clutched Pru's arm.

"Take too long. I got directions. I'll take her. You stay here with the kid."

Billy prayed between sobs as they carried her out to the car. "Everything will be just fine." Rosie's voice eerily soothed Billy as they laid her down on the back seat and covered her. "It's all right, baby doll, you'll get through this."

As Rosie took off in his Stutz with his wife, Billy ran back inside to the only other person he loved more than life itself.

He sat with Victoria cradled in his arms, rocking back and forth, till the phone rang. Like last time, he didn't remember getting to the hospital or who got him there. But he later found out that Rosie was a better babysitter than Nurse Pertl ever was.

****

It was daylight by then. I only remember a nurse or a doctor, somebody in white, telling me something about a heroin overdose, and me rushing up to her bed and nobody stopping me. She was connected to all kinds of tubes, barely recognizable.

"Pru! Honey Bear! What happened?" I grasped her hand, with a needle stuck into it, adhered to her with a bandage, attached to a long tube. Her hand was like ice. I squeezed. She didn't respond.

"Pru, you know how much I love you. Please— don't let these drugs mess you up. You have to quit. Not for me, for the baby." She was now a blur through my tears. "We'll go someplace far away and start another life together, if you'll just get better. Please!" I begged, tears streaming down my face.

Her lids fluttered and my heart jumped. "Pru! You're awake! Pru, it's me, Honey Bear!"

"Snuggles," she whispered, her dry lips barely moving. I came closer. She opened her eyes halfway and tried to focus.

"Yes, it's me, I'm here, Honey Bear, I'm here." I squeezed her hand again, and ran my other hand over her arm, trying to warm it. "I love you, Honey Bear."

"I—lo—love you—t—"

"Don't talk, you don't have to talk. Save your strength. Save it for when you get out of here."

"The—baby—"

"She's fine."

"Make sure—Vicky—"

"Honey, don't talk—"

"—takes care of—"

"Please, honey, save your strength—"

"—care of you."

Make sure *she* **takes care of** *me? She meant the other way around. "I'm taking very good care of Vicky, honey. She's home right now with Rosie's driver."*

"No, Snuggles—when you get—get old, she—has to take care of you." Her voice faded till I could barely hear her.

"Oh, come on, we'll get old together. Don't talk like that." I smoothed her hair back from her face. "I can't wait to play with your hair again." But her eyes closed. "You want to go to sleep? I won't talk anymore. I'll just sit here right by the bed."

"N—no, Billy, I have to go," she whispered, and I lowered my ear to her lips to hear.

"Go? You're not going nowhere. Just back home with me, when you get better, and you can finish your painting…"

"I have to go, Billy. It's my time…"

"No, Pru. Don't talk like that." My heart started hammering. I removed my sweaty palms from her arm. "Please. I love you, Pru. You're my whole life." I struggled to keep my voice even as I sobbed. "Don't leave me!" That was an order—the only one I'd ever given her. I turned my head so she couldn't see me bawling and swiping at my tears.

"That painting—with the sunshine and the flowers—"

"Bright Eyes! It's still on the wall over the mantel. It's the most beautiful one you've ever painted." Keep her talking, I thought; keep her mind off all this talk of leaving and it being her time. *"I'm bringing it to the beach house as soon as I leave here."*

"That's where I'm going," she whispered.

"Where? Into the painting?" I brought my hand back to cover hers. It felt even colder, if that was possible.

"I'm going there, Snuggles." This time her voice was near normal. It wasn't a whisper anymore. It was happy, with a trace of strength.

"Pru, don't die, you hear me? I need you!"

She let out a long sigh, and for the first time in months a genuine smile formed on her lips. A look of contentment, of peace like I'd never seen before softened her face.

I stared at her for a long time.

"Honey, Bear, I love you." I sobbed openly.

A nurse came into the room, checked her pulse, then wordlessly walked away. A doctor stood at her side.

"She's gone, Mr. McGlory. I'm sorry."

I stayed on my knees, shaking my head, then lowered my lips to hers. I kissed my Honey Bear one last time.

****

He had to sign forms and releases and make arrangements, but mercifully it all went by in a blur and he didn't remember any of it. He just remembered a doctor with sympathetic eyes telling him what a shame it was, yes, a terrible shame that Mrs. McGlory had been three months pregnant when she died.

Billy felt like dying right beside them.

Chapter Fifteen

"The average suicide rate for the previous thirty years had been 17.8 per 100,000 people. That rate rose to 20.5 in 1931, with a total of 20,000 suicides for the year.

—The Spectator

The Twenty-First Amendment put an end to Prohibition.

The *Mala Femmina* was in drydock for repairs and closed to the public, so Billy had her all to himself. He boarded her, stood at the bow, and looked out over the river, into the vast blackness and the lights from Jersey in the distance.

He went down to his stateroom, poured himself a Scotch, and unlocked the safe containing his journal. Taking it and the drink with him, he entered the empty casino. It seemed eerie without the jangling bells and rings and dings, the calling out of numbers and thick cigarette smoke, the energy, the sweat. This was the first time he'd seen it closed at night. Yet it was oddly peaceful, like it welcomed a rest. Where were all the gamblers now? Indulging in other vices, or doing some good in the world?

He entered the empty theater, turned up half the house lights, and took a seat in the back. He got out his journal and started to write.

Summer of 1934, I don't know the date. Who cares?

I have that same feeling of abandonment here in the Mala Femmina*'s theater as I just did in the casino. Of course it'll end some day. I still have my dreams: get that orchestra formed, do some recording, and keep writing songs. Too bad it can't end when I'm ready, not when someone else pulls the plug. But that's lunacy— once you're in this business, you relinquish your free will. Looking around, I'm still astonished how much I've accumulated in such a short time. Hell, I'm not even thirty yet. This is all mine—the boats, the casinos, the staterooms, the theaters, all of it. But you know what? I really don't give a damn, because I lost the only thing that mattered to me in my whole life.*

An ear-splitting explosion ripped through the silence. He jumped out of his seat and shot out the door to the starboard deck. Looking down the pier, he saw a brilliant burst of colors light up the night sky—and another boom, followed by another, then another. "Ah, jeez, it's the Fourth of July!"

Without another thought, he swept off his cap and saluted the American flag fluttering from the mast in the gentle breeze. At that moment, he had to pay his respects to those who had come before him, so he could be born here and have a better life than they did. With his hand over his heart, he sang the only song that brought tears to his eyes: "America the Beautiful."

Craning his neck, he saw her: Lady Liberty, arm held high, bearing that torch beside the golden door. He pictured his mother leaning over the ship's railing and seeing that statue for the first time. He knew how they'd suffered so they could be free. So he, his children, and his children's children could be free.

But he was not free. He was the property of the organization. And those soulless bastards had killed his wife and unborn child. The organization, who elevated cold revenge to an art form.

It would be cold enough for him.

"This is payback time, Honey Bear," he vowed.

Chapter Sixteen

"When the Eighteenth Amendment was passed I earnestly hoped that it would be generally supported by public opinion...

That this has not been the result, but rather that drinking generally has increased; that the speakeasy has replaced the saloon, not only unit for unit, but probably twofold if not threefold; that a vast army of lawbreakers has been recruited and financed on a colossal scale; that many of our best citizens...have open and unabashed disregard for the Eighteenth Amendment; that crime has increased to an unprecedented degree—I have slowly and reluctantly come to believe..."

—*John D. Rockefeller, Jr., 1932*

"We'd knock off some older bosses and they'd promote younger, more vigorous men. They kept growing richer and stronger."

—*the FBI, on the Mafia's smuggling of heroin*

"Hey, Chickalazoo," Billy asked one of Louie Q's deputies, "you think you can get the boss out to the *Mala Femmina* for a surprise birthday party next Saturday night?"

"Yeah. Whose birthday?" he asked.

"His." Billy curled his lips.

"Hey, how'd you know it was his birt'day?" Chickalazoo asked.

"I have ways of finding things out." Billy displayed his craftiest smile.

"Yeah." The deputy nodded. "I bet he don't even know it's his birthday."

"So then he'll be twice as surprised." Billy winked.

****

Not a day later, Rosie phoned up.

"Hey kiddo, I know you well enough to ask this. Why didn't I get an invite to the party you're throwing Louie?"

"Because it's a surprise party, and to be honest, you're such a *chiacchierone* you'd blab it to him. I was gonna tell you. I wouldn't leave you out. Look—just meet me on the pier Saturday night at eight-fifteen sharp." He hung up and got busy.

The party would start at eight. But he didn't want his only friend in the world anywhere near that yacht when the party started.

****

Explosives were easy enough to get. He went to his buddy Vincenzo who blew up old buildings for a living. Vinny didn't ask any questions, just got Billy what he wanted. Even delivered them to the *Mala Femmina*, so all Billy had to do was set a clock. He set it for nine, an hour into the party. The guests would be half squiffed by then, but they wouldn't know what hit them anyway.

****

He went out to the *Mala Femmina* in the speedboat to greet the birthday boy and his guests—the bigwigs and their thugs. No women had been invited; he'd told the lugs there'd be wads of strippers on board, so leave the wives and molls home. He'd planned every detail with painstaking precision: the captain had orders to anchor the *Mala Femmina* in New York Harbor and vamoose in the life raft. Four of their other gambling boats lay anchored nearby, with fireworks aboard, waiting to mark the special occasion.

"I'll be back. I'm going to my cabin to shave and shower," were Billy's last words to his boss. But he couldn't help adding, "Hey," as he looked at Louie, "Happy birthday. And many more."

"How'd you know?" Louie cupped Billy's cheek with the same hand holding a cigar. "*Madonne*, was I surprised!"

"You ain't seen nothin' yet," he muttered as his guests made their way inside. Then he turned and slipped back into the speedboat. He got to the pier at 8:15, as Rosie's Lincoln pulled up. "Is Louie out there yet?" Rosie asked as the driver opened the door for him to step out.

"Yup." Billy stood facing the *Mala Femmina*, taking a drag on a cigarette.

"Was he surprised?"

"Hell, yeah." Billy blew out a stream of smoke.

"Well, we goin' aboard or not?" Rosie gestured at the speedboat.

"Nope. We're taking a stroll to Battery Park," Billy told him.

"What for?" Rosie screwed up his face, baffled.

"You'll see when we get there."

****

Billy and Rosie sat on a bench in Battery Park, waiting. As Billy ate a hot dog, Rosie stared out into the harbor with his binoculars. It wouldn't be long now.

Billy finished eating and took a slug of beer. "What time is it?"

Rosie glanced at his watch. "Almost ten to."

Billy bought another hot dog from the vendor, sat back down, and took another slurp of his beer.

"Hey, you hear Capone's in the slammer?" Rosie asked idly as Billy bit into his second hot dog

"No, I can't imagine whatever for. Yuk, yuk." He chomped away.

"Tax evasion."

Billy halted in mid-chew. "You're joshing."

Rosie shook his head. "Shame. He threw the best parties."

Billy had no comment for that one.

At one minute to nine, Billy started counting off the seconds.

The explosion made the Statue of Liberty's teeth rattle.

"It's all over," Rosie commented, like he was talking about the bottom of the ninth in a Yankees game. "You want to see it close up?" He held his binoculars out to Billy. "Better view than any horse race I ever seen."

"Nah. They're all in hell now anyway." He didn't bother looking up, just heaved a satisfied sigh and finished his hot dog. "Let's get outta here. I'm meeting Greta at her place. I'll drop you off first."

He went home to shower and change, but when he got there he poured himself a glass of good strong legal whiskey first. He held the glass up to the world outside. "This is only the beginning."

Epilogue

"I say to you, that from this date on, the Eighteenth Amendment is doomed!"

—Franklin D. Roosevelt,
Democratic National Convention, 1932

To my grandkids, and if you're reading this, I hope I'm already dead.

I'm bequeathing this journal to you, to read after I'm dead. It's in the will I drew up when I was twenty-five and starting to accumulate some serious wealth. As you know by now, I also had other reasons for making up a will at twenty-five.

I might rip this part up when I get old enough to realize my days are numbered. But it makes for good gossip, and if the family ever gets famous enough to make history books, then it'll become one of those legends.

Well, I pulled it off. Cleaned them all out. They're rotting in hell, and this city will be a better place for it. I hope Pru's smiling down on me from up there. She hated those thugs and what they were doing. Don't worry, Pru, they're going in the opposite direction from where you are; they're sweating where it's real hot.

Sometimes, when I walk down that street or hear a certain song, my eyes tear up. Not so much out of sadness but nostalgia, when I remember the good times, the booze, the money, the cars. Yeah, I really did get used to that life, lethal as it was. But I've seen the evils of all I thought was harmless—just business. It's not just business. You can do business and not be a criminal.

Now I'm free. I can do anything I want—anything. Not everything. I'm too old—and sensible—to go after everything. I'm still young enough to tour. And young enough to have a few more kids. Forgive me, Pru, but I need to get my life back.

After the boat blew up, I settled in Bronxville, close enough for the Sunday visits home but far enough from my former life that it didn't haunt me whenever I went to fetch the paper or the milk bottles.

My daughter Vicky was with me, and since I didn't exactly have a regular job, I was able to spend a lot of time with her. She did have a nanny, though—Miss Benson, Susan's former nanny, now that her kids were old enough to walk themselves to the park and ballet lessons.

I had to leave Vicky with Susan occasionally when I went on the road with my makeshift band. I still hadn't completely formed the William Amadeus McGlory Orchestra. I couldn't find musicians good enough to pay full-time salaries and trust they'd stick with me for the duration. So the band had a high turnover, but we did fulfill that Carnegie Hall dream of mine, as well as concert halls all over the U.S. and a few Europe dates. I cut records for RCA and did some radio. I was still playing in clubs at night, and indulging all my vices. Except one.

I hadn't looked at another woman since the day Pru died. I didn't even look at Greta that way, and I'd looked at her that way plenty when Pru was alive. But now that she was gone, it just didn't seem right. I felt her watching over me with those sad eyes, reflecting on her pitifully short life, and I couldn't bring myself to make a move on any woman.

So Greta saved me the trouble. She waited a respectable year, to the day, after Pru's death, and showed up at my door. Nothing dramatic like being naked under a mink coat. She just came over with a copy of her latest book—she'd penned a rather intimate sentiment to me on the title page—and we mosied over to the couch with our cocktails.

The conversation went the usual way: politics, music, industry gossip. Then she asked the loaded question:

"Billy, have you thought of dating again?"

"Greta, I haven't looked at a woman since…you know."

"You're looking at me." She stated the obvious.

I turned my head away fast.

"Listen to me," she said. "I think you know what I'm trying to say here."

I cracked a smile. "It's nice of you to wait the protocol year."

"I've been waiting fifteen years, Billy."

She had me there. "Huh?"

"We've known each other long enough I can tell you this. I've been crazy about you since that first dance in the school basement when we were what, thirteen? It's only gotten more intense the older we got. But of course I couldn't do anything about it—you were going with Pru, she was my best friend, and I had to live my own life—but I never gave up hope. Working

together on the show intensified it—cooped up together, watching you sleep on the couch, the intimacy of creating together—but I think it was the song that did it."

"What song?"

"Our song. 'Yes, I Can.' The one we wrote together. Something magic happened that night, something I'll never be able to explain. It was like that song was part of both of us, waiting for us to come together and put it to words."

I sighed at the memory. "Yeah, that hit us like lightning, didn't it?"

"And by opening night, I was madly in love." She paused for a heartfelt sigh. "I never actually wished you and Pru would split up or anything, but I always knew if you did, I'd want to be there for you. So here I am."

This whole revelation stunned me. I knew we'd always had a warm, affectionate thing going, and she'd let her guard down that night at the beach house. I was falling in love with her back then, but this was a ton of bricks smacking me in the face.

"I just don't know what to say, Greta." All I could do was stammer and shrug and tug on my chin and get up to pour another drink. She followed me. When I turned around, there she was. We fell into each other's arms, and I became hers.

We got married in the Maryland wilderness on our way to start a new life in Miami Beach. Our first daughter, Theresa, was born nine months later. I want to grow old with Greta, have a few more kids and see them grow up. Pru's paintings and sculptures went into storage for Vicky. Except the "Billy" statue. That I gave to Les Fontaine. He wept tears of joy, and now it's a fixture on top of his piano.

I thought I wanted a change of scenery, to get out of New York. But after two years, I couldn't take any more of Florida's heat and humidity and bugs, so we moved back. With the Depression over, it wasn't so depressing, and we settled in Westchester with Theresa, our new son Thomas, and my daughter Vicky, who looks just like me, but that's where the similarity ends. We're as opposite as yes and no.

So there it is. I'm going to do my damndest to make sure nobody sees this till long after I'm dead. I only wish I could be there in forty, fifty years when you read this and can say your grandpappy was a real hero. The newspaper clippings merely speculate. But here it is, from the horse's mouth—well, pen. I did it, kids! I wiped the thugs out—took 'em out and blew 'em to kingdom come!

By the way, that hit-and-run driver who put me in a body cast—two days later, they found out it was a little old lady who'd knocked back one too many after a Bingo game and went for a spin in her Nash. She also accidentally hit somebody else that night, but he wasn't so lucky. He was Ralphie Russo, from the family who ran Staten Island. So all that paranoia was over nothing. "They" never came after me. I guess "they" never found out it was me who blew the yacht to smithereens, the dumb shits.

I'm starting a new journal now, but it won't be anywhere near as interesting as this. I'm leading a clean life, and who the hell wants to read about that? But do me a small favor—whoever reads this journal: it wouldn't hurt to make the rounds of the publishers with this and give them a shot at it. Hell, it might even be better if you tell them it's a novel, but they probably won't believe you. Who could make this stuff up?

Bibliography

Books:
Altman, Richard, *The Making of a Musical*
Blumenthal, Ralph, *The Stork Club*
Furia, Philip, *Poets of Tin Pan Alley*
Galbraith, John Kenneth, *The Great Crash of '29*
Green, Harvey, *The Uncertainty of Everyday Life*
Homberger, Eric, *The Historical Atlas of New York City*
Lester and Kerr, *Historic Costume*
McCutcheon, Marc, *Everyday Life from Prohibition through World War II*
Mitgang, Herbert, *Once Upon a Time in New York*
Morris, Lloyd, *Incredible New York, High Life and Low Life*
Novak, Elaine and Deborah, *Staging Musical Theatre*
Peacock, John, *Fashion Sourcebook*
Time Life, *This Fabulous Century, 1930-1940*
Walker, Stanley, *The Night Club Era*
Watson, T.H., *The Hungry Years*
Websites:
www.civil/auc.dk/lupo97/Newyork.htm
www.crimelibrary.com/hoover
www.ettnet.se/twin/whoswho/ny.htm
www.harcourtcollege/com/history/ayers/chapter24/chapter24.html
www.history.ohio-state.edu/projects/prohibition/laguardi.htm
www.history.ohio-state.edu/...cts/prohibition/whyProhibition/htm
www.history.ohio-state.edu/projects/prohibition/student.htm
www.hoboes.com/html/Politics/Prohibition/Notes/Illusi

on/html
www.home.eznet/net/dminor/NYNY1931.html
www.laborers.org/Digest_11-86.html
www.mcwilliams.com/books/aint/402.html
www.retroactive.com/vices/guinan.html

A word about the author...

Diana has written several historicals set in England and the U.S., a vampire romance, and two time travel romances.

Diana is a member of Romance Writers of America, the Richard III Society, and the Aaron Burr Association. In her spare time, she golfs, plays piano, bicycles, hikes, and devours books of any genre. She's been pursuing a master's degree in archaeology and loves to visit historical sites all over the world. Diana and her husband own CostPro, Inc., an engineering business based in Cambridge.

Visit Diana at:

http://www.dianarubino.com,

www.dianarubinoauthor.blogspot.com,

https://www.facebook.com/DianaRubinoAuthor,

and follow her on Twitter @DianaLRubino

Thank you for purchasing
this publication of The Wild Rose Press, Inc.

If you enjoyed the story, we would appreciate your
letting others know by leaving a review.

For other wonderful stories,
please visit our on-line bookstore at
www.thewildrosepress.com.

For questions or more information
contact us at
info@thewildrosepress.com.

The Wild Rose Press, Inc.
www.thewildrosepress.com

Stay current with The Wild Rose Press, Inc.

Like us on Facebook

https://www.facebook.com/TheWildRosePress

And Follow us on Twitter
https://twitter.com/WildRosePress

www.ingramcontent.com/pod-product-compliance
Lightning Source LLC
Chambersburg PA
CBHW070804030726
47504CB00003B/695